Torkil Damhaug studied literature and anthropology in Bergen, and then medicine in Oslo, specialising in psychiatry. Having worked as a psychiatrist for many years, he now writes full time. In 2011 Torkil's third Oslo Crime Files novel, FIRERAISER, won the Riverton Prize for Norwegian crime fiction – an accolade also awarded to Jo Nesbø and Anne Holt – and his books have been published in fifteen languages. He lives with his wife and children near Oslo.

There are four deeply dark thrillers to discover in Torkil Damhaug's Oslo Crime Files series: MEDUSA, DEATH BY WATER, FIRERAISER and CERTAIN SIGNS THAT YOU ARE DEAD.

By Torkil Damhaug

Medusa
Death By Water
Fireraiser
Certain Signs That You Are Dead

TORKIL DAMHAUG

CERTAIN SIGNS THAT YOU ARE DEAD

AN OSLO CRIME FILES NOVEL

HEADLINE

Sikre Tegn På Din Død © Cappelen Damm AS, 2013
English translation © 2015 Robert Ferguson

Excerpt from 'Quietness' by Rumi from *Essential Rumi* © 1995 Coleman Barks

The right of Torkil Damhaug to be identified as the Author of
the Work has been asserted by him in accordance with the
Copyright, Designs and Patents Act 1988.

First published as an ebook in Great Britain in 2016 by
HEADLINE PUBLISHING GROUP

First published in paperback in Great Britain in 2017 by
HEADLINE PUBLISHING GROUP

Published by agreement with Cappelen Damm AS, Akersgata 47/49, Oslo, Norway

1

Cataloguing in Publication Data is available from the British Library

ISBN 978 1 4722 0689 3

Typeset in Granjon by Palimpsest Book Production Limited,
Falkirk, Stirlingshire

Printed and bound in Great Britain by
Clays Ltd, St Ives plc

HEADLINE PUBLISHING GROUP
An Hachette UK Company
Carmelite House
50 Victoria Embankment
London EC4Y 0DZ

www.headline.co.uk
www.hachette.co.uk

CERTAIN SIGNS THAT YOU ARE DEAD

My father killed three times. The last time I saw it happen. He had sent me on ahead to the shop to buy a newspaper, a loaf of bread and an ice cream. But when I put the money down on the counter, I was told it wasn't enough, the price of bread had gone up. I ran back to ask my father which I should choose, the bread or the ice cream. Questions like that used to make him laugh out loud. I caught sight of him just inside the park gates. He was standing by the cedar tree and looking round, but he didn't see me. He started to walk across the grass. As I set off after him I saw that he was carrying his gun. I had played with it several times; he kept it in a drawer in his bedroom. Now he was holding it in his hand, behind his back. The man waiting by the rose bushes noticed me, he recognised me and smiled. I remember that. I had just turned eight. The man was holding a paper bag in one hand, I remember that; it was light brown. The way my father moved his arm as he pointed the gun at him, I remember that. Not a single sound, apart from maybe a tiny click. But the man is still looking at me as a small flower appears on his forehead. It buds and grows. No one shoots better than Father, I remember thinking. And then the man shakes, twists, falls face down into the bush. That's what I remember most clearly, how the sharp thorns tore open his cheeks.

What makes you think of that now?

Maybe because I'm sitting looking out the window, I can see a part of the street down there. Children passing by. Roughly about the age I was.

From the expert witness's notes, 1 August 2014

PART I

7–13 June 2014

1

ONE HALF OF her face was in shadow, divided by the light that fell through the room from the open window. He raised himself up on his elbows to get a better look at her. The eyes were closed, she wasn't moving, had been lying like that for a long time. A lock of hair had separated itself and lay across the cheek that was in the light and had an area of thin, tiny scars. He raised his hand to lift the hair back into place, but stopped midway through the movement, resisting the temptation to touch her. Instead he moved his gaze down her neck and the shoulder with the tattoo, a small figure; it might have been a letter from some foreign alphabet. He'd asked her about it but got no answer.

A slight movement in the thin curtains, a touch of wind through the warm room. She breathed slowly and deeply, the way she did when she was sleeping. But maybe she was lying there and knew he was looking at her. Her breasts moved in a way that suggested as much, raised up a little too high each time she breathed in. Carefully he transferred his weight to his left arm so that he could turn and let his gaze take in the rest of her naked body, all the way down to the feet that were so small and narrow; around one ankle the gold chain he had given her.

And at the sight of those feet the thought suddenly that it could end here, that there was no need to go on. The indistinct sense that there was nothing better up ahead, nothing that could equal this particular moment, and that in going on he would only lose it again, like when you let go of a balloon filled with helium and watch it vanish up into the clouds.

He extricated himself from the foam mattress, the hollows made by his palms and his knees gradually disappearing. She liked this mattress, it was one of the first things she said after she came home with him the first time. She'd sat down on it, obviously enjoying the way it shaped itself around her body. It was the evening they met each other. He'd been at Togo with Siri and a couple of her friends from med school. Later on that evening an old friend showed up, and with him the woman now lying in his bed. For some reason he had got to his feet the moment he saw her, almost offered her his hand as though they were at a reception and she was the one everyone had been waiting for. For a second or two she had looked into his eyes, then turned away with a smile that he was unable to interpret.

He and Siri had been together a year that night at Togo; they had probably gone there to celebrate. She wasn't jealous, constantly assured him that she trusted him and had no need to keep tabs on everything he got up to.

But at a certain point this new woman had gone to the toilets, which were down in the basement. He waited half a minute before getting up and following after her. Counted the fourteen steps down the black stone staircase. Suddenly it was as though he could hear his own footsteps with astonishing clarity through the buzz of talk and the electronic distortion of the djembe drums. His bladder was almost empty, and he finished quickly, washed his hands, quick look in the mirror, used a paper towel to open the door the way Jenny had taught him to when he was four or five, something he still did when he had to use public toilets.

The ladies' toilet was directly opposite. She emerged at the same moment, that same smile as when he first said hello to her, but this time she didn't turn away, she stood there looking straight at him.

– Sigurd Woods, that's your name, isn't it?

When he nodded, she repeated the name as though testing out the sound of it. He had never heard it said that way before. She must be from somewhere in the south of Sweden, where Zlatan and Timbuktu had grown up, but he didn't ask, didn't want to appear curious. As she was about to turn away, he held a hand out, touched her bare shoulder with the other, as a way of showing her she could go first.

Then she put her arm around his waist, pressed herself up against him as they walked the few paces to the stone staircase.

– And your name is Katja, he said, to regain his composure.

In the afternoons, the bedroom lay bathed in sunlight. It made its way through the tree crowns in the back yard and the heat inside could become tropical. Sigurd Woods got up and switched on the ceiling fan; it turned slowly a couple of times before accelerating and filling the air with a deep murmur. If Katja had opened her eyes now, perhaps she would be looking at him from behind as she lay there in his bed. *Our* bed, he corrected himself. Said it aloud in a low voice, to hear what it sounded like. Three weeks ago, when she arrived with her bag, he'd said it was stupid to waste thousands on a box room in Tøyen that she had to share with lots of other people. As though it was all about the money. A few days later she'd let herself in carrying two large suitcases.

He stood there looking at the branches of the huge oak tree. Imagined what he looked like to Katja, his silhouette in the sunlight, the broad back, the biceps. Even when she wasn't there, he would sometimes try to see himself with eyes that might be hers.

The phone on the table started blinking. It was Jenny.

He did nothing, knowing that the call would be followed by a message. When it arrived, he waited a minute before reading it. His mother wanted to talk to him. He knew what it was about.

As he turned back towards the bed and saw that Katja was indeed lying there watching him, he realised what he had to do. Sooner or later the two of them would have to meet, her and Jenny. It was a ritual they had to go through. It had become necessary to reveal more of himself, like where he came from. It also meant Katja telling him more about herself. In the early days, it was part of the excitement to know as little as possible about each other. She appeared from somewhere or other to stand in front of him that night at Togo, went ahead of him down to the basement, as though knowing that he would follow her. But now that phase was drawing to a close. She lived with him, he needed to know more about her, a sort of map to relate to. For the time being it was a simple sketch, with a few details prominently marked. She had grown up in Malmö, was a couple of years older than him, had worked as a model, wanted out of it, which was why she had come to Oslo, *city of opportunities,* as she had several times referred to it, without a trace of irony in her voice. One twilight evening in the bedroom she had revealed that she was adopted, and he had expected to hear more. But each time he approached anything to do with family, she placed a finger over his lips, or turned away with the same smile she had given him that first evening at Togo.

He stepped across the room, stood in front of her beside the bed; she stretched, touching him at the conclusion of the movement, acted surprised at his reaction to the touch.

– Let's go for a ride, he said as he glided down on to her, grinning as he noticed the idiotic and unintentional pun.

* * *

The previous year, Jenny had moved away from the farm and into a small apartment at the hospital where she worked. Sigurd helped her; it had to be him, otherwise his father might have ended up doing it, in spite of the fact that Jenny's moving out had crushed him. Sigurd had been expecting it for years, but it seemed to hit his father like a bolt of lightning.

Sigurd had made four or five trips, taking clothes and personal possessions, kitchen equipment, but no furniture. Jenny intended to buy everything new. He'd assembled it all for her, and connected up the washing machine, the TV and the stereo. Jenny couldn't thank him enough for all his help; she seemed to take it as a statement of support for her decision to leave his father. That wasn't the case, but he didn't make an issue of it.

Nor had he revealed how he felt about the new man in Jenny's life. On the two or three occasions when they had met, he had been polite but without showing any particular interest in who the man was. The fact that it was him who opened the door to his mother's flat when they arrived that evening didn't surprise him at all.

– Hi, Sigurd, said his mother's partner and held out his hand.

Sigurd took it and shook it, a little harder than he usually did, remembering as he did so that this Zoran was a man who lived through the work of his hands, and that to damage them would have a dramatic effect on his life.

– This is Katja, he said, ushering her in front of him in through the tiny hallway.

As the two of them shook hands, he studied Zoran's face. A friendly, relaxed expression. Definitely the type she would like.

The muted sound of music from the living room, someone laughing out loud. He had been prepared to find Zoran there, but not other guests. Just then Jenny emerged from the bathroom. She had a new hairstyle, the bleached hair hanging in a bob on each side, shorter at the back. She brightened as she saw him, until she realised he had someone with him.

– This is Katja, Sigurd said again, and this time studied his mother's face. It had always been easy to read. She blushed, and a muscle above her brow bulged and flickered.

– Jennifer Plåterud, she said quickly. People she liked call her Jenny, and for a moment or two Sigurd wondered whether she would invite Katja to do so.

She didn't know about Katja. Over the last four weeks, Sigurd had spoken to his mother less frequently than usual on the phone. The last time he had hinted that he and Siri were no longer seeing as much of each other, and Jenny had reacted with surprise. *What are you saying*, and *surely you can't mean it*, and *but she's so nice*.

The two of them had hit it off at their very first meeting, and soon it was obvious that Jenny felt a closer bond to Siri than Sigurd ever had. It wasn't just that Siri was studying medicine and could share the codes and secrets of the profession with his mother; there was something in the way they talked together, not least when talking about him, as though they were joint owners of something, some rare object, or a holiday home.

It wouldn't be like that with Katja. And bringing her here, on Jenny's birthday, was a pretty dubious idea, he didn't need to read his mother's face to realise that.

– You've got guests, he said. – We won't stay long.

It looked as if she was still struggling to get over her shock. She tidied the two bobs of her newly cut hair behind her ears and they immediately sprang free again.

– Now don't be so silly, she said. – Zoran. She turned to him. – This is . . . was it Kaja?

Zoran smiled with his whole face. He was two heads taller than her, taller than Sigurd too, with cropped greying hair and a powerful jawline.

– Katja, he corrected her. – I've just said hello to her.

For a moment they stood there looking at each other, mother and son, each with a new lover. There was a break in the music from the living room; no one spoke. Sigurd usually brought flowers on his mother's birthday, but on this occasion he had not done so.

– But come on in, for goodness' sake, Jenny exclaimed, her voice a little too loud. – Are you Swedish?

A coolness had descended into Katja's eyes, making them even darker. Sigurd held her back, pulled her close and tried to kiss her. She turned aside with a look that reminded him of that first evening at Togo, and it occurred to him that perhaps it wasn't so much the smile as the way she turned aside that had made him follow her down into the basement.

Three candles were burning on the dining table. A couple sat there; they looked to be about the same age as his mother.

– The only thing that was missing to make this into the perfect birthday, Jenny enthused. – A visit from one's son . . . one of them at least. Zoran, will you fetch some chairs from the kitchen.

Introductions ensued. The balding man was Knut Reinertsen. He wore rectangular spectacles with a green frame and had a surprisingly limp handshake.

– Knut is a psychiatrist, Jenny explained, and Sigurd wondered why that had to be the first thing he knew about him.

– And this is Lydia, his wife, originally from Russia.

Making that the most important thing about her, rather than the fact that she was a gynaecologist heading a research project into childlessness in which Jenny was involved, all of which he later learned. He smiled at his mother's clumsiness. She was doing her best, and he was the one who had put her in the position in which she was struggling. Suddenly he felt for her.

He turned to Katja. – And this is Jenny, my mother. Apart from also being doctor to the dead.

– I already gathered that.

– I've always got on well with the dead, Jenny announced. – The relationship's really quite simple.

– I couldn't agree more, Knut Reinertsen chimed in, his voice a rumbling bass that didn't match his handshake.

– Although right now I'm working as much with those not born yet, Jenny went on.

– They're not all that demanding either, Knut Reinertsen boomed. – Although sometimes I wonder. Days can go by with that being all Lydia ever thinks about. In a world threatened by overpopulation, women like you spare no attempt to ensure that there are even more of us, even quicker.

Sigurd sat down next to Katja, pinched her thigh below the edge of her skirt. She removed his hand.

They were offered some of Jenny's moussaka. Sigurd took one look at it before declining on behalf of both of them. But he couldn't refuse the cakes when they made their appearance on the table, a sort of sweet and sticky Australian delicacy that he'd grown up with and never had the heart to admit he couldn't stand. They were accompanied by a Russian dessert wine that Lydia Reinertsen had brought along. She was a little grey mouse of a woman who could have come from anywhere, though it turned out to be St Petersburg. As he sat there, it occurred to Sigurd that of all of them sitting round that table, only the psychiatrist Knut Reinertsen was a hundred per cent Norwegian. They had obviously made a point of the fact, because there was something from each person's country of origin on the menu. Zoran produced a bottle of slivovitz to go with their coffee, apologising that it was the only speciality he'd had time to produce after a week on duty in the surgical ward. Sigurd stuck to fizzy water; he was driving and anyway didn't feel a need to get intoxicated in this company. Katja clearly did, draining her glass in two large swigs and unhesitatingly accepting Zoran's offer of a refill. She seemed to be getting on better with Jenny's new partner than with any of the others.

Knut Reinertsen was knocking it back too, his deep rumble acquiring an increasing nasality as the evening wore on. Clearly a man who was used to being listened to. Apparently he was doing research into the ways people who had been exposed to war and torture found of coping. He lectured away for a while in an increasingly loud bass, but then suddenly decided it was time for him to arrange for contributions from others. He began by asking Sigurd what it was that *he* did.

– Business, Sigurd answered, knowing that his brush-off would not be enough to discourage the man's persistence.

– Business? Well, well—

Zoran interrupted: – Sigurd is twenty-three years old and already earns more than you and I will ever earn, Knut.

It wasn't completely true, but Sigurd had no objection at all to Zoran's saying it.

The mention of money seemed to make the psychiatrist genuinely curious; he wanted to know more. Network marketing was clearly a concept that made him turn up his nose.

– Isn't that some kind of pyramid scheme?

Sigurd declined to be provoked; he'd fielded the question many times. He described the idea behind Newlife. Every month recruit three new people with the motivation to sell specific products, these recruits in turn bringing in three more, and so on. Working like that, you could quickly make a million.

He looked at Katja as he said this. The first time he'd explained to her what he'd achieved with Newlife, she found it hard to believe and he had to show her the books. Then her jaw dropped. Now she sat there with this cool look in her eyes and no apparent interest in the conversation.

– What kinds of products? the psychiatrist wanted to know, and Sigurd gave him a couple of examples and a brief account of some of the research behind the health products.

– Newlife is the second-fastest-growing company in the USA, well ahead of Apple.

Knut Reinertsen dried around his mouth with his napkin. Sigurd could see that he was disguising a smile. – Research that has produced skin products that can *completely reset* the genes? What does that mean—

Jenny interrupted: – Besides earning a fortune, Sigurd studies at the business institute. By the time he finishes, he'll have a master's in business and economics.

He'd teased her a number of times by saying this wasn't necessary. That for him it was a waste of time to sit for exams he didn't need. That it was actually all about one single thing, *succeeding*. This time he couldn't be bothered to correct her. He wasn't there looking for recruits for his business.

As in all such gatherings, the evening was dominated by those who preferred to talk about their own affairs rather than pay attention to what others had to say. Sigurd reckoned he was a good listener. It gave him several advantages. Now he sat listening to what they were all saying, and the way they were saying it. Zoran with his accent, not really more than a dislocation of the rhythm, even though he'd only been in Norway a few years. Jenny, on the other hand, still spoke with a broad Australian accent even after a quarter of a century, and had given up any attempt to get rid of it a long time ago. It had occurred to Sigurd that there might be an element of protest in it, an admission of the fact that she would never become a Norwegian. He glanced over at Lydia Reinertsen. Her eyes would be all he would ever remember of her. She had an outward squint, and it was fascinating to try to decide which eye was looking at him. As he attempted to work out the way to meet her gaze, he engaged her in a conversation about Russia, a country in which he had never been interested.

– What about you, Katja?

Knut Reinertsen leaned across the table. Sigurd had noticed his gaze flickering over her on a couple of occasions, as though trying to find out whether her breasts were the real thing.

– What about me?

She stared back at him. Knut Reinertsen drank some slivovitz; she did the same.

– What do *you* do?

Sigurd groaned inwardly, but Katja gave a tolerant smile, a hint of that teasing light back in her eyes. – I work as a waitress.

Knut Reinertsen nodded as though he had guessed as much a long time ago.

– She's starting to study in the autumn, Sigurd interjected, to his own annoyance. There was no need to decorate her with a bit of status. And she could speak for herself. Which she did, announcing that she had applied to do a course in film and TV at Westerdal's media college. Sigurd knew that her answer wasn't meant as an invitation to proceed to further enquiries, but the psychiatrist did not. He wanted to know where she was from, and failed to pick up her signals to the effect that this was not something she intended to talk to him about.

Sigurd tried to move the conversation on to another subject, but Katja interrupted him.

– I'll mail you my story, she said to Knut Reinertsen. – Or perhaps it would be better if you send me a questionnaire that I can fill in.

She was still smiling, but it was not a smile Sigurd recognised. It struck him how quickly she could turn into someone quite different from the person he thought he was in the process of getting to know. He balled his napkin and dropped it on to his plate alongside the half-eaten cake, determined to leave now and get her out of there.

– Because I think it's about time to pay some attention to your wife, she went on, still staring straight at the psychiatrist. – You haven't said a word to her all evening.

In the car he said to her: – Well, at least you made him shut up.

– He didn't shut up enough.

He felt she'd gone too far, tried to work out the right way to say this to her.

– I thought you'd taken your mother's name, she said before he'd found it. – But her name isn't Woods.

– She still calls herself Plåterud, my father's name. I don't know why, they've been separated for over a year.

That his name was Sigurd Woods and not Sigurd Plåterud had nothing to do with the ongoing divorce proceedings. He had decided to use the name years ago; it felt like it had always been his real name. In taking it he didn't become someone else, he became himself. Moved differently, thought differently, took decisions that he had previously postponed.

– Does it bother you? she asked.

– Does what bother me?

– That they split up?

He smiled, shook his head. – I'm twenty-three, he said

as he turned down on to the motorway and put his foot down, letting the BMW use up some of the power that had been accumulating under the bonnet. – I'd been waiting for it to happen. For thirteen years at least.

Suddenly he saw an image of the room in the loft of the barn back home. The peephole in the wall through which they could follow everything that went on in front of the house.

– Why exactly thirteen years?

He shrugged. He'd put it behind him. And if he was going to start talking about something like that, he'd need to know more about her. As though it were a game: don't reveal your best cards before the other person does. Don't be left there with nothing more to show.

– I'm not sure it was necessary to make such a fool of him, he said instead.

– Who the hell are you talking about?

– The psychiatrist.

He could feel her gaze boring into him from the side.

– If you're going to start talking shit, you can just let me out right here.

He moved out into the overtaking lane, accelerated. The sky above Groruddalen was a shading of pink and orange light dotted with grey-black smoke and shafts of blue. He imagined the air full of swirling grains whipped up from the asphalt, and metal shavings so finely fibred they could scarcely be seen, glinting in the light from the fjord far ahead of them, like tiny flakes of snow in the warm evening.

He didn't turn to her until they had passed through the toll ring.

– Sorry.

A word he didn't intend to use too often, but right then it was the best he had, even though he didn't quite know what he meant by saying it.

2

SIGURD WOODS ALWAYS took a walk around the hall before
a lecture. He spoke to as many as possible of those who had
turned up, got some idea of who were the sceptics, and who
would be the most easily persuaded.

– How many people here want to be in charge of their
own lives? he said once silence had descended on the large
auditorium. It was full that evening, more than seventy in
the audience, and extra chairs had been brought in. The
usual assortment of students, pensioners, tired dental assis-
tants, nurses and secretaries, all there because they needed
something new in their lives; a *restart* was the word he liked
to use.

– No one here who wants to take charge of their own
life? His eyes alighted on a woman about Jenny's age. She
was suntanned, too much peroxide in her hair, and pink
wrinkles on her chest above the neckline. She looked away,
and he realised he hadn't phrased the question properly.

– How many of you want to earn a huge amount of
money? he asked, and one hand went up, followed by a
couple of others.

– Of course you do, that's why you're giving up over an
hour of this beautiful summer evening to listen to me. He
smiled broadly. – You will not regret it.

He looked at the woman again. This time she held his
gaze.

– And how many of you want a good income and at the

same time be able to spend as much time as you like doing what you really want to do?

He said it with just a touch of irony. A forest of hands shot up into the air.

– I thought as much. Smart people.

From this point onwards it would have been sufficient to proceed as he usually did, but he chose to improvise. That was why he was successful, that ability to surprise even himself.

– My father, he said as he filled a tumbler of water. – My father owns a farm.

As he said it, he visualised Katja. Her face as she lay in bed, divided in two by the light streaming in through the window. The thought of taking her to the farm. Showing her where he came from. Showing her the barn loft where you could stand on a chest and look down on to the grass in front of the house, see who came and went. He shook his head, shook the idea away.

– Running a farm is a lot of hard work for very little return. He took a sip of water. – That's a given, in a country that consists of mountains with a few wind-blown acres of arable land in between them. Everyone knows that, including my father. So he got himself a teaching qualification. Hard at it all week, with just a few hundred thousand to show for it at the end of the year. Most of it goes in taxes, the rest in expenses. He'll carry on like that until he retires, wearing himself out for nothing. My mother is a doctor, works long hours, always having to get up in the night, and she doesn't make much more.

They liked this, the way he was getting personal.

– You know what I earned last month?

He turned and wrote a figure on the whiteboard. A number followed by five zeros. Someone in the audience expressed disbelief, and the figure was a touch too high, but not much; the last couple of months had actually been very good.

– And I earned this much simply by doing things I like doing, he continued. – Such as standing here talking to you. I'm studying at BI; in a couple of years' time I'll be a qualified business economist. And I won't owe a krone in student loans. And this is only the beginning. The two people in this country who've been with Newlife the longest earn the same money as me. Times ten.

He let that sink in for a few moments.

– In the final analysis, it's all about one thing: time.

He was careful to look serious now. – Your own time. Time you can spend doing what you want to do.

He was about to go even further but reined himself in. The one word he hadn't mentioned was left hanging in the air, because he knew it wasn't appropriate for this gathering. He had tried it before and discovered then that it was best to leave it unsaid on the introductory night, because those who followed what he was saying so far knew that everything led up to this one word.

Freedom.

Afterwards he walked out on what was one of the lightest evenings of the year. It was past eight thirty, but the sky was only a slightly deeper shade of blue than it had been at midday. He had bought new shoes. They cost three thousand and weighed nothing. The wind up from the fjord carried a damp heat with it. He had made one of his best presentations, recruited a dozen new members for the network. And two days before the deadline he had handed in his exam paper on finance and economic strategies. Not exactly a masterpiece, but certainly good enough. And he wouldn't be opening another book until the autumn. He had been checking out holiday options on the internet. Maybe surprise

Katja, book something without telling her. An island off the west coast of Mexico with hardly any tourists. Katja sitting on the edge of the swimming pool, her red swimsuit soaking wet, her hair too, looking right at him, the same look as that evening at Togo. Katja wading naked out into a lagoon. He stands watching from the beach, and waits a few seconds before following her. She starts running but he catches up with her, puts his arms around her from behind, lays her down in the warm water.

People were sitting on Aker Brygge wearing T-shirts, women in flimsy strapless dresses. Someone from BI waved to him, one of those with shares worth millions, a present from his father. He used to laugh at Sigurd's network trading, because what was the point of working that hard for a lousy few million? What was the point of starting from scratch? And now the guy sat there waving him over. Sigurd smiled back at him. He'd started buying shares too, but using money he'd made himself. He made a sign with his index finger that was supposed to mean something like *enjoy it while you can*.

The only vacant table with a view of the fjord was of course reserved, but he knew the head waiter at L'Olive, it could be fixed. Sigurd slipped him a two hundred and sat down, hung his Moods jacket on the back of the chair, stretched his legs. He was early, ordered a Bonaqua while he waited. Didn't like waiting, but that was one of the things he intended to work on. It was always about that, about pushing forward, encountering new obstacles, overcoming them.

After a quarter of an hour he'd worked enough on it. He drank the rest of his Bonaqua, picked up his mobile, no message from Katja. He sent one to her. Not impatient, just making sure she hadn't made a mistake about the time and place.

He needed to move, got up and went to the toilet. Twenty

minutes now. No answer to his message. He felt something that might be anger. Decided he needed to work more on that. To show anger was to show weakness. He logged on to Facebook, scrolled down through a few dozen happy messages. Clicked on her page. Not been updated for some weeks. He'd checked out her friends there, didn't find out much. No information about her he didn't already know, nothing about her family. A reference to a film she was in. He'd asked her about it, she'd laughed it off.

It had been a mistake to take her along to his mother's birthday party. The imbalance in what they knew of each other had become even more distorted. He was behind, spending far too much time trying to work out who she was, trying to pin her down. But sooner or later he'd manage it.

His phone rang, he picked it up, in his mind's eye seeing the stone staircase in Togo, the fourteen steps down to the basement.

It wasn't her. He took the call anyway.

Trym didn't ring that often. Sigurd knew at once what it was about. First all those preparatory phrases. *You've got to come back and plant the potatoes*, that was one of them, an inside joke they'd kept up from childhood, from the days when their father still planted potatoes. *Self-sufficiency*, that was another one. Their father's belief that a time might come when they would have to provide their own food. But Sigurd wasn't in the mood for joking. He conveyed as much to his brother, that he was busy.

– Can you lend me some bread?

The sixties slang was supposed to take the edge off the question, normalise the painful truth that Trym was still living up there on the farm, still in the same bedroom and almost twenty-five years old, with nothing else to do but sit in front of a computer screen, and what made things even worse: that he had to call up his kid brother and ask for a loan.

– I already have done, Sigurd reminded him.

Brief pause.

– I ain't forgotten. Just need a bit more time.

– You've got too much time, said Sigurd, but then didn't go on. Didn't say: what you need to do is move away from your father, get yourself a job, get yourself a life. – Fuck, no, Trym. I'm not lending you any more until you've paid back what you already owe me.

– I've got something going, his brother offered, his voice weak.

– Sure you have. You've gambled away every single krone.

For a moment he was tempted to relent. It wasn't big money they were talking about, maybe a thousand or two. Had he thought it would help his brother he wouldn't have hesitated, but giving him money only made things worse and tied him ever more firmly to the farm.

Again that image: standing on a crate by the eyehole in the barn loft, peeping down at the lawn in front of the house. A car parked by the tool shed. A blue Renault. If he makes an effort he can still recall the registration number. And Trym holding him back as he's about to climb down from the loft and do something or other, still not knowing what that might be.

– Gotta go, he concluded. – Got someone waiting for me. Keep in touch.

He headed towards Vestbanetorget. Needed to walk. Seven weeks now since he'd met Katja at Togo. Close to four since she'd moved in. He thought about her too much. Even when he was supposed to be working. That was okay, probably had to be that way for a while. The first phase and all that. But this was the first time she had failed to keep a date. He pulled out his phone again.

That was when he saw her.

She was getting out of a car, a black Audi with tinted

windows. He stood on the edge of the dock. She ducked back inside again, wearing a short black dress, too short to be standing like that; he could almost see her G-string, and every guy staring over in that direction wanted to have his hands round those thighs. Maybe she was retrieving something, or saying something to the driver, or kissing him. Because it was a *he*, Sigurd was in no doubt that it was the outline of a man's head he was seeing in the driver's seat.

She emerged again, closed the car door and started walking up along the dock, and he noticed the looks she was getting, felt certain she noticed them too, that they did something to her, affected the way she walked, the way she held her head. He ducked behind a play frame on the quayside and followed her after she passed, saw her take out her phone and start tapping. A few moments later he received her message. *Delayed, sorry, something came up.*

She stopped outside L'Olive; the head waiter opened the door for her. He explained something to her, gesturing with his hands.

Sigurd strolled up to them.

– Back again, chief? said the head waiter.

Katja turned and saw him, put an arm around his neck, brushed her lips against his cheek.

Sigurd let her do it. – Is that table still vacant?

– Sorry, chief.

– Can you fix it?

He moved his hand in the direction of his jacket pocket, and the head waiter winked.

– Just give me a minute or two, I'll see what I can do.

After they had sat down and he had ordered a bottle of champagne, she put her hand on his arm.

– Are you annoyed?

She spoke differently from the way she had done in the

very beginning. She adapted quickly, though her accent was still unmistakably southern Swedish.

– I never get annoyed, he told her, touching the tattoo on her shoulder with his finger. Angry, he might have added, but never annoyed.

She looked out across the fjord. In the evening light her eyes seemed to contain ever-deepening layers of colour. He watched them as she made her excuses. Apparently some Vanessa or other had called her, and the battery on her phone was flat, and there were other problems, but mostly it was because this Vanessa wouldn't let her go before she'd helped her with her nails. No Audi, no male driver whom she had to bend over and whisper something or other to, maybe touch his lips, meanwhile showing off her arse to half the men in Oslo. For a moment he was tempted to ask who the man was, but decided against appearing to be a vulgar peeping Tom.

Back home she undressed in front of the bed. The thought of that Audi had still not left him. It would not disappear as he lay there on the blue sheet, already naked, watching as her clothes were loosened and dropped to the carpet. As she bent over him, head shaking, eyes wide in exaggerated admiration, he could still see the car in his mind, and he continued to do so for the rest of the night, no longer as a disturbance but now something that fired in him the desire to conquer her, obliterate who she was and create her as something new. She showed him things he had never done with any girl before, drove him to do them. And who was it showed *you*? he thought somewhere inside, but he could see that it worked, twice, three times, and then for a moment it was as though the black Audi had been worth it.

That was what he needed it for.

3

SIGURD'S OWN VIEW was that he had made a lot of progress in working out his strengths and weaknesses as a fighter. First and foremost was his ability to read his opponent. This prepared him for what was to come, meaning he could change his guard so quickly that any attack often evaporated completely. MacCay seldom offered praise, but in various ways showed him how valuable this quality was, that it was perhaps the essence of what it was he was trying to teach others. Not just to see the movements, but to read the opponent *as a person*. Interpret a look, a stance, realise what an opponent was going to do even before he knew it himself. Most people moved according to set patterns, which they found difficult to change, leaving them easily exposed. The best varied things the whole time, changed things unexpectedly, made themselves hard to read. The good were able to make use of an opponent's mistakes, the best were able to create them.

Three times a week MacCay gathered a few pupils he had faith in. It wasn't often that new members were admitted to the group, but on this particular Wednesday he'd put Sigurd up against someone he didn't know, a guy with a Moroccan background who was also a brown belt. Someone said his name, but Sigurd didn't want to think of him as a name; the Moroccan would have to do. That was part of the training too, to make your opponent nameless. Later they might talk, or they might not.

The Moroccan had taken part in tournaments in Sweden and was said to have done very well. Now he'd gone up a weight class. The first round was spent checking each other out. The Moroccan was quick, but no quicker than Sigurd. His forward-leaning stance showed that he was more of a wrestler than a boxer and would probably aim to get his opponent onto the floor.

To keep all other thoughts out was a part of the training. The person who thinks about the sex he's going to have later on is going to lose the bout, MacCay used to say, and he'd taught them a few simple tricks of concentration. There was one thing they were allowed to take into the bout with them. Not as a thought but as an image. Something imagined that they could put aside and pick up again after winning. Recently it had been Katja who appeared when Sigurd concentrated and allowed an image to form. Katja lying on the blue sheet, with her eyes closed, face divided by the light from the window.

Things changed in the second round. The Moroccan began to look tired. Something half-hearted about his attacks; he tried a scissor takedown, pulled back, but not in the same way, always varying things, going right, left or moving backwards. A step forward, a medium-high kick, predictable. And then suddenly he left himself open. Sigurd saw into the opening, waited for maybe a microsecond. Then something exploded in his temple and the next thing he knew he was lying on the mat with the Moroccan over him and his arm locked in a kimura hold. The Moroccan applied a little pressure, as if to show how easily he could break the arm if this were not training.

Sigurd had to tap his submission. He looked up at the silhouette in the light from the window. The Moroccan removed his helmet and spat out his gumshield, smiled down at him, not in mockery, just to register that in the group's inner ranking he was now above Sigurd.

He wanted them to eat out, a new sushi restaurant near the city hall. Stroll down through the park in the evening light with his arm around her.

Katja couldn't. Had to meet a girlfriend. She offered details, the friend's name, the same Vanessa he'd already heard about but never met. She talked about what they were going to do, even where they were meeting, and the keenness with which she provided all these details made him doubt.

While she was getting ready, he sat at his computer and looked at a lecture he was to give at the weekend. He could still feel the blow that had knocked him down, had seen it coming; it was as though he had let it happen deliberately. The Moroccan was no better than many others he had beaten. Sigurd was quick enough; there was nothing wrong with his reactions and reflexes, nor his strength and precision. It was something else he needed to work on.

Your greatest weakness is also your strength, and vice versa. MacCay had drummed this into him from his very first lesson. Pain causes anxiety. If you can keep this anxiety separate, keep it compartmentalised, you can endure a great deal of pain. Sigurd thought he was good at this. But it was also about anxiety at the prospect of *causing* pain, a fear that the aggression accumulating inside you would take over, that you would lose control, and therein lay the key to understanding his weakness, MacCay said. That hesitation about entering the space that opens up in front of you, exploiting the advantage you've fought your way towards, making the decisive strike.

Katja emerged from the bathroom, stopped behind him, read over his shoulder. He concentrated on the keyboard.

Participants in the weekend seminar were already network leaders who had been on board for some time. They knew the Newlife products and would be capable of asking questions it made sense to be ready for. Was it correct that the tablets they sold to postpone the onset of ageing affected the genes in the skin? Might there not be serious side effects if they started altering people's genes?

– You're so clever.

She smelled of a new perfume. It gave him a jolt somewhere in his head, more or less the same place where the strike from the Moroccan had hit him. He held her round the neck, kissed her; she pulled away.

– Vanessa's waiting, I promised—

She interrupted herself, lifted her skirt, sat across his lap.

– Stay awake and wait for me.

He grunted, glanced down at the few lines he had managed so far.

– Promise me.

Her steps across the floor, listening to them, as though there might be something in the way she moved that could tell him more about her. When he heard the click of the front door closing, he got up and stood at the window. Moments later she appeared. He watched her walking away, the motion from the slender heels up through the pelvic arch. He imagined holding her back, lifting that thin crimson dress up above her arse. Forbidden to others, permitted to him.

Her mobile phone lay on the dresser in the hallway.

He picked it up, put it down again. The keyboard lock hadn't turned itself on yet; a message had arrived just before she left. He opened the toilet door, turned suddenly, pressed a couple of keys, postponed the lock for another few minutes.

While he was pissing, he thought about it. Did he need

to know who had sent that message? Or who she'd called while she was in the bathroom? He flushed. Let the idea of looking through her phone disappear along with the water from the cistern.

On his way to the kitchen he picked it up again and activated the screen. Took a Bonaqua from the fridge, drank, realised he was actually thirsty. The bottle was half empty by the time he put it on the table, next to her iPhone. He opened the settings, navigated through to the screen lock, turned it off.

Just then, it rang. He dropped it; it landed in the middle of the table and lay there with the display uppermost: call from a number beginning with 93.

Half a minute later, his own phone rang. The same number. He knew it was her.

– I must have forgotten my mobile phone. You haven't seen it, have you?

– No.

– Not heard it, either? I just called it.

He imagined the look on her face when she realised she had no phone with her.

– Seen nothing, heard nothing. Have you checked your bag?

– Of course, she groaned. – Can you have a look round?

He wandered through the flat. Heard the sound of her breathing, as though she'd been running.

– Found it. In the bathroom.

– Shit.

– Can you manage without it?

– What do you think?

He opened the contacts list. Apart from his own and a couple of others, the names were unfamiliar. This was necessary, he told himself. Find out those tiny details that she refused to reveal about herself, a little bit here and a little bit there, a jigsaw puzzle in which she would presently appear complete. And once he had that whole picture? The thought almost made him laugh. Siri and the other girls he'd been with had wanted him to know as much as possible about them. But every relationship ran the risk of turning into a series of predictabilities. When it reached that stage, it was already over. Maybe what was needed was for him never to cease being surprised, for the things he thought he had discovered to turn out to be wrong after all.

He found a message from Vanessa. It was still possible to put the phone down without transgressing any limits. The message was four hours old.

You coming to Malmö this weekend?

He read it twice, maybe three times more. Tried to square it with the fact that this friend was actually in Oslo and due to meet Katja in a few minutes. He opened the message that had been sent at 17.12, four minutes after Vanessa's.

Have to know this evening. Egertorget six o'clock.

The recipient was in the list of contacts as IH. He heard the key in the door, put down the phone, remembered he'd fiddled with the lock setting, navigated, turned it on again.

She was standing in the doorway.

– Is it still in the bathroom?

He took it over to her, held her by the arm, pulled her towards him.

– Sigurd, she protested, – I really don't have time for this.

He kept hold of her, didn't relent. He had her pressed up against the wall.

– Vanessa can wait, he murmured.

He left the car in the car park below Tinghuset, jogged over to Øvre Slottsgate, found a table next to the window in 3 Brothers with a view across Egertorget. Ordered Bonaqua and coffee. He'd picked up a newspaper from somewhere, began leafing through it. She was lying. He had a right to know why. It wasn't the thought of spying that made him uneasy. What bothered him as he sat there was the danger of being caught, of looking like a loser, someone out of control who'd left himself exposed and would just have to take whatever got through his guard.

His phone vibrated. Message from Jenny. When had he started calling her that? Long before she moved away from the farm. When had he realised that this was something she was going to do? Long before he stood on that crate up in the barn loft and looking down saw the blue Renault outside the house. He'd always known.

He was on the point of calling Katja's number when he saw her. She was walking up past the government building. Stopped at the entrance to the metro, looked round, sunglasses, hair gathered at the back in a ponytail that glinted black in the evening light. In his mind's eye he saw the basement steps at Togo, fourteen of them, black stone. For an instant he thought of crossing the square, putting his arms around her, holding her tight and taking her back home again.

One minute passed, two. She paced up and down, small, restless steps. He picked up his phone again, took three or four pictures, knew he'd have to delete them. A man walked past, sort of half stopped. She looked at him, and maybe she nodded. But then he carried on walking and Sigurd decided to quit this sneaking about and go home and do something useful. Then he saw her set off walking in the same direction as the man. Sigurd slapped a hundred-kroner note on the table and ran out. Looking for that crimson dress and those bare shoulders, the black ponytail that swung from side to side like a pendulum. All those looks when they were out had made him feel proud. And alert. He'd traced an invisible line around her, patrolled it. But she wasn't a trophy. He wanted to figure her out. Know everything about her. That's why I'm walking along here, he thought, because I want to know. I'm not jealous, but I do want to know everything about you, Katja.

He walked a little faster, risked getting closer to her. A stream of people out in the warm evening sunlight, but if she turned round she could easily pick him out. She didn't turn round. Crossed Kirkegata. He crossed after her on red. Caught sight of the man she had nodded to, still a few metres ahead of her. Black jeans and a leather jacket. He was tall, neck like a bull. Didn't look Norwegian. Eastern European, he guessed, as if guessing something like that was any help at all. He still didn't know if this man had anything to do with her. He held up his mobile, took a few pictures of him, and another one of her. Loser, he muttered to himself. Pervert loser.

The man turned down Dronningens gate. Four seconds later she reached the turn. Walk on, he whispered, Katja, please walk on, doesn't matter where you're going, but please don't follow him.

She disappeared round the corner. He stopped at the pedestrian crossing, caught sight of her as she climbed into a car, the black Audi. For a moment he felt relief. Could go home now and wait, get ready for when she returned.

As they drove up towards the crossing and stopped to wait for green, he squeezed into the back of a shop doorway. The number, he thought, and ducked forward enough to see the licence plate, repeated the number over and over to himself.

As though through a grey mist he could see the two silhouettes in the front seats. The man on the driver's side. Her next to him. Katja, he muttered to himself, repeated it louder. Because now it was over.

* * *

She returned home at two o'clock. He propped himself up one elbow, was going to get up, go out and stop her in the hallway, ask her to pack her things and leave. Had made up his mind to give her money for a taxi and a hotel room for a few nights. Unless of course there was someone else she could move in with.

Lay there listening to her in the bathroom, the tinkling in the toilet bowl, the flushing, the hissing of the cistern, the tap turned on, the electric toothbrush.

She entered the bedroom quietly, slipped under the blanket. He lay turned towards the wall but could feel the prodding of those alien smells as they spread around the bed, his bed. Strongest the smell of cigarette smoke; she didn't smoke. Perfume, the same one she had used the first time they met, that evening at Togo. And something indistinct behind it, not sweat or any other body smell, something less sharp, perhaps just the faintest scent of engine oil.

He couldn't contain himself any more, turned towards her.

– Can't sleep? she whispered.

In the light of the night sky filtering down through the sheer curtains he looked directly into her eyes, two dark holes in a greyish ellipse. Like a death mask, he thought.

– Had a good time?

She grunted, as though to convey that she didn't want to talk about the evening and half the night she'd spent somewhere or other, at the end of her car drive.

– Yeah, was okay, she yawned.

– Vanessa's all right?

She nodded, he could see that; it angered him, but within his anger there was a relief that she didn't speak, that she contented herself with this nod when she lied to him. He half sat up, ready to tell her that he knew all about the man in the leather jacket, about the Audi, ready to show her the pictures he had taken. And then his anger might turn into something quite different, something he hardly recognised. To hold it back he laid a hand on her shoulder, let it slip down to cover one of her breasts. She squeezed it, holding it there. He moved towards her, inhaling her smells, that indefinable one closer now, the one like oil that yet still might be sweat, but not her sweat; hers was light and acidic, with a sharp edge inside it. He pressed down on her; she parted her lips slightly, reluctantly, he noticed; he moved his tongue inside her mouth, as though searching for a taste, a sign, proof, and then suddenly he was on top of her.

– Sigurd, I'm just totally worn out now.

She said it in Swedish, and he thought maybe that was to show him that she really meant it.

– Me too.

She usually slept naked, but now she was wearing panties. He began to peel them down.

She took hold of his hair, drew his head away. – I *must* sleep.

There was no invitation to talk her round. He pushed even closer, was very close to passing the limit. She jerked under him, twisted away. He lay there breathing into her ear.

– Tomorrow, she murmured. Reached her hand down under his waistband and pinched him hard, twice, and then snuggled up in the duvet.

He lay there staring up at the ceiling. The light created different patterns as the curtains moved. Waves of brown that turned white. Was still lying there when he heard the city sounds pick up again outside, as though someone were slowly turning up the volume control.

Abruptly he got out of bed and went into the living room. The punchbag lounging in one corner. He picked it up and hung it from the hook in the ceiling, and then began punching, harder and harder, his fists leaving deep pits in the dense fabric.

4

She had to be out of the house by eight. – The job interview, she said, as though it was something he should have known about. She was in a rush, into the kitchen and kissed him, first on both cheeks and then, after a look at him, on the mouth, a quick nip at his lower lip.

– Tonight, she said, pressing a finger to the tip of his nose. – You and me.

He looked at her without speaking.

– You're not cross, are you?

He poured more coffee.

Once she was out of the door, he called the DVLA.

– A rental car, said a female voice once he had given her the registration number.

I thought so, he murmured to himself. – Do you have the name of the firm it is registered to?

– It's registered with Europcar.

He found the number, didn't even take the time to work out a credible story.

– I work in a shop in Dronningens gate, he said, improvising. – One of my customers left . . . some papers behind when he was in here. I ran out after him, managed to note down the registration number of his car. Can you help me to trace him?

Without waiting for her answer, he gave the number.

– Sorry, but we're not allowed to give the names of customers.

– These look like important documents, some kind of application form.

– Then perhaps you have the name there yourself?

He sat at the kitchen table. – It's a little hard to read—

– I'm sorry, but I can't help you, the woman interrupted. – But if you'd like to bring the documents in here, we'll make sure they get to our customer.

He went to the bathroom, bent over the tub and splashed cold water on his head and chest. Stood dripping wet in front of the mirror, imagined himself following that black Audi. Got closer, until he could see the two shapes, Katja's head with the ponytail, and the man with his bull's neck. They were driving along a forest road.

He swore out loud and returned to his desk. It was past twelve, the day was already half gone and he'd done nothing but let his thoughts idle.

He woke his computer, wrote: *Don't let your thoughts turn you into a loser. It all starts with your thoughts.*

His phone rang; it was Jenny. He sat looking at it, didn't feel like talking to her right now. She always asked questions, wanted to know how things were. And he might give himself away. She would comfort him then, relieved that the thing with Katja hadn't worked out. Tell him that from the moment she laid eyes on her she knew it would end like this. And she'd suggest he got in touch with Siri again. In this imaginary conversation he tried to explain to her why there was no future in the relationship with Siri. There was nothing wrong with her. She was pretty, good body, clever, in every way a good person. And when he was with her it was as though he always knew what she would say, how she would react, how her body would respond to his approach. Everything turned into a confirmation of what he had already discovered about her a long time ago.

He made himself an espresso. As he watched the thin brown stream being pressured down into the cup, he had an idea, and before he had finished his coffee it had become a plan.

He opened his list of contacts, called a number.

– Hey, boss.

– Been a while.

– Follow you on Facebook. You're doing fucking brilliant.

Sigurd put another espresso pod in the machine, switched it on.

– Kent, buddy, listen, I need to find something out. It's actually very important for my work. You know someone who knows all about filters and firewalls and stuff like that, right?

Silence at the other end. He looked out of the window. The branch of the oak tree on the pavement, the sharp sunlight flickering through the leaves.

– And which side of the wall are you going to be on?

Sigurd let his silence speak for itself.

– He'll be well paid, he said finally.

The guy who opened the door wasn't much older than he was. He was about five or six kilos overweight, with droopy eyelids and a chin covered in a well-trimmed beard that thinned out and followed the lines of his jawbone.

– You the guy Kent called about?

Sigurd confirmed it and was invited in.

They passed through an open-plan office. Three or four of the desks were occupied. *Consultants*, the sign on the door said, without specifying a field.

– You work here? asked Sigurd.

The guy shrugged, clearly a sign that he wasn't interested

in answering questions like that. He looked at the note.

– Europcar? Should be doable. It's a question of money. How soon do you need this?

– How soon can you let me have it?

The guy thought about it. – That's a question of money too.

– Everything is a question of money, Sigurd said.

– Give me a couple of days and we'll say five sheets.

Sigurd ran a finger along his lower lip. – Five is okay, he decided. – But I'll expect it today.

He was eating at Eger's when the guy rang.

– Come on over. Bring your bedclothes.

Sigurd shook his head. As if he was being invited to a gay pyjama party.

Twenty minutes later he was there, walking through the same open-plan offices, only two other people there now. Neither of them looked up from their screens.

Sigurd dropped the envelope onto the table. The guy with the manicured beard glanced inside, put it away in a drawer.

– Take a look now, he said. – This information will be available on screen for fifteen seconds and then it's gone for ever.

Sigurd took out pen and paper and made a note of the name, mobile phone number, driving licence number and address in Malmö.

Out in the street he took out the sheet of paper.

Ibro Hakanovic.

He said the name over and over again, like a formula. Felt suddenly that familiar sense of relief. This is what it's about, he thought. Always be looking for the openings.

He got into his car, picked up his phone, called Kent.

After he'd told Kent what it was about, he could hear

the smile at the other end. That smile was the real price, not the lousy few thousand kroner.

The Moroccan was just opening his locker as Sigurd entered the changing room. He was wearing a light summer suit, looked like linen, well pressed, white shirt, shoes that might well have been Italian. He continued to undress without even glancing at Sigurd.

They lined up down in the hall, the group of five whom MacCay was calling his A students. And the Moroccan. Sigurd knew who he would be sparring with. He'd looked for something new in the changing room, something he might have missed last time. The Moroccan was almost as powerfully built as he was, but he moved like a man who weighed half as much. He was slightly smaller, with a slightly shorter reach.

Some likened this kind of fighting to chess. MacCay would have none of it. It was more like putting together a three-dimensional jigsaw puzzle, the movement of a body in space, reading it but not with your thoughts; you had to learn to read quicker than thought.

Sigurd was determined to get the Moroccan on the mat this time. He backed off, allowed himself to be hit on the head. Breathed more heavily than he needed, quickly put a hand to his forehead as though he'd been shaken. He repeated the sequence, took an even harder hit, retreated, as if he'd tripped. The Moroccan closer now, something new in his eyes, something that said he was sure of the outcome. Sigurd encouraged his advance, parried the first strike, took the second, let the pain surge through his body. When the third blow came, he ducked, hit back, but a little too hard; for an instant he was too far forward, the distance between his elbows too great. The Moroccan, driving his fist in from below, an express train with three coaches on, caught him under the chin, across the bridge of the nose; his head jerked backwards.

MacCay stood leaning against the wall. Said nothing, seemed uninterested, but Sigurd knew that afterwards he would be able to describe every single movement. Situations in which his hip had been placed too far forward, or his punch hadn't come from the shoulder.

His gumshield was dislodged; he forced it back into place with his tongue. In that instant the Moroccan mounted a second lightning-fast attack and Sigurd could hear the thought as though a voice were speaking to him: *Gonna get a thrashing now, Sigurd Woods, this is gonna hurt.* He raised his guard, drove the thought away, looked for something to replace it, found nothing but that image of the black Audi, the two figures outlined in the front seats.

He took a hit to the temple, the sweat spraying off him, some landing in his eyes, but when the next strike came, he saw it, like a door opening up in front of him. He dodged to one side, and then he was there. Four blows in succession, the Moroccan staggering backwards, raising his hand in a futile attempt to protect himself. Sigurd kicked him in the side, and as the Moroccan bent double, grabbed him in a headlock, brought his knee up under his chin and twisted him onto the floor, locking him with his thighs and unleashing another salvo of punches. The feeling was different now. The tension in the body he was hitting was gone; it was as though he was punching a sack.

He didn't keep count of the number of times he hit him. The Moroccan raised his hand, and Sigurd knew he was about to tap the floor to concede defeat. He grabbed hold of the hand and twisted it aside and kept on hitting until it was no longer himself doing it but something inside him. He felt an iron grip around his shoulder.

– That's enough now.

MacCay dragged him up, kept his hold on him.

– Go take a shower.

Sigurd pulled off his helmet and slunk towards the door. Realised it was the last time he would be going there, because what he had been doing was something very different to sparring.

– Wait for me down in the cafeteria.

He had not lost control. He had given it away. It had only happened once before. He could remember the occasion clearly. Didn't fight much at school, didn't need to; he wasn't among the ones who got picked on. But that day he'd known in advance. Known it from the morning onwards. Who the other person was didn't matter. As long as he was big enough and strong enough. There mustn't be any taint of cowardice in what was going to happen. He picked the boy out at the morning break, started a quarrel. That same feeling then, hitting and hitting until someone pulled him off. It was thirteen years ago. The day after he saw the blue Renault parked in front of the house. Never experienced it since. Not even had a real fight since then, not until now. As though there was a connection. He tried to laugh it off. But still a splinter was left, nagging away at him.

Almost a half-hour passed before MacCay appeared in the doorway. He took a coffee from the machine before sitting down.

– What's the matter?

Sigurd shrugged.

– Were you trying to kill the guy?

– Wasn't trying to do anything special. It was a fight.

MacCay leaned across the table. – A broken nose and two broken teeth.

– Sorry.

– You know what something like that costs?

– I'll pay you.

MacCay hit the table with his fist.

– Fuck you, boy. You think you can pay your way out of everything in this life?

Sigurd didn't think that.

– And just how many enemies do you think you can manage to live with?

– I'm not looking to make enemies.

– Then don't do things that mean you have to keep looking over your shoulder every time you have a night out in town.

Silence for a while. They drank, he his water, MacCay the coffee.

– We have to look at the other side, Sigurd. MacCay was calmer now. – Always look at what's on the other side.

He pointed at Sigurd's forehead. – You think too much. You've been missing the most important thing. Been too scared. Of yourself.

– I guess you're right.

– Of course I'm right. But today you showed something else. Dug deep. Too deep. But I saw what's inside you.

– It was a surprise to me too.

MacCay smiled quickly, and just as quickly turned serious again.

– I'm going to have to throw you out. Suspend you for a while at least.

Sigurd drank the last of his water.

– Take a week to think things through, Sigurd. How to find that balance. Get access to what you had today, but without killing your opponent.

He stood up.

– I think you might amount to something. Maybe you weren't lying about being half Australian after all.

He shook his head and left.

5

SHE HAD COME home late and was still sleeping when he got up. He sat in front of the computer. Worked on the lecture. Things went better this time. He wrote about dreams, allowing yourself to have them, not letting people who are envious of you, or unable to dream themselves, stand in your way. Dream thieves, that was what they called them in Newlife. People who live off the dreams of others by destroying them.

Not for an instant did he forget that Katja was lying there behind the closed bedroom door, but it no longer prevented him from working. A sense of being invincible. This was what life could be like after her. He threw open the window on the warm summer morning, listened to the city, the cars and the people, the sparrows that had settled on the lawn. Windless, and yet the oak leaves fluttered ever so slightly, as though it were the light that made them tremble.

He carried on writing; it flowed along by itself. Some he could use in the lecture, the rest he would cut. Newlife offered the world products that prevented cells from ageing, that gave their lives a *restart*, constantly renewing the genetic material and keeping the bitter face of old age at bay. It was a unique combination of the dream of financial independence and the dream of eternal youth. Who could say no to that?

Around ten, he heard the bedroom door open. He carried on writing about how to triumph over everything that gets in the way of reaching your goals. Bare feet across the floor. Carried on writing about the dream thieves. Hands on his shoulders, lightly caressing. Carried on writing.

– Hi.

Her voice full of anticipation. As though he were the one she had been lying there thinking about.

He turned. She was naked, smelled of sleep and yesterday's perfume. He looked up, struck once again by her eyes, as if he had forgotten how dark they were.

– Hi, she said again, and slipped down into his lap. – I want you, Sigurd Woods. Do you understand?

Wearing nothing but the orange blouse, she sat at the table. He stood in the bathroom door, watching her. Thought of the evening they had first met. How she had turned away, with a smile no one else noticed. He could've made a different choice that night. Not followed after her. When this is over, I'll be stronger, he thought. The kind of thought he should have written down.

She sent a text message, a long one, then pushed the plate with the half-eaten slice of bread to one side, put her mobile phone down, drained her espresso, refilled it. A pling from the phone; she picked it up, read. Is that Ibro Hakanovic you're exchanging messages with? he thought, and was about to walk over and ask her. But that wasn't the way it would end. Not with an ordinary quarrel. That might make her think he was jealous.

He sat down in the chair next to her. Looked at her in the late morning light, the olive skin against the orange material, naked from the waist down. He placed his hands on her knees, pressed them apart.

– Vanessa? he asked.

– What about Vanessa?

– The one you send all the messages to?

She looked at him for a moment. A new message arrived; she crossed one leg over the other.

– I have to go to Malmö.

He felt his face crumple and collapse.

– Now?

She read on, put the phone down again, leaned over and kissed him quickly, stood up and crossed to the window.

– As soon as I can.

– Has something happened?

– It's my cousin. She needs help.

He didn't ask what kind of help that might be. He didn't ask who this cousin was. If indeed she even existed at all. She'd spoken of a cousin before, maybe the same one, though never of anyone else in the family.

– Something only you can help her with, he said. Not as a question; it was an observation, a reminder to himself of where he was and where he was going.

– What do you mean?

He stood up and crossed over to her. Even in the summer light her eyes were darker than any others he had ever seen. He pulled her close. This is the last time, he thought, and felt relief.

But then it was on him again.

– I'll come with you.

– Where?

– To Malmö.

She pulled away, tensed. – That would be cool. But this time I have to go alone.

He didn't say anything more, just let her carry on digging herself into it, all on her own.

– It's sort of private. She doesn't want . . .

He smiled now, and maybe she could hear herself how feeble it sounded.

– I'll explain. When I get back home.

So home was here, his place, his flat.

– Okay, he said, and had to smile again. – I'll give you a lift to the bus.

She looked away. – No need, Sigurd. You've got so much else to do. She nodded towards the computer.

– I can take a half-hour break.

She shook her head firmly, turned and went into the bedroom. He heard the sound of a suitcase being placed on the floor, the zip being opened. She won't be coming back, he thought suddenly. As though the zip had told him.

Her mobile phone was on the kitchen table. He sat looking at it for a while before picking it up. Felt like opening the window and throwing it out. Instead he stood up, put it in his pocket, walked once round the table, was about to take it out again, put it back. Then she was standing in the doorway. Wearing pale yellow trousers, a blouse the same colour, suitcase in her hand.

He forced a smile. – So this is goodbye.

She wrinkled her eyebrows. – Back Sunday.

– Sunday. He nodded slowly.

She looked around, glanced over at the clock. Went back into the bedroom. He could put it back now, not on the kitchen table because she'd just looked there. On the windowsill, he thought, half hidden behind the curtain.

– Sigurd.

He stood there, pushed a hand into his pocket, put his fingers round it, found the mute button and pressed it with his thumb.

She came back in again. – Have you seen my phone?

He shook his head, parodied exasperation. – What you need is a servant to look after your things for you.

She ignored him, bent down and looked under the table, glanced around the room. He sat at the computer, not watching her, monitoring her mounting frustration.

– Have you checked the bathroom? Where you usually leave it?

She hurried back into the room, rummaging about, swearing out loud now.

– Can't you help me instead of just sitting there laughing?

– I'm not laughing.

– Call the number.

He walked into the bedroom, picked up his own phone from the bedside table, hid hers under the mattress. Back in the living room, he scrolled down to her name. It occurred to him as he did so that maybe it would still vibrate, even though the sound was turned off. He didn't make the call, just to be on the safe side.

She went back into the bathroom, back into the kitchen, even looked inside the fridge. He might at least have laughed at that, but didn't.

– Either it's on mute, or the battery's flat, or you've left it somewhere else.

– I was just using it, she groaned.

– Where?

– Here. At the table. She turned and studied him. – *You* haven't by any chance . . .

He strode across the floor until he was standing right up close to her.

– What are you trying to say?

– One of us must have put it somewhere.

He narrowed his eyes, but not too much. – Are you suggesting I might have stolen your mobile phone?

She scratched her neck. – Not stolen it.

– Then what?

She was looking directly at him now. Her eyes changed all the time in the sharp light, layer upon layer of dark shadow.

– Bloody hell, Sigurd, I'm in a hurry. I can't go without my phone.

Heard something in her voice he'd not heard before. Helplessness, a confusion on the verge of panic.

Then you'll have to stay here, he thought. Stay here until it turns up again.

She didn't stay. After another round of successively less systematic searches she suddenly grabbed up her suitcase and was gone, slamming the door behind her. He was on the point of running after her, giving her the phone, but it was too late; she wouldn't believe him if he claimed he'd just found it.

He slumped down in front of the computer again, but all hope of work was gone now. She was the one who was the thief. Had stripped the flat of thoughts and willpower. Not thoughts. He was full of them. Of the kind he didn't need. He should have called Trym. Had promised to, promised they'd do something together. Had promised Jenny that he'd take his big brother out. As if he was a fucking care worker. Trym who should have been bigger than him, stronger, who should have been able to beat him up and run off with all the best-looking girls, who should have finished his education a long time ago, who should have travelled the world, climbed in the Himalayas, gone diving in the Caribbean, gone parachuting. He sat there at home on the farm. Not even waiting for something. Other than a win on the online casino. For someone to come driving up to the house with a truckload of money and dump it outside his front door. And what would he do with all that money? Keep on gambling.

He called him. His brother's sleepy voice. Sigurd felt his anger rise.

– Fucking hell, are you still sleeping?

– A bit late getting to bed.

– Well, what do you expect if you sit up on the internet half the night?

Pause. Then Trym's voice, hesitant.

– Has something happened?

– Yeah, something's happened, something's happening all the time, but you've shut yourself away on a fucking farm in deepest Sørum, in Norway, closed off from the world, and you sit there and sit there while your life rots away from the inside.

– For fuck's sake, Sigurd, I don't have to put up with this.

– Great, then don't. Get up and fight back.

Trym hung up. Sigurd was left standing bent forward and staring at the table. Of all the idiotic things he might have thought of now, it turned out to be the barn loft that came into his mind. Why did he climb up on to that crate and look out? Because Trym had called to him. Trym had come home from school before him. Now he was standing half hidden behind the barn bridge, calling to him in a low voice and beckoning him.

Don't go in.

Course I will.

Come here.

Trym takes hold of his arm, drags him into the barn, over to the steps.

Come up with me.

Tell me what for.

Not until you're up in the loft.

Trym climbs up after him. Closes the door behind them. This is their room, their hideaway. Neither of their parents ever comes up here.

Look outside.

Sigurd positions the crate on its end below the wall vent and hops up on to it. There's a car parked by the shed. A blue Renault Mégane. Nice name, crap car. He can see the number plate, repeats the number in his head a couple of times, not easy to know what one ought to remember.

Whose car is that, then?

Dunno.

Why is it parked there?

Dunno.

The thought hits like a bolt of lightning: *Is it a burglar?*

Trym shakes his head.

How do you know?

Mum's home.

A new thought, even worse: Mum alone in the house with the thief.

We've got to help her.

He hops down from the crate, takes a screwdriver from the shelf, drops it, picks up the hammer instead.

Trym blocks his way.

You better stay here.

No bloody way. Let me out.

He pulls at the door. Trym wraps his arms around him, holds him firmly. He's two years older and weighs ten kilos more. Sigurd has to give up. He kicks out at the crate and it hits the far wall with a loud crash. Trym slides down in front of the door, blocking it, as if it's the entrance to the world's most dangerous room.

Mum has a visitor. *You get my meaning?*

He doesn't, but he sits down too.

Well, then, never mind whether you understand or not. You're staying here. Until that car has gone.

Sigurd looked out. A fine drizzle had settled on the window, but he couldn't see any clouds. When he called his brother back, Trym didn't answer. He tried again, left a message. Apologised for his bad mood, didn't mean to be a shit, suggested the cinema.

He would leave all this behind. That was what it was about. Break away, move on. Australia. He was half Australian. Eighty per cent Australian, as Jenny used to say. He'd never been there; all the same, he knew it was the place for him. But first he was going to make it here, not go out there like some loser on the run.

His phone rang, a jazz ringtone he'd downloaded the week before. He looked at the display: number not recognised. It was her.

– Sorry, Sigurd.

– For what?

– I was so pissed off about that phone. And then I blame you.

– You got yourself a new one? he grunted.

– Well I had to.

– Are you in Malmö already?

– Nearly.

He couldn't hear any background noises. It was though she was sitting in a quiet room. At any rate, not on a bus.

– I care about you, she said.

– Well that's something.

Short pause.

– Can you accept me the way I am?

He didn't know. Was still sitting there thinking about what that might involve when his phone rang again.

– Got some stuff for you, said Kent.

– Stuff?

Sniggering at the other end.

– What you asked for. And a bit more. People always get more than you ask for.

He pulled into a parking bay along Ullevålsveien. Kent wearing a suit jacket in this warm weather, sunglasses and an attaché case. Jumped in.

– Drive on.

Sigurd was a little too quick on the accelerator pedal, nearly knocked down a cyclist.

As they passed Bislett Stadium, Kent opened the case, took out an envelope, looked round like someone pretending these were state secrets changing hands. Sigurd knew him from secondary school. He had dropped out in his final year. Tried his hand at this and that but mostly lived off social security. Had a couple of conditional discharges, Sigurd knew, and spent a summer doing community service for taking hundreds of photos of mostly underage girls who believed him when he told them he could get them jobs as models. He was still trying his hand at this and that.

– I think we can call this hitting the jackpot.

Sigurd didn't respond.

– What you need is in this envelope. Ten to twelve snapshots. Most of them taken at a villa in Nittedal. The address is on the accompanying paperwork. And a map. And everything we've got on this guy. From Malmö. Bosnian, it looks like.

Sigurd heard Kent's snigger and felt like putting a fist straight through it. Got a hold of himself, swung into a street behind Sankthanshaugen, opened the glove compartment, took out the envelope with the thousand-kroner notes.

– Eight, he said, – if you want to count.

– Eleven for this job, said Kent.

Sigurd glared at him. – We agreed on eight.

– There's more there. More than the deal.

– You want three thousand for a map you've downloaded from Google?

– Okay, okay. Kent backed down. – Let's say eight. Special price for a friend.

He'd studied the map until he had it memorised. Knew there was a Shell station right after the turn-off, pulled in there, parked in the customer car park, in a vacant spot behind the station, next to a container. Not that she'd immediately think of him if she saw a BMW that was like his. If she was thinking about him at all. He allowed himself to dwell on the question: did she forget all about him when she was with Ibro Hakanovic? She wasn't the type to indulge feelings of guilt. It was part of what made her who she was, that she didn't respond like other people, didn't say what others said, didn't feel like others. As though she were always somewhere different from where he expected to find her.

It was five past nine. He pressed the screen washer, started the wipers, turned them off. Tried to list his alternatives. One was to go home. Sit down in the living room. Wait for her. He wasn't the type to wait. He took the envelope out again. Indistinct photos on cheap paper, but clear enough. The black Audi. Katja getting into it. The guy with the neck like a bull in the driving seat. Both of them at the entrance to a brown detached house. Picture of the house from a distance, a wood in the background. Close-up of someone behind a window, two silhouettes that didn't need further identification.

He jogged up the road. It swung through a stand of trees, then across a farmyard and up towards a residential area closer to the edge of the wood. He took a short cut across a field. There was no sign of the Audi in the housing area. All the houses had garages and he couldn't open every single one of them.

Further up the road was a house standing on its own. Not until he was about two hundred metres from it did he recognise it from the photo. Brown detached house, large lawn out front, trampoline in the garden. He walked on through the bright evening light, knew that he was visible from the windows, knew she could be standing in one of them and catch sight of him. Again he began to run, sprinted past the house without looking in that direction.

A little further on, the road was blocked by a barrier. On

the other side it continued on up towards the wood and disappeared among the trees. He turned round and studied the brown house. No sign of light in any of the windows. They'd probably already gone to bed. Lying there in the half-dark.

The garage door was open, but the car wasn't there. It was time to turn and go back. Then he saw it. The rear end sticking out beyond the far wall of the house. He went as close as he could to make sure it was the same car. It was getting darker, but evening light still penetrated the clouds. He was easily visible as he stood there and studied the number plate. She could have spotted him ages ago. Still he stood there. As though giving her a chance to come out, to go with him. It was nine thirty.

He sent a message to her new number. *All okay in Malmö?* Was startled to get an immediate reply.

Better now.

He squeezed his phone, raised his hand suddenly as though to hurl it against the garage wall. Took a hold of himself. For another minute he stood there, watching the first-floor windows, before crossing the yard.

The door was locked. He walked around the house. Took out his phone again to call her. Stand by the garage and peer up towards what could be the bedroom, hear her voice, get her to lie about where she was, what she was doing.

At the back of the house he passed a cellar door, tried the handle. It opened, and the unlocked door was what decided the matter. He would find her, stand there in the dim light of the bedroom and look at her, smile down at her as she lifted her head from the pillow and said his name. And then he'd go, never see her again.

He crept up the basement steps. Opened a door. A pair of shoes in the corridor, some rubber boots. Jackets hanging on a hall stand. No female clothing. A door ajar on the right. He entered a kitchen. No lights on. Stood there listening. The sound of voices from an adjoining room. He peered through the keyhole. Dark in there too, just the blue flickering light of a television. A couple shouting at each other, then he recognised the voices; he'd watched the series many times.

At that instant, the door was thrown open, Sigurd staggered backwards and crashed into the stove. The light went on. The person standing there was wearing a vest and boxer shorts, had a towel round his shoulders.

– What the hell?

Sigurd raised a hand, a guard maybe; he certainly didn't intend to shake hands.

– What the hell are you doing here?

The man turned and grabbed something from the living room, straightened up again, still standing in the doorway, a golf club in his hand.

– You won't find what you're looking for here.

– I don't believe you, said Sigurd, the words burning in his throat.

– I'm not stupid enough to keep it in the house, the man shouted.

– Katja? said Sigurd in surprise. He said it loud enough for her to have heard if she was sitting in the adjoining room.

– What about Katja? growled the man in the boxer shorts. He had highlights in his hair, and was even bigger than he looked from a distance, muscles bulging, eyes small and angry. For a moment Sigurd saw the situation from the outside. He was in a stranger's house, uninvited. Maybe he'd made a mistake.

– Ibro Hakanovic, he said, and realised it wasn't very clever to say the name, but right now he wasn't feeling very clever. And maybe it was the sound of the name that galvanised the man. Suddenly he took three steps forward, raised the golf club and hammered it down on Sigurd's shoulder.

He shrieked.

– How stupid can you be? the other man growled, and raised the club again. – I told you, I don't have it here.

Sigurd held both his hands above his head, saw the blow coming, threw himself backwards, hit his neck against the sink as he fell. The man was on top of him, Sigurd rolled aside, the club hammered into the wooden floor right next to his head. He got to his feet, bent double, on the other side of the man, the door out to the corridor blocked. He backed into the next room, a living room, the television still on, *CSI: Miami*. On the table was a frying pan with the remains of a meal. He grabbed hold of it, pushed with all his weight against the living-room door, kept pushing as it opened slightly. Then he stepped aside, and at once it burst open and the guy came stumbling in. In the split second it took him to regain his balance, Sigurd lifted the frying pan and brought it down on the man's back with all his might. Hakanovic fell flat on his face, bits of sausage and potato raining down all over him as he dropped the golf club. Sigurd grabbed hold of it, hit him again, on the back and on the arm. Then he caught sight of the small tattoo on the back of the shoulder, a letter from a foreign alphabet maybe, and he knew where he'd seen one exactly like it before. Don't hit his head, the thought flashed through him, *not the head*. He shouted out loud as the last blow landed.

Yesterday you told me you witnessed a murder when you were eight years old.
  What I told you was that my father shot a man.
  Correct . . .

My father shot him in the head. He was the best marks-man in the club. He won more prizes than anyone else.

Did you talk about it afterwards?

Father wasn't angry that I came running up, if that's what you're asking. He never got angry with me. I think maybe he even wanted me to follow him that day. I distracted the attention of the man he was going to meet. Or maybe he wanted to show me how quickly life can end. Because afterwards that's what he said to me. That I should always be prepared. Always be alert. Always have a plan for what to do if a threat suddenly appears.

Did you think much about what you saw him do?

Now and then I thought of the man's face. What the sharp thorns did to it, because he couldn't protect himself when he fell. I'd met him before; he was a handsome man, about the same age as my father, but with hardly any wrinkles and always clean shaven. If he'd had a beard, it would have protected him from the thorns. Father didn't want me to look at him, but I had to go over to the bushes, and he was lying there with his cheeks all ripped up.

What happened after that?

I played for a while with the other kids in the square. It was a Sunday; we went to church. Like always on Sundays. During prayers I peeked up at my father and I saw he was crying. I'd never seen that before. And he spent longer there than he usually did. Outside, two men were waiting. As soon as I spotted them, I knew they didn't belong there. I realised they were waiting for someone and grabbed my father's hand to get him away. But it was too late.

From the expert witness's notes, 2 August 2014

PART II

13–15 June 2014

PART II

13–15 June 2014

6

Arash's phone beeped. It was from Emergency. He was on the floor above, parked the empty bed and hurried down there.

– You should answer the telephone, the nurse scolded him. She had a neck like a turkey and was at least twice his age. Her voice often sounded as if she was angry about something or other.

– Quicker to come straight to you. He smiled.

She shook her head and didn't seem completely impervious to the smile. Once or twice, on evenings when things were quiet, she'd invited him into the office behind the counter where she sat and offered him coffee and biscuits. But this evening was very busy. New patients in, all the examination rooms in use, a chaos of beds and screens in the corridors, nurses and doctors running around with stethoscopes waving and telephones to their ears, into one room, wrong patient, out again, as though no one knew what anyone else was doing.

– Examination room four, she said. – Patient to the orthopaedic ward. She handed him a note with a name on it.

– Will do, he said with another smile; she told him once he had such a nice smile. Women in this country could say that type of thing to anyone at all. He had no objection to it, once he got used to it.

– Asap, Arash, she growled, but with a twinkle in her

eye, and he put his hand to his mouth and blew her a kiss. She turned sharply away. He saw that she was grinning.

In examination room four, two nurses were standing bent over a bed while a third was hanging up a drip. The woman in the bed suddenly began to howl, like a wounded beast. The sweat was pouring off her and she was rocking backwards and forward. The two nurses tried to hold her down.

– I'm supposed to pick up a man, Arash began.

– Does this look like the man you're supposed to be picking up? the third nurse chimed in.

Arash didn't think so. Another long-drawn-out howl from the patient, deeper this time. The nurses talked among themselves, about a doctor who hadn't arrived, about ringing again.

– There's supposed to be a patient for an orthopaedic bed here, Arash tried again.

– This is not a surgical patient, groaned the nurse who had connected the drip and now reached for a telephone.

She tugged at the sleeve of his jacket. – Try room three, she said, sounding a little more conciliatory. – We had to move her. She added in a lowered voice: – Pregnant.

Arash knocked on the door of the next room before entering. A man was lying alone on a bed inside. He was enormous, feet sticking out from below the blanket that had been tossed over him. He was wearing only one sock. There was a bandage round his head and one eye was bloody and swollen and tightly shut. He peered up out of the other eye.

Arash held up the note and pointed.

– Is this your name?

– Yes.

He pulled the brake-release. – Then you're coming with me.

– Coming where with you? the patient said in Swedish.

– You're going to a bed in an orthopaedic ward.

– Who the hell says so?

Arash thought about that a moment.

– The doctor who examined you. They've decided you should be admitted.

The patient raised his finger and waved it in front of him. – No doctors have examined me. And who the hell are you?

Arash looked more closely at him. The sound of that threatening voice reminded him of something, it made him uneasy. He tried to explain what his job was, to make sure patients got safely from one department to another.

– Once you get to the ward, you'll be given a more thorough examination, he concluded. He placed the bag with the saline drip by the bedhead and pulled the bed towards the door.

– You're not taking me anywhere.

The patient tried to get up. Grimaced and slid back down again with a groan.

– You're in pain, Arash comforted him as he straightened the blanket that was about to fall on to the floor.

– Where did you get that ring from? the patient asked suddenly, seemingly released from his pain for a moment. – Are you a Muslim?

– Yes, Arash blurted out, and the unease that had retreated to somewhere in his neck now flooded through his whole chest. He glanced down at his hand, the ring with the black enamel and the three words smelted in gold on to it.

– I must get Katja somewhere safe.

Arash parked the bed again. – Do you have a cat?

It wasn't uncommon for people who ended up in hospital to be worried about the pets they'd left at home.

– They found out where I live. They were asking about Katja.

The voice was not the same as the man he had been reminded of, Arash reassured himself, nor did the patient have an Iranian accent. But the reference to a cat made him feel uncertain. And what business was it of this stranger's if he was a Muslim or not?

Suddenly the patient grabbed him by the arm.

– Katja isn't safe. I have to bring her here.

Arash pulled his arm free. He realised that he must have misheard, the patient wasn't talking about his cat. – We'll let your relatives know, they'll come and look after things for you.

The patient shook his head; it seemed to cost him a great effort, and he grimaced again in a way that made him resemble even more the man Arash did not want to be reminded of.

– Where is my phone?

Again the patient raised his arm and reached out to grab him. To calm the man down, Arash bent over and felt in the pockets of the trousers that lay folded below the bed. There was a phone in one of them. He handed it to the patient, who peered at it through his one good eye.

– She's got a new number, he grunted, tapping on the screen, putting the phone to his ear. – Hi, Katja, are you still in Stockholm?

He waved Arash away. – Get out of here, he growled, and pointed towards the door.

Arash let himself out into the corridor. There was no limit to the amount of patience he needed in this job.

One of the assistant doctors came hurrying by. Not many years older than him, but already thinning on top. His name was Finn Olav and he was the type who stopped for a chat when he had the time. He and his wife lived on the floor above Arash. A couple of months earlier, Arash had taken one of their kids home when she fell off a swing and lay crying in the grass.

– You just standing here waiting? Finn Olav asked, and half opened the door to the examination room.

Arash explained the situation: that he'd been sent from one room to the next and was equally unwelcome in both.

Another beast-like howl came from room four.

– Ectopic pregnancy, said Finn Olav, nodding towards the door with a crooked smile. – Neither you nor I have any business in there. We leave it to the tribe's own elders. Now as for this guy here . . . He pushed the door open and peered in. – He's probably right to say that he's untouched by medical hand so far.

He laid a pale and freckled hand on Arash's shoulder.

– We need chaos pilots like you. Whatever you do, don't give up. If you do, the whole place will collapse in an instant. Promise me that.

He winked and closed the door behind him.

It was impossible to take even a five-minute break that evening. After the supervisor went home at ten o'clock, it was Arash who manned the phone. But he liked that. Perfectly okay to sit in the mess room playing cards, but it was better when things were happening; time passed quicker. Soon it would be night, then morning. And then Saturday morning. Thoughts of what was going to happen then welled up in him, only to be interrupted yet again by the telephone. Emergency. Why had he still not fetched the patient from room four?

– He wasn't in room four, he was in number three.

– Are you trying to be funny?

– No.

– I don't give a damn what room he's in. They were expecting him in orthopaedic two hours ago.

Arash knew there was no point in trying to explain. He had done his best to deliver the Swedish-speaking man with the head injury to his destination. Half an hour after he got there, he'd even popped his head in on his own initiative and the patient still wasn't ready; one of the other doctors was giving him some medication and he was waved away once more with a bewildering urgency.

– Do you think the idea is for him to spend the whole night here in Emergency? groaned the voice on the phone.

Arash didn't think so.

– Well then, get the man to where he's supposed to be.

He parked an old lady with a broken hip outside the X-ray lab and returned to Emergency. Sure enough, the patient with the bandaged head was still lying there in room three.

– So the doctors are finally finished with you, said Arash as cheerfully as he could.

The man didn't answer. He lay with his eyes closed and looked as if he was asleep.

– Now I'll take you to where you're supposed to be going. Trust me.

Arash released the brake, manoeuvred out through the doors and headed down towards the end of the corridor.

– There was no accident.

The patient's voice was slurred and feeble.

Arash stopped and leaned forward. – What did you say?

– Has Katja been here?

– Kat? Is that your girlfriend?

– She didn't die in a car crash.

The patient opened one eye now, still seemed more asleep than awake. Just as well, thought Arash. At least this way he's not so frightening.

– When you get to the ward, they'll help you get in touch with your family.

– Ring Katja, the patient snuffled. – She isn't dead. I have to tell her that. It's the eyes.

– You probably have to tell her she's not dead, said Arash, and permitted himself a little smile.

– The eyes are the same. She has eyes you never forget.

The patient was snuffling even more, the pupil in the half-open eye hardly larger than a pinprick. Arash was used to seeing patients under the influence of strong painkilling drugs. Some behaved like drunkards; others were already that way when they arrived.

– Did you call Katja? Is she on her way?

– I'm sure she'll be here, said Arash comfortingly.

– It isn't like you think.

– Okay then.

– She's in the photograph. Third from the left. The patient lifted one hand and pointed, as if the photo were being held up in front of him.

– We're going up to the ward now, said Arash firmly. – Once you get there, they'll sort all this out. They'll ring this girl you want to get hold of. Don't worry.

– Give me the phone.

Arash found it under the pillow, handed it to the patient, not sure that he was capable of holding it, still less finding a number on it and making a call.

The duty phone beeped.

– You forgot the papers.

The woman from reception again. She hadn't said a word about papers until now, but he didn't argue with her. A couple of times before, he'd arrived at a ward without papers. Same thing every time, he was the one that got the telling-off. The papers were not his responsibility but the doctors' and nurses', and it was not uncommon for them to get mixed up. Every single day there were a thousand opportunities to get into a quarrel with someone in this place, and right from the start he'd made up his mind to avoid it. One day he would be a doctor here himself. And then he wouldn't be down on anyone, not nurses nor junior doctors and definitely not porters.

He glanced at the patient. Both eyes closed now. Didn't look so good, should probably not have been given so much painkiller without someone to keep an eye on him afterwards. This was not Arash's job, but he cared, had already started training for the day when it would be his responsibility, and he'd spoken up a couple of times. On at least one occasion he'd prevented a death, he was pretty sure about that.

He bent over the patient. – Can you hear me?

No reaction. He laid a finger on the man's neck, above the tunic. Felt the regular beating. At that moment the man opened his good eye wide and stared at him.

– Who are you working for?

Arash started, straightened up. Realised that this was the look that made him think of the guard he prayed to God he would never have to meet again.

– I don't trust anyone in this place.

– I . . . I've got to go and get your papers, Arash managed to say. – You just lie here for a few moments.

The patient tried to grab hold of his arm.

– You're not going to kill me, are you?

Arash moved away. – You're safe here. Do you know where you are?

The man turned his head. The bandage slid up his forehead; there were cakes of dried blood in the close-cropped hair.

– My wallet, he gasped. – They took my wallet.

Arash bent down and picked up the plastic bag from the tray under the bed. There were some clothes in it, shirt, jacket. There was a wallet in the jacket pocket. He handed it to the man, who struggled to raise his hand.

– Okay, I'll put it somewhere safe for the time being, said Arash, and slipped it into his own pocket. He pushed the bed up against the wall next to the lift, put the brake on and went back to reception in Emergency.

– There's enough going on as it is, the nurse scolded him when he put his head round the door.

– The papers are usually on the table; sometimes they're in the bed, said Arash without raising his voice.

She handed him an envelope. – Not this time they weren't. Pay attention and we won't have any more cock-ups.

And again he managed to produce a smile. This was not his final destination. This was a station along the way. It helped, to think that. With a little bow he took the envelope, walked back along the corridor, pulled on the string; the door opened with a noise that made him think of a choir of the dead whose souls had just departed their bodies. It was almost twelve o'clock. He'd said yes to overtime: another two hours to go before he could crawl in under his duvet.

The phone rang, his own this time. He fished it out of his back pocket. She had insisted on ringing him, even though he had told her he would be working late.

– Hi, Marita. Aren't you usually asleep at this time?

He could hear her smile.

– I'm sitting here with a glass of wine. Alone.

Arash stopped, flattened himself against the wall as one of the other porters came by wheeling a bed.

– Alone?

– He's already left.

– With the shooting club?

– Gone all weekend. This is about the first time I haven't had to go along with him.

– What are you going to do?

– Meet you.

He stared at the corridor wall on the other side. A picture hung there. Flowers beside a lake.

– Is that wise?

– I'm not wise. You're wise. And you said we should have a cup of coffee together.

Yes, he had done. It was a week ago. After the lesson, he'd stayed behind in the classroom. She usually came in as his pupils were making their way out, pulling the trolley with the buckets, a mop in her hand. The first time he was surprised when she started a conversation with him. The next time he was slow packing away his books; she was obviously waiting until they were alone in the room. And once they were, they'd talked more. It was on the fourth occasion that he'd said this about having a cup of coffee together. After that, they called and sent each other text messages every day.

– I want us to meet tomorrow.

– Marita, he said, happy at the chance to say her name. It was lovely. She was lovely. Her eyes were grey-green and mournful, even when she smiled. He wanted to say this to her. He was not the least bit afraid of telling a woman straight out that she was lovely. But he didn't; she was married.

When he'd hung up, he felt calmer. He rounded the corner, stood there looking down the empty corridor. Had to smile. The thought of meeting her had caused him to go in the wrong direction. He'd been training himself not to let his thoughts occupy his mind so much. But she was more than a thought. *Your path begins on the other side.*

He went back through the doors, back down towards Emergency. Stopped by the lift where he'd left the bed, hurried on, peered down the next corridor, stood there trying to think. Someone from the lab came by, pushing a trolley, rows of clinking test tubes.

– Here you are, then, she said.

– Here I am, he muttered, confused.

– Right, then, she said.

– Have you seen a bed with a patient in it?

She looked around, under the trolley with the test tubes; finally she looked in the pocket of her jacket. – Not there either. Suddenly she put her head back and laughed loudly. – Have you lost your patient? Then we'd better organise a search party.

He half ran up to the orthopaedic ward. The duty nurse was sitting in the staffroom.

– Any new patients?

– Lots of them.

– I mean just now, a few minutes ago.

– Who are you talking about?

He pulled out the wallet. Inside was a credit card and a driver's licence. He put the licence down in front of her along with the admission papers. – His name is Ibro Hakanovic.

– He was booked in an hour and a half ago, the duty nurse confirmed.

– But someone from here must have fetched him and taken him up to the ward, Arash insisted, his voice a little louder than he would have liked.

– Well that's your job.

– Yes, he said. – It is my job.

He raced down the stairs and back to Emergency. It is my job, he repeated to himself.

The nurse with the neck like a turkey was on the phone, but she hung up when she saw him.

– Did you deliver the patient *with* his papers this time? He wiped his forehead. – I delivered the papers.

– Good. We can't run a hospital like that.

– But not the patient.

She wrinkled her brow, then gave a strained smile.

– I haven't got time for jokes right now. She turned to the computer.

– I have delivered the papers, but not the patient, Arash blurted out.

She spun round on the chair, stared at him, put on the spectacles that were dangling in a loop around her neck, stared again.

– You're messing me about now, Arash, aren't you? You're messing about with a country lassie.

He explained. The spectacles came off and went on again, her eyes getting smaller and bigger by turn.

– Well, then, off you go and find him, man, don't stand around here gawping. This is a casualty admissions I'm trying to run here, not a lost-property office.

At that moment Zoran entered. – High voices mean high blood pressure, he said. – Not good for you, Brita.

– I've seen a lot of things go on here, she sighed, blushing, – But never porters who manage to make patients disappear.

Zoran turned to Arash. – I knew you were a man of many talents. So now you've taken up conjuring, have you?

He laughed, and Brita laughed too, just briefly, then she puffed out her cheeks and was suddenly not a turkey any more but some bigger bird, ready for a fight.

– Which patient are we talking about?

Zoran was probably on his way from one operation to the next, but he took his time. Arash had never seen him rushed.

Brita peered at the screen. – Ibro Hakanovic, Swedish citizen. Admitted two hours ago, moderate injuries.

– Heard about him. Broken ribs, back pains, concussion. We're keeping him in overnight for observation.

Zoran laid an arm around Arash's shoulder. He was a powerfully built man with greying hair and even greyer stubble, and eyes that missed nothing. It was thanks to him that Arash had got the job.

– We'll get this sorted out. He smiled at Brita, and she sat down again, breathing heavily, but said no more.

– What do you mean? Patients don't just vanish into thin air.

Benjaminsen was from somewhere away up in the north of Norway, and usually when he spoke he sounded so cheerful. Now he sounded more like a tired dog trying to bark into a phone.

Arash explained once more.

– Have you spoken to the security guards? his boss wanted to know.

– They're waiting. Want to know if they should call the police.

– Give over, Arash. The guy must be around here somewhere. We can't have the police running about all over the place every time there's a cock-up. That would look just great.

The head porter said nothing about just who was responsible for the cock-up, but there was no doubting what he thought of the whole business.

– Take one of the guards with you and have a thorough look around.

– We've had a thorough look round. All the wards and corridors around the casualty department.

– Then expand the search, every floor, search the whole place.

– And if we don't find him?

Benjaminsen groaned, a waft of his sleepy exasperation seeping through the line.

– Of course you'll find him.

* * *

Arash was joined by one of the security guards, a stocky little man of about his own age. His face was round and featureless, and his huge forearms bulged through the short sleeves of his uniform shirt. The man made his voice deep and spoke in an abrupt bark. They met in the vestibule, and the guard decided they would head off in different directions and meet up in the middle of each floor.

Half an hour later, they wound up in the security guards' room in the basement. Arash put the wallet on the table.

– Are you walking around with his wallet?

– He gave it to me. I was supposed to be looking after it till he got to the ward. He was scared and full of morphine.

The security guard emptied it: a credit card, a driver's licence. – Ibro Hakanovic. Born 1980. Doesn't sound very Swedish.

He put the cards back, handed the wallet to Arash. – We won't mess about with this any more. Best leave it to the police.

– But we're supposed to find him.

The guard rubbed a hand over his close-cropped hair. – The guy's done a runner, he said with finality.

Arash shook his head. – He's injured, he's bleeding, he's full of painkillers, he could hardly even manage to turn over in the bed.

A low growl from the guard.

– Maybe we should check the cameras, Arash suggested, nodding towards the large bank of computer screens where the movement of people around the hospital could be followed.

The guard looked at him a moment. – *I'll* be the one to decide that.

He turned to the instrument panel, pressed a few buttons. Checked the clock, ran the films backwards and forwards for a while. Corridors with nurses and doctors rushing by and, much more slowly, patients in dressing gowns, some with crutches or Zimmer frames. Now and then someone going in or out of the main entrance.

– Don't see anything here. But a couple of the cameras are out of order.

Arash stood up and peered over his shoulder.

– Stand over *there*. The guard waved him away with his finger, as though he didn't want anyone, or at least not Arash, standing behind him. – They're trying to trace the fault. They've been at it a week now and got nowhere, and now here's the weekend. The matter's been raised at the highest level, but there's cuts here and cuts there. Idiots.

– Where are the ones that aren't working?

The guard rewound the film. – Down in the basement. By the ramp.

Arash leaned heavily against the table. – He can't have got down into the basement.

The guard turned and looked at him for a moment. In the sharp light, his eyes took on an indefinable watery colour.

– Tell me something I don't know, he yawned. – You who are supposed to be looking after the patient, for example, you tell me what you've done with him.

When Arash didn't answer, he added: – You better take a look around in the basement while I check everyone who's left the building in the last hour.

As the lift door glided shut behind him, Arash stood peering down the basement corridor. First in the direction of the staff entrance and the chapel, then the other way, towards the tunnel and the ramp. Began walking in that direction, past the changing rooms. A few stands with white coats and tops hanging from them along the walls. He stopped at a junction, a corridor leading left; he wasn't familiar with it, didn't know where it led to, even though he'd been working there for almost a year. Should've brought a compass, he thought, and peered down through the light reflected in the linoleum from the neon strips in uneven grey puddles. At the far end of the corridor a couple of the strips were gone. There, in the half-dark, he glimpsed something that ought not to have been there. Part of a bed was visible. He hesitated a few seconds, then headed on down.

The bed was empty. The blanket lay there in a heap. Beneath it blood had stained down into the sheet. The bag of clothes hung from the bedhead. First thought: call somebody, call the guard, call the nurses. He rejected it. The patient was injured and debilitated by all the morphine he'd been given. Best to find him without asking for help. It was his duty to make up for his mistake.

– *Onjai?* he suddenly called out in Farsi.

The corridor swallowed up his shout.

– Are you there? he tried again.

He stood there listening. The distant rumbling of the ventilation system. All those other sounds that penetrated down through the enormous building. Even now, at night, the place was full of sound, groans and cries from the floors above, surgical saws and forceps, beds and trolleys being wheeled along, orders and questions, the slapping of footsteps, chat and backchat, the low hum of coffee machines, newspaper pages rustling, the clicking of knitting needles. But in this corridor it suddenly seemed very quiet, a quiet such as he had never known in the hospital before. It reminded him of another basement, in a building filled with sounds that would live in his memory always, voices shouting, the groans and screams of bodies in pain too great for anyone to bear. And suddenly silence. The silence after a gunshot. A silence in which you still don't know that was a blank in the gun held to your head.

Arash rubbed at both temples, as though to erase these

memories from another time, another place that had suddenly surged up to become part of what he was seeing and hearing now.

He tried a door just up beyond the bed. It wasn't locked. A storeroom. Shelves of towels and packs of paper serviettes and cartons of plastic cups, a junction box that gave off a low growling, another door at the far end. He hurried through the room. *Exhaust fan*, the sign said. He closed his eyes. The image of another room, in that other basement. They called it the cold room. For three days he'd sat there in the dark, naked, as the cold penetrated into every cell of his body. *Silence is the surest sign of your death*. He blinked hard a few times to rid himself of these shadow thoughts, but it only made them stronger.

When he tried the latch, it didn't move. He bent down, peered through the gap. It didn't look as if it was locked. He tried once more, still it wouldn't move. He breathed more easily, made his way backwards through the room again.

As he was about to leave the storeroom, he stopped abruptly. Bent down slowly. Two stains on the shelf next to the bottom, neither one bigger than a coin. He touched one with a fingertip.

Blood, still damp.

On the floor, another drop, almost brown against the grey linoleum. And along the wall to the left, more drops.

A cupboard in the innermost corner, the ventilation shaft. The drops of blood led towards it in an almost straight line.

– Ibro, he called above the drone from the junction box. – Ibro Hakanovic?

He followed the drops, walking on tiptoe so as not to tread on any of them. Took a step back as he jerked the little cupboard door open. Another step, but not far enough. What had been doubled up inside followed the door out and tumbled over on top of him with a gush of wind, like air escaping from a giant bellows. Arash was knocked off his feet, the half-naked body pressing him into the floor, pushing him through the floor and on further down.

He screamed, but didn't stop falling.

7

JENNIFER HAD PULLED down the blackout curtains and the
thick velvet curtains, slipped naked into the bed, put on her
sleeping mask, twisted her earplugs into place, wrapped the
summer duvet around her and turned so that her face was
away from the window. The tiredness was still there, but
already it was weaker. An army of thoughts was ready and
waiting to roll in over her, take possession of her and drive
sleep away. She'd learned a counter-technique that involved
directing the attention towards one part of the body after
another, starting with the toes and moving upwards. Now
she was concentrating as hard as she could on a point beneath
the sole of one of her feet.

Something moved. A sliver of light had managed to pene-
trate the fortress walls of the curtain and the rearguard
defence of the mask, and from there straight through the
thin eyelids. Imagining things, she told herself, but it was
enough to disturb her concentration on the sole of her foot.
She raised the mask and turned towards the window. Sure
enough, a slender beam of evening summer light had
threaded its way in through the veranda door and across to
the wall. She groaned in exasperation at her own carelessness,
closed her eyes again, determined to ignore the strip of light;
it could hardly amount to more than a few photons.

Too late, of course. She would have to get up and deal
with it. In a few hours' time the sun would reach that side
of the house and then she'd find herself bathed in light; it

penetrated everything. And if she woke at five, it would be completely impossible to get back to sleep.

She leaned over, tugged at the blackout curtains, so hard that a gap now opened up on the other side. Using an English word, she cursed loudly and shamelessly, then climbed abruptly out of bed. She dealt with the problem, went back to bed again, searched again for that point beneath her foot she had just been concentrating on, knowing all the while that her battle against the superior forces of light was now irrevocably lost.

She had been living in this country for more than twenty years. The first summers had been magical. She and Ivar in the apple orchard with a glass of wine on the table. The light that never went away. The feeling of not even needing sleep. And when she did finally go to bed, she would fall asleep within minutes. Not until years later did the light start to bother her, in the beginning just the occasional night, but then gradually getting worse and worse.

For a while she let her thoughts wander around this memory of the orchard, even though it was such an obvious trap. Seemingly restful, the way it recalled the smells of those still summer evenings. Ivar beside her on the garden sofa, always quiet. The boys in bed. Sigurd, who never slept; he'd inherited her restless wilfulness and could never manage to wind down in the evening. Never any problem with Trym. Not until he grew up. And she realised now that this was where her thoughts had been driving her all the time. Into this sticky web of worries about her elder son.

She sat up, rubbed her hands against her cheeks. The time was quarter past one. Even with the window open, the heat in the room was oppressive. As she heard the sound of a helicopter taking off from the emergency pad down by the hospital, she gave up and went into the kitchen, phone in hand. She called Zoran, hardly expecting he would be able to take the call. He'd gone on duty at eight, and Saturday night was usually hell. She was about to text him a message. Jumped as the phone began to vibrate in her palm, like some little animal woken by the few words she was thinking of sending him.

A hospital number on the display. Why not? she thought. The night's ruined anyway. She'd had a hectic day at the end of a long, hard week. She was behind in her research and would have to work Saturday to catch up. But what bothered her most was the thought of all the other things she should have done. First and foremost called Trym. Ideally driven out to the farm and talked to him.

– Plåterud, she answered, a hint of irritation in her voice. Before too long she was going to stop using that surname, reclaim her own.

It was the chief physician, and she dropped the irritation at once. He would never call her after midnight unless it was something really important.

– We've got a situation at the hospital.

– Situation? she said. – Isn't that why we have hospitals?

– Murder.

She had received similar telephone calls many times before. In all the years she had worked at the forensic institute, it meant she had to drop everything and make her way out to a crime scene. But now that she had stopped working there and found a quiet haven as an ordinary pathologist and researcher, she'd fallen out of the habit of being always prepared.

– I contacted the forensic people, said the chief physician, probably reading her thoughts. – There's complete chaos there at the moment.

She knew all about that. But that wasn't why she had quit. She didn't mind chaos. As long as she could grab a few hours' sleep now and then.

– They're asking if you wouldn't mind helping out. Of course, they say they're not taking it for granted, but there's no one more capable of dealing with the situation than you.

She grunted. She had no objection at all to flattery, even if the ulterior motive was as obvious as it was on this occasion.

– Okay, she said. – I'll get down there.

It took her two minutes to find what to wear, another two to put on make-up, three to walk over to the Akershus University Hospital staff entrance. Several police cars were parked there. A uniformed constable guarding the door. Broad shouldered and shaven headed. The former she liked, not too keen on the latter.

– I'm going to need to see some ID, he said with what sounded like a deliberate attempt to be polite.

She pulled her ID out of her bag. – I've been asked to come down here.

He glanced at it, then at her, coolly assessing her, then back at the card again before nodding and letting her pass.

Several policemen in the basement corridor. One of them with a huge dog on a leash. The chief physician appeared through a door. He wasn't much taller than her, with a halo of hair of indeterminate colour encircling his head and a nose that was much too big for his sharp-boned face.

– Jennifer, he exclaimed, as though they were old friends who hadn't seen each other for a long time. – So happy to have you on board.

She wasn't quite sure what he was on about but didn't bother to ask. He touched her arm and pointed down the corridor. Two policemen there talking to someone sitting on the floor, a young man wearing whites, obviously an employee, looked Turkish or Arabic. He had blood on his face and on his shirt front. As Jennifer passed, he looked up at her, and only then did she realise it was the porter who Zoran had got the job for.

She stopped and retraced her steps.

– Are you hurt?

She'd seen him quite often wheeling beds about but had never exchanged more than a couple of words with him. Zoran said he was an Iranian and that he'd arrived here after a dramatic flight from the ayatollahs.

The porter moved his lips but didn't answer her question. Looking into the wide-open eyes, she wondered for a moment if he was insane.

The chief physician touched her arm again, a polite reminder. Only the exceptional circumstances could justify his constant touching.

– He's in shock, naturally, but otherwise unharmed.

– He was the one who found the body? she asked as they walked on.

– As far as I know. I'm still not clear about exactly what happened. He's had a sort of panic attack. A doctor's going to take a look at him.

– Why does he have blood on his clothes?

The chief physician shook his head and showed her through an open door that led into a storage room.

In one corner there was a huge lamp. Three technicians busy in the harsh light. She recognised one of them, had worked with him during her time as a forensic pathologist.

– Hi, Jenny. He flipped two fingers to his cap.

The guy had spent half a year down under and always felt obliged to show her that he'd managed to pick up something that just might pass for an Australian accent.

– Thought you'd got away with it slipping off into the bush, did you?

The hospital in Akershus was all of fifteen minutes away from the centre of Oslo, and she gave him a little smile, thinking how one of the things she missed was working with crime-scene technicians on a job. She had always enjoyed the banter.

– I'll go and put some work clothes on, she told him.

He looked her over. She had on a light blue summer frock, but two minutes with a make-up pouch wasn't enough to work miracles.

– Don't disturb anything here until I get back.

She was shown into an office where she could change. Again she passed the porter sitting on the floor. This time he didn't look up, just sat there staring straight ahead.

She pulled on her overalls and cap. Took a last look in the mirror hanging above the sink. Her face still looked like a building site, but as soon as she entered the storage room, she put these useless considerations aside.

By the far wall, in front of a closet, the twisted body of a man. Powerful upper-body muscles, cropped black hair with bleached highlights. His face was turned to one side; she could see one wide-open eye. He was wearing a black T-shirt and boxer shorts. Blood across the linoleum around him, but not much. She bent down, noted that the shirt was ripped in the belly region, lifted it and saw that there were four stabs wounds and another one directly below the costal arch, this one in an upward direction so that she realised at once the liver had probably been damaged. Carefully she lifted the head with one hand. A crackling sound as the cartilage parted in a gap that went directly across the larynx.

– We haven't touched him, said the technician she knew from earlier. – Had to wait for a doctor to make quite sure he's dead. Not something your average half-witted copper is capable of.

– You just do your job, you, she grinned back at him.
– And let me take care of the patient.

By the time she let herself out of the pathology lab, it was gone three thirty. Tiredness had caught up with her again, now in the form of a vague heaviness in the region of her sacrum; soon it would be making its way up her through her back. If she hurried, she might get at least a couple of hours before having to start on the autopsy. Every once in a while sleep did in fact manage to break through, like some sneak thief, no matter how much light there was in the room, and that was what she really needed now, to have every last one of her thoughts and concerns stolen.

As she was about to enter the lift, a voice behind her.
– Jenny.

She turned, recognised him at once, even though years had passed since they last met. And even though the years had left their mark on the face she looked up into.

– Hi, she said, feeling herself blush.
– Hi, he said, not letting go of the hand she had held out in her confusion.

She pulled herself free. – Are the Oslo police involved in this case?
– No, just me. Pastures new.

She remembered now, hearing somewhere that Roar Horvath had gone back home to Lillestrøm.

– You too, I see. Got a minute?
– Why not? she murmured, annoyed that she wasn't able to come up with an excuse.

She made him instant coffee in a plastic cup back in the office.

– I hear you're doing the autopsy.

She hesitated a few moments. – I'm finished with forensic medicine. I was asked to do this as a favour. And you, she went on, to change the subject, – detective with the Romerike district police?

He looked straight at her, smiled quickly. – Section leader, actually.

She hooked her hair behind her ears; it fell forward again immediately. – A leader who gets up in the middle of the night to visit a crime scene?

She recalled him as an averagely talented and averagely committed police officer. As something else too, from the times when she had been to his house, even though she had done all she could to forget it.

– I like to be involved. I see the job a little differently now to how I did before. Something happened a couple of years ago. A friend of mine . . .

He moved the coffee cup around in his hand.

– He died in a fire. Actually, the best friend I ever had. A lot of other things happened too. I ought to have known . . . Still, that's the way it goes, there's a lot we should have known.

He seemed changed somehow, more serious; she didn't know if she quite liked it. Had no intention anyway of spending the rest of the night in true confessions and doesn't life just tear us apart and all that. He was sitting in her office, it was almost four o'clock; she should have asked him to come back during the day, or preferably ring.

– What happened down there in the basement? she said as she drank her coffee, thin and tepid.

Roar Horvath scratched his neck. – Swedish citizen, thirty-four years old, admitted to hospital last night. Injuries to his back and head, none of them serious. And then he disappears.

– Disappears?

– He vanished before they could get him to his ward. They looked everywhere. Then this porter's wandering about down in the basement, comes across a trail of blood, opens the closet door and the body falls out on top of him. At least that's what we've got out of him so far.

Jennifer put her cup aside, more curious than she had the energy for.

– What the hell sort of story is that?

Roar Horvath ran his hand through his thin quiff. His widow's peak was more prominent now than it used to be.

– You can say that again.

– You believe his explanation?

– It's not really a question of belief.

Was he being patronising? Suddenly she felt annoyed. Wanted to end the conversation and go home.

– Do you know him?

She shook her head. Didn't know any more than what Zoran had told her. The guy wanted to study medicine. In Zoran's opinion he was certainly bright enough, if they'd give him the chance.

The thought of Zoran made her pick up her phone. Maybe have a few minutes with him, if he wasn't busy in the operating theatre.

– Apparently he's been working here for a year, said Roar Horvath. – From Iran. Refugee, apparently.

Jennifer got up. – Must try and get some sleep before I go back to work.

– Not a bad idea. You have somewhere here you can get your head down?

– I live here now. Close by. Been here for a while.

The lines in Roar Horvath's brow deepened. To her they still looked like three gulls in flight. – Moved from the farm up there?

She drained her cup and put it down in a way that was supposed to say they needed to end this conversation now, that from her point of view it had ended, that she had no intention of sitting there in the middle of the night or at any other time discussing her private affairs with Roar Horvath, former detective sergeant attached to the violent-crimes section of the Oslo police. She didn't want him to know anything at all about what she'd been through over the last few years, about leaving Ivar and the farm, leaving two sons who should've been adult enough to understand what she could never explain to them, that it was all over between her and their father and had been for years, that she was leaving him in order to survive. Not because Ivar in any way bothered her, or ever had done; on the contrary, it was all the things he *hadn't* done, all the things he wasn't, that was driving her crazy. In his helpless fashion, all he ever wanted was for her to be happy. As though that made leaving him any easier.

– I'll be in touch with the police tomorrow, she said, opening the door.

– You can call *me*.

He handed her a card. She dropped in into her bag without looking at it. – I'll be doing the autopsy before lunch. You can expect a provisional report sometime in the afternoon.

– I don't doubt it. He didn't take his eyes off her. – You're one of the best I've ever worked with. It's a pity for forensics you quit.

Maybe he was being sincere. To avoid having to use the lift with him, she opened a drawer and turned her back, pretended to be looking for something.

He stood there in the open doorway. – The chief physician would prefer it if we don't announce the cause of death just yet. No hint at all of what might have happened down there in the basement.

She turned to him. – Can something like that be kept a secret?

He smiled in a way she recalled from the days when they

worked together. And not just worked together either, she had to correct herself, but that was as far as she would go in conceding what had happened, even in her thoughts.

– Of course not, he said. – But you know how much trouble there's been here. Patient security and all that. They're asking for the weekend to work out the best way to handle it. Fine by us. The longer we get to work in some sort of peace, the better we like it.

8

It was the woman who started asking him questions. She was wearing a uniform shirt, with her fair hair gathered at the neck. How long was he away when the bed with the patient disappeared? Was it common for the papers to be left behind at A&E? How was the search conducted? Simple questions, simple answers. She let him speak without interrupting, nodded now and then, and her eyes were friendly. Why had he gone down into the basement alone? What did he think when he saw the trail of blood on the floor, and why hadn't he called for help? Hard to answer that one, but he managed it. Avoided saying what he knew he mustn't say, not at any price. That the stairs down to the basement reminded him of the stairs in the prison at Evin, that he couldn't shake the thought that the patient in the bed resembled one of the guards, someone whose name he didn't want to remember, someone he'd tried to remove every trace of from his thoughts but who nevertheless appeared in his nightmares, sometimes in broad daylight too, in visions, and then suddenly in a hospital bed. Because it was the guard lying there, but at the same time not him, and he couldn't reveal any of this.

You'll be all right, Arash.

He said that inside himself, over and over again, until the words came from someone else, someone who had helped him before.

In the car on the way down to the police station, he hadn't

managed to say anything. Not even when they took him into this room. Only when the woman in the light blue shirt came in was he able to speak. He felt as though this woman wished him well.

But when the other one started asking questions, things changed again. This policeman was wearing a leather jacket with a white T-shirt below it; he had a moustache, and a fringe that accentuated the egg-like shape of his head. His eyes were grey-blue and slightly protruding. Just now and then, certain things about him seemed to resemble the patient. The look in Ibro Hakanovic's eyes as he lay in the bed talking to him. Arash drove the images away, forced himself to return to the place where he actually was, an interrogation room in the police station in Lillestrøm, a room painted grey and white, no windows, no pictures on the walls. They'd said they wanted him there for a conversation. When the man in the leather jacket started asking questions, it wasn't a conversation any more but an interrogation, because he gave nothing in return. Sat in his chair with an expressionless face and noted down his answers. And then the questioning took another direction. Who were his contacts in Norway? Did he move in Iranian circles? How long had he been in the country? When he answered *three and a half years*, the woman interjected that he spoke unusually good Norwegian for someone who'd been there such a short time. He turned to her in gratitude, and perhaps her face coloured a little when he looked at her. He wished she could have been there alone with him.

But it was still the man with the bulging eyes who was asking the questions. He had introduced himself, and Arash knew quite well what his name was but avoided thinking about him as anything other than a policeman. The woman's name was Ina Sundal. He held on to that.

– You came here as a refugee three and a half years ago,

said the policeman. – You claim that you travelled via Turkey and Germany.

Arash felt himself nod. He had retraced the route of his flight many times when waking up in the middle of the night. The mountain pass in the winter darkness. The group of fifteen approaching the border step by step. Their guide had been given most of his money before they started and they didn't know whether they could trust him. He was a Kurd, and if he betrayed them he would be paid a lot more money than they would ever be able to afford. Besides his own rucksack, Arash was carrying the pack belonging to the oldest man in the group, a seventy-year-old who could hardly breathe in the blizzard.

– Why did you come to Norway?

He glanced across at Ina Sundal.

– Nothing happens by chance, he said to her.

– I see, said the policeman.

– I could have stayed in Germany. But a friend I made in Frankfurt knew someone in Norway who could help me. A hospital doctor.

– Whose name is?

– Zoran Vasic. He got me the job as porter.

Ina Sundal noted something down on her pad, must have been the name. He could have told them more about Zoran. Asked if he could ring him. Thinking about Zoran helped. Made it easier to answer questions. No, he wasn't married, had no close relatives in Norway, lived alone, had no girl-friend.

The policeman interrupted. – A few minutes ago you told us you got a phone call from a woman. That was one of the reasons you were away so long.

He had said this to Ina Sundal; now he regretted it.

– Yes.

– Yes what?

– A woman. Someone I know.

– But not a girlfriend?

– No, not a girlfriend.

– What is her name?

– What do you mean?

He knew perfectly well what the man meant. Had to do all he could to keep Marita out of this, but it was too late. They could check his phone at any time, find her number.

– I'm asking you to let me have the woman's name.

– Is it important?

– That we don't know.

– Her name is Marita.

Her husband was a policeman too. He might get to hear everything that was being said in this room. He thought that he could never meet Marita again.

– What else?

– Does this have to be written down?

He looked at Ina Sundal, saw the shadow of a smile in her eyes.

– Don't worry about it, Arash. What you say in here stays within these four walls.

He was going to have to trust her.

– Marita Dahl.

– How did you meet her?

– She works at the same school as me.

– Teacher?

– She cleans the classrooms.

– And what do you do there?

– I teach.

– Teach what?

– Norwegian. For people from other countries. Like me.

– Have you been back to Iran since you came here?

Ina Sundal wanted to know this.

– I can't go back.

– You can't see your family?

She cared about that kind of thing.

– No—

– Why can't you go back? the policeman interrupted. He had a printout on the table in front of him. Arash could see it was about him, and yet still this question, as though he didn't believe what was almost certainly written there. Or he was choosing to ignore the fact that Arash had taken part in protests at the university, had even been named as one of the leaders. *Silence is the surest sign of your death*. The words were there again now. They had been with him through all the hundred and eighty-four days he had spent in the Evin prison. He could have shown them the marks on his body from each and every one of those days; they would never fade.

– I am a wanted man, he contented himself with saying. – I am on a list of enemies of the Iranian state.

This unleashed a new round of questions. Again, how much contact did he have with other Iranians in Norway? What about asylum seekers and refugees from other countries? Arash couldn't imagine what all this had to do with what had happened earlier that night. And then it hit him: he wasn't just a witness, not just the person who happened to have found a dead body in a cupboard in the basement floor of the hospital. He was a suspect, and his background strengthened the suspicions against him. Suddenly he saw things from the outside, as though he were standing behind the people on the other side of the table. He was no longer the person sitting in that chair but a refugee from Iran whom he knew all about. No, Arash was not attached to any mosque in Oslo, yes, he would call himself a Muslim, though not many imams, either back home or here, would.

– And the dead man, do you know his name?

– Ibro Hakanovic. Swedish.

– So you knew him?

– No.

He repeated what the refugee Arash, who was sitting in the chair had tried to explain, that he had found the driver's licence and the credit card in the patient's wallet.

– And what were you doing walking around with his wallet?

He had already explained that too. And what the man had said when he gave it to him.

– You said he seemed afraid? And yet you left him alone there in the corridor?

Having placed himself outside of events, he was breathing more calmly now and following closely every movement in the face of the Arash who was sitting in the chair. Whispered in his ear what he should answer. He'd been through so many previous interrogations and that was the way he had always survived before, by stepping away from Arash and into the other, the protector able to take care of everything.

– The patient had been assaulted a few hours earlier, he said, letting Arash look directly at the policeman. – He was very confused. I have seen many patients with head injuries. They arrive, particularly over the weekends, they've been fighting, been beaten up. Nothing unusual about it. Happens all the time.

In this country, he might have added but didn't. Thought this wasn't the right time to start talking about alcohol and violence. Felt no call to either, didn't need to start saying what was wrong about Norway. The Arash in the chair came from something worse, from a place where an interrogation like this could be a matter of life and death. He disliked this policeman, his persona, the part he was playing, but not more than he liked Ina Sundal's persona. Something happened to her eyes when they met his, the pupils grew larger, and twice she'd adjusted the hairband around her blond ponytail. From his position there, outside of Arash, he saw the two officers so clearly that it almost made him burst out laughing. It had always been easy for him to see the ways in which people dealt with their insecurities, those who lived with them, and those who wrestled against them, like an enemy to be overcome. Again he thought of Marita. Perhaps he would meet her again after all, talk more to her without other people being around. Just talk; anything else would be idiotic. But when it came to women, he had always been an idiot. If it hadn't been for a woman, he might never have joined the struggle against the ayatollahs, or even the protests over the corrupt elections. And Arash the refugee would never have ended up precisely where he was now, in a plastic chair, in an interrogation room, in a country a thousand miles from his home town.

It was past five when he let himself in and flipped off his shoes in the hallway. Finn Olav and Tonje's baby was awake and crying on the floor above. From his own kitchen he heard the sound of a boiling kettle.

Ferhat was sitting at the table.

– *Guten Morgen*, said Arash.

Ferhat looked up from the week-old newspaper. – *Arbeit?* He preferred to speak German, spiced with a few Kurdish and Norwegian phrases.

Arash nodded. He said nothing about the interrogation, nothing about what had happened at the hospital.

– Have you eaten? he asked. – *Gegessen?*

Ferhat pointed at the fridge. He was frugal when it came to food, usually had to be persuaded to help himself. Coffee was his only indulgence, half a jar of instant a day, maybe more.

This wasn't the first time Arash had had an illegal living with him. He often said yes when someone he trusted asked him. Checked the background as far as possible, said no if he picked up any hint of narcotics or prostitution. Felt he had an obligation to help others. He'd been extraordinarily lucky himself. Without the aid of others he would never have made it here. Would never have made it anywhere.

He put bread and turkey sausage on the table.

– It's halal, he assured him, and Ferhat grimaced, revealing the stubs of his teeth. Arash didn't know if it mattered to him; he hadn't seen him praying once in the three days he'd been there, but he never asked people about things like that.

– I've got a job, the Kurd revealed as they sat there with their plates. The first day he hadn't said a word; since then there'd been a few brief, halting conversations.

– *Arbeit macht frei*, he added, and Arash looked closely at him, to see if he was joking. There was nothing to indicate it, and he wondered if he should ask the man if he knew where the phrase came from.

– Where have you got a job? he said instead.

Ferhat thought about it. – He runs a firm. *Gesellschaft*.

– In Oslo?

– Club. Ferhat nodded. – *Tanzen*.

He made a movement with his shoulders, probably trying to illustrate what dancing was.

– Drive. Fetch things. *Vielleicht*.

– Without a driving licence?

Ferhat thought about it. – He'll fix it.

Arash stood up, put his plate in the sink. – Does a place to live come with it?

– *Bald*.

– Well, you can stay here until then.

Ferhat looked at the untouched slice of bread. Maybe that downcast look was his way of saying thank you.

9

MARITA WITH HER back to the big window looking out on to the square in front of the station. Arash, facing it, could see the hills rising on the other side of the river behind her, and the afternoon light that almost broke through the thin cloud layer. He could follow all the figures crossing the square and coming closer.

– Ham roll, please, he repeated after her, putting more stress on the *ham*.

– I think your Norwegian is amazingly good, she said without looking up from the menu.

– It's a strange language, said Arash. – Not difficult, but strange.

She glanced up at him. Her eyes were grey and green and suited the timbre of her voice.

You are in love, Arash. For the first time since you came here, you are in love. You have met thousands of women. Iranian, of course, Arabic and African. Many of them understood that they can look at you as they sit behind their desks in the classroom; they don't need to be careful about where they're looking. And all the Norwegian women who greet every man with a smile, as though he were the love of their life. Of all these women you could have fallen in love with, you picked one that is married.

This is a great test for you.

This last thought took him by surprise, and he tried to

discover where it came from. Peered at the people passing on the street outside as though among them there might be someone who had the answer. An elderly man pushing a pram, heading away from the station. Maybe he's minding his grandchild, he thought, or it could even be his own child. Two young people, their arms around each other, she wearing a short shirt that left her whole stomach visible. A woman crossing the street from the car park. She was tall, with longish dark hair, walked with a slight limp.

– How come you speak it so well? After only three years?

He shrugged. – Each time you learn a new language, the next one gets a little bit easier.

– How many languages can you speak?

– Farsi, of course. Pashtun, Arabic, French, English, Norwegian. And a smattering of Russian.

He liked the way she drew breath, to show how impressed she was.

– I've always been interested in languages.

– How long does it take you to learn a new one?

He weighed it over.

– I could probably discuss quite a few things within a couple of weeks.

– What would be the first word you learn?

He put down the menu, looked across at her, the thin dress with its tiny heart-shaped buttons down the front.

– *Pretty*, he said. – *Pretty*, and then *woman*.

He was on the verge of leaning forward to touch the hand resting on the table, or her forehead, the reddish hair. The thought that he might actually do it at any moment was almost unendurable.

– Marita.

She looked inquisitively at him. The sound of her name floating in the air between them.

– I asked you if it might be difficult for you to sit here. He glanced around. – I mean, if someone you know sees us together.

Again she appeared to direct all her concentration at the menu. – I don't often come to Lillestrøm. Don't know anyone here. Is it difficult for *you*?

He shook his head. That was the way it was in this country. It was his business if he went to a café with a woman, regardless of who she was, if she was Christian or Jew, rich or poor, no matter what country she came from, which family.

– You're married, he said in a low voice.

– Do you want me to leave?

That was the last thing he wanted.

– I'm very happy that you and I are sitting right here right now. As for what happens later, I have no idea.

A tiny furrow appeared in the middle of her brow. – I feel the same way too.

– But I can't help thinking about the fact that you have a home. A husband. I don't want you to get hurt in any way.

It didn't come out well. If he really was concerned for her welfare, he would not have asked her out.

– Okay then, let's talk about it, she said. – Since you think about it all the time.

The waiter approached their table.

– Have you decided yet? he asked.

Marita opened the menu yet again.

– We'll order drinks now and come back to the food.

– Of course, said the waiter, and Arash could hear that he was Swedish. The way he spoke reminded him of something. He knew what it was: the patient's voice, the one who had asked if he were a Muslim, the one who'd asked about his ring, the one who'd disappeared and was murdered in the basement. He saw in his mind's eye the steps leading down, couldn't help it, but it wasn't the same basement as the Evin prison. He clung on to that, closed his eyes for a few seconds, rubbed his forehead with his hands.

– Is something wrong?

He looked down at the table, at the uneven brown stains.

– Nothing wrong.

The sun had broken up the cloud and was shining in through the window, burning on his neck.

– He's very suspicious, said Marita, and realising he didn't understand what she was talking about added: – My husband.

Not without good reason, thought Arash, but didn't say it.

– Does he want you to be happy? he asked instead.

She appeared to be thinking this over. – I don't know, she said at last. – I don't know what he wants for me.

Their coffees were served. She sipped from hers, patted her lips with a serviette and left a small brown mark on it. He felt he wanted to pick it up and press it against his own lips.

– How did you meet him?

– Do we have to talk about this?

– No. I'm sorry.

She turned her head and looked out of the window for a few seconds. He was about to change the subject when she continued speaking.

– I was with somebody else, but it wasn't good for me. My husband seemed very different. Again she used the serviette to pat her lips dry. – We started sending text messages to each other. One day he called. And then he came to see me. And, well, you know.

Arash didn't know, but didn't ask.

– At first it was really good. Much too good. I should've realised. He's a policeman, after all, and I really trusted him

. . . I can't carry on the way things are now. She leaned forward and lowered her voice. – Is that wrong of me?

– No, he said, looking into her eyes. – No, he said again, as much to silence his own doubt, to drive it off into some dark corner where it was invisible and inaudible. He felt a strong urge to tell her what he felt when he saw her, what he felt when he woke up and thought of her.

– We are two people, he began, and maybe because that was such an obvious thing to say, it made her smile. – Two grown people, he added. – We live in a country in which grown people make their own decisions about almost everything affecting their lives. If someone had told me before I came here that such a place existed, I would probably have said it was impossible. Maybe I would have said such a place would be dangerous.

– Is it dangerous?

He raised his hand and could have placed it on her bare arm. Her fingers almost touching his, so much paler. They had marks from rings, but she wasn't wearing any. He forced himself to look outside, at the sharp light above the hills, the last scraps of cloud disappearing, the people coming and going.

– Your ring, she said. – There's something written on it. Is that Persian?

He nodded. Pronounced it slowly: – *Sokoot, sokhæne khodast*.

His father had given it to him. Arash remembered him standing in the doorway, watching as he packed the few things he intended to take with him. It was his father who had got him released from the Evin prison. He'd gone to the imam, who had friends in high places. His father had done that for him even though his imprisoned son had already cost him his job. He hadn't spoken of it afterwards. Hadn't spoken to him at all. And then there he was, standing in the doorway as Arash was preparing to leave. He held out his hand. Arash took it, hesitantly. When he drew back, he was holding the ring. At first he thought it had slipped from his father's finger.

Your ring.

His father shook his head.

It's your ring now.

He wanted to hand it back. But it was impossible.

Put it on, it will protect you.

He did so, slipping it on to his finger.

It was the last time they saw each other.

– What does it mean? Her finger was still touching the black enamel.

Arash hesitated before he said: – Silence, God's language.

She nodded, as though this were a truth she immediately recognised.

– There's something I have to tell you, Marita. But I don't know if I should . . . He tried again: – At the hospital yesterday. Last night. A patient died.

It felt so wrong to be talking to her about this. If he let her in any further, told her about the basement, and the dead patient who fell on top of him, as though the whole thing were his fault, if he took her down into that basement, she would never come up again.

He glanced over towards the open door, felt the breeze, a warm hand touching his neck. Again looked out across the square in front of the station, checking to see if there was something out there that could hold him back, stop him from revealing any more about what had happened. A taxi stopped and a woman got out; the driver lifted her red suitcase out for her and the woman began wheeling it towards the station entrance. Her trousers and jacket were red too, and it was as though the colour was a warning that something terrible was about to happen. Two men stopped on the pavement on the far side and spoke to each other. One had his back towards the café. The other had on a suit and a white shirt open at the neck. He was unshaven, a handsome man. Arash sat watching him. Marita said something, it seemed to come from far away, and he took out a handkerchief, dabbed at the side of his neck where a drop of sweat was about to trickle down inside his collar.

The two men outside concluded their conversation. The one in the suit headed right towards the station while the other, in jeans and a T-shirt, stayed where he was and pulled something from his back pocket, a packet of cigarettes. He lit one, turned and glanced across the street towards the café window. For a few seconds he stood there, looking at the table where they were sitting, and Arash met his gaze and recognised him immediately. It couldn't possibly be him, but he was no longer able to doubt it; he never forgot a face, and this was one he had seen just a few hours earlier.

– What is it? Marita twisted round and followed his gaze.

– Don't turn round. He grabbed her arm and she did as he said.

– Wait here, he told her.

– Arash, what's going on?

Her voice seemed far away, as though she was sitting in the next room. She sounded scared.

– Don't go anywhere. Don't be afraid.

She tried to protest, but he was already at the door.

Outside, he saw the man crossing the roundabout. Arash half ran after him. The man turned down into the station underpass; he was tall, quite well built. Arash knew he ought to leave it. A voice, maybe his own, kept telling him he was making a mistake, that it must be someone else. He kept muttering to himself as he ran.

He caught up with him halfway through the underpass.

– Hello.

The man stopped and looked down at him. Arash saw it then, in the eyes, the way the pupils expanded.

– Yes?

– I know you.

Again he studied the face, the muscles flickering in the forehead, in the jaw.

– Don't think so, the man said in broken Norwegian.

– Ibro Hakanovic.

The man's eyebrows gathered, the eyes narrowed.

– You are mistaken.

Arash didn't stop looking at him. If he backed off now, he would never get rid of him, he would see this man in others who passed him by, more and more often, every minute, every second.

– I am not mistaken. You were at the hospital. You were injured. I followed you down into the basement.

The man shook his head, carried on walking. Arash followed him for a few steps, until the other whipped round.

– Get lost.

Arash raised a hand. He was holding something in it, a knife; he must have taken it with him from the café.

– I know who you are, he shouted.

The man took a step towards him, then he backed away, turned and ran.

Arash slumped again the wall of the underpass, buried his face in its rough surface.

She was standing outside when he returned to the café. When she saw him coming, she went to meet him and took hold of his arm.

– Arash, you must tell me what's going on.

She was right, he had to tell her, he no longer had any choice. She was afraid, and he didn't want her to be afraid.

– I've paid. You said you had a car.

He nodded and led the way to the car park, got in, didn't start the engine. Sat there staring through the windscreen, out into the car park. People passing on the pavement. They've got nothing to do with me, he thought. Don't let them into your story. An elderly man putting bags of shopping into the boot of a car. Someone younger, in a tracksuit, walking a dog. A tall woman with dark hair and a slight limp; maybe he'd seen her earlier that day. Marita, beside him in the front seat. And when he said her name inside, he started to talk, as though the name had been a switch. He told her about the patient who had disappeared. Who before he vanished had asked him about his ring and said something about a car crash, like a warning. He described how he had to search down in the basement. And the man tumbling out of the storeroom, the heavy body forcing him down on to the floor. He smelled of sweat and blood and dead flowers, and maybe that was what Ibro Hakanovic was trying to do, warn him about something that was going to happen. Because he sort of had his arms around Arash as they lay there on the floor, as if he was trying to stop him from getting up.

Afterwards he realised he was dead.

– If he's dead, then you can't have seen him walking along the street in Lillestrøm.

He was still glancing round. Today was even warmer than the ones before, the sun even sharper.

– You're probably right.

She didn't take her eyes off him. – Of course I'm right.

– I can't have seen him here.

She put an arm around his neck, pulled his head towards her, resting it against her neck, hugged him.

– It must have been awful, Arash.

He inhaled the smell of her warm skin. Her voice had

come closer again; she was no longer in an adjacent room. He told her about the basement, the other basement, the one in Evin jail. He managed to control his thoughts again, light and shadow parted.

He didn't tell her everything; most of what happened couldn't be spoken of. She was a good person. The two of them had come together for a reason. He must take care of her. There were people in the world who wanted evil. And there were people who wanted to protect others. Maybe everyone had something of both in them. Maybe it was he himself who turned the people he met into one or the other. That it was because of him that she was now sitting beside him as his protector. He held on to that thought. She was good because he had made her good.

– We'll take a drive, she decided.

It wasn't his car they were sitting in; it belonged to Finn Olav from the floor above. That time he had walked the crying young girl home, Finn Olav had invited him in for coffee, thanked him, and over and over again insisted that if there was any way at all in which he could repay him, he mustn't hesitate to ask. And that afternoon he had not hesitated. *Borrow the car?* Finn Olav had echoed, his forehead creased in wrinkles. Arash was on the point of withdrawing the request, but then the doctor smiled broadly and slapped him on the shoulder. Of course Arash could borrow a car. Which one, Tonje's Golf or his own new Prius hybrid? Take that one, think green.

That was the thought he clung on to as he started the silent car. Everywhere you went there were people who helped each other. Small things, large things. And people with evil intentions. He had to make sure he was always in a place where he was able to see who was what.

– Of course, I can't drive you home, he said.

The light was still not completely divided from the

darkness, but he felt safer now. She sat there, still stroking his hair.

– We can go back to your place. I never got round to drinking my coffee. Didn't eat anything either.

He tried to think it through. Ferhat was going to be out all day. For some reason or other he'd asked the Kurd about that before leaving the flat.

– Coffee. He nodded. – Coffee and food.

The door wasn't locked. He understood why, and for an instant he thought of turning round and taking her somewhere else. She was already standing in the hallway.

Ferhat was sitting in the living room. No newspaper on the table in front of him, only a bag of chewing tobacco, a kettle, a jar of instant coffee, half full. He looked up as they came in. Looked at Arash, looked at Marita, no reaction at all showing in his face.

– This is Ferhat.

The Kurd didn't react, carried on slowly chewing the tobacco or whatever it was he had in his mouth.

Arash turned to Marita. – Ferhat's staying here with me for a few nights, he explained. – He doesn't have anywhere to live.

He took Marita into the kitchen. – He's having a hard time of it, he told her.

She nodded. – You like helping people. I noticed that about you at once.

He put out cups, found some biscuits in the cupboard, fetched the kettle from the living room where Ferhat, barefoot and wearing only a shirt and a pair of stained tracksuit trousers, still sat motionless on the sofa, chewing and staring into the air.

– We'll go for a walk and take our food with us, Marita decided. – I like walking.

10

Before starting the autopsy, Jennifer described the corpse lying on the table. Male, 193 centimetres tall, powerfully built, cropped black hair. External injuries: five stab wounds in the lower belly with a pointed sharp weapon, probably a knife, the deepest of them 8.3 centimetres. Laceration to the throat, a thin cut 7.5 centimetres in length, the cartilage, nerves and vessel in the thyroid gland severed, but none of the main arteries in the neck, which explained the limited amount of blood at the scene. She also described the blunt-force traumas, presuming that most of them were inflicted before admission to hospital, almost certainly the cause of his admission.

At about eleven, Zoran appeared. He had one of the junior doctors with him. Jennifer tried to move some of the strands of hair dangling down over her face without using her hands, felt herself blushing from the edge of her cap down.

– This is Finn Olav, said Zoran. – He was the one who admitted the patient yesterday.

She held up the bloody gloves to show why she couldn't shake hands.

Finn Olav repeated his name, and his surname, Kiran. He didn't look to be much over thirty but already showed signs of a double chin and an emerging bald spot. In the pathology lab lighting his face looked a pale yellow colour. It made her think of how she herself must look, standing there in the green gown, glasses perched on her nose and a face puffy from lack of sleep.

– Everyone's talking about this down on the wards, said Zoran. It must have been a long time since he'd had any sleep too, but it didn't show, and the stubble on his cheeks that turned grey at the point of his chin and then black down his throat suited him. – There are rumours that someone stabbed him.

Jennifer opened her arms wide in exasperation. – The management is trying to keep it quiet. They're hoping to have the weekend before they need to give details. Not a good idea, if you ask me.

– And they did, presumably? Ask you?

– Of course not. But I said so anyway, to the chief physician himself.

She had seen a brief report on the net under the headline *Died at Akershus as a result of injuries*. Not exactly wrong, but nothing about the murder that had taken place in the basement. Did management think that people's confidence in the hospital wouldn't be shaken if it took several days for the truth to emerge?

– Just wait till the press gets hold of this. And yes, it *is* true that a man was stabbed to death. She thought there was no harm in revealing at least this much to the doctors responsible for the patient. – But you didn't hear it from me.

She stepped aside and let them see the body with the now opened chest.

– Stab wounds to the lower belly, she indicated.

– Look fatal, Zoran observed. He had now put his spectacles on.

– He died of drowning, Jennifer informed him with a slight smile.

Finn Olav turned to her. – The man drowned? Where?

She lifted the sheet covering the head and neck. Zoran studied the cut in the throat. – I presume blood from the severed thyroid gland ran down into the lungs, he said.

– He drowned in his own blood.

Finn Olav bent over to look at the lungs, which had been removed and laid separately on the table. –That's crazy. Though wouldn't the lack of blood to the brain be fatal before that?

Zoran nodded. – But all the main arteries seem to be intact. Is that correct, Jenny?

– If you want to take over and finish the job, then be my guest, she sighed, feeling a desire to cuddle up to him.

– I wish I could. You need to get some rest.

– What about you? You've been on duty for over twenty-four hours.

– I'm fine. I'm off in another hour. When are you finished for the day?

He looked at her, and the question turned into an invitation. Finn Olav glanced quickly at each of them in turn, an angled wrinkle forming over one eye. In the beginning, Jennifer had done what she could to keep the relationship with Zoran a secret, but now the whole world might as well know it.

By the time she was finished, it was eleven thirty. Still not tired, but feeling a tenacious exhaustion that prickled all over, mostly in her neck. She thought about having lunch, decided to dictate her preliminary report first. It took ten minutes, on autopilot; she'd lost count of how many of these she'd done over the years.

She should have spent the afternoon on her research project. The project group had arranged a meeting for Monday, the scholarship student had shown her something that was possibly a new discovery and Jennifer had promised to run the tests again, see what came up and get a presentation ready. Despite the student's enthusiasm, she didn't really believe they'd have anything new to offer. Nothing that could help to explain why some women got pregnant time after time whilst others, for no apparent reason, tried and tried without success, with their biological clocks ticking away all the time and getting reading to stop.

She was in no state to deal with such matters right now, and after dictating some eight or ten notes that had been lying around on her desk for a little too long, she stalked out through the vestibule on her thin heels. More like wobbled, she thought, and straightened up in her new sandals. She'd found them a couple of days earlier in an English internet shop. They suited her, but in her state of chronic exhaustion they were not easy to manoeuvre in.

She sent a message to Zoran. *He* would definitely be asleep. Could get his head down anywhere, sleep for five minutes or six hours and get up refreshed, always refreshed.

He wasn't sleeping, and she headed past the garages and down in the direction of the block where he lived. It felt as if she'd been drifting for a long time. She'd made the break, left Ivar, left the farm, quit the job with forensics. The beginning of a journey, that was what it was. She didn't know where it would end. Recently she had started thinking that the road would perhaps lead back to where she'd come from, to a town on the far side of the world, the one she had left nearly thirty years ago. But that town was no more. Her parents were both dead. An older brother had moved to Darwin, her little sister was living in one of Sydney's posher suburbs; they kept in sporadic touch through Facebook. The friends she had once had in Canberra were now scattered to the four winds.

The door to Zoran's flat was locked. She wondered whether she should ring the bell, decided to let herself in with the key he had given her a long time ago. As she closed the door behind her, he emerged from the bathroom, bare chested, his face covered in shaving foam.

She reached up and scraped an opening around his mouth.
– Santa Claus here in the middle of summer?

– Well, I need to keep in practice.

She followed him into the bathroom, stood there watching as he finished shaving.

He wiped off the rest of the shaving foam, turned to her, shaking his head.

– They're working you to death, Jenny.

She let herself collapse on to him; he caught her and held her tightly.

– But not you? she murmured into his chest. He was working five-man twenty-four-hour shifts. If any of the others were ill, he sometimes had to take a double shift. And surgeons couldn't exactly doze their way through shifts. She had never heard him complain.

He led her into the living room, let her slump down into the sofa. – Shall I fix you something to eat?

She grunted something that was probably a yes.

– Perhaps you'd prefer to sleep? he said, leaning over her.
– I'll carry you into the bedroom.

She considered giving in to the desire to be lifted up and taken to bed. The first time she'd been there he had carried her into the bedroom, and quite a few times since then too.

– Think I'd better eat first, she yawned.

He disappeared into the kitchen, and she curled up and lay there looking out into the warm light. Drifted into a doze, but as if her eyes were still open. Someone calling to her. It's Trym, not more than five years old. He's standing in the doorway; he can't sleep either.

Are you asleep?

No.

Not Trym that answers, but a little girl.

She forced her eyes open wide, remembered where she

was, in Zoran's front room. Frugally furnished. A print on the wall, a landscape, that was it. If she were to move in, the flat would change pretty quickly; she was no minimalist. Zoran didn't have a single photograph on his shelves either. In her own flat, however temporary it was, she had several pictures of the boys as children. Zoran had a daughter, but Jennifer knew nothing about her. Lying there on the sofa, she thought they ought to meet, her and the daughter.

He came in carrying a plate, put it down in front of her. Bacon and egg, sliced tomatoes, fresh bread with Dutch cheese. Espresso coffee. Olives in a little glass bowl. He bought them from a Turkish shop in Lillestrøm. She had never liked olives until she met him; now she could almost have lived off them.

– When did you last see your daughter?

He shrugged his shoulders. – A few years ago. Why do you ask?

– Just wondered. You said once she lives in Germany.

– That's right.

– Well that's not so far away.

– Not in terms of geography.

He didn't say anything else, and she thought she ought to.

– I always wanted a daughter.

He nodded; she'd said that before.

– All the things we never got and never did.

– I think lack of sleep is bringing out the melancholy in you. He smiled.

– Not at all, she protested. – I'm the sanguine type. A bit choleric. But never melancholic.

– Well all right.

– Don't you agree?

– I'm not much interested in theories about bodily fluids, Jenny.

– I'm not disposed to be depressed, is what I mean.

He sat in a chair at the end of the table, his back to the window and the sharp light.

– We change, he said. – You're not the same now as you were ten or twenty years ago.

She didn't want to admit that he was right. For a while, mostly for fun, she had tried to categorise the people she met according to the four temperaments. It was the lightness of spirit she always felt somewhere inside her that led her to define herself as sanguine. It never left her, not even at the darkest times. But in recent years an undercurrent of something heavy and stubborn had begun to manifest itself. Maybe it was age, maybe it was this country and the mad extremities of light and darkness in its seasons. Or maybe that undercurrent had always been there and she had refused to recognise it.

– I'm getting old, Zoran. And I'm not ready for it.

She sat up, punctured the egg yolk. It formed a dark yellow pool on the blue plate.

– It's okay, she sighed. – You don't have to say anything.

He leaned forward, stroked her hair.

– Did you finish the autopsy?

– I've done the preliminary report.

– You're amazingly efficient.

She could feel herself blushing. She blushed all the time, like a schoolgirl. Even in situations that weren't in the slightest embarrassing. But it didn't matter much if it was him seeing her like that.

– It's an okay job, she said. – If I slice off the wrong thing, it's not going to kill anyone.

She glanced across at him. He was leaning back in the chair, freshly shaved and showered. Coffee cup balanced on the tips of three fingers.

– Not every day patients get murdered over there.

– Only by lousy surgeons, she rejoined. – And nurses who can't figure out the correct dosages.

During the time she had been working there, there had been a steady stream of stories in the press about the hospital. It had more patients than it could handle, the routines were inefficient, they lacked qualified staff, all things that could result in fatalities among the patients. But what had happened last night was something completely different.

– It was Arash who found him.

– I know, she said, and had to yawn.

– Been trying to get in touch with him. But he's not answering his phone.

– Smart guy. After a night like that. She thought about it. – Think he might be involved?

– In the murder, you mean? A faint rough edge to his voice.

She looked up at the ceiling, studied a crack in the plaster. She had fled too, it struck her, but not from any religious dictatorship. Or, like Zoran, from a war in which neighbours suddenly began to kill each other.

– I know you like him, Zoran. You want to help him.

– Arash is bright. Speaks five or six languages fluently. He was studying for a master's when he had to get out.

She pushed the plate to one side. – I guess that's why they've got him wheeling beds about over in this country.

– We're lucky, you and I, he said, looking thoughtful.

– Is that offer still good? That you'll carry me?

She got him smiling again. – It's good all day. All week.

– That's it?

– Longer than that.

Without looking up, she felt his gaze. A couple of weeks ago he'd hinted that she might think about giving up her own flat and moving in with him. When she didn't respond, he'd let it go. If he'd asked again now, she would probably have said yes, I'll move in, I want you to take care of me. No matter what happens, I'll be able to handle it with you at my side.

Abruptly he stood up, held her around her neck and beneath her knees, swung her up into the air, swaying through the room and into his big bed. There he undressed her and tucked the duvet around her.

– You don't need to leave straight away, she murmured.

– Aren't you going to sleep?

– You can lie here with me a little while, until I do.

11

They came to a farm. Arash had walked that way before. The track continued around the back of the barn and on between the fields. The corn in the fields was green. A sudden wave through it, loosed from an invisible hand, because as they walked past and on towards the forest, he felt no wind.

He had walked there in winter too. Like walking through a house someone had moved out of, white sheets draped over everything. That first winter he had felt uneasy the whole time. Like sinking to the bottom of something and struggling to get to the surface again.

– Shall we go back? he asked.

She looked at him. – Why?

The forest path slanted away upwards. It was a gravelled track and easy walking, but Marita was wearing sandals made of suede.

– Your shoes are much too good for a walk in the forest.

She waved away his objection.

They came to a clearing where the trees had been chopped down and stacked in piles. There was a smell of bark and sap. Marita stopped and picked a flower from the side of the track. – This plant can cure deadly diseases. She held it up to show him. It was purple with white patches. – But if you take too much of it, it'll kill you.

He examined it closely. The stalk had tiny hairs on it; it was beautiful, but apparently dangerous too.

– And this . . . She pointed to another one, yellow, with large, smooth petals. – If you want someone to tell you the truth, you put this in their drink.

– You know such a lot, Marita.

– I know almost nothing. Nothing about things that really matter.

But she carried on showing him plants and telling him about their secret lives. – Did you know that flowers need sleep just as much as you and I do?

There was a stream running along one side of the path. He remembered that its source was a tarn. The sun was almost directly over their heads. She was breathing more heavily; her forehead was shiny, tiny droplets of sweat just below the skin waiting to emerge.

– Did you know that plants dream?

He had to laugh. The light filtered down through the branches, not a breath of wind, only the singing of the birds and the flies buzzing around them, and the smell of the newly chopped trees, mingled with moss and marsh.

Images flashed through him: the patient in the bed, the man he had followed in Lillestrøm. But there was nothing threatening in it any more, just thoughts. He could put them to one side, he could turn to Marita; it was she, no one but she, who walked at his side, and nothing of what he had just seen was real. He laughed again, and she leaned into him, without asking what he was laughing about. Today something new started, he thought. It wasn't by chance that he had come to this land, and walked in a light that was never absent, not until deep into the autumn.

He touched her.

Her summer dress felt like silk; it had thin shoulder straps. He would look after her. A piece of his life that had been missing, the thing that would make everything else fit. Suddenly he felt stronger than he ever had before. Could have told her there and then what was in his mind, but could also wait. There was a certain order to things. But what was gathering inside him was so strong that it tossed him about in all directions, and he saw the same thing in her eyes too, in the way her body moved, her breathing.

They walked around the marsh and he led the way over the little bridge, three logs laid across the stream, and up the hill on the other side. If he listened out, he could distinguish the songs of five or six different birds. Many of them spent the winter in countries like his own. But they never sang there the way they did up here in the summer light.

– Here it is.

They passed through a gap in the rocks that gave on to a grassy hill leading down to the tarn. – This is your place.

– Are you giving it to me? she laughed. – That's very generous of you.

He said no more about what he could have given her. Not just the tarn and the forest behind, but the hills beyond them, and everything he could see.

– I'm hot. She walked down towards the bank. – Join me in a swim! she shouted up to him, stepping out on to a large boulder that sloped down into the black water.

He shook his head. – We don't have our swimming costumes.

She turned towards him, stood there for a few seconds, hair full of light, the dark water behind her. Then she pulled off her dress.

He looked away. Had to keep watching out of the corner of his eye. She stepped out on to the edge of the stone and into the water.

– It isn't cold, she called up to him.

He stood by her clothes, looked down at them, the thin

frock on top, white, with big red flowers, almost like blood-stains. Hesitantly he undressed.

She swam round in circles, watching him as he stood there naked on the boulder. He had never liked to swim in places where he couldn't see the bottom. Put one foot down; it sank into mud that swirled up and clouded the water. He dived in and swam out towards her. Only her head was showing above the water. Her face a few centimetres from his, her breath ruffling the surface of the water between them. Something was about to happen. The shimmering light told him, and the clouds that pulled further and further away towards the horizon.

She had packed the bag. He took out one of the blankets, allowed her to dry herself first, laid the other one on the grass. Flies gathered in a cloud around them, and there must be an ant heap somewhere close by. He took out bread and cheese, the bottles of water.

She wrapped the blanket around herself. – I could live here. In your forest.

He nodded, as though he agreed.

– That's the first time I've ever bathed naked with a man.

He placed his hand next to hers. Again she touched his ring.

– There's something about that, she said.

There was something about it. His father had got it from a *pir*, a Sufi teacher he wanted Arash to study under. Arash had always gone his own way. Now here was where he had ended up.

– Can I try it?

He could feel himself frowning. – The ring? Why? he thought. – Why not, he said. He eased it off. – Give me your hand.

His father's voice spoke to him from a distance, warning him, something about a curse, all the things that could be set in motion if he went ahead and did this. He didn't hear the words, didn't want to hear them.

The ring was much too large. She tried it on one finger after the other; the thumb was the only place where it stayed put.

– It brings happiness to the person wearing it, he said, managing to smile.

She sat down in front of him, the sunlight in her eyes, all the grey gone from them, only the green left, flecked with brown. She waited. He leaned forward and let it happen. Her lips were cold and tasted of the water; it reminded him of blood, and he could feel something else about to take over, as though the hands holding her were not his.

He let go.

– Are you afraid?

He was on his knees in front of her, naked. He wasn't afraid. The thing growing inside him was a little like anger, but it was possible to make it head off in another direction.

– We must take our time.

She looked at him for a long time. – You're wise, Arash. Let's have something to eat first.

First before what? he should have asked, but said nothing.

– Have you got something to slice the bread with?

He handed her the knife, watched as she sliced. Her pale fingers with the marks of the rings she wasn't wearing. Instead she was wearing his on her thumb. The sun was high above the treetops on the far side. Made her red hair glow redder, her white skin whiter. The black enamel in the ring blacker. He reached out a hand, touched her cheek. You are beautiful, he thought in Farsi. The same words came out of him in her language. He said them again, because this moment had to be attached to something, and all he had were these words.

– Don't be afraid of me, she murmured, and wriggled out of the blanket until she was almost beneath him. He bent over her; she sank down into the grass without his touching her, and through what might be anger he could feel a need to protect her against everything that could happen, against anything he might possibly do to her.

– Wait. She sat up. – I have to . . . you know. She gestured vaguely in the direction of her stomach. – You'll wait for me?

As though she was giving him a choice. As though it were still possible to leave this place without her. He closed his eyes, could feel that he hadn't slept for more than twenty-four hours, shut out the light, the sound of the flies buzzing ever more densely around them, the smell of the water, and the wind crossing the surface to remind him of something he must never forget.

– I'll wait for you.

He didn't open his eyes again until she was over in the trees. He lay on his back and looked up into the sky. If he could have followed his gaze up there, he would never have found his way back again.

Silence is the surest sign of your death. He couldn't manage to turn his head to see where the voice was coming from; somewhere above him, or from the water. Further off, a woman screaming, and he felt for the knife, raised it to the sky and cut it open, and maybe it was then that she began to scream, but he couldn't wake up, not yet. There was something his father wanted to say to him, and he couldn't wake up until he heard what it was.

The ring.

I have it.

You've given it away. Now anything can happen.

He jumped up, the knife in his hand, staggered a few steps to the water's edge and tossed it into the tarn.

She might have been gone ten seconds, or an hour. He took his phone from his trouser pocket. Five past four. Some unanswered calls. One from Zoran. Put it down again, walked a few paces in the direction of the trees. Didn't see her, didn't hear her.

– Marita.

A sound somewhere off to the right, a path in that direction, just about visible. If she needed more time, whatever it was she had to do, he wouldn't intrude on her. He stood there for a minute, two minutes. Then he headed up the path. There was a swarm of tiny frogs beneath his feet; he trod on one, jerked his foot back.

– Marita.

There was a different sound to her name. It sounded thinner. Something was missing. The path ran alongside the stream before crossing it. And in that moment, he knew he had walked there before, walked those exact steps. He froze.

She was lying on the other side, where he knew she was lying. Head down towards the water, auburn hair lifting in the faint current, just the way he had imagined it. He ran up to her, bent over her. He had seen everything before. The eyes staring up at him, the broad band across the throat, as though someone had hung a chain of red gold around her neck, but something was running from it in a dark red stream, down into the moss.

He opened his mouth. No sound emerged. He sank to his knees, leaned across to the other bank, grabbed at the moss by her head; it was saturated with blood that stuck to his hand, and he withdrew it quickly. Then the image of her disappeared, as though it were something that had arisen in his thoughts and belonged only there. But when he opened his eyes she was still there, lying on the other side, and he was still bent across the stream, like a bridge that never quite made it.

Then he noticed something down in the water. A head covered in a black hood, with an opening just for the eyes, like a woman wearing a niqab. The head rose up from the bed of the stream, took on a body, arms, and a hand that was holding something shiny, and he realised that he was looking at a reflection in the water, and that the figure was approaching him from behind.

The arm he saw reflected in the water rose slowly, like a snake about to strike. As the blow came, he rolled to one side, was on his feet and running, leapt over on to the other bank of the stream, up towards where a tree had fallen across it. It grew dark around him, and he glanced over his shoulder, saw the whole figure there, in front of the sun, right behind the fallen tree stump, the black-clad and faceless figure, the head completely covered, the hand raised, and in it a gun. He heard a twang, like the sound of an arrow leaving a bow, felt the burning in his arm that ran all the way up towards his throat, and then the splashing sound of something falling into the water. I've been shot, he thought, but he didn't fall over, carried on running in a zigzag between the trees, knew the black shadow was following him. Another shot, the bark ripped from the tree trunk right by his head. Is this the way you're going to die? he shouted as he dived in between two spruce trees. Something grazed his ear, showering him with bark and splintered wood. He crept through the heather, the ground shook, an escarpment opened up beneath him; he felt himself sucked down into it, fell several metres, landed on something hard. The edge of a stone cut into his leg; he knew it hurt but he felt no pain. Blood was gushing down on to his bare foot as he got to his feet and hopped on. From the pond he had landed in he saw the outlined figure in black between the trees at the top of the escarpment, and he plunged on through the water, across a gravel track, on into the forest.

He stopped when he came to a bog, stood there gasping for breath. As he bent to examine the wound in his leg, he heard a sound behind him, a twig snapping, a metallic click. Bent double, he staggered out across the bog. On the far side an area of tall bracken, on the right two large boulders leaning against each other. It would be possible to squeeze under them, a little hollow there. The deep notes of the birdsong suddenly grew more urgent, as though warning him. Not there, he mumbled, and wriggled his way backwards into the bracken.

He lay there listening as the ground sucked the warmth from his body. He became nothing but this listening. Listening away from his pains. Listening to the drops of light falling from the needles of the trees. He clasped both hands around the gaping wound in his leg, as though to stop the sound of the escaping blood giving him away. He could hear four different birds now. Two of them warned him away, two tried to tempt him forward. *Get up, get up*, said one, and that told him that there were two kinds of birds, those that wanted to help him and those that wanted him to die. After a while, he was also able to distinguish the rippling of a stream, though it must be different from the one he had run alongside, away from the place where he had found her, where she still lay. He listened himself away from what he had seen. Concentrated on the sound of the birds that warned and the birds that tempted. A shivering through the trees, but no wind, must be something else moving the branches, and then her name was there. Marita. She puts on the ring. He lets her do it. Marita is dead.

Another sound penetrating. Like a foot being pulled free

of the bog, and he thought that it was her name that had betrayed him; perhaps he'd said it out loud. The sound came again, closer now. The trees in the area where it came from stood close together, and he felt vulnerable, lying there in the falling light, chalk-white amongst the green. He started to count, because that helped. These seconds were his time, and the thought made it possible to lie like a rigid corpse between the fronds of bracken.

The shadow emerged from the trees, stood in the midst of the clearing, half turned, the black hood pulled up. Like an alarm sounding, freezing everything into silence, not a twig in the forest moving now. Arash saw how the sunlight gathered itself into a cone that searched for his naked body. Then the figure bent over, looked to be examining something on the ground.

The silence ended. It was the evil birds he was hearing, the ones that tempted him to go on. And the bracken laid its leaves flat and would no longer hide him. But the figure in black was busy searching over by the boulders, examining that little hollow he had so nearly crept into. Stood up straight again, took a few paces towards him, backwards, turned around slowly, stared in his direction. Arash closed his eyes, unable to bear the thought of meeting the other's gaze at the moment of his discovery. Now I'm going to get up, he whispered to himself, because the waiting was unendurable. Better to crawl across to the one waiting there and get it over with. Then Marita's face was there again, the empty eyes, and suddenly he felt something else, something stronger than the longing to give himself up to the figure in black. Anger was what made him release the grip on his leg, dig with his hand into the moss he was lying on, free a lump of it, dig deeper until he felt something hard, the edge of a stone.

He opened his eyes as the dark figure turned away again and began crossing the clearing. Tall, and powerfully built, the gun in the left hand, and as the figure disappeared between the trees, Arash noticed something about the way it walked, one leg dragging slightly. If this was a dream, he would not have seen that particular detail, he was certain. Then that thought paled and faded, and the warning songs of the good birds came back, drowning out all other sounds.

12

A BIRD SAT on the telephone wire outside. Jennifer, still half asleep, was looking at it. The smell of roasting meat wafted in to her. The bird was a magpie, she saw as she woke up. Her distance vision was still good. It was when things came too close that she had trouble.

She found Zoran in the kitchen.

– What time is it?

He glanced at his wristwatch. – Five thirty.

– Have I slept the whole day away? she wailed.

He dried his hands, put his arm around her.

– Not the whole day. And not my day, at any rate. Don't you remember anything from before you fell asleep?

She remembered every moment. He had crept in under the duvet. Naked. Sneaked his way inside her. Lay like that for a long time completely still. Moved a little each time she was about to fall asleep. Finally she came almost without a muscle tensing.

She leaned up and kissed him. He smelled of onions and olives.

– What are you making?

He opened the oven door, a joint sizzling inside. – I asked Lydia and Knut to come over.

– This evening?

– You're invited too.

She gestured with her arms, looked down at her half-naked and unwashed body.

– Come as you are. He smiled. – That's fine.

– You're impossible.

She went to the bedroom, opened a cupboard. She had left some clothes there over the last few weeks, a couple of summer dresses, so she wouldn't have to go home first if she was late in the morning. And shampoo and conditioner, a travelling make-up bag and underwear. All of it in bags, nothing unpacked on to the shelves.

– When are you going to open a restaurant? Knut Reinertsen exclaimed as the roast appeared on the table.

Zoran was wearing an apron. He sliced the beef, thin and neat.

– I wouldn't rule it out.

– Then I insist on a regular table there, said the psychiatrist.

Jennifer's contribution had been to lay the table, light the candles, put the roses Lydia had brought into a blue vase. Now she sat there wishing she could have spent the evening alone with Zoran.

With another bottle of wine opened, she drifted into mild intoxication, secretly watching him across the table. In the evening light from the window, his face was younger and more beautiful than she could remember having seen it before. Not too beautiful, fortunately, and not too young. There was something else about it, a quality that would not vanish with the passage of the years. She had always been attracted to men who were older than her. For some reason or other an image of Roar Horvath came into her mind. *He* had been almost ten years younger. There were other, younger men she couldn't even be bothered to remember. Maybe all those mistakes had been necessary in order for her to sit there and look at Zoran like this. If that was the case, then it was all worth it.

– You lot seem to have found a good way of getting rid of your patients, Knut Reinertsen mused aloud. He was the only one at the table who didn't work at the hospital, and the only one who could not resist alluding to what had happened there the previous evening.

– Why don't we talk about something else? Jennifer suggested, trying in vain to stifle a yawn.

– Long day? asked Lydia.

–This light, said Jennifer, with an exasperated gesture in the direction of the window. – I can't sleep.

Zoran filled people's glasses. – Before she goes to bed, she has an extensive routine designed to keep it out.

He described the procedure she went through every evening that was supposed to prevent event the faintest sliver of light from getting through.

– It's true, Jennifer admitted. – I must have complete darkness. I never used to be like that.

– What do you say to that, Mr Psychiatrist? asked Zoran.

Knut Reinertsen dabbed around his mouth. – There's a biological explanation, of course, he began. – But the psychological one is more interesting.

He took a sip of wine and glanced round, probably to make sure he had everyone's full attention.

– The desire to block out light indicates a deep-seated desire not to see. The symbolism is simple, not to say blindingly obvious.

– Thank you for that analysis, Knut, said Zoran. – Send your bill to me, since I was the one stupid enough to raise the question.

– It's nothing, really. But I looked through the newspapers and didn't see anything about what happened at the hospital yesterday—

– Wasn't the idea to talk about something else? Jennifer interrupted, aware of her own slight irritation.

– Knut doesn't take hints like that, said Zoran.

– Dangerous place, that hospital, Knut went on, – even for those in good health.

– Was it you who examined him? Lydia asked, directing her question to Zoran.

He raised his wine glass, glanced at it. – One of the junior doctors. I didn't get a chance to look at him before he disappeared.

Knut pointed at him with his fork. – Then it's true that the man was admitted with minor injuries?

Zoran glanced across at Jennifer. – It's probably not unlikely that the people who started the job before he was admitted came back to complete it.

– Then presumably they would show up on the security cameras?

Jennifer had had exactly the same thought. – Some of the ones in the basement are out of order, she said.

– Yet another thing that doesn't work, Lydia sighed. – At management meetings we spend all our time discussing things like that and almost none at all on the medical side.

– Someone got into the basement, Jennifer went on. – A window by the entrance to the psychiatric department was broken, and the lock on the basement door forced.

Lydia shook her head. – I heard it was one of the porters who found the patient.

– He's a good bloke, Zoran interjected. – Iranian.

Lydia folded her serviette. – Do you know him?

– Zoran got him the job, said Jennifer. It was one of the things she admired about him, his concern for the welfare of others. – He was still there when I arrived last night. He looked as if he'd had a breakdown.

The sight of the porter on the corridor floor, the blood on the white shirt.

– He's probably a refugee, Knut nodded, – since he's Iranian.

– He was imprisoned in Tehran's most notorious prison, Zoran said. – I don't even like to think about the sort of things that go on in there.

– So he suffers from some kind of post-traumatic stress disorder, said Knut. – And what happened at the hospital yesterday triggered it off again. Poor bastard.

He started talking about various programmes he had taken part in, providing emergency help in disaster areas; the unspeakable cruelties people were capable of inflicting on each other. – Has this porter been offered professional help?

– I wish I knew, said Zoran. – I haven't been able to get in touch with him today.

– How can someone break into a hospital unnoticed? I mean, there are hundreds of staff swarming all over the place.

For some reason or other Knut Reinertsen was looking at Jennifer as he said this. He had a way of speaking that always made her feel inadequate.

– Maybe because we have other things to do besides going round checking doors, she said, aware herself of how sharp her response sounded.

– That was a dreadful shift, Lydia interjected, perhaps trying to smooth things over. – Inexperienced junior doctors who have to ask about everything, nurses who can't handle the workload. You have to chase round after things they haven't had time to lay out. Typical that something so gruesome and absurd should happen on an evening like that.

She sipped at her wine. Jennifer said no when Zoran offered her more, she'd had enough. Could feel that she would be able to sleep and hoped the guests would leave before she became wide awake again.

Lydia was talking about something else that had happened the previous evening. A pregnant woman with severe pains in the abdomen.

– We did an ultrasound on her and found a normal foetus five months old. The only problem was, it wasn't in the womb, it had attached itself to the lining of the stomach wall.

– There, you see, said Knut.

– See what?

– You don't need to be a woman to carry a child. We all have a stomach wall. Soon we'll have the technology that will enable men to become biological mothers. That must surely be of interest to you in your studies of childlessness.

Lydia laughed quietly.

– But it's paradoxical, he growled, his voice even louder now. – At the same time as we spend billions helping people to have more children, we're doing nothing to prevent over-population, which is the greatest threat in our time.

Zoran opened another bottle of wine and topped up Knut's glass. He seemed to find the psychiatrist's improvisations entertaining.

– Don't you agree, Zoran? That is the real cause of all the wars and the environmental disasters, that there are quite simply too many of us. Imagine what it's going to be like here in fifty years' time, with less food, less energy and a population that carries on growing at an explosive rate.

– It won't do that, said Zoran as he topped up his own glass. – It'll even out.

– But not enough, and not quickly enough. It will be like a game. Somebody has to leave, because there isn't room for everyone.

– There's probably something in what you say, Lydia agreed.

– Says you, who spends all her time trying to counter nature's own natural braking mechanisms. If you really are worried about the future, why are you helping those who are unable to have children?

Zoran shook his head. – Lydia is one of the best researchers we have, Knut. Give her a little cred now and then. He leaned over to her, patted her arm. – Actually he admires you just as much as the rest of us here do. Knut has a weakness for intelligent women, same as me.

Suddenly it was as though Jennifer could see Lydia with Zoran's eyes, the strips of grey in the untidy medium-length hair catching in the evening light, even the slightly diverging eyes making her attractive in a mysterious way. Jennifer felt a twinge of something she hadn't felt for a while, something that might have been jealousy, the faint edge of a thought that Zoran might like Lydia more than her. He meant what he said about intelligence, and Lydia was an unusually talented researcher, with a passionate interest in the outcome of this project to find the genetic reasons for childlessness. Jennifer couldn't manage quite that same degree of involvement.

She stood up. On her way to the toilet she passed so closely behind Zoran that one breast brushed against his shoulder. He glanced up at her, and in her mild intoxication that twinge of jealousy came as a reminder of how her life had been so far. A sort of passion had driven her on, she thought distantly, a longing for everything that lay just beyond her reach. Maybe that would have to burn itself out before peace became possible for her.

By the time she returned to the dining room, the slivovitz was on the table. Knut was still talking about the murdered man, that perhaps they should search the whole hospital, just to make sure there were no more bodies hidden away in cupboards and closets. Or skeletons, he added, just in case they hadn't got his point.

– This man thinks about death the whole time, Lydia said, raising her eyebrows. – What is it about psychiatrists?

Jennifer's phone began vibrating in her handbag. She

ignored it. Just wanted to carry on sitting there feeling slightly tipsy, waiting for the moment when she could have Zoran all to herself, sleep next to him. Maybe something else first, but then sleep, so close to him that not even the light could bother her.

Ivar was the name on the display. He didn't often call, and she really didn't feel like answering. But a little worm had begun nibbling somewhere inside her. If she didn't get rid of it at once, it would just eat itself bigger and bigger.

She took the call out in the kitchen.

– Where were you? he asked, and hearing the accusation in his voice, she remembered.

– Was it today?

– You know perfectly well it was.

That wasn't true. She had forgotten. Got the days mixed up.

– We've been waiting over an hour.

– Sorry, she stammered. – I'm really sorry. Is Trym there?

An exasperated heavy sigh from the other end. – He's sitting here on the sofa. Waiting for you.

– Ivar, please listen. I'll call you back in two minutes. Go somewhere where Trym can't hear you. Sorry, she repeated, and she really was. – Honestly.

She went into the bedroom, called back.

– The boy is in trouble, and you can't even be bothered to come and have a chat with him.

– I thought we had agreed on tomorrow.

She should have told the truth, that she'd been at work all night, that she was exhausted, that their arrangement had escaped her mind completely.

– Have you thought about him even once since the last time I called you? Ivar wanted to know. – Have you any idea of just how serious this is?

– I think about it all the time, she sighed as she sank down on Zoran's bed.

The silence at the other end was unendurable.

– I've spoken to a psychiatrist, she lied.

– Oh yes?

– He's going to be able to offer him something. Soon.

She returned to the dining room. Walking a little unsteadily. Not because of the wine. All three of them looked at her.

– Everything all right? asked Zoran, reaching out a hand, pulling her in.

– Yes. She slid down into her chair. – That is . . .

There was a slice of tiramisu left, a spoon with cream.

– It's my son, she said suddenly, pushing the plate aside. – He has problems.

She was overtired and had drunk more than she should have. Didn't usually involve other people in her problems. She had discussed Trym with Zoran, but not even he knew everything.

– Borderline, said Knut Reinertsen.

She was startled. – What the fuck do you mean?

She didn't often swear in Norwegian; it always sounded as if it was someone else speaking.

– Your son is going with a woman with a borderline personality disorder.

Everyone was looking at Knut. He didn't appear to have any objection to that at all.

– Aren't you being just a bit trigger-happy now, Knut? said Zoran.

– Listen. If a patient comes to you with chest pains, let's say an elderly man, he's nauseous, cold sweats, shooting pains in his left arm, what would you say?

– That's different, Zoran protested.

– Is it? If I talk to someone for two minutes and the

person in question has all the symptoms of a particular diagnosis?' The fact is, most diagnoses are made within the first minute. In your field too.

Zoran shook his head.

– This Katja, or whatever her name was, Knut continued. – Not meaning to offend you, Jenny, but it wasn't hard to see that your son would have problems.

– Katja, exclaimed Lydia. – Was that her name?

Zoran looked at Jennifer. – Is it Sigurd that's in trouble?

She was still upset. – You're wrong, Knut. Sigurd is in full control of his life. I'm talking about my elder son. He's the one who needs help.

Knut Reinertsen's face fell. A lopsided smile that came and went.

– You have another son, he said. – How old is he?

She looked at him. He'd been sitting there showing off all evening. But she'd promised to help Trym, had even lied that everything was arranged.

– Twenty-five. Almost.

Knut nodded, as though he already knew that. Jennifer glanced at Lydia, who also looked on expectantly, as if waiting to hear more. Jennifer felt a sense of relief. There were people who cared and wanted to help. Not just Zoran, but Lydia too. Even Knut Reinertsen, for all his insufferable pomposity, was leaning towards her, a friendly expression in his eyes.

– If there's anything you want to share with us . . .

– He lives with his father. He began studying, was always good at school, but now he's dropped out. Sits on the net all day every day, or rather all night.

Rather than try to work out a solution for himself, Trym was the type to give up and call for help whenever the going got tough.

– Mostly it's gambling, she explained. – At first we thought it was the sort of thing that all people of his age do these days. But then we found out he was losing a lot of money, really quite large amounts.

– How much?

– Not sure. He's had a few thousand kroner from me, and from his father. But a week ago we found out he owes a lot more. Maybe ten times more.

– Do you think he's addicted?

They had been avoiding that word. Trym had repeatedly said he would get a job, pay back what he owed, give up gambling. He'd been saying it all spring, and now it emerged he'd been borrowing money from people they knew nothing about.

– Do you think you . . . She looked straight at Knut. – Or do you know someone who might?

– I'll see what I can do. He met her gaze. – We think we know those closest to us. But the closer you get to someone, the more blind you are.

Jennifer blinked a few times, not sure where he was going.

– Of course I'll help you, he added.

13

CERTAIN SIGN THAT YOU ARE DEAD 146

DARKER NOW.

Arash wriggled out, turned over on his side, still listening. How many hours had he been lying there? Two birds conversing, one on each side of the rushing stream. All the others fallen silent.

It had clouded over, the tree trunks shrouded in a thick grey light. He stood up, the pain searing from his leg and down into his foot, but the one on the inside of his arm no more than a distant burning. He limped around the boulders he had been lying near, clambered up on to a little hill. It was lighter there, and he crawled on, to avoid being seen. It was a few hundred metres down to the main forest track. He didn't take the chance of using it, kept to the trees. Couldn't tell if he was heading towards the edge or deeper into the forest, the light moving away from him, sounds growing fainter.

At some point in the grey night he came to the bank of a tarn. Outline of a cabin on the far side. The forest behind rising in a dense wall towards the brow of a hill, the sky above it now visible through gaps in the clouds.

He listened out. No signs of life. Waited, listened again, limped slowly in the direction of the cabin. He walked round it twice, peered into the dark interior. Down by the water he found a stone, broke a window at the back of the cabin, the glass shattering the silence. At that moment a wind up from the water, as though warning him. He retreated into the trees, sat on his haunches and waited. Nothing. Still he waited. The grey light was turning to white by the time he risked returning to the cabin wall, put a hand through and released the window catch.

Two rooms, one with a bunk bed, one with a sofa and three chairs. A kitchen surface in the corner. A washbasin, a mirror. A shelf with biscuits and tinned food. He found bedclothes in a cupboard in the bedroom. Pulled off a strip and wound it round his leg. The material was at once saturated with his blood. He tore off more, tied it tighter. Examined his other wounds in the mirror, avoiding looking into his own eyes. The bullet had grazed his arm, a little flap of skin dangling, just a flesh wound. A gash at the top of his forehead, deeper, but hardly bleeding. Someone had been looking out for him. The same someone who had let Marita die. Suddenly he began to shake. He crept into the lower bunk, pulled the blanket over him. Around him the whole room was shaking.

Perhaps he was asleep. The ceiling was dotted with black patches, possibly knotholes. They were signs he would have been able to understand if only he could read the language. Someone was communicating with him through these signs. About his chances of getting away. If he could only learn how to interpret them. Can you do that, Arash?

He drifted away again. Or it was the light that was changing, seeping in across the threshold. Sounds audible on the other side, a door being opened, steps across the floor. Someone standing there breathing, more slowly than him. He held his breath. Heard a dog sniffing right next to his ear. He mustn't let anything out, close off his body, release neither sounds nor smells into the room. Someone coughed close by. Unless it was from the other side of the outside wall. A bird hopping around out there, a raven or a crow.

He started. A chair being moved in an adjacent room. He was paralysed, couldn't seem to open his eyes.

Then later, everything was silent again. He was standing by the bed, it was light in the room. He was no longer bleeding from the cut in his leg, but the back of his wrist was still caked with her blood. He took a few steps towards the window. It was ajar. Deep birdsong from outside. Silence a moment, then there it was again. He tried to work out if it was warning him or luring him on.

The ring.

She'd taken it with her. Was that why she died?

Marita, he mumbled. I can't go back without the ring.

Marita, if you're here somewhere, talk to me.

He opened the door into the tiny living room. The smell in there was different. Reminded him of the smell by the stream where she lay. Then he saw it. The mirror covered in spots.

Don't look in that direction, Arash.

He couldn't stop himself, held on to the bench and looked into it, unable to see his own face there. Only those red spots, thick and glistening, as though made of half-dried blood. If he looked closer, they turned into letters.

Letters that became words as he stood there.

He began to read them out loud, but the voice that sounded in the room was someone else's, pronouncing the words in Farsi.

Silence is the surest sign of your death.

As he read, he heard children's voices, thinner and sharper than the voice in the room. They came closer, were right outside, a darker voice there now too, and a dog howling. He opened the cabin door wide and stormed out.

A woman stood there and stared at him, a key in her hand. Three children frozen on the ground behind her. One of them started to wail, and the dog continued howling, as though to drown out the scream. He took a step towards them. The other children were crying now, and he realised how naked he was, that he was bleeding. He turned and ran off in the other direction, across the lawn, into the trees.

The surest sign. He shouted the words over and over as he ran, until they turned into a tune he could sing. He knew exactly where these words came from. And the thought of his father made him stop and press his cheek against the trunk of a pine tree. Stand there with eyes closed, listening to the racing of his own breath.

When he came to again, he saw it in the bright sunlight. It lay coiled on a flat stone between the trees, its head rising from the centre of the coil. A black zigzag pattern running down its back. He hadn't seen snakes since arriving in Norway, but knew that this one was poisonous. He took a few paces towards it. The snake stretched its head and showed its tongue, staring at him, its eyes two tiny coals framed by grey scales. A look that had followed him for longer than he could remember. Abruptly he was consumed with anger. As though some huge hand had ladled it down into him. He looked around, saw three stones lying on the slope, picked up the largest, carried it over to the rock. The snake made a deep, frothy sound, as though puffing into a moist bellows. The head was erect now, the neck a rod that moved in small, pendular circles. It continued to hiss, and the sound threw him into a frenzy. He took two running steps and hurled the stone at the snake's head. He scored a direct hit. The head was crushed against the surface of the rock and split open with a popping sound.

He bent over it. The body was still in motion, a spasm that passed from the squashed head and down through the abdomen. He grabbed hold of the tail, ran back towards the pine tree and whipped the snake's body against it, over and over again.

Not until he realised he was standing there with only sinewy shreds left in his hand was it possible for him to stop. He threw it away, fell to his knees and buried his face in the soft moss.

How did you cope after your father died?

I coped.

Last time you mentioned someone your father worked for. Someone who protected you and helped you after you were left alone.

My father didn't work *for him. He was bound to him by ties that could not be broken. That was why he did the killings. He had nothing personal against the victims.*

Can you tell me who that was? The person who protected you?

He doesn't have a name. Or he has a hundred names. He was my protector even though you won't find it written down anywhere.

He must be quite old?

Yes.

Where does he live?

I don't know.

But you are able to get in touch with him when you need to?

Not any more. Not now that I've told you all this.

Are we talking about a physical person, someone who is of this world?

You're asking if I believe in God.

Do you?

I can believe in any god who offers protection, and who divides the world into good and bad. And I can take a step back and look at this god and smile to myself. When someone says to me that they can't do this or that because God forbids it, I can agree with them. Or I can turn away and laugh at them.

From the expert witness's notes, 3 August 2014

PART III

15 June 2014

14

Sigurd Woods stood in front of a group of Newlife leaders. About fifteen of them. He knew what he needed to know about each one of them, he knew what he ought to say, how he ought to say it, had been through it so many times before it had become routine. Now he stood there and the words just wouldn't come.

Man died at hospital as a result of his injuries.

It was almost twenty-four hours since he'd seen the report on *VG*'s net edition. Not much more than that, beyond the fact that the man had been found unconscious in a villa in Nittedal. On the local paper's website, a picture of the house. At first he refused to believe his own eyes. And then he refused to relate to what he saw. And then he gave up, and it swept over him, forcing its way in everywhere. He could hardly stand upright, had to lie down on the floor with his eyes closed. An hour passed before he opened them again. A mere hour, of all the time that was left to him.

He had killed a man.

Now another twenty-two hours had passed, he thought as he stood there in front of the fifteen leaders and heard the sound of his own voice. The words were more or less the same as usual, but they sounded different, as though he were reading from a script somewhere inside himself. The downcast eyes and almost inaudible restlessness in the room confirmed that they were experiencing it the same way.

He cut it to the minimum. Concluded with a few words about Donald Trump. The man who forges on past all obstacles. Donald Trump doesn't play by the rules; he's free to make his own.

Subdued applause once he had finished.

– Questions? he offered, hoping no one had any, because he had to get out of there. Or should he stand there and start talking about freedom? The freedom to choose whether to hand yourself in or not, a day and a half after you had beaten a man to death.

He'd get a few years. Three. Maybe less. He'd googled verdicts in cases of assaults leading to death. Because they must surely believe him. That he'd gone to that house in Nittedal with no thought of killing anyone. He hadn't been armed. Had gone there on completely different business, wanted to clear things up, get her to tell him what was going on, so he knew where he stood. The text message he'd sent her from outside the house should be proof enough of that. He'd ended up in a fight with another man, had hit him a few times with a golf club. Maybe he'd get away with self-defence. A good lawyer should be able to manage that, even if he had broken into the house where it happened. That he'd called the emergency services and requested an ambulance before getting out of there would tell in his favour. Why had he carried on hitting the man after he was down? they might object. Why had he run off if it was a simple case of self-defence? Why had he waited several days before giving himself up to the police? The penalty for murder was eight to fifteen years. For premeditated murder up to twenty-one.

One of the women approached him. One of the most loyal. She wasn't much older than him.

– Not feeling too good today?

He shook his head. — Coming down with something.

If he was going to lie, then lying that he was ill was about as contemptible as it got.

— I noticed.

Sigurd glanced at the empty chairs. Might as well go the whole way with it now, the being ill. — Should probably have stayed in bed.

He *had* done that. The whole of yesterday he had lain there looking out through the closed window. The baking hot summer's day outside that hardly moved. At some point or other a message from Katja. As though nothing had happened. Hearts and smileys. That told him one thing: she had not been in that house, hadn't been there with Ibro Hakanovic. Had gone to Malmö just like she said she would. There was a moment's comfort in the thought. But no more than that. He had killed a man. On account of her. Bullshit. It was on his own account. There it was in all its banality: he had beaten a man to death because he couldn't endure the thought that she wanted someone else and was going to leave him. Maybe it had never been part of her plan to stay. Not once she didn't need him any more.

The girl was still standing right in front of him. He looked down into her face. She was pretty in a way that was meaningless to him. But there was that adoring look in her eyes. The kind of look that usually gave him strength. Now he found it repellent.

— Do you need someone to talk to?

He forced a smile. Should he go home with her, lie on her bed and tell her what he'd done? The thought made him blank out, but only for a moment. He would never be able to free himself from this thought: he had not swung out with that golf club to protect himself, because he could have run off as soon as the guy went down. He'd carried

on hitting him. Many times. Harder and harder. Ibro
Hakanovic was dead.

He stopped outside the street door, couldn't face going up
to the flat. The phone rang: caller not recognised. Sooner
or later it would be the police. It was Sunday, early afternoon; they'd had more than a day and a half to find him.
If they didn't have fingerprints and DNA, which would
take longer, they probably already had witnesses. Someone
who had seen his car at the petrol station and made a note
of the number.

It would still be possible to get away. That was the other
thought he had been playing with over the preceding hours:
get on board a plane. Australia, maybe, Jenny's country, the
one she'd always talked about but never taken them to. How
long would he be able to wander about down there before
they caught up with him?

– Is Katja there? said the female voice on the phone, and
he didn't know whether what he felt was relief or disappointment. It was a postponement. Indefinite. This time did
not belong to him. It was borrowed. Sooner or later he
would have to pay it back.

– She isn't here, he said. – Who is this?

– A friend, said the female voice. He could hear the very
slight accent. – Do you know where she is?

Did he know that? Did he actually know anything at all
about her?

– In Malmö, he offered.

– When will she be back?

– Not quite sure.

He had begun to get used to the thought that she would
never come back.

– Maybe this evening. Can't you call her?

– She's not answering her phone.

He almost burst out laughing. Of course she wasn't answering; her phone was still up in the apartment, hidden between the mattress and the base of the bed.

On the steps he stopped, turned, went back to the car and set off driving. Anywhere. Realised he was heading out towards Gjelleråsen. Had no business out there but kept going anyway, through the tunnel towards Nittedal. Turned off at the petrol station, up the gravelled track, through the farm. Stopped at the barrier into the forest, wound down his window, sat there looking out in the thick morning light, down towards the house he had broken into. Security tape had been placed around the property, but he didn't see any signs of life. He could go down there, into the kitchen, into the room where it had happened. Sit in a chair, or on the floor, and wait until someone arrived and asked what he was doing there. It would be a release, and his confession would happen by itself.

His phone rang again. Jenny. Hearing her voice, he knew that it was his mother he had to tell. That he had killed a man. Put it in her hands. Let her do what needed to be done. She knew the system, she knew the police, she could go along with him. This is my son, he's here to confess to a murder.

– Have you talked to Trym? she asked.

– Trym? he said, as though he couldn't quite work out who that was.

At the same time, a flash of anger because it was Trym Jenny wanted to talk about, Trym who never got anything right, who gave up the moment he encountered resistance, lay there whimpering and calling out for someone to help him get up, help him put on his clothes, help him hit back when someone bullied him. But then this image too: Trym sitting in front of the door of the barn loft, blocking it with his huge body, refusing to let Sigurd out, preventing him

from racing down into the driveway and slashing the tyres
of the Renault standing there, scratching the metallic blue
paintwork, smashing the windows and wing mirrors with
a hammer.

– Has he mentioned anything about going to see a psychiatrist?

Sigurd woke up. – I don't think so.

– I've arranged some consultations for him. If he changes
his mind, could you perhaps make sure he gets there?

He grunted, and she added: – I know you're busy. It's
not easy, always being the one who can do everything.

Are you referring to me? he felt like shouting. Is that
supposed to be me you're talking about? Bit his tongue. He
needed her. He sat there and needed his mother.

– Is something the matter, Sigurd?

Impossible to answer no. He couldn't manage any other
answer either.

– Katja?

– What about her?

– No, I just wondered . . .

– She's in Sweden.

– For good?

She couldn't hide the fact that that was what she wanted.
If she was even trying.

– We needed to take a timeout.

He made a face. That was the expression Jenny used
when she sent either him or Trym to their room. To give
them the chance to have a good think about things and
come back a little bit wiser. If he could've, he would have
laughed out loud. As though this was all about child-rearing.

– You've probably got plenty on your plate too, he said,
to avoid any further conversation about Katja.

He heard his mother's heavy sigh. – Oh yes.

Silence. He had nothing to fill it with.

– I started at the hospital to get away from murder and misery. Do research, work that might make the world a better place to live in.

– What do you mean?

– I can't say too much about what's happened here.

Another sigh. He knew it was a sign there was something she wanted to confide to him. That was fine, because he wasn't ready yet to make his own confession.

– I had to take on an extra bit of work for the forensic people. And there's such a lot of baggage that comes with murder. But of course I already knew that.

– Murder, he said, staring straight ahead. – Has there been anything about it in the papers?

– Just a short paragraph.

He opened the car door, stepped unsteadily on to the track. – A man in his thirties?

– Correct.

He had to walk twice round the car. He heard the song of a chaffinch from the trees, and the hissing of cars down in the valley, a steady stream on their way home from a weekend in the country. He felt the urge to roar, forced himself not to. – But that's not your job any more, he managed to say.

Yet another sigh. – I guess I'll never get away from cases like that. They pursue me. The dead follow me.

– You could always have said no, he said, and could feel that what he had to tell her was on its way up and out, like vomit. He was back inside the car, but got out again, staggered past the barrier and on towards the edge of the forest.

– Listen, I have another call, I have to take it, she said. – Don't forget to call Trym.

It raced through him again, that anger over his brother's feebleness, over a mother who was always on the way somewhere else. It thickened inside him and shaped itself into a name. Ibro Hakanovic.

– Sure, he said quietly. – I'll make sure Trym gets to see the psychiatrist. It's the least I can do for him.

He could hear her smile at the other end, see her in his mind's eye, the quick movements as she flicked her hair back behind her ears. – You're the best brother anyone could have, she said, and he could tell by her voice that she meant it.

– And the best son, she added.

She's home, he thought as he let himself into the apartment.

– Hi, he said, looking into the front room, standing in the doorway. The smell of someone, but not her. – Katja?

The bathroom door was wide open, the bedroom door too. She often left the apartment like that, maybe with the kettle plugged in, or the TV still on. He always unplugged everything before he left, closed all the doors.

The wardrobe doors in the bedroom open too, bedclothes slung across the floor.

He took out his phone. Started rehearsing what to say, report the break-in. When did this happen? Sometime today. What's missing? He went back into the living room. His computer was on the table. The flat screen on its pedestal. The drawer with his passport and extra credit card untouched.

Katja, fucking hell, have you been here?

He tossed his phone on to the table, slumped down into the sofa, pressed both hands against his cheekbones, hard, dragging the skin up and down, as though it were a mask that had got stuck.

Have you been here? he repeated. Been here and gone again?

15

THE CALL WAS from the Institute of Forensic Medicine. When Jennifer finally took it, a secretary on the line transferred her to the head of the institute, a man whom she had not missed for one second after handing in her notice there. After a few preliminary courtesies, she was expecting to be offered her old job back and had her answer ready.

– You did us an enormous favour last night. I've spoken to the Romerike police. They said the service they got was even better than the one we can offer.

She listened out for any trace of irony in his voice.

– It wasn't a particularly demanding job.

– Maybe not. But you're one of the very best we've ever had here.

She could feel herself blushing.

– Could you do us another favour?

She hadn't expected that type of question. – Favour?

– Murder.

She had to laugh. – You want me to do a murder for you?

He laughed too, a little uneasily. On one occasion she had told him straight out what she thought of his qualities as a leader, and he was not the type to forget a thing like that.

– Someone has done that job already. Not too far from where you're working right now.

Give them an inch, she groaned inwardly, though she felt pleased rather than annoyed.

– Second time in less than forty-eight hours, a stabbing. What's the matter with people out there in Romerike?

– You don't have the time to handle it yourselves?

He started making growling sounds, a habit of his. It sounded as if he'd been holding it back for a long time.

– We've got two off long-term sick and one short-term.

Maybe it's about time to ask why, she thought, not without a certain malicious pleasure.

She was picked up by a police car, a young woman in uniform. Sundal she said her name was, first name Ina according to her ID, so that was what Jennifer decided to call her.

They turned off the main road, not many minutes' drive from the hospital, and bumped along a farm track. A tractor was parked behind a barn with an elderly man in a boiler suit sitting on it.

Ina Sundal nodded to him; the man glared back at her without returning the greeting.

– He found the body.

– He lives here?

– Owns the farm. And the forest.

Ina Sundal drove on along a rutted track between fields. Deeper into the woods the track was even more uneven. The afternoon sun shone somewhere up between the crowns of the spruce, and in the flickering light Jennifer observed the young policewoman as she eased the car up a stony hill. She was naturally blond and quite pretty. A little mascara but no sign of foundation. Jennifer recalled her own face the way she had seen it in the mirror before leaving home.

– Have you been to a crime scene with a murder victim before?

The policewoman glanced at her. – A couple of times. How about you?

Jennifer had to smile. – I worked as a forensic pathologist for over twenty years. There's not a lot surprises me.

– So you get used to it?

– When you're in the company of dead bodies every day, you have to get used to it. It helps to be methodical.

– I'm thinking the same. That I need something to do there, not just stand around and watch. But I don't know how I would deal with it if I was around death the whole time. Especially not children. The thought of them never growing up.

Jennifer thought about this.

– Children aren't the hardest.

Ina Sundal gave her a quick look. – No?

– I suppose losing a child is the worst thing that can happen. But for the child it isn't like that. They've lived such short lives, they lose so little. I think the hardest is young people who have just grown up, that's the worst. They've found a direction in life, somewhere they want to be, they have a lot ahead of them, and a lot behind them.

Suddenly she saw Sigurd's face, maybe because she had just been talking to him on the phone. The sense of unease invaded the car and enveloped her for a moment, as if she could actually smell it.

Two cars were parked at the end of the track. Ina Sundal parked next to them and they went the rest of the way on foot, reaching a tarn. At a point where the path split, Ina Sundal pulled out her phone and made a call. – Do we carry on around the lake?

She got a reply and walked on ahead down to the water's edge, following it round. Behind a headland they saw figures in white, moving slowly around an inlet, like animals with big, clumsy bodies.

Roar Horvath was standing on a large stone inside the cordoned-off area. He was peering out across the water, as if looking for someone out there. Jennifer wasn't sure how she felt about having to work with him, concluded that she didn't need to feel anything at all.

He turned and saw her, seemed surprised. – You caught this case too? So you're back in the fold?

– Temporarily.

– Everything is temporary, he said.

The observation seemed out of place, but as he turned and nodded in the direction of the wall of silent trees, it took on a meaning he probably hadn't intended it to.

– I'll show you where the body was found.

Clothes lay strewn across the little grassy slope leading down to the bank of the tarn. A summer dress, a bra, a G-string and a suede sandal. It must have had a cork heel, because the other shoe was floating upside down at the water's edge. A bag was half covered by a blanket. Jennifer could also see two glasses and a paper plate beneath it.

– Picnic?

– Looks like it, nodded Roar Horvath. – A picnic with death.

She made a face that might have passed for a smile and followed him into the trees. He was wearing a crumpled shirt, jeans and dirty trainers. Never was a very elegant man, she thought, but his outfit was more appropriate than hers, in particular the high-heeled sandals she'd bought three days earlier, which were intended for more urbane pursuits.

– Woman, probably in her twenties.

– Judging by the clothes, I wasn't expecting to see a man, she responded.

He turned and smiled back at her. It was five years now since there'd been something between them. It felt like centuries. Or as though it had never happened.

They clambered up a mossy slope. From the top they

could see down into a creek bed. The first thing she saw were the white legs sticking up over the edge, like branches of a tree from which the bark had been stripped. The stomach and upper body remained obscured until they began moving downwards. She felt dread, but with an element of something else in it, an expectation of finally seeing the very worst, the sight that would mean she would never again have anything to dread.

The hair lay swaying in the creek, green algae at the tips. The eyes were open and partially mutilated, probably by birds. Blood had run across the face and stiffened in large patches at the hairline. The woman lay with her head bent backwards, her whole throat slashed open. As though a red-painted clown mouth were laughing in their direction, the clustered flies like rotting stubs of teeth.

Jennifer stood a metre away, at the edge of the creek. In her mind she was already systematically organising what she was looking at. The woman was naked, and by no means slim. Later, when she sat at her keyboard, she would probably describe her as heavyset. Roar Horvath's guess was that she was in her twenties, and he could be right. Her hair was auburn, and Jennifer assumed that her skin had already been quite pale before death had stopped all circulation of the blood. Superficial scratches were visible around one wrist; also in the palms of the hands. The fingers were swollen, with signs of depressions caused by rings on several of them. There was only one actually on the hand, oddly enough on the thumb. It looked like gold, with an inscription in black enamel that might be Arabic, or Hebrew for that matter. If the other rings had been stolen then it struck Jennifer as odd that this one, which looked quite valuable, had not been.

One of the technicians, crouching, was making his way up the course of the stream. Perhaps looking for a murder weapon. It was not uncommon to find it close to the victim. But something told Jennifer that this hadn't been done by someone who threw away the knife or other sharp implement and ran. The way the throat had been cut reminded her of another body she had investigated less than forty-eight hours earlier, even though the technique used had been different.

The crime-scene technician disappeared with Roar Horvath. Jennifer spent a few minutes taking the rectal temperature, assessing the rigor mortis and the post-mortem lividity. It had started drizzling slightly, but the forest was still steeped in sunlight; it looked to be swarming out of the tiny drops of water. Quite a warm afternoon, but suddenly she felt cold, and it occurred to her that she might be getting sick. She had never liked the forest. Been surrounded by it all those years on the farm with Ivar and the boys. Never went into it unless she had to; it had always been Ivar who had taken Trym and Sigurd out walking.

She peered down into the creek, saw the outline of her own body, the face ruffled and reassembled in the slight currents. A rotten branch was sticking down into the water, covered in fungus. She could feel how the forest lived on death. Had it not been found, the body in the creek would have been chewed by carnivores, torn into pieces of different sizes. Bacteria and fungus, already starting to grow into the skin and the mucous membranes, would gradually cover them completely, eating their way inwards, dissolving everything into their invisible components.

Abruptly she stood up, put her equipment into her bag, followed the stream down towards where Roar Horvath was standing talking to Ina Sundal and two men who must also be police officers. She joined them.

– Cause of death pretty obvious? One of the policemen made a swift movement across his own throat.

– It wouldn't surprise me if her throat was cut while she was still alive, Jennifer agreed.

Roar Horvath scratched his forehead. – When?

– About twenty-four hours ago. I'll probably be able to pin it down a bit more than that.

– We were just talking about another throat that was cut. A couple of days ago.

Jennifer nodded. – I'll bear that in mind when I come to write my report. She looked at Ina Sundal. – I'm about ready to return to the world of the living.

The policemen guffawed, and she laughed a little with them, more like a shiver that rose up through her and made its way out.

Roar Horvath touched her arm lightly. – Good to have you on board, Jenny. I'll call you.

She didn't ask why it had to be him who would call. He was section leader, but obviously wanted his hands on the wheel all the way. It wasn't her problem. That he might have other motives for appointing himself pathologist's contact was something she couldn't even be bothered to think about.

16

ARASH FOLLOWED THE movement of the sun behind the clouds. The bleeding continued from his leg, and from the cut between his toes. He was still barefoot, but had found some clothes in another cabin he wandered past. It grew dark and then light again. He came to a road, the asphalt rough and grainy, not as yet warmed by the sun. Round a corner he saw houses he had seen before, the shopping centre and the blocks on the hillside. Later he was standing outside the flat. The clouds were gone by then and the sun burned on his neck.

He didn't have his key. Rang the bell and ran further up the stairs, waited on the floor above. Finally the door opened. He peered down between the banister railings. Ferhat was standing there.

Arash limped down.

— Are you my friend?

Ferhat didn't meet his gaze.

— *Dein Freund*.

Ferhat opened the door, let him in. As though he were the one who lived there and Arash the refugee who needed to hide.

— Blood.

Arash pulled off the tracksuit top, showed him the wound in his arm. — Shot, he said, managing to keep his voice calm. — They shot at me.

Ferhat nodded, as though he was in no doubt what it

was all about. – He was here, he said. – Ask for you.

Arash jumped up, ready to run. – Who was here?

– A man. Ask where you are. Search all the rooms.

– When?

– Hours ago. He says you'll be helped.

– What did you say to him?

– He asked me to call when you get back. Call number. Ferhat shrugged. – I won't do that, he added. – He gives me money. *Nicht mein Freund.*

Arash crossed to the window, stood behind the curtain, peered out into the sharp light. Abruptly he ran to the door, opened it, listened out in the stairwell. Sounds from the neighbouring flats. Shrieking infants, people quarrelling. Then silence. He closed the door and went back inside.

– I have to go.

Ferhat looked at him. His gaze wasn't as empty now, as though something had woken him up while Arash was away.

– *Wohin?*

Arash shook his head.

– You are not well. Best to sleep. Ferhat pointed towards the bedroom. – *Schlafen.*

Arash glanced over at the half-open door. Maybe someone was in there.

– I found a poem, he muttered. – Written on a mirror in the forest.

Ferhat carried on looking at him, said nothing.

– The patient didn't die that evening when he fell on me. He isn't dead.

Instantly the thought came again: – The ring!

He held up his hand in front of Ferhat.

– The ring is gone, the Kurd nodded.

– It all adds up, muttered Arash, but he didn't understand how. They were after him in the forest. Ibro Hakanovic was cut up, but walking around in Lillestrøm. Now they'd done the same thing to Marita, cut her up. Was she not dead either? If it wasn't Ibro Hakanovic lying in that hospital bed, it could have been the prison guard at Evin. They had done as they promised: to come after him even if he fled to another country, find him no matter where in the world he was.

– You're sweating, said Ferhat. – *Du bist krank*. Ring the doctor. *Krank*.

Arash shook his head. Don't ring. The ring. Without the ring he was nothing. His power would desert him, he would shrivel. Sit there and watch them come.

– You must sleep, Ferhat said again, and now Arash could see that he was lying. They had been there. Paid him to wait. Paid him to ring and tell them. He, Arash, was the one they were after. They had sent the pursuer into the forest to find him. The eyes in the opening in the black hood. He had seen that look in the stream, when the one in black stood over him with the knife in his hand. The knife that slashed Marita. She lay and bled to death at his feet. His ring on her thumb.

He had to find it.

In the bathroom, he washed away the blood that was still trickling from his leg and from his arm where the bullet had caught him. Ferhat came in. Talked more than he had done in the whole week since he had first shown up, and using a lot more Norwegian words. Arash let him. Not for one second could he trust Ferhat. They had given him money.

He dressed, took his old shoes from the back of the wardrobe, the spare keys from the drawer.

– Where are you going?

He waved three fingers in the air, back and forth five times, studied the Kurd, watching for signs. The traitor revealing himself.

– Ring them, he said, suddenly had to laugh out loud.
– Ring and tell them I was here. Ferhat, *Freund*.

Ferhat took a step closer, had the same look in his eyes now as the patient in the bed, as the guard at Evin.

– *Man tara nemikosham*, muttered Arash. I'm not going to kill you.

Ferhat tried to touch his arm. Arash whirled round, stared into his eyes, deep into them, beyond the traitor, beyond the basement at Evin, beyond the darkness when they took him out into the yard and pressed the barrel of a gun against his head.

He ran. His leg wasn't painful any more, nor his shoulder. Light flared across the sky, grew fainter, flared up again. As though it were his own pulse that made it flash. Are you still there, Marita? Are you sitting by the stream looking at me? Did you go there to drink, and something in the water spoke to you and made you sleep? Because you cannot walk around wearing that ring.

He crossed the main road, carried on up the farm track where he'd walked with her over twenty-four hours ago now. But that might have been a dream too. He ran past the farm furthest from the main road, his breathing quicker, the pulses of light through the sky too, but he didn't tire. Could carry on running like that. Then he heard the hum of an engine and knew it was a sign, because cars weren't allowed up here in the forest. He stopped and listened. It came closer. He turned towards the rocks on one side of the track, took hold and pulled himself up, climbed three metres up in a straight line. Snaked over the top and curled into a ball. Peered out between two thin birch trunks. A car appeared around the corner, a police car. He lay beneath the trees, listening. The sound of the car faded. No voices, no footsteps through the moss.

He could hear every sound in this forest. Insects and predators. And birds, not only those close by, but all of them. As though they were singing simultaneously, warning and gossiping, the ones he could trust, the ones he must avoid. He had learned how to understand them now, and followed them further up the track. Stopped when the warning notes grew loud, continued once the volume had dropped. Turned off the track, clambered up a rise, saw the tarn through the branches, approached in an arc. Suddenly the sound of voices. Two white-clad figures by the stream. They were wearing hoods. The kind of suits policemen wore. But they were something more. It occurred to him that he had seen similar figures clad in white long ago. Maybe it was in a dream, and maybe they were still part of that same dream. If I don't wake up soon, he whispered, if I don't wake up now, and his voice had become loud, as though it had flown down to the people in white, along with the gossip birds, the ones who were announcing his presence, the ones telling everyone he was to be picked up and shot. He turned, ran on into the forest.

Darker by the time he approached the flat again. He waited behind the wall of the neighbouring block. No lights in the windows. Maybe Ferhat was sleeping. If he crept up on him while he was asleep, he could end the wretch's life before he had a chance to ring the number they'd given him.

He sneaked into the kitchen. The drawer made a scraping sound as it glided open; he sucked it in, held it down, wouldn't let it out into the room.

Listened. No sounds, only the birds, those that warned him. But Ferhat always slept soundlessly. Maybe he never slept, maybe he was always watching him. Maybe Ferhat had been sent to make all this happen.

He took out the breadknife. As soon as he felt it in his hand, he didn't need to breathe, didn't need to draw breath for a long time, had enough breath to do what he had to do. The curtain in the room closed. The sofa in the darkest corner. Ought to say something first, wake Ferhat, ask a last question, let him confess. But then he remembered the look in his eyes, the same as the patient's, and the guard at Evin. And now Marita was dead. If he closed his eyes, he could see her. And the snake coiled on the flat stone, the little back-and-forth of the head. The same rage overcame him, and he charged across the floor towards the sofa, ripped away the blanket.

No one there.

No Ferhat. No Ibro Hakanovic. Everything still. Even the birds had flown.

The phone in the bedroom rang, making him jump. He dropped to the floor. The light was dimmer again, as though the day was suddenly over before it had begun. Or as though someone had recalled it. The morning he had seen coming had still not arrived. Silence from the floor above now, no crying child.

The ringing didn't stop. He crawled over to the window, couldn't answer the phone, but if he didn't answer, they would come and check. The temptation birds were still there, on the roof right outside, a magpie gossiping, another one a little further down spreading it.

– Arash? Are you there?

He had to calm his breathing before he could speak into the phone.

– Why aren't you at work? Are you ill?

– Not too good.

– Why didn't you tell anyone?

He had no answer. But it was okay to carry on. Benjaminsen was his boss, but he wasn't one of them, he could hear that at once.

– If you're ill, that's all right, but you have to let us know so we can rearrange things. Will you be in tomorrow?

– Yes, Benjaminsen. I'll come if you need me.

That was a good thing to say. He was going to be able to manage this. Get through it. Sleep. Back to work. Because on the other side of sleep, everything would fall into place again.

– I realise it hasn't been easy for you after what happened in the basement, said Benjaminsen. – Have you talked to anyone about it?

– Yes, I have talked to someone.

– So it's probably just as well if you don't come today. More bodies keep arriving. They arrived with another one just a few minutes ago.

Benjaminsen said this as though he were proud of it. As though he stood there directing all these vehicles arriving with bodies inside, telling them where to go with them.

And in that moment, Arash could see the scene. They were arriving with *her*.

– A woman? he asked.

– Correct. They found her up in the forest.

She lay in the stream, blood pumping from her open throat, down into the water. On her thumb she was wearing his ring.

– She's going for a post-mortem? he managed to ask.

– A full-scale investigation. Call me early tomorrow, Arash, so I know that you're coming in.

– I will do that, Benjaminsen. Trust me.

A promise should not be given if it couldn't be kept. But he was into the lie now. Needed more cunning than the magpie balanced on the guttering. More venom than that snake.

He turned to look into the mirror on the wall. Saw no one there.

– The ring, he said in Farsi.

– I quite agree, Arash. Get well soon.

Long after Benjaminsen had hung up, Arash stood there staring. Then he opened the drawer, took out his ID and his keycard.

17

the ring, he said and put...

light green. A red...ret wellroom...
and after being unseen had happened. Went a road there
saying. Then beeped and the...screen took out his ID and
the...yard.

JENNY REMOVED THE canisters with the test material from the fridge where the student had put them, took them into the lab, sat there looking out at the greying sky. If the clouds kept low and thick, the evening would be dark, which meant the possibility of a few hours' sleep.

The student had spent the week comparing results from fertile women and women unable to have children. She was obviously unsure what she had seen and wanted Jennifer to have a look at five of them. Jennifer sighed at the prospect of everything that had to be excluded again, and then again, before arriving at some conclusion they had already reached. It was evident that Lydia Reinertsen never for a moment doubted the importance of the research they were conducting. She remained a source of wonder to Jennifer. Lydia was colourless and formless, the kind of person who never stood out in any way. But she had real ambitions for this research project. She seemed to be convinced that they were on the verge of discovering a type of genetic disorder that predisposed to childlessness, and that it was going to be possible to demonstrate the condition. If she was right, it would be possible to develop a treatment.

Jennifer had allowed herself to be persuaded, and yet her involvement remained only moderately enthusiastic. And every time Zoran asked how the project was going, she felt the same pang of jealousy. Every time he praised Lydia's intelligence and perseverance. Once he said that it was researchers like her who helped us really progress. Not at the individual level, because that was our own responsibility, but as a species. Lydia was childless herself, and her involvement in the research was easy to understand. And maybe in the final analysis this was why the really good researchers succeeded, because something hugely important was at issue for them personally, something that was a matter of life and death. But no matter what the final results, Lydia would be too old to benefit from them herself. She was working for other childless women, others who felt that growing emptiness at being unable to bring forth a life formed and developed within their own body, the material inside them, the proteins, fatty acids, membranes, the DNA codes, cell by cell. And Jennifer had no problem in understanding a need that she herself had satisfied. Because the thought of withering away and disappearing was countered, to some extent, by the thought that she herself had been a nesting place for the life that would take over from her.

She turned on the microscope and entered the world of events in the Petri dish. Egg cells gliding slowly around, big as whales, seemingly impregnable for the little suitors swarming around them. But they were not impregnable. The most persistent of the sperm cells forced a way in through the membrane. At the same instant this membrane closed up again, preventing other sperm from entering, a complex system of signals that caused the proteins to bind together and form a barrier against competitors. The start of a new life, that was what she was sitting there watching, and she could not understand why it was she had devoted herself to the other end of life. Why death had always preoccupied her more than birth.

Within a few minutes she had seen it. Half an hour later she was certain. In three of the five dishes something was happening that shouldn't be happening. It was clear that the cell membrane was not closing up again after the first sperm had forced its way inside. Several others passed through, meaning that the fertilised egg would fail to develop. Maybe Lydia would turn out to be right, and they were on the trail of one of those countless tiny and crucial mistakes nature made all the time, marking the difference between a life that would develop, and one that would die out within the first few seconds.

She looked up, suddenly aware of how alone she was in the room. It was almost six o'clock, and there was rarely anyone around on a Sunday. She wouldn't have been there either if she hadn't been delayed in her work and expected to present the results at a meeting the following day. And if she had not been thoughtless enough to accept the two forensic jobs over the weekend. She stood up, packed away the dishes she had marked, satisfied that she would now be able to ring Lydia and tell her that they had probably made an important discovery.

As she was heading for the staff exit, she heard footsteps behind her.

– Excuse me, you're a doctor, aren't you?

The person addressing her was a thin, pale boy wearing white work clothes. Across his forehead a broad band of infected pimples.

– That's right.

– In pathology?

She confirmed that too.

– Something's happened. Can you come and take a look?

– Is someone hurt?

– I'm not quite sure.

Jennifer couldn't work out what that meant, but followed him down the basement corridor. He stopped outside the door to the cold storage room.

– You're a porter?

He nodded. – I was fetching some empty bags. His lip was trembling. – Can't get hold of my boss. Not quite sure what to do.

– About what?

He slipped the keycard into the lock, opened the door to let her in. – Can you have a look?

She hadn't been in the cold room before. It was like entering a winter's day, and she pulled the thin jacket closer to her body.

One wall was covered with metal shelving. There were cloth bags occupying some of the bays. She knew they contained dead bodies.

The door slid closed behind her. She grabbed the handle, couldn't open it from the inside, knocked hard.

– Sorry, said the pale youth when he had finally got the door open again. – Didn't mean to . . . He held the keycard up in front of him, as though it was to blame for her being locked in.

– Bit early to be leaving me down here, don't you think?

He shook his head, probably more from confusion than as a response to her comment.

Jennifer looked round the room. Only now did she notice that two of the bags on the uppermost shelf were open. She could see something in one of them, a glistening white scalp. From the shelf next to the wall, an arm dangled towards the floor.

– Crazy, muttered the boy.

His phone rang.

– Can I take this outside? His eyes were remote and terrified, as though he were about to have a panic attack.

– Okay, just so long as you don't lock me in here for good.

As she approached the shelf, the smell of putrefaction

grew even stronger. The protruding arm was bluey-black, with some dark fluid slowly dripping from it on to the linoleum floor. A little of the hair was also visible. Jennifer lifted the edge of the bag, uncovered the face.

It was easily recognisable. A few hours earlier she had been bending over it out in the forest. The auburn hair, the gaping neck. The gases escaping into the room had not yet been muted by the cooling process. The woman lay there almost squinting at her, a glimpse of grey showing between the swollen eyelids. Does death have a special gaze? Jennifer thought. Doesn't it just have a smell? Thoughts like this suddenly surprised her. But they led nowhere, because death wasn't an opening to anything else at all.

She was about to turn away, but stopped, her attention caught by the arm hanging out of the bag. It took her a few moments to realise that the hand had been mutilated and something was missing.

The thumb.

18

Sigurd stood by the window. The wind took hold of the trees outside. An old woman opened her umbrella, but he couldn't see that it was raining. His mobile rang several times as he stood there. Must be Trym. Sigurd had sent him a text; he was going to cover his brother's debts. A lot more than he had imagined: forty-nine thousand kroner. He knew he ought to be present when Trym paid off the debt, because the temptation to use the money to gamble would be great. Sigurd was going to help him, he was going to give his brother more support. Standing there looking out on to the summer evening, he knew it. Saw it in the green light in the trees, in the movement of the wind. Not because he had killed a person, but because the life he had been leading was over. An ache in the feeling, a faint nausea. And somewhere behind it, something that might have been relief.

He turned and looked at the apartment, seeing it as though for the first time. As though he were at a flat-showing and was wondering if this were a place where he could live. That was something else he'd have to think about. He didn't need a living room and two bedrooms, could manage with something half that size. Less furniture. Not fashionable designer names chosen so that other people would notice them. As if the apartment, and the rest of his life too, had been nothing but window-dressing.

He glanced at his phone. It was Katja who had been calling. He rang her back.

– Something happened? he said, getting in before her.

– I've been trying to get hold of you all day. Why don't you answer?

– Is anything wrong?

He shouldn't ask that, shouldn't open up areas in which it would be easy to trip himself up. Unless that was what he wanted.

– I don't know. Someone I know. From Malmö.

– What about him?

She hadn't said it was a *he* she was talking about.

– I can't get in touch with him.

Sigurd bit his lip, forced himself to keep quiet.

– Something must have happened. I've sent texts. There was something he was supposed to be doing for me.

– Maybe he's away somewhere.

– Actually he lives in Oslo. Or very close. If I don't hear from him soon . . .

She didn't say what would happen in that case.

– I must try to talk to someone from his family.

– Is that so difficult?

She didn't answer. Seemed far away. So she didn't notice that something was the matter with him too. He breathed more easily. This was at the heart of it, breathing as calmly as possible, surmounting the challenges, one after another.

– Who is he? he asked a little too abruptly, and struggled to control his voice. *Ibro Hakanovic deserved to die*, he might find himself saying. *He tried to take something that wasn't his.*

– Why do you ask?

Her voice was full of suspicion, and those suspicions could head off in several different directions. They could lead to a place in which he would be forced to confess what he had done. Be the first to tell her something she clearly didn't know. That the man she couldn't get hold of, who wasn't replying to her text messages, the one she may have had something going on with, that this man was now lying in a cold room somewhere in a hospital on the outskirts of town, his body opened up and examined, organ by organ. Even better, that it was Jenny who had done the job, mapped the damage her son had done to the dead lover. Or whatever he was.

But Katja wasn't the one he would be telling this to.

– When are you coming home? he managed to ask.

Silence for a long time. He thought she'd ended the call, but then heard her breathing.

– I don't know. Right now, I don't know anything, Sigurd.

19

ROAR HORVATH STRETCHED out his legs in the tiny box room of an office. Not until Jennifer picked up the steaming mug and took a large sip did he speak.

– Nothing else was done to the woman's body?

– Only the thumb. But I'll take a closer look when I do the autopsy.

– And none of the other corpses were mutilated?

– It doesn't look like it.

He rubbed his cheek, leaving a red mark on the skin. – So we're talking about desecration carried out here in the hospital? Less than two days after a murder in the basement?

Suddenly Jennifer remembered. – The ring!

She squeezed the plastic cup so hard it split.

– When I looked at her body up in the forest, there were marks from rings on her fingers. But she was only wearing one, the one that was on the thumb. It looked quite strange.

– Very observant, Jenny, Roar Horvath exclaimed. He leaned across the table, much too close to her. – Bloody good. Can you describe it?

She pushed her chair back as far as she could, tried to summon up a mental picture of what she'd seen. – A gold ring with an enamel surface and an inscription of some kind, in Arabic or something.

Roar Horvath noted this down on a folded sheet of paper. – Can we take a look over there?

She called the porter. A minute later, they met him outside

the cold room. His eyes flickered up and down the corridor. Maybe he should have been given the rest of the evening off.

– You don't have to come in with us this time, Jennifer reassured him.

The porter unlocked the door and waited behind them in the doorway.

– You said earlier that the bag was open when you came in?

He nodded. – One arm was hanging out.

– Who else has authority to come in here?

– Ask the chief, Benjaminsen.

Jennifer's gaze swept over the body bags on the shelves. The police technician had finished his work; the bags were closed up again and back in place.

Roar Horvath walked round looking at the name tags. – I've spoken to the security guards. They're stationing a man on the door for the time being.

He turned to the porter. – Do you guys come in here a lot?

– Now and then.

– What does that mean? Once a day? Twice? Ten times?

– Once, maybe. Or twice. Ask Benjaminsen—

– I will do the autopsy tomorrow morning, Jennifer interrupted. – I can't do anything more today.

– No one expects you too, said Roar Horvath. – Even you have to allow yourself a break now and then.

She accompanied him out through the staff exit. At the top of the steps he stopped and looked round. – Do you think that kid might have pocketed the ring?

She recalled the pimply youth, his thin back as he disappeared in the direction of the porters' room.

– It wouldn't be the first thought to cross my mind. Fortunately, it isn't my job to suspect people.

He smiled, was serious again. – We think we know the woman's identity.

He could have mentioned that earlier, she thought, or not bothered at all.

– Thirty years old. Lives in Enebakk. Married to a policeman, as it happens. Not reported missing until this evening.

– What's her name?

She didn't know whether she wanted the woman to have a name and a story. But it wouldn't be long before the newspapers were full of details about the life that had been so brutally torn away.

– Marita Dahl. Can we send the husband up here tonight?

– For identification?

He nodded. – By tomorrow morning the press will know that the patient you admitted was murdered here in the hospital. There's going to be a media storm. Not a bad idea to be prepared.

She met his gaze. By comparison with the cold room, the humid summer air outside seemed almost tropical. She should have called someone else, it struck her, reported the mutilation to the body in the usual way. But she'd had his mobile number to hand, and in her haste it was him she had called.

– The husband wants to get this out of the way too.

– That's perfectly understandable.

He looked as though he was thinking.

– Could you handle it?

For some reason or other she felt that she could. She had always been good with the bereaved.

– What about that other case?

– You mean the patient you found in the basement? Roar Horvath glanced round again, as though it was important to demonstrate that he was talking to her in confidence.

– No need to tell me if it's very hush-hush.

He gestured with his hand. – Don't worry. As I say, you're part of the team.

– You flatter me.

She could feel herself blushing, and turned away, pretended to be looking at something over by the roundabout.

– The victim, the patient, that is, was originally from Bosnia. Roar Horvath drew his fingers through his thin fringe. – He grew up in Malmö, and our colleagues down there have information that connects him to criminal gang activities in the city.

– That's not going to come as any surprise. First beaten up, and then someone enters the hospital and finishes the job off. Jennifer forced a yawn. – And the woman in the cold room, does she have any connection with these circles?

– Well, that's what you'll be helping us to find out.

He was still standing there looking at her. It was then that she realised that in her hurry she had not done her blouse up properly. At least two buttons were open, like some eight-year-old in a rush to get to school. She couldn't bear the thought that this man had seen her on several occasions with no blouse on at all. She blushed again.

– I'll deal with the husband, she said, and headed in the direction of the pedestrian crossing.

– Thank you, Jenny. He was silent for a few moments. – Maybe we could—

– Oh fuck, she interrupted, looking at her watch, remembering the appointment she had made with Ivar.

He laughed.

– Bugger, she said, tempering her language. – I'm supposed to be somewhere else right now.

– Oh that's too bad, he said. He sounded as if he meant it. – What about identifying the body, shall I ask someone else?

She thought about it for a moment. – Probably better if I postpone the arrangement I had.

She called Zoran on her way home, needed to talk to him. He was on his way to the operating theatre.

– Weren't you supposed to be up at the farm having a chat with Trym?

– Yes, I was.

– Dropped the idea?

She hadn't dropped it but put it off for another day.

– Am I a bad mother?

– On the contrary, Jenny. You've always been there for those boys of yours.

Zoran obviously understood that that was what she needed to hear. And there was some truth in it too, she added in her own defence. Year in and year out she had done what she could for them. Got up in the middle of the night, comforted, washed, bandaged, driven them to practice and training. And yet still this feeling of having let them down. She knew only too well where that came from.

– Something came up, that's why I had to change my plans.

She told him about the body in the mortuary, and the thumb. The only thing she didn't mention was the conversation with Roar Horvath.

– Cut off a thumb?

She could hear that he was curious, so maybe that meant her excuse for postponing the meeting with Ivar and Trym was good enough.

– Probably to remove the ring she was wearing. The swelling meant that it couldn't be removed otherwise.

– Why would anyone break into a hospital to remove a ring?

– It doesn't look as though it was a break-in. But that's a job for the police.

– By the sound of your voice, it's a job you'd like to do for them.

– You know me far too well, she laughed in relief, wanting it to be true. – I noticed that ring when I examined the body at the crime scene. I was able to describe it to them. Quite unusual. With an inscription in Arabic or something.

A long silence at the other end.

– Zoran?

– Can you describe to me exactly what that ring looked like?

She did so.

He muttered something or other, in Serbian, it might have been.

– What is it?

– Something I have to check on. Don't worry about it.

– You think I'll accept that as an answer?

It took a while for him to reply. – I might possibly know something about that ring. She could hear him hesitate. – Or maybe not.

– What is it you might possibly know?

– Who it belongs to.

She fumbled for the door key in her handbag.

– The description matches a ring belonging to Arash.

– The porter? The Iranian?

A few more seconds passed before several other connections became evident to her.

– I have to let the police know about this immediately.

– Can't I have a word with him first? He's had a pretty tough time of it. And if I'm mistaken . . .

That was what Zoran was like. Didn't like making trouble for people who had enough already.

– They're going to have to look into it regardless, she told him. – If Arash doesn't have anything to do with that woman, they'll soon check him out of the case. I'll talk to them; that way you won't have to.

He sighed heavily at the other end.

– I'll ask them to be careful, she reassured him.

By the time she finally let herself in, she had just concluded yet another conversation with Roar Horvath.

She emerged again an hour later. It was pouring with rain and she had to go back in for an umbrella. It kept off the worst of it, but by the time one of the guards let her into the chapel, she felt like a drenched cat. Inside, she collapsed the umbrella and left it by the door. She smoothed her hair back with both hands. Was wondering if there was a mirror where she could repair the worst of the damage when a man rose from the sofa in the small antechamber. He wore a police jacket and a peaked cap with a badge.

Jennifer looked round; no one else was there.

– I think it's probably me you're looking for.

– Sorry, she said, thinking mostly about what she must look like. – I'm Jennifer Plåterud. She held out her hand, which was wet too. – Doctor, she added.

The man towering in front of her was in his forties, thin and with a bent neck.

– Dahl, he said.

– I'm sorry, Jennifer said again, thinking now of the other's situation.

The policeman drew his first finger over his greying moustache a few times, as though something were stuck there.

– A colleague of yours is supposed to be coming too. We can wait.

Dahl nodded towards the entrance. – She got a phone call. She's sitting out in the car.

Jennifer glanced at her watch. – Then we can go on ahead. If that's okay by you.

He looked at her a moment. His eyes were strong and light blue, the blood vessels like a network of fine twigs in the whites.

Two lit candles on a table at the front of the chapel. The rain beating against the large windows was the only sound that could be heard.

Jennifer looked at the coffin standing in the middle of the floor. – As a policeman, I'm sure you've seen many injured and dead people. But it's something completely different when you yourself are . . .

She was usually good at this, finding the right words to say, but now they knotted up.

Dahl stepped over to the coffin. Before Jennifer could say anything, he had lifted the sheet, exposing not only the pale face, sallow but not yet swollen, but also the throat with the gaping butcher's slash across the neck.

He muttered something or other. *It's you*, she thought she heard him say. A few other words too, forced out between the tight lips.

– Death was instantaneous, she said; that was the kind of thing bereaved people wondered about, but the man in police uniform showed no reaction. He stood there bent forward, as though examining the cut across the neck. Then he pulled the sheet off her, all the way down to her knees.

Jennifer stepped forward, assailed by an unpleasant thought. The man hadn't shown her any ID. Suppose it were someone other than the dead woman's next of kin who was standing there, scrutinising the body . . .

– This is her? she said, keeping her low voice.

Still no answer. The man seemed far away. He ran a

finger over the dead woman's shoulder, squeezed hard, leaving a deep indentation.

Jennifer took hold of the sheet. – I am sorry, Herr Dahl, but it's important that you answer the question.

He seemed to come back from his faraway place. Again he looked at her, the red twiglets in his eyes wider now, and at last she managed to feel pity for him.

– This is Marita, he said loudly. – My wife, Marita Dahl.

The voice was without resonance; it sounded as though he were introducing her to strangers at a social event he wanted to leave as soon as possible.

Suddenly he took hold of the corpse's left hand.

. – What the hell is this?

Jennifer slowly and carefully began to cover the body with the sheet again. – You mean the thumb?

He studied the mutilated hand.

– Herr Dahl, she said, more firmly now. – As you know, this is now a police matter.

It sounded odd. He glanced at her, his lips parted momentarily. Then he let go of the hand, and it fell with a muted slap on to the dead woman's stomach. He turned abruptly and walked out.

Jennifer found him in the dark antechamber. He stood with his back to her.

She closed the door behind her. – I do understand what a strain this must be.

He turned to face her. – Are you American?

She shook her head. – Australian. We have to wait until your colleague arrives. Those are the rules. You have to confirm what you said in there. The ID.

Movement around his lips. – Formalities. He nodded. – I've been involved in this before.

– But perhaps not as a next of kin.

– Not as next of kin.

He bunched and opened his fist several times.

– Were you up there?

– Where?

– Up in the forest where they found her.

Jennifer thought about it for a few seconds.

– I examined her. That's my job.

– Isn't it the forensic pathologist who does that kind of thing? You work here.

She nodded in the direction of the exit. – Usually.

– So then this isn't usually?

– Herr Dahl, I can't give answers to all your questions.

– My wife's been raped and cut up. He closed his eyes tight for a few seconds.

Jennifer said nothing. Could have said she saw no signs of sexual assault, but it seemed clear to her that this was one of the details that were not to be made public yet.

– How do you think he got her to go all the way up to the tarn with him? Dahl looked up through the small windows, out at the pouring rain. – D'you think he tied her up, carried her, or forced her to walk in front of him with a knife?

20

ARASH DOESN'T MOVE. He doesn't even move his eyes any more, stares only at the same point on the wall. Sit like this tonight, through the night, the next day, the night after that. Sooner or later it will pass. He knows that now. This that might be a dream. Though it isn't a dream. Because in his hand he is holding something. A thumb. Not his. The ring still on it. *That* is his. Or hers. It binds them together, she who is dreamt, or dead, or dreamt dead, and he who sits here staring into this wall. The ring is a gateway. Go through it; there on the other side she is still alive. Smiles at him as she steps out of the water.

In his other hand he holds a knife. *Silence is the surest sign of your death.* Maybe it was she who gave him the knife. This is the thought that causes him to move his head, look down at her thumb, stained now and much thicker than when she had stroked his forehead with it. He lays the blade against his wrist, presses it flat against the skin, so hard that it makes his fingertips throb.

The window is slightly open. He hears a bird outside the house. Tries to work out what it wants him to do. Twice before he's been pulled across that boundary, to the place where birds talk to him and give him signs. He still has the tablets that help him sleep. And other tablets too, that turn his thoughts heavy, make them move so slowly he is able to control them. Sleep for forty-eight hours, and when he wakes up, all is clear again, and he can use his thoughts as he did before, decide for certain things and against others, understand what people are saying, understand what he himself is saying. *Silence* . . . I'm not going there, he mumbles. But talking is the last thing he should have done, because these words, said out loud in the bright room, are not directed at him but her, and they make her visible. He sees her inside the ring, he takes it off her thumb, lifts it up and holds it before his eye, and she emerges from the tarn in the green light of the ring and he cannot not speak to her. You shouldn't have taken me there, he whispers. Not to that tarn. You shouldn't have taken that knife. The birds warned you, and still we bathed. And that was wrong, because you belong to another. I belong to you, says Marita. And you belong to me. He knows that this is right: he belongs to her, and he cannot return as he has done before; he must follow her to where she is going.

He raises the knife again; it *was* she who gave it to him. He presses it against his wrist, now with the blade towards the skin. The outer layer is penetrated, just as hers was, and when he sees the bleeding start, he knows that he will never be coming back again. A bell rings. The doorbell. It could be anyone at all outside; the neighbours, Finn Olav and Tonje, maybe they heard him shouting, because he may well have shouted, or it could be the same people as those who sent Ibro Hakanovic after him, come now to fetch him themselves. They released him from Evin prison, but followed him all the way, through the streets of Tehran, on the bus to Tabriz, followed him across the mountains, sat in a café in Ankara. And every day since he came to this country they've been keeping track of him, watching him. He cuts into the wrist now, it's hard and sinewy, and this knife isn't as sharp as the one that cut Marita. I'm sorry, he says, speaking to her, and to his father, who is now also within the ring, standing there silently rebuking him for everything he's done.

Someone is knocking, someone shouting outside. He seems to hear his name. And then a buzzing noise, like a drill. They had to find him in the end. He cuts deeper and feels the penetration, and the blood that comes out is no longer a thick and dark stream but a thin shower. He leans his head backwards; someone is holding it. These are her hands he can feel around his neck. She talks to him in a language he has never learned and yet he is still able to understand her.

The door has been forced open and someone is standing there, wearing a dark coverall. Several others behind him, weapons in their hands, but they cannot reach him in the place he is on his way to, not if he takes one more step and the gate closes behind him.

This is our penultimate conversation.

And you want me to talk about who I was and who I am.

That is one possibility.

You want to know if I am damaged in a way that confirms the image of the world you have. You would prefer to come to the conclusion that there is something wrong with me, that I lack empathy.

I have never said that.

You think it. That I am incapable of feeling the pain of others. But that is not the case, not at all, and if you understand yourself then you will understand that. After our first conversation, for the remainder of that day all I thought about was the man who fell into the rose bushes. I dreamt about him at night. He stood by my bedside and looked at me, not saying a word. He was bleeding from his torn cheeks.

You felt for him, that time in the park.

I am good at reading other people's feelings. Not simply reading and understanding as a thought. I can enter into the feeling, no matter what it is, feel the grief in it, the pain, the fear. And then, when I wish, leave it again. As a child, I cried easily with a friend who hurt himself, or with those who were grieving over the loss of someone. But I was able to decide for myself when there had been enough sorrow, and then I would stop crying. I am still like that.

You have control over your empathy.

I feel sure you can do this too. In your thoughts you can decide to turn away when you have had enough. Otherwise you wouldn't be able to do the job you do. You would be swallowed up in the feelings of others.

From the expert witness's notes, 3 August 2014

PART IV

15–17 June 2014

21

Zoran served a pasta dish. It was simple, he assured her, just a few shellfish, olives, tomatoes and herbs.

– You spoil me completely, Jennifer complained as he poured white wine into her glass.

– Weren't you spoilt long before you met me?

She had to laugh. From the moment she had entered Zoran's flat, she had felt as though a burden had been lifted from her shoulders. She had next weekend off. They should go away somewhere together. Knut and Lydia had a place by the sea not more than a few hours' drive away; they could borrow that. Just the two of them naked in the sun on a big flat rock by the water. He had never seen her this naked before, not outdoors, not in a light like that. She drank the wine, and just the thought of that nakedness made her want him. But this wanting was different from before. She could sit there and feel calm and enjoy the wait. It was almost thirteen years now since Sean. Sean could have done anything at all with her life and she wouldn't have been able to lift a finger to stop him. If he'd asked her to leave home with him, leave the farm and the boys and the job, she would've done it. But Sean left without asking, without saying anything at all. It tore her into tiny pieces; the whole of the next year was spent trying to put them together again. It was only now that she was able to think about it without being torn apart again. If she'd gone to Dublin with Sean back then, she thought, she wouldn't be sitting on Zoran's little balcony, looking out over the lawn and the birch trees between the blocks, hearing the traffic in the distance, an ambulance approaching, sitting there waiting for the light night she would spend together with him.

On the table, her phone vibrated and she picked it up.

Sigurd, she noted, relieved it wasn't somebody else.

– Thanks for what you're doing for Trym, she said before he could speak. – I hear you're lending him the money and making sure his debts are paid off once and for all.

Zoran stood up, picked up the plates and went inside.

– What you're doing for him, you're doing for me too.

– Isn't it tomorrow he goes to see the shrink? Sigurd sounded a little ill at ease. – Since it's the first time, I can go with him. Have lunch with him afterwards. He needs to get out.

– With a brother like you, things have to work out for him—

– That isn't why I'm calling, Sigurd interrupted her. She heard an undertone in his voice that made her pull her jacket tighter around herself. Because what he was about to say had something to do with her, she was certain of it. Sooner or later it would all have to come out, all the things he could reproach her for.

– How are *you* keeping? he asked, and it was like a confirmation; he would follow up his concern for her well-being with something she couldn't bear to hear. Not this evening.

– I'm working, she said quickly. – Not actually at this moment, I've finished for the evening. But you know.

He couldn't know. Not about crime-scene examinations, or corpses with their thumbs cut off, or encounters with next of kin filled with rage and despair.

– I'm doing several jobs for the forensic department, she continued, still keeping the conversation at a safe level. – You know how it is, give them an inch. First this Swedish Bosnian who got butchered. And now there's another case. Read about it in the papers, I can't tell you any more.

– What did you say?

– I said, murders are being committed, and for reasons I will never understand, I chose the line of business I chose. I'm a peace-loving person by nature. I like what's safe.

– What did you say about the Bosnian?

– What did I say?

– Something about him being sliced up.

If her intention had been to distract Sigurd from his real purpose in calling, she appeared to have succeeded. She wasn't the best mother in the world, but she had done her best, she consoled herself. She had always loved him unconditionally. Admired him more and more as he grew up. As long as he needed her, he had been the most important person in her life. Him and Trym, she added in her thoughts. She had been unfaithful several times, and it wasn't something she could regret; without it she would have withered away. But she hadn't been unfaithful to the boys, and she had made sure this other life was kept secret from them. They didn't even know about Sean, who had been completely unpredictable and had twice visited her at the farm. Maybe one day she would try to explain to them why she had made the choices she did in her life. But she needed this evening for something else.

– That's right. He was stabbed to death. It was a pretty nasty business.

She felt she could reveal this much to Sigurd; he wasn't the type to pass things on. And in only a few hours' time, the hospital authorities and the police would be holding their press conference. In the nick of time, too; a journalist

on a local paper had already received a tip-off about what
was coming.

– What do you mean?

She sipped her wine. It was her third glass. The second
was always best, and she usually stopped there. But after a
day like the one she'd just had, a third seemed called for.
A harmless increase in the dosage.

– Of course I'm not allowed to talk about this to anyone,
Sigurd. But I know I can trust you.

She had always enjoyed sharing secrets with him. From
when he was a child, there were things that only the two
of them knew. This shared intimacy connected them still,
and would always do so, no matter what sort of complaints
he had about her. And maybe she made too much of it.
Maybe he didn't reproach her for the way she'd never been
able to share her life with his father. Not the most mean-
ingful part of it.

– This man, this Bosnian, was murdered here at the
hospital. A few floors below the department where I work.

– What the hell are you saying?

– I'm saying he was practically delivered to my table, all
ready for his autopsy.

She knew it wasn't funny, but she laughed a little at her
own joke anyway.

– But the man was seriously injured; it said something
about him dying as a re-re-result of . . .

She had not heard him stammer since his primary school
days. Not often then either, only when he got so agitated
he couldn't handle it. She felt a strange warmth at the
memory of it.

– They've put a news blackout on the case. God knows
why. I guess the hospital is worried about its reputation and
all that, and the police want to be left to work in peace. The
excuse is probably that the next of kin have to be informed

first. And now something else has happened, so there's going to be a media explosion.

– But didn't he d-d-die of the injuries he had when he was admitted?

– Sigurd, you're not to say a word about this to anyone.

– Yeah, sure, I mean, of course I won't.

– The man was injured, as you say, that's why he was admitted. But not seriously. Beaten, concussed. He died of something completely different. Someone obviously decided to follow him to hospital to finish the job.

Silence.

Then he said: – Are you completely sure of that?

She laughed, feigning exasperation. – It's my job to find out things like that. I've been doing it since before you were born. They've arrested a suspect. Now she felt she had said too much. – The online editions will have all this in a few hours' time; you can read about it there. Why did you call me?

– Nothing really. Just about Trym.

She could tell from his voice that this wasn't true. Relieved that he wasn't going to bring up all the other stuff, she poured herself another half-glass of wine. She would make things right. Pay the debt she owed them. That was exactly how she phrased it to Zoran when he came back in with the espresso.

– You go round with this idea that you owe some kind of debt you have to repay, he replied. – Not the kind of debt Trym had, but all the same. Maybe the two types of debt are connected.

– Now you're talking like Knut Reinertsen, she protested. – Maybe you've been spending too much time in his company recently.

Zoran laughed. – Maybe so. I'm sure you remember what he said about parents and children last time he was here.

– Don't remind me.

– The role of the first child is to live up to the father's ambitions. The role of the second child is to live up to the mother's emotions.

– That man is a clown, she groaned. – And he's never had any children of his own to raise. Thank goodness.

– Now you're going a bit too far. You don't know him.

She snorted. – Father's ambitions. The man who was father to my boys never had any.

Zoran shook his head. – Does it never occur to you that you're a trifle unfair on him too?

Of course she was unfair. Always had been. Had condemned Ivar for being who he was and not who she wanted him to be.

– I'll tell you a story, she said. – When Sigurd was in primary school, he often got into fights with other boys.

– Hardly an unnatural propensity.

– One of the boys in class used to terrorise the others. Most of them put up with it, but not Sigurd. One day he had had enough, and there was a fight.

– I'm sure Sigurd handled himself well.

– The other boy was a head taller than everyone else, but Sigurd gave him a thrashing. And I mean a real thrashing, lips, teeth, bruises. The bully was off school for several days afterwards.

– You sound proud.

She gestured with a hand. – I had always told the boys that they had to hit back if the situation ever arose. And now we had to sit through one of those conflict meetings and apologise for Sigurd's violent tendencies. Everything had to be done the Norwegian way. Rather than deal with something themselves, children absolutely must go to the grown-ups and report it. And the grown-ups would then *talk about it* and *work on changing attitudes*. As though reporting something like that ever helped.

– And you made this very clear to those at the meeting,
I imagine.

She nodded firmly. – Suddenly my patience just ran out.
So we're supposed to teach our children to be victims instead
of looking after themselves. I can still remember the looks
I got.

– I can imagine the scene, Jenny.

– Ivar didn't often get angry with me, but he sure was
after that meeting.

Zoran poured out their espressos. – Decaff, he informed
her. – Nothing must be allowed to disturb your sleep
tonight.

– Not even you?

He sat beside her. – I heard you talking to Sigurd about
the murder. Is that such a good idea?

– He won't say anything about it. And he's very curious.

– Everybody is.

She snuggled into him. Again that thought of getting
away. She'd mentioned it to him. Move to another country
together. She'd suggested Germany, where his daughter
lived. He rejected the idea, for some reason or other didn't
want to talk about her. But the US was a possibility. Or
even Australia, if Jennifer wanted to go back. And Sigurd
was part of the picture too. Australia was the country for
people like him.

– You're still thinking about the Iranian, she said.

He sipped his coffee, glanced down at her. – He has a
name.

– Of course he does. She felt a touch of shame at the way
she was always trying to keep her distance. – You're still
thinking about Arash. It bothers you.

– Doesn't it bother you?

– Of course.

– Arash is no killer.

– I never said he was. But sooner or later they would have arrested him. Best that it was sooner.

Some swallows came towards them, cheeping, pulled away at the last instant in an arc and rose into the sky again.

– You're probably right there, Jenny.

– I think it's hard to imagine he's killed anyone too. But he was at the scene of two murders, and then that thumb . . .

– He's in utter despair.

Zoran picked up the wine bottle. She placed her hand across her glass, and he poured into his own. They heard the rescue helicopter starting up down on the landing bay, the air cut into slices that came scything towards them. Once it had taken off and disappeared, he said: – Being locked up is probably the worst thing that could happen to him.

– The psychiatrists will keep an eye on him. They think he's psychotic.

– So would you and I be if we were exposed to the same things he was. Tortured every day for six months. Threats, electricity, punching, mock executions.

She thought about this. – Might *that* be the reason this had happened?

– Are you suggesting that he's killed two people?

– I suppose that's what I'm asking myself.

Zoran looked up into the bright sky, followed a cloud with his gaze as it slowly unfolded and assumed another shape.

– I'd very much like to have spoken to him myself.

She stroked his powerful forearm, left her hand there. – He won't be allowed mail or visitors.

– Might *you* be allowed to talk to him?

She felt as if her whole face frowned. – Why should I talk to him?

Zoran shrugged. – To see how he is. Let him know that

someone out here is thinking of him all the time. I'm afraid this might end very badly for him.

Jennifer stood up, leaned against the balcony.

– I doubt if they'd let me. She bent down and pressed her cheek against his. Nothing calmed her down like the smell of him. – But I can try.

22

Sigurd drifted through the streets on the June evening. When he looked round, he was in Frogner Park. He carried on through the graveyard, crossed the ring road and headed up the hill. Only then did he begin to run. In his thoughts he repeated what Jenny had said. *He was stabbed to death.* Are you sure? *He was stabbed to death.* But what about the injuries he had when he was admitted? *He was stabbed to death. They followed him to the hospital and stabbed him to death.* Are you one hundred per cent sure? *He was stabbed to death. It's my job to find out things like that.* He left the road and headed into the forest. A thin veil of rain, grey and warm; he hardly registered it. Suddenly he stopped and shouted into the trees. *He was stabbed to death. They followed him to the hospital.* He squatted down, tipped over and landed face first in the damp grass, inhaled the smell of the earth it grew in.

Back home, he pulled on the gloves and started on the punchball, a few loose jabs, a series of quick feints, then moved on to the bag. Didn't have to think while he was punching. He needed that thoughtlessness. Punch his way into it, his arms heavier and heavier, his head lighter and lighter.

When his hands couldn't take any more, he stopped, opened the window wide and breathed the evening air with deep breaths. Stood looking down into the street. Someone standing by his car, a man in a short jacket bending to look at the bumper.

– Hey, you, he shouted, but the guy didn't react, and he ran to the door and down the stairs. The thought of what MacCay had said, that he made enemies for himself. Someone planning to do something to his car, scratch the paint or whatever the hell guys like that did.

No one there when he reached the vehicle. He noticed a vague disappointment, because now he was ready, ready to draw a line and beat the shit out of anyone who crossed it. He took a walk around the car, checked the paintwork, checked the mirrors and the lights. Didn't find any marks that weren't there before.

In the shower, he could let his thoughts run. The other thoughts.

When he was with Katja, he turned into someone he didn't recognise. A person who put up with everything she said and did. As though in the instant he had followed her down the basement stairs at Togo he had become another. But she had barely gone out the door before he felt he was finished with her. As though she had passed straight through him and left no imprint.

A couple of things remained to clear up. Report to the police station. Tell them what had happened that evening. That he had broken into a house. Been attacked and fought back. That he had called for help as the other man lay there.

He picked up his phone from the mirror shelf. For an instant, but no more, the thought that she might have rung after all, that such an abrupt break wasn't necessary. He felt a twinge when he didn't see her name on the call list, but then it went away. With her it was impossible to have a direction, he saw that now, the moment she was out of his life.

Trym had rung. He called him back.

– You out minding the cows?

Trym laughed. He had an infectious laugh. That was

something they'd always shared, laughing at the same things: at their father's frugality, that he never threw out a pair of underpants even when the seam in the crotch was torn; at the fact that he always made an effort to believe the best of people, never got angry. So easy to parody. And their mother's restlessness and impatience, her preoccupation with make-up and clothes, and how everything was better back home where she came from. But why she had left the best country in the world to live in a mud hole on the other side of the planet was something they could never get out of her.

– I've hired four milkmaids to do the dirty work, Trym answered. – You should come and say hello to them.

– That's what I was planning on doing. It's tomorrow morning you're going to see this psychologist, isn't it?

Trym hesitated. – I'm not sure.

– Come on, you know perfectly well it is. You're not thinking of backing out?

– Guess not.

– Get a grip.

Sigurd thought about it.

– I'll come up to the farm early tomorrow. I'll drive you there.

– You're bloody keen. Don't you have a shrink of your own? You can have my appointment if you want.

– Thanks, maybe he can take us both at once. Couple counselling.

He heard Trym grin.

– Did you transfer that money?

Sigurd emptied the used capsules from the espresso machine and poured in fresh water.

– I'll do it now, just as soon as you hang up.

He did so, transferred the forty-nine thousand kroner. It felt good to get rid of it. At least he thought it felt good, but he needed another shower. Be there for Trym. It started there, everything that was going to be different.

He stood naked in the living room, fiddling with the sound system, the ice-cold water pooling on the parquet floor around him. Had just navigated to the Foo Fighters playlist when the phone rang again. It was still in the bathroom.

He ran to take it, knew it was her.

First to see the bridge lives. The loser dies.

Sigurd had passed Strömstad and was approaching Uddevalla bridge. It was after midnight. Hardly any other cars out on this summer night, and after crossing the border he pushed the speedometer needle up round a hundred and fifty.

Years since he'd driven south along the E6. Not since the time the family went to the big amusement park at Liseberg. He and Trym in the back seats, Ivar and Jenny sharing the driving. There are a lot of bridges along the way, but one in particular that outshines all the others. They talk about it long before they get there, as soon as they cross the border at Strömstad.

First to see the bridge lives. The loser dies.

What an awful wager. It's Jenny who says that. *Can't you find a different prize?*

Trym isn't interested. Live or die, that's all that matters.

A few kilometres before they reach it, they pass a mast. From that point Sigurd can follow the second hand, because he knows from the last time they drove this way precisely how long it takes before the bridge comes into view.

There it is! His shout of triumph comes moments before he can actually see it.

You cheated, Trym yells, and the accusation starts a quarrel that can easily last all the way to Gothenburg, because if there is one thing Sigurd can't stand, it's being called a cheat.

You'll both get a helium balloon when we reach Liseberg, Ivar mediates. Trym protests. *No point in betting if everybody wins.*

Jenny always wants there to be one winner. Ivar wants everybody to win. But Sigurd gets first choice; there can't be any arguing with that.

In Liseberg, the balloon seller only has three balloons left, two pink rabbits and a yellow lion with a silver mane around his head. Sigurd stands studying them in the sunlight, watching their slight movement in the wind. Thinks he should take one of the rabbits, let Trym have the lion.

And all these years later, it was that lion balloon he thought of as the masts of the Uddevalla bridge came into view above the treetops, towering up into the light night sky. The bridge still made him think of a ship with enormous masts and cables stretched out like sails.

Jenny agreed with him, it was like a ship, while Ivar thought it resembled a cathedral.

He said it as though cathedrals were holy places, he who always claimed to believe in people and not gods.

What do you think, Trym? Ivar wanted to know.

It's a bridge, said Trym, *and it looks like a bridge.* To say anything else was nonsense, because he'd read about it, he knew how long it was, how wide and how high, how much steel and concrete was used in building it, how many metres of cable.

The windsock hung limp, and Sigurd accelerated up the curve of the bridge. As though the masts gathered the light in the air around them, bundled it and sent it off in all directions. Jenny was afraid of heights, the only thing he knew she was afraid of, apart from spiders, and Trym would always try to get her to look down into the fjord that seemed to be several hundred metres below them. She sat there in the front, her gaze fixed on the road ahead, letting her breath out in an exaggerated sigh of relief once they'd reached the other side. Sigurd didn't like her doing that, because it reminded him that one day, even she would be gone. He could remember a fantasy he'd had at that time. Jenny alone in a car out of control, smashing through the railings on the bridge and out into the blinding evening light. The vision was so clear to him that he could literally feel the drop down towards the fjord.

As he was driving down off the bridge, he remembered.

– Shit, he said aloud, and took out his mobile, called Trym, couldn't reach him, tried Jenny instead.

Her voice sounded sleepy.

– I woke you, he said, realising that it was past midnight. – Sorry.

– I hope this is important, she muttered.

He apologised again; he'd called without thinking. – It's about Trym.

– Anything wrong?

The voice was awake now. He knew she had trouble sleeping, and now he was causing her unnecessary worry.

– Just this psychologist he's going to see.

– Psychiatrist, she yawned.

– I promised to drive him there tomorrow.

– That was kind of you, Sigurd.

– But it turns out I can't after all.

– That's a shame. Then Trym will just have to make sure he gets there on his own. He should be able to manage that at least.

It was naïve of her to think like that. Left to himself, Trym would never go.

– Or else Ivar can help him. Are you in the car?

That must be easy to hear. It occurred to him that there might be another reason why he had called her.

– I'm in Sweden.

– All right?

– Just crossed the Uddevalla bridge. The one that looks like a ship. I'll hang up, you need to sleep.

– I'm well aware of that, Sigurd. Very considerate of you to wake me up to remind me of the fact.

He heard her closing a door.

– You're not going to Malmö, are you?

– Not exactly.

– This is something to do with Katja, isn't it? You don't have any other business in Sweden?

– Not unless it's a trip to Liseberg.

– Are you trying to be funny?

He thought quickly, working out what he could say and what he had better keep quiet about.

– Katja's in some trouble. She called me earlier.

– And so you just drop everything and leave?

– I have to help her.

She had not exactly begged him to come, but after everything that had happened, he felt he owed it to her.

– What kind of trouble?

– Not quite sure.

That was almost true. Katja's voice had sounded afraid, but she wouldn't say what the matter was. He gathered it had something to do with Ibro Hakanovic. She wouldn't even tell him where she was. Not until he was close.

– This is not something you need to worry about, he reassured Jenny. – I'm going to talk to her.

– I thought it was over between you two?

That was what she had been waiting for.

– Yes, he said, and didn't know whether that was true, didn't know anything about what was going to happen. – It probably is.

He could hear Jenny's sigh of relief, and it annoyed him. He hung up before she could notice.

Once he'd passed Malmö, he received a text from Katja, an address and a few lines that were probably supposed to be directions. They weren't much help. Instead he used GPS to locate the house, in a forest just east of a little harbour town on the Baltic coast.

It was after four in the morning when he arrived. He passed several cabins as he drove through the forest; they looked like summer places, their windows dark. He turned into a field, cut the engine, opened the car door. A slight wind in the fir trees, and the pounding of the sea somewhere close by. A bird on a bare branch, its harsh, guttural screech; judging by its silhouette, an owl.

He left the car, walked a few metres along a grassy track. The house was behind a hedge. At least he thought that must be it. Two storeys, painted white, she'd written in her text; in the pale dawn light it looked dark grey. As he crossed the lawn, he saw that the paint on the walls was coming away in large flakes. A Swedish flag hung limply on a pole by the front door.

He walked around the house. The curtains were drawn tightly in most of the windows, but next to the veranda he found one with a gap he could look through.

Someone curled up in a chair.

The veranda door wasn't locked. It was her sitting in there. She jumped once he was inside. – It's you.

The voice was toneless. He hadn't expected her to throw her arms around his neck. Wasn't sure what he'd expected.

– How did you get in?

– The door, he said.

– But it was locked.

He crossed the floor, stopped by the sofa where she was sitting. There was a faint smell of rot inside the place. She didn't move when he kissed her on her cold cheek, sat there staring straight ahead, muttered something he didn't catch.

But he understood.

Someone was dead. Someone she had known well, someone she'd always known. He could have told her now, given her the details she didn't know. Instead he began asking careful questions, got fractured answers in response.

He sat down beside her, managed to get an arm around the narrow back, and straight away began stroking her neck and hair. She didn't move, and he sat there holding her and looking out through the window, towards the brightening sky above the fir trees.

At some point she rested her head on his shoulder. – Why? he heard her murmur. – I don't understand. They couldn't have known anything. I'm the only one who knew.

– Do you want to talk about it? he said.

She didn't reply. Just as well, because he was struggling to control his own words. Something in him might just start to talk by itself. Reveal what he was sitting there thinking. She had lied. Had used him. Had been with another. A stream of dark joy at the thought, or the opposite, a bright sorrow. For would it not after all be possible to carry on as before? Not as before. Ibro Hakanovic was no longer there. His shadow was. Shadows disappeared. Hold on to her, he thought. That was what she wanted. Someone to hold her so tight she couldn't get away.

But she pulled herself free, struggled up, bare legged and wearing that clinging red dress, not even a G-string underneath as far as he could tell. She let herself into what was probably the bathroom. Running water, at first into an empty sink, and then a more powerful and deeper sound as it filled.

Afterwards, she disappeared into one of the other rooms.

He heard the creaking of a bed base. Then silence. He waited half an hour, then he went in. She was lying on a double bed, curled up. He stood watching as her outline became clearer in the morning light that fell through the thin curtains. Still she didn't move. He crossed over to her, bent, his ear next to her face. Felt the tiny puff of breath that came from her, mingled with an almost inaudible moaning, like the echo of a cry from far away.

23

JENNIFER FINISHED THE autopsy well before lunch. She'd found things that would interest the police and decided to call Roar Horvath, but had something else to do first. Maybe she'd even have time for a bite to eat.

She knocked on the door of Lydia's office. Heard voices from inside, opened it anyway. Lydia was on the phone. She held it away from her ear. – Won't be a sec.

Jennifer was on the point of withdrawing, but Lydia signalled no and pointed to a chair.

The conversation was in Russian, as far as Jennifer could tell, and when Lydia ended the call a minute or so later, she said with a smile: – The good thing about Russian is that you can say what you like. No one here understands a word.

– Well you never know, said Jennifer, and Lydia glanced at her, apparently trying to look worried.

– So next time I'm talking to my lover in St Petersburg, I'll have to ask you to wait outside?

Jennifer laughed, hadn't expected that from Lydia. Even when she was joking she seemed reserved and correct.

– Did you get my notes?

Lydia nodded. – I've just been looking at them. If you're right, this might be the breakthrough we've been waiting for.

– If so, it's no credit to me.

– You're much too modest, Jenny. I'm very happy with your work. I'm going to spend the rest of the day checking your findings against the DNA profiles.

She sounded like a girl who'd been given a present of something she'd always wanted.

– I was a little late in letting you have those notes, Jennifer apologised. – As you know, my past has caught up with me.

Lydia looked at her, wrinkles gathering above the rim of her spectacles. – The forensic institute not letting you go? That I can well understand.

– I'm a little rusty, Jennifer answered. – But I'm probably still usable.

Lydia got up from her office chair. She was wearing trainers and an outsize T-shirt under her doctor's coat.

– I hear a hospital employee has been arrested, she said.

– I heard that too.

– Is it Zoran's friend?

Jennifer didn't want to say anything about the severed thumb.

– That's what they're saying.

Lydia took off her glasses and put them on the table; her gaze changed, the eyes getting smaller, one pointing outward even more noticeably. – D'you think it's that porter who killed the patient? If that's the case, then he must be terribly disturbed. I mentioned it to Knut. He knows several cases of people very badly damaged by torture who do the most dreadful things in a panic. He says hello, by the way. Apparently your son had an appointment this morning but he never turned up.

Jennifer groaned. Of course Trym hadn't gone. She should have called Ivar and asked him to take care of it, had forgotten.

– Sigurd, my other son . . . yes, of course, you met him. She pushed her hair up behind her ears; it fell forward again. – Sigurd was supposed to be taking him, but something came up.

She told Lydia about the telephone call the previous night.

Sigurd who had broken up with his awful girlfriend but still jumped into his car the moment she called and drove to Malmö or wherever it was. It was a kind of relief to talk about it. Lydia was a listener; she was interested in what she heard, asked questions that showed she cared.

– I can hear you've got a lot to think about, Jenny, she said as Jennifer stood up, her hand resting on the doorknob. – But I'm so happy with the work you're doing. That you're so involved.

Jennifer could feel herself blushing.

– I wish I could ask more of you, Lydia went on. – If you had the time. This project needs you.

This research project of yours is all you live for, thought Jennifer, but then regretted it. Lydia was easy to work with. And she obviously accepted that not everyone had the same passion.

– There's talk of expanding the field. It would be particularly interesting to look at younger women who miscarry. Compare them with those over thirty.

– Is there any money?

– Someone up there is interested in what we're doing. Lydia nodded in a vaguely upward direction, as though such matters were decided on the next floor up. – Childlessness is something that affects everybody.

A lot of people with life-threatening and painful conditions are further back in the queue because they don't have anyone to plead their case, thought Jennifer, but didn't want to contradict her. It wasn't her job to moralise about the ordering of priorities.

– If you want to, you can work closer to the area I'm dealing with.

Jennifer glanced at her, forgetting for a moment that it wasn't Lydia's right eye that was crossed. It must be strange for her, being practically blind in one eye, with people seeming to stare straight past her.

– Genetics has never been a speciality of mine, she pointed out.

– You've learned an incredible amount in a very short time.

Jennifer liked hearing that kind of thing a little too much, and made no protest.

– Someone of your ability picks things up at once. And our lab technicians are actually very skilled.

– I'll think about it, Lydia. And have a chat with my departmental head.

– She thinks it's an interesting idea. I already mentioned it to her.

Jennifer didn't quite know what to make of this. She was glad to feel needed. But she wasn't going to be staying. The time to break camp was approaching.

She managed a quick trip to the canteen, picked up a bagel, as they called the roll with sweaty cheese. Back in her office she called Roar Horvath. He sounded stressed. Not hard to understand why.

– I had a quick look at the newspaper, she said, as though that might calm him down.

– They've turned everything upside down, he groaned. – We invited them to a press conference, but those rats got in ahead of us.

– Funny they didn't get hold of it even sooner. Loads of people around the hospital know what happened to that patient.

– That's what I told them. We should have let the press have it straight away.

He was hardly the sort of leader who always got his own way.

– And now we've got people from the NCIS here, he sighed. – Not that we asked for them. We're going to be treading on each other's toes the whole time.

Her concern for his logistical problems was less than minimal, and she was even less interested in being his confidante.

– I'll be sending a preliminary post-mortem report some time this afternoon.

– You've always been quick on the draw, Jenny. I like that.

– It's going to interest you, she told him, determined to stick to the matter at hand.

– I am all large wet ears.

– Ugh. You need a prescription for eardrops?

– Ha ha. Let's hear what you have.

She pushed away the plate with the thing that was supposed to be a bagel, couldn't sit there chomping away into his already wet ear.

– We talked about the modus operandi. The more I study the murders, the more alike they seem.

– The knife?

– Not impossible it was the same weapon. Very pointed, very sharp. But there's something about the way the cut was made, at a slight angle to the left. If our theory is correct, that the victims were attacked from behind, there's a lot to suggest that in both cases the perpetrator was left handed.

– Excellent. Thanks for that, Jenny.

She smiled to herself. – Of course, the cut on Marita Dahl's neck was much longer. The artery and the jugular on one side have been severed.

– Making it messier.

– And a quicker death. You'll get pictures of the throats. And an assessment of the murder weapon. Whoever did this knew exactly where to cut. And how. Clinical precision, to coin a phrase. It makes you wonder what he practised on. Or who.

– Excellent, Roar Horvath said again. – Any biological traces?

– Sent for DNA analysis. Particles of skin beneath the nails, blood, hair.

A phone rang; she heard him take the call and give a message. One or two short sentences and he was back again.

– What about the Iranian? she asked.

– What about him?

– How is he?

– Do you know the guy?

– Only that he works here. I'm curious by nature, you know that.

He chuckled; it sounded strained, but he didn't end the conversation.

– We've taken a long and confused statement from him. For the moment at least it looks as though he's able to cope with being held in a security cell. Sits there staring at nothing. At least he isn't any trouble.

– Has he said anything about what happened?

Roar Horvath didn't answer for a few seconds, as though wondering how much he could tell her.

– It looks as if he confesses to having been at the scene. Claims he was attacked by a person with a knife and had to run away naked through the forest.

– Was he hurt?

– He claims he was shot.

– That'll need treatment.

– Not as far as we can see. He's covered in scratches and small cuts. The deepest is one across his wrist, and that must be self-inflicted. We got a doctor to stitch it up.

Jennifer spun her coffee cup round on the table, watched

the wave motions from the centrifugal force. Suddenly she said:

– I can take a look at him.

– The Iranian?

– He says he was shot. What if I have a look at it? Maybe the doctor who sewed him up doesn't have much experience of gunshot wounds.

In her mind's eye, she could see Roar Horvath, the deepening wrinkles in his brow, like three seagulls in flight. Even if he had his doubts, he would agree to it. He was the type to give in. People change, she thought, but the personality stays the same. How does that add up? Why would that be?

24

As THE LIGHT through the living-room windows grew sharper, Sigurd sat in his chair and studied a withered plant on the windowsill. Katja was lying curled up on the sofa, a blanket over her, her face half covered by her black hair. The outside door was ajar; the owl could no longer be heard, but other birds had woken up now. Somewhere behind the trees, the breaking of the waves. The distant drone of traffic. A deep note that sounded as if it came from a ship. Now and then human sounds. Children laughing, people talking on the track along the side of the field.

He took a walk. Followed a path through the forest that emerged on to a road with a petrol station a few hundred metres away. He bought rolls and cheese, a Pepsi Max, instant coffee and some fruit. As he came back in through the veranda door, she opened her eyes. An almost imperceptible smile when he put the rolls and some spreads on the table in front of her, but she didn't touch any of it.

He poured her a glass of Pepsi, ate half a roll.

– How long are you planning to stay here?

She turned slightly, looked up at the ceiling. – Don't know.

– Is this because of the man who died?

She nodded.

– Does being here help?

She glanced across at him. – You don't understand.

– Perhaps you could help me out. So I understand some of it at least.

Abruptly she sat up. – I don't understand it either. Why they killed him.

He waited for more.

– There's someone I must get hold of. Can't leave here until I know it's safe.

– Has somebody threatened you?

Without answering, she stood up, wrapped in the blanket, took her phone from the table and let herself into the toilet. He heard her speaking to someone, but not the words; her voice was low. When she came back, she was wearing the red dress but was still barefoot, her hair tangled.

She grabbed the bottle of Pepsi and drank.

– I'm trying to get in touch with a member of his family, she said once she'd put the bottle down. Her voice was stronger now, maybe a sign that she was ready to talk about it.

– Do they live here too?

– Who?

– The family of the man who's been killed.

She nodded, and again he felt a jab. But he was in a different place now. He was not a killer; he wasn't the one who had killed the man she was sitting there thinking about.

He eased down beside her on the sofa. – Does Ibro have relatives in Malmö?

He'd crossed the line, it was something that had to happen, but she answered without looking at him.

– An uncle.

For a moment he thought he'd got away with it. But then she pulled away and turned towards him.

– How do you know his name?

He felt himself turn cold, and then hot.

– I found out.

She stood up. – They came to your house. They came to your house and asked, right?

– Which they?

– You know. You know who I'm talking about.

He was about to protest, but it was as if the breath had gone out of him.

– You're lying, she shouted.

He slumped back. All he could manage was a shake of the head.

– If you lie to me, I don't ever want anything to do with you again, nothing. She was bent over him, every word screeched down into his face.

– What are you talking about? he managed to say at last.

– I'm talking about you ratting him out. I'm talking about you helping them to find him. I'm talking about you killing him.

She raised her hand, and for a moment he thought she was going to hit him.

– How did you know his name?

– Calm down, he said feebly. – I checked up on it.

She launched herself at him, scratching his face, pulling his hair. Not until he felt the pain did he twist round and trap her wrists and hold her down on the sofa.

– You mustn't, Katja, do you hear, you mustn't do that.

– Fucking Judas, she sobbed, and tried to break free. He kept her pinioned. Kept on holding until he felt the strength drain from her arms. When he let go, she sank to the floor.

He sat on the table. Sat there watching as the sobbing took hold of her, first a couple of gasps, and then waves that looked as if they might rip her apart.

It was midday. She still lay curled up on the floor. He tried to think a step ahead. He had lost her. Had never had her. But he needed to know. If there had been anything at all. Why she'd come to him, why she'd stayed.

– I'll tell you what I know, he said.

She didn't respond.

– If you tell me everything else.

– None of your fucking business, she snarled.

He squatted down beside her. – I've been an idiot. But it's not my fault that he's dead. I had nothing to do with what happened to him at the hospital.

He caught her gaze. Forced himself to hold on to it while he told her. Decided as he was talking not to gloss over anything, not even the thing he was most ashamed of. He would look at her the whole time, make it impossible for her to get up and leave before he had finished. Didn't know what he was seeing in those dark eyes. Fear still, disbelief maybe, anger, contempt again, but not for an instant did he take his eyes from hers.

– You hit him.

– I was defending myself.

– You ran off.

– I picked up his phone. Called the emergency number.

– You left him lying there.

– I waited in the car until I saw the ambulance arrive.

– He died.

– Not because I hit him. He wasn't badly injured. Concussion. Minor injuries.

– And how do you know that?

– I . . . I know someone at the hospital. I talked to them.

– Your mother.

He hesitated. – Ibro was killed after he was admitted.

– You spy on me, you lie to me. Why should I believe you now?

– Someone followed him to the hospital, Katja. They managed to get inside and they stabbed him. It'll be in the newspapers.

When she didn't protest, he carried on.

– I think it's some kind of gang feud or something.

He saw again the black Audi, Ibro Hakanovic in his leather jacket and shades behind the wheel, her beside him.

– What the hell do you mean by that? she snarled.

– Mean?

– Just because he was Bosnian, he was in a gang and doing drugs and trafficking, and that's why he was killed, is that what you're trying to say, something like that? Are you actually a tiny little bit fucking racist?

She sat for a long time with her face turned to the ceiling. He saw her eyes move behind the lids, tiny sideways jerks.

Finally he said: – Now I've said everything. If you do the same . . .

– I don't owe you anything, she spat.

He didn't answer. Said nothing about how she had moved in with him without so much as a by-your-leave. Nothing about how he had never asked her for a single krone; on the contrary, it had been his pleasure to buy her all the things she needed, as well as a lot of small things she didn't need.

– I'm not going to ask what you did together. Those times you didn't come home until the middle of the night.

– Good. Don't ask.

– But I want you to tell me.

Now she looked at him. – He was my first boyfriend, she said.

– But he ended it?

She shook her head. – We never ended it. Not him and not me.

As though someone had started a drill, pushed the bit into his chest, pressed deeper and deeper. So painful he squeezed his lips together.

– I never promised you anything, she said. – I never said I belonged to you.

He stood up suddenly, upending the Pepsi bottle. A brown

puddle spread across the smooth tabletop. She looked up at him, and it occurred to him that she was waiting for something. She stared into his eyes for a long time. As though she were silently mocking him. Then she stood up too, went into the bedroom.

He found a cloth, dried up, drank the last flat mouthful that remained in the bottle.

– Are you leaving? he asked when she reappeared.

Without answering, she stepped across to the veranda door. It slammed shut behind her so the glass shook. A dead leaf fell from the plant on the windowsill. He followed its slow descent to the floor.

25

JENNIFER HAD BEEN inside a security cell many times before. In her first years as a doctor she earned extra money by taking blood samples from suspected drunk drivers.

This particular security cell was not all that different from the others. A small air vent and a camera high up below the ceiling. A zinc toilet in one corner, a mattress against the wall.

Arash wasn't lying on it, but next to it, on the stone floor. He didn't look up as the guard let her in; he stared at the wall, barefoot, unshaven, longish hair hanging down over his eyes and a bandage around one wrist.

– I am Jennifer Plåterud, she said. – I work at the hospital. I've seen you a few times. I'm a doctor in the pathology department.

Now he looked up at her, large black pupils. No sign of recognition.

– I am a good friend of Zoran's, she added, and she could hear herself how feeble it sounded. Zoran is my lover, she could have said. And the best friend I've had. And so much more than that.

– I've talked to the police. They've told me what happened. What they think happened, she added. – I'm here because you've harmed yourself.

She thought she saw him nod, turned to the guard.

– You can wait outside.

The guard's eyes narrowed. – Are you sure?

– It'll be fine. I'm just going to take a look at some of his injuries.

A tiny break in her voice as she said this. She didn't know if it would be fine. Knew almost nothing about this man. It was not unlikely he was psychotic. Not impossible that within the last forty-eight hours he had cut the throats of two people. But she put her faith in what Zoran had said.

The guard shut the door, opened it again. – I'll be here, right outside. He pointed to the window on to the corridor. – Watching.

Once he was gone, Arash sat up.

– I know who you are, he said in a clear voice. – You are Zoran's girlfriend.

She was surprised. – So he told you that.

– I've got eyes.

She held his gaze, but not for long. He still looked frightened. She knew that fear was a more common motive for murder than anything else.

– Zoran says hello, she said, her voice low. It struck her that was the kind of thing she shouldn't say. She was there as a medical expert, to help the investigators. – He is thinking of you.

The Iranian leaned his head back. Something else appeared in his eyes, like something forcing its way forward that had to be blinked away.

– No matter what you've done, Arash . . .

Again he glanced up at her, and beneath the long lashes the expression in his eyes changed again, hardened. For an instant she thought of calling the guard.

– I have not done what they say.

She didn't reply to this. – You let yourself into the cold room yesterday evening, she said instead. – Even though you weren't supposed to be at work. You were looking for the dead woman, the one who was found in the forest.

– The ring, he muttered.

She took a quick look at his hands, couldn't see it on any of the fingers.

– I have to have it back, he said in a loud voice.

She took a step back from him. – I can't help you with that.

He answered something or other.

– I didn't get that. Can you repeat it?

His lips moved; she stepped closer again.

The surest sign . . .

She was certain he had said that, but the rest was in-comprehensible, as though he were speaking in a different language.

– If you want to talk to the police in Iranian, we can get you an interpreter.

– Do you have a pen? he said, so suddenly that it made her jump. – Pen and paper.

She thought for a moment, opened the door.

– Do you have a pen and a sheet of paper?

The guard looked at her quizzically.

– It might be important, she urged him.

He pulled a pen from his pocket, and an envelope, looked at it, tore off the back.

– Everything all right in there?

She nodded firmly, pulled the door to again, turned towards Arash. He grabbed the pen and paper she held out to him.

– As I was fleeing through the forest . . . I came to a cabin. Had to hide there. It was light everywhere. I had no clothes.

He held the paper up against the wall, wrote a few lines.

– Someone came in the night, he said. He gave the paper back to her. – In the morning, I found this message.

She studied the letters for a few moments, presumed they were Iranian.

– Rumi wrote this. Have you heard of Rumi?

She thought for a moment. – Isn't he a poet?

– This was written on a mirror in that cabin. I think it was written in blood, but I can't be sure about that. I've read it many times before. How is that possible?

She looked at the piece of paper again. – What does it mean?

Arash took it from her, studied it for a few moments before writing on the other side.

– Read, he said. – Read aloud to me.

He pushed the note into her hand. She had the feeling he was testing her.

– Read, he repeated.

– Walk out like someone suddenly born into colour. She fumbled for her spectacles in her jacket pocket, put them on. *Silence is the surest sign of your death*. As she read, he never took his eyes from her.

– How is it possible? he asked again when she had finished reading. – That is what I want you to help me with, Jennifer Plåterud. – Find the explanation for why this particular poem was written on that mirror.

She put the note into her pocket. – I'll have to think about it.

– I want Zoran to have that, he said.

She pushed her hair behind her ears. – I have to give this to the police. I'm not allowed to take anything out of here.

Suddenly she remembered why she had come. – You said that you'd been shot at.

He said nothing.

– Can I see the wound?

Now he moved his lips as though forming soundless words. Then he unbuttoned his shirt, slowly removed it. He gave off a tangy smell; it made her think of the forest he'd run around in, bogs and rotting trees.

He was broad shouldered, but his biceps were not pumped

up like those of so many other young men. They were criss-crossed with scratches, some of them running on to his back.
– Turn round, please, she said, careful to keep her voice friendly.

His entire back was covered with bulging scars, the remnants of deep wounds. She thought of what Zoran had told her, what this man had been through before coming to Norway. Felt a sudden urge to stroke his ruined skin.

She composed herself. – Old injuries.

He didn't answer.

– Where did the bullet hit you?

He seemed to hesitate briefly before raising his arm.

Again she put her glasses on, examined the zigzag pattern that might have been caused by a branch. She had seen the marks of a bullet across skin many times; they ran in a straight line. This didn't look anything like one.

– So you were shot at? Are you sure you were hit?

He pointed to the marks below his arm.

– That's from a branch or something like that, said Jennifer, fearing for a moment that her observation might enrage him. But he dropped his arm, slumped slightly.

– On the other side of the stream. I turned just as the figure in black shot.

She didn't contradict him. – Did you hear the shot?

– Didn't hear any shot. Just a crack.

She didn't know much about weapons, but had tried shooting with a silencer.

– I heard something fall into the water.

She looked at him. A shell casing, she thought. If he was lying about this, would he have said that?

– How far away was the man standing when he shot? She realised she was asking questions that weren't part of the brief she had been given. – I mean, how far away was this from the woman who was killed?

Arash closed his eyes, shook his head, as though seeing something he didn't want to see.

– Some distance, he muttered finally. – I ran up alongside the stream.

He waited for a few moments before continuing.

– The figure in black was standing on the other side, by a fallen tree. I felt a burning in my arm. I ran as fast as I could.

The guard peered in. – You okay in there?

– Everything's fine.

To Arash she said: – You can put your shirt back on.

He didn't react, and she picked it up for him.

– That patient, he said suddenly.

– Which patient?

– Ibro Hakanovic was trying to tell me something.

– Then you must inform the police.

– He had head injuries and they gave him morphine. Arash gestured with his hand as though administering an injection. – Tiny pupils.

She nodded. The observation was probably reliable. Zoran still believed that, one day, this man would go on to study medicine at university.

– Ibro Hakanovic was talking about someone he called Cat. He said there was a car accident but Cat wasn't dead after all.

She wasn't sure she'd heard him right. – His cat wasn't dead?

Arash nodded. – That's the reason he was murdered.

Jennifer glanced at the guard. No reaction there.

She turned back to Arash. – Because of a car accident?

– *If* he's dead. Can you tell me, Jennifer Plåterud, is Ibro Hakanovic dead?

– He's dead.

– And Marita?

– Her too.

She looked into his eyes. Different mental states swirling around each other in the darkness there. She saw fear, confusion. Grief.

– I'll manage, he said, as though he knew what she was thinking.

26

Katja returned late in the afternoon. For the last hour Sigurd had been sitting at the kitchen table in the alcove, his iPhone in front of him, scrolling the latest updates on Facebook without seeing what was written there, clicking on *Like* to every piece of news.

Without looking at him, she disappeared into the bathroom. He heard the swish of water from the shower. She came out again, her hair wet, no make-up and wearing the same dress as before.

– What's happening?

She didn't answer, slumped down on the sofa, sat turned away, looking out through the window. He got up, put his phone in his pocket. – I'm going home.

He wasn't expecting any reaction, but she looked at him.

– You must help me.

He felt he needed more air, crossed to the door, opened it wide.

– You can either help me or not help me.

She needs you, he thought out into the light wind. Katja needs you for something. The way she had done all along. The reason they were together.

– If you don't help me, something very serious will happen. But it isn't your fault, Sigurd.

The way she said his name, as though none of this had happened. As though there had never been any Ibro Hakanovic.

He turned to her, waiting to hear more. It took a while
before it came.

– The people who killed Ibro are after something.

She ran both hands through her dripping hair.

– Ibro had something they will do anything at all to get
their hands on. When they don't find it, they'll come after
me.

– Who are *they*? he asked, and knew that was something
he shouldn't have done. Don't ask any more, just withdraw.

– I'll tell you everything. Once I know what you've
decided.

He had decided. He would leave and not see her again.
Not yet quite sure how.

She looked directly at him, her eyes in the afternoon light
almost black, yet translucent.

– Tell me, he said, his voice sounding much harder than
it felt. – Everything that's happened. He closed the door.
– Exactly what has happened. Afterwards you'll get my
answer. Whether I'll help you or not.

He stood in the middle of the room listening to what she
had to say. Things he had previously tried to find out,
parts of her story he had filled with his own imaginings
because he had to know. He no longer knew whether he
still needed to know them, but he let her speak anyway.
About growing up in Malmö, dropping out of school and
hanging out in dangerous places, a mother she obviously
couldn't talk to, younger brothers and sisters. Nothing
about a father, he noticed, but didn't ask. Maybe it was all
the things he didn't know about her that had turned him
on. Maybe this woman who sat there telling him about
herself would grow more and more like others he had met
and broken up with.

– Where we grew up, you were either with someone or

against them. Ibro was friends with someone who joined the R-Falange.

– What's that?

– A gang of Bosnians and Albanians. They were at war with the V-Falange, Serbs and Macedonians, and with the MC gangs. That's what it's about, you get respect or you're dead.

– So Ibro Hakanovic was in one of the criminal gangs? Did you call me *a little bit fucking racist*? he added silently.

– He didn't much like it. He wasn't the type. He got promoted through the ranks, but all the time he wanted out.

– He had no choice?

She ignored him.

– Kreshnik, brother of the leader of the R-Falange, got stabbed in a bar in the centre of Malmö. He shot back. It was self-defence.

– And Ibro was involved?

She shook her head firmly.

– Ibro wasn't like that. But he was nearby when the guy was shot.

Sigurd resisted the temptation to ask what being *nearby* might mean.

– Kreshnik ran off and gave the gun to Ibro. Ibro was supposed to make sure it disappeared for good.

– Not such a hard job.

– Ibro owed him a favour. But he didn't do it.

– Didn't do what?

– He sat there with the murder weapon. The police would have no doubt about who had used it; the butt was covered with blood from Kreshnik's wound. It was the chance Ibro had been waiting for, you see?

Sigurd didn't respond.

– He was going to take this chance to get away from all that shit. I suggested he come to Oslo. Plenty of jobs there.

That was what I was doing those days when I was away. Helping him with all these fucking forms. But the most important thing was to secure the evidence he was in possession of.

– And he needed you for that?

She glanced up at him. – He was in danger. He knew everything about everyone. You don't live long on the outside like that. Understand?

– He needed you, said Sigurd. – And you needed me.

He had reached the place he had been looking for. Hearing what was most painful to hear, what would make it possible for him just to turn around and leave.

– I got him a place outside town where he could stay for the time being, a house belonging to someone I knew who was away. Yes, well, you know about that house.

He looked away.

– Ibro was careful. No one was to know what he was planning to do before he had secured himself. The murder weapon was to be deposited in a bank box. Someone he could trust was to make sure the police got a key if anything ever happened to him. But somehow or other it got out. They found him before he got that far.

Sigurd nodded reluctantly. It fitted with what Ibro Hakanovic had said that evening at the house. That he didn't have what they were looking for.

– And how am I supposed to help with all this?

She sat for a while, breathing deeply; he saw how her nostrils widened and then narrowed.

– They're bound to think that I'm the one with the gun now. I have to go to Malmö and give someone a message. I have to go there before they find me.

She pulled her hair back so hard her hairline whitened.

– If I don't, then they'll do the same thing to me as they did to Ibro.

He didn't know which parts of her story were true and which she had made up. But her fear at least was real. He sat down beside her on the sofa. She rested her head on his shoulder.

– We'll manage this, Sigurd, no matter what.

Don't say that, he thought. It's too late to say something like that.

She listed the names of streets and squares as though she expected Sigurd to know exactly where they were.

– Right here, she shouted as they were in the middle of a busy crossroads.

– Get a grip, he growled and swung into a bus bay. He had never been in Malmö before.

– What is it now? You want me to drive?

She had become more and more agitated and ill tempered the closer they came to the city, snapping at him or else refusing to answer.

He turned on the GPS. – Give me a name.

She rolled her eyes. – I did that ages ago. Möllevångstorget. Do I have to spell it?

He got it up on the screen, ran the windscreen wipers a few times before pulling out and turning down the next street.

– Wait. Drive back.

– Aren't we going to Möllevångstorget?

– I want to show you a few places first, so maybe you'll understand.

Another round of pointing and last-minute directions. Sigurd received confirmation of something he had long suspected, that she wasn't good at telling left from right.

– Slow down here, she said, and directed him down a narrow road with red-brick high-rises on both sides. They cruised down to the end. – That's where it began, she said, nodding towards a gate. – A few years ago. Someone we knew very well was shot. Shot twice.

She demonstrated on herself where the bullets had hit, one in the chest, one in the neck. – Everybody knew who was behind it.

– So you went to the police?

She snorted.

– What would *they* have done? Everyone knows. No witnesses. Why should they? The police don't give a shit anyway. In the papers it says *gang related*, and that means there's nothing more to say, it's not something that affects most people. Do you know how many people have been shot here over the last few years?

He didn't know.

– Nineteen. Murdered in broad daylight. Only a couple of the cases ever came to court. So maybe now you understand why people have to take care of themselves to survive.

They drove out on to a main road again, and she told him to take a right.

– So you don't mean left?

– Pack it in.

She pointed again, this time at a building a little further up the street. – The reason we're sitting here now is because of what happened right there a few months ago.

He peered out at the frontage they were passing. A sign read *Chess Club*. Another said something about health foods.

– Someone in the V-Falange shot Hasan, Ibro's best friend. They were like brothers.

Sigurd thought about it.

– And so it was avenged in the bar you were talking about. That's why Ibro Hakanovic was *nearby*.

She ignored the sarcastic tone. – Ibro didn't want there to be any killing. He knew people on both sides. They all grew up together. He tried to mediate. Prevent a full-scale

war breaking out. After Hasan got shot, he decided he had
to get out of here.

  – And run to Norway.

  – Back then, he couldn't. Not until he had that gun.

  – The murder weapon from that bar?

  – Ibro could prove that it was Kreshnik who shot. It
didn't help him much. They killed him anyway.

She sat silent for a while, looking out of the side window,
the wet stone walls gliding by in the afternoon light.

  – Do you begin to get some idea of what this is all about?

He didn't reply. Then she placed a hand on his knee and
squeezed hard. He put his on hers to remove it. It stayed
there.

27

TV2 NEWS DEVOTED the first eight minutes to the murders, and returned with more towards the end of the broadcast. Twenty-four-year-old man charged. Originally from Iran. Photo of Marita Dahl, footage of the forest where she was found, the police tape, car tracks. The item continued at the hospital: patient murdered in the basement, almost three days before the newspapers were informed. A short interview with Roar Horvath, who had reason to believe the two cases were connected. He held up surprisingly well, thought Jennifer, looked to be enjoying himself in front of the camera.

The reporter had managed to get an interview with the chief physician himself down in the lobby. In a statement that was thereafter repeated in various ways, viewers were told that it was the police who had made the decision to keep the matter secret. Along with party leaders and government ministers the chief physician had obviously attended one of those courses designed to teach people how to avoid difficult questions without appearing to be evasive. It was amazing what you could get away with once you mastered that technique, thought Jennifer as she switched off the TV.

It had clouded over. She stepped out on to the balcony, glanced hopefully up at the sky above the blocks on the opposite side of the lawn. But no matter how dark the clouds were, they would never block out this light that forced its way in everywhere.

She fetched her coffee, sat on a rust-spotted veranda chair

that the previous tenant had not thought worth taking with him. The air felt clammy, but the rain that had been threatening all afternoon had evidently changed its mind. She needed to talk to Zoran. Fought against a desire to ring. He was on duty but answered her text: he'd be in the operating theatre for the next few hours. Before he had to leave she'd managed to tell him about her conversation with Arash. Zoran wanted to know everything they had said; he really cared about the Iranian. A moment's jealousy. She wished he would care more about her and a little less about everyone else.

One ridiculous thought led to another, one that was nothing to laugh about. Something the Iranian had said. The person who allegedly shot at him in the forest had dropped something in the stream. She had mentioned this to Roar Horvath. Though she had found no evidence of a bullet wound, it might still be that Arash was telling the truth and that there was a shell casing up there somewhere. His response was that the technicians were now finished at the crime scene, and that they had combed a large area. He didn't say that they would not go back up there again. Made a note of what she told him and clearly had a lot else on his mind. Probably also thought that it was not her job to be conducting interviews. Or to get the accused to write down poems, be they in Iranian or Norwegian. He would make sure her information was passed on to the investigators working on the case. But what truth was to be had in the words of a psychotic man? The Iranian could well believe his own story without it having actually happened.

Only now did Jennifer find a good answer to this, and for a moment she considered calling Roar Horvath. But it was past ten, he might get the wrong idea. Instead she put on jeans and a jacket and a pair of trainers and headed out.

Not until she was down in the stairwell did she realise where it was she was going.

She stopped behind the barn. There was a *No Parking* sign hanging on the wall, hardly legible. She stood looking up towards the brow of the forest for some time. Her phone rang.

– Are you at work?

Sigurd's voiced sounded odd, hectic.

– Yes. Or actually, no. I'm on my way up into the forest.

– With Zoran?

– Alone.

– This late in the evening?

He sounded worried. She liked that, that he was concerned for her safety.

– I'm actually on my way to a crime scene. Where the woman was found.

– Are you investigating this case?

– I'm not an investigator. I'm a doctor.

– Then what are you doing there?

He had always tried to look out for her.

– Take it easy, Sigge. I'm going for a stroll in the woods. I need the exercise. And it's light, and the sun is still shining. At least behind the clouds it is. She had to laugh at the optimistic tone of voice she had adopted.

– Do you know any more about the man who died at the hospital?

– Of course. It's my job to find out more.

– They're saying on the news that there's a connection to the woman who was killed.

– I heard that.

– They've arrested someone. What do you think?

She started up the muddy path between the fields.

– I can't tell you what I think, Sigurd.

– That means you know something. That there is a connection.

This curiosity was something he had inherited from her. He never gave up if there was something he wanted to know. Always managed to get her to tell him things she had decided to keep to herself.

She heard the sounds of traffic in the background. – You out driving?

– Yes.

– You alone too?

– No.

– You got hold of Katja?

– We're in Malmö.

– I see, she said, careful not to let her tone betray her. – Staying there long?

– Just one day. A few things to sort out.

Walking on through the forest, she was still thinking about the conversation. Australia was the country for Sigurd. He had that drive in him. And boldness. And her mixture of impatience and stubbornness. If she ever moved back, it might well be along with him. Him and Zoran.

It was almost pitch-dark where the trees came closest to the gravel track. The cloud cover had thickened and she felt a few drops. Up by the tarn, it was lighter again. A family of ducks by the banks. A mother with four young who swam off as Jennifer approached.

The security tape was still in place, from the stone sticking out of the tarn on up to the stream. Small drops of rain soundlessly ruffled the black surface of the water. For a few seconds there was a silence so dense that she felt a chill pass through her. And suddenly the sensation that someone was standing somewhere in the forest behind her, following her every move.

She turned, overwhelmed by an aversion to continuing on

through the trees, up to the place in the stream where the woman had been found. Saw again the head against the dark green moss, the hair waving in the flowing water, the gaping throat.

She forced herself to carry on along the indistinct footpath. This was a kind of exercise, exposing herself to her own unease, getting in touch with her own fear. She reached the point where the woman had been found. In the half-light she could see that the moss by the bank of the stream was still red. She tried to imagine the sequence of events. The blade of the knife was at least ten centimetres long. Marita Dahl was probably squatting a few metres away, emptying her bladder; there was a smell of urine on the moss the technicians had taken away with them.

She carried on up the bank of the stream where Arash had said he ran. A person with a knife behind him, face hidden by a balaclava. Turning, he saw his pursuer by a fallen tree.

She found it a little higher up the stream. It lay parallel to it, and probably so far from the crime scene that it was unlikely that the technicians had been there. Arash may have been hallucinating, or lying. But if what he said was true, his pursuer had stopped by the roots of this upended fir tree and pointed a gun at him, fired, and something fell into the water.

She didn't have a torch with her. Took out her phone, walked on a few paces, bending as she directed the light down into the running water. Turned and went back to the upended fir. Was about to jump over to the other side when her eye was caught by something glinting among the dark, algae-coated stones. She squatted down, leaned out across the water. Saw a shadow reflected in the mirrored water, next to her own. It grew larger and assumed a form, became a body, a head bending over her.

She spun round, holding the phone up in front of her, as though it might protect her.

28

They passed an amusement park where a big dipper could be glimpsed through the trees, found an empty parking space.

Again Katja tried to ring someone, still no answer.

– What now, Katja Värnholm? Sigurd asked as she put the phone away. – We've made it unobserved to the centre of Malmö. What is your plan? You have a mobile phone number, but the man who owns that phone doesn't seem interested in talking to you. Shall we kidnap him?

She shook her head. – Let me run things here. Just don't fuck up, that's all I'm asking you.

He could have laughed at her. She clearly thought that things could carry on as before, that she could treat him as her chauffeur and her personal handyman.

She turned a corner, headed up along a street that looked exhausted. Dusty windows facing the traffic. They passed a nightclub, a gym next door. She stopped, nodded in the direction of somewhere called Aladdin's Grill, according to the sign. Pictures of different dishes hanging in the window, falafel, salads, chicken kebab.

Inside, it smelled of spices and meat. They hadn't eaten since breakfast, and Sigurd thought they might get something here. But when they sat at the table nearest the door and he brought the subject up, she brushed him aside. She was wearing shades, even though the little place was dimly lit and they were the only guests.

The sound of a toilet flushing. A small, thin boy emerged from a room next to the bar; he couldn't have been more than fourteen or fifteen. Light skinned, with straw-coloured hair and a thin matching moustache on his upper lip.

Sigurd ordered coffee and mineral water, had to repeat himself a couple of times before he could make himself understood. And a beer for Katja.

When the boy returned with the bottles and glasses on a tray she said:

– Is Tariq here today?

– Seventy-six. The boy turned towards Sigurd. – Kroner, he added, perhaps unsure whether the foreigner understood the currency.

Sigurd took out a hundred note, sceptical about the wisdom of using a credit card in a place like this.

– I know Tariq, Katja continued.

The boy shrugged his shoulders.

– Is he here now?

Another shrug. Katja removed her shades. – Someone says hello.

– Wait.

The boy disappeared through a curtain behind the bar. A couple of minutes later, he was back.

– Who says hello?

– Someone he knows very well. I would very much like to say it to him in person. Understand?

The boy glanced at Sigurd. – He has to leave.

– What do you mean? Sigurd wanted to know.

Katja nudged him. – Do as he says.

He took a walk around the block. It was still drizzling; not enough for him to get wet, just a layer of damp across his forehead and his bare arms. He carried on past the railings of the amusement park with the big dipper. A few battered old roundabouts there too. *People's Park*, it said above the entrance. A car he thought he might have seen before was parked further up the road, engine running, a black van with graffiti on its sides. It pulled out, drove towards him. The windows were tinted; he couldn't see who was sitting inside. Not difficult to feel paranoid here, he thought. Finding patterns in random events. He grinned to himself and headed for the park gates.

Not many there in the finely blowing rain. Two women in hijabs wearing black at the centre of a flock of children. Young people drinking beer on the grass under the trees. He glanced impatiently at his watch. Sent her a text. Was he supposed to wait the whole evening? Did she expect him to ride the roller coaster while she sat around talking to old friends?

A man wearing a clown's outfit walked around selling helium balloons. Sigurd looked to see if there was one with a lion's head, didn't see one in the bouquet that wafted in the scarcely noticeable summer breeze. He leaned against the gate, seeing in his mind's eye the fairground stalls at Liseberg, Jenny suddenly furious because he had let go of the balloon he'd just been bought. But now he remembers. It isn't her anger that causes him to freeze at the sight of that silver and gold lion rising and rising as though being sucked up above the city, up through all the layers of the atmosphere. It's the thought that it will disappear away into nothingness and never come back.

29

JENNIFER TOOK A step back, almost tumbled into the water, her foot slipping on a stone. The man who had approached her stood looming above her on the bank of the stream.

– What are you looking for?

She looked up at him, had seen him before, in the chapel where he came to identify his dead wife. It was the voice she recognised first, then the long face, the blue eyes beneath the peaked policeman's cap.

– You work with the dead, he insisted. – You carried out the autopsy on her. You've got no business up here.

Her voice had locked solid; now it freed up again. – I . . . like to do a job thoroughly.

– This isn't your job.

– I often walk in the forest, she lied.

It didn't sound convincing, but he took a step away.

– You're looking for something.

She clambered up from the stream. – That's correct. Something I lost while I was up here. An earring.

That sounded even worse, and she cringed. Dahl peered intently at her, and she looked away.

– And you, she responded. – *You* are presumably at work, since you're wearing your uniform.

He straightened up, no more than three paces away from her. She began fiddling with her phone.

– You don't need to ring anyone.

He gestured abruptly with his arm, as though to stop her.

– Have to make a call, she answered quickly. – Someone waiting for me.

She scrolled through her call history, found Zoran, remembered he was in the middle of an operation, found Sigurd, scrolled on.

Roar Horvath had his answering service turned on. She left a message saying where she was, mentioning Dahl, saying that he was there with her. She watched him as she said this. He moved his head slightly, teeth just showing between his lips.

She started to walk back the way she had come. He followed a couple of metres behind.

– I frightened you.

She took a few steps aside and indicated that he should pass her.

– Did you see me arrive?

Now he smiled, the slightly pointed teeth fully revealed.

– I know you've arrested someone. He walked on by her. – An Iranian.

– I haven't arrested anyone. As you know, I'm a pathologist.

– Who is this person they've arrested?

Jennifer squeezed her fingers around the phone. – You're a policeman, she began. It seemed like a good thing to say.

He stopped, took a step closer. – It was nearly three days ago. She rang and said she was going for a coffee with a friend. Damn her.

Jennifer started playing with her phone again and was startled when it began ringing.

– Hello, Superintendent Horvath, she almost shouted.

Dahl turned away.

– Jenny, you better tell me what's going on, said Roar Horvath.

She carried on walking towards the tarn.

– I'm up in the forest.

– Still? At the crime scene?

– Marita Dahl's husband is here too. He arrived as I was . . .

She glanced up through the trees; he was no longer there.

– I've found something. She lowered her voice. – Something that shows Arash was telling the truth. Someone shot at him.

Roar Horvath didn't interrupt while she explained. When she was finished he said: – I'll send a patrol car out to pick you up. Keep this line open until they reach you. Don't hang up, you hear me. Don't even think about it.

The police car arrived as she had almost reached the farm. Less than two minutes later, another car turned up, a black station wagon. Roar Horvath jumped out.

– Typical Jenny, he exclaimed.

He had no justification for saying such a thing, but she let it pass.

The patrol car was sent away. Then she remembered. – I saw something in the stream.

– You said that.

– A spent shell. At the place where someone shot at Arash. We have to go up there and get it.

– I'll get one of the technicians to do it.

– Tomorrow? It might be gone by then.

He took out his phone, hit a number, explained the situation.

– Where did you say? he asked her.

She described the place, the fallen tree trunk, estimated how far up the stream it was.

– They'll be up there within an hour, he said after ending the call. – Now I'm driving you home.

Still embarrassed at having been the cause of an emergency call-out, she got into his car.

Something wet between the seats touched her fingers. She yelled and yanked her hand back.

– Pepsi, said Roar Horvath sternly. – Lie down.

Jennifer turned her head cautiously. A dog crouched on the floor in the back. It did as it was told, jumped up on to the back seat and curled up.

– I see you got a dog.

– Sorry. Should've warned you before you got in. She's so bloody nosy, has to lick everything. Wouldn't harm a fly.

– When did you become a dog-owner? she said, and immediately wished she hadn't. She didn't want to talk about anything personal with him, nothing that would bring up the fact that they once had a thing together.

– A couple of years ago. He turned the car in the space in front of the pile of chopped tree trunks. – The dog belonged to a friend of mine.

He manoeuvred down on to the path between the fields.

– And now it's yours.

– He died just over three years ago. Burnt to death in his house. His wife had the four kids to take care of. Couldn't manage the dog as well. I offered to look after it, so the animal ended up with me.

She looked at him. – That was one of the fires in Lillestrøm?

– Correct.

– It was your friend who . . .

– My best mate.

He swung round behind the barn, down on to the farm track.

– Not exactly obedient, but I've managed to train her up a bit.

The dog whimpered restlessly in the back seat.

– And how are you? he asked. – You sounded pretty shaky on the phone.

She felt herself blushing, but he kept his eyes on the road ahead.

– Fine now. It gave me a real shock suddenly to see him there.

– He didn't threaten you?

He hadn't done that. Even though she had felt threatened. She seemed to see him, bending over the bloodstained moss by the stream.

– He's just lost his wife. It's not surprising he'd want to see the place where it happened.

She was thinking of someone else, something she couldn't quite put her finger on. She looked out over the fields in front of them, towards the church tower in the distance.

– If we do find a shell casing where Arash said it should be, then it makes his statement a lot stronger.

Roar Horvath changed gear and accelerated. – He hasn't really managed to give us anything we could call a statement.

– But if we believe him when he says someone shot at him . . .

– That doesn't mean that he isn't involved.

He pushed away the dog, which had rested its snout on the back of the seat and was sniffing at Jennifer's hair.

– Some way or other the Iranian is connected to this, Jenny. What are the odds of him being at two separate crime scenes over the last forty-eight hours by sheer chance? Alone with two victims at about the time they were killed, same method, possibly same weapon.

– What would his motive be?

Roar Horvath glanced over at her. – The guy is damaged, he's suffering from some serious psychiatric disorder after being tortured. We can't really say with any certainty what's going on in his head. If we start looking for rational motives, there's no guarantee we'll find any.

– Maybe not.

– We've also considered the possibility that the madness is an act. But we've had an interesting statement from a witness. A woman out walking with her three children yesterday morning, on their way to the family cabin in the forest, about five or six kilometres from the place where we found Marita Dahl. Just as they arrive, they get a helluva of fright when a man comes charging out. Naked apparently, and roaring. Waving his arms about. On the point of attacking them. She says he was like a wild animal, but judging by his appearance, it was our Iranian.

Jennifer thought about this.

– Well, he did say he ran naked into the forest, and that fits with the cuts on his body. But in that case his clothes ought to have been at the scene. I didn't see any. Only the woman's.

– You've always been a good observer, Jenny. None of the clothes were his.

– So he went back and fetched them?

– Seems a reasonable supposition.

– Or the man with the knife, if he exists, took them.

– Possibly. But then we have to ask why he should bother to take the Iranian's clothes and leave the victim's behind.

– Maybe because he was determined to find Arash before we did.

They turned on to the main road.

– You ask for a motive, Jenny. I'm saying he might have experienced a panic attack before both killings, become psychotic, felt threatened, who knows what. Or we can start looking in a completely different direction.

She waited for him to go on. Roar Horvath drummed on

the steering wheel and seemed to be weighing something up, perhaps wondering how much he was able to tell her.

– Ibro Hakanovic lived in Malmö. We've spoken to our colleagues down there. The guy was part of a criminal network of, for the most part, Albanians and Bosnians. Narcotics, gambling, possibly people-trafficking. He also had his own sideline as a debt-collector.

– So the murder was gang related?

– It's not impossible. Or someone in debt may have decided that they didn't want to pay him after all.

She thought for a few moments. – Are there any reasons at all for believing that Arash might be involved in stuff like that?

– That remains to be seen. We're keeping our options open. All the footage from the cameras is being examined second by second. Any person who entered the hospital that evening will be studied as though they were on a catwalk.

She had to smile.

– But we have no images from the entrance where the break-in was, she objected.

– The Iranian might have known that several of the cameras weren't working. Isn't that the kind of thing porters know?

– Could be.

– We've asked around at the hospital. A lot of people knew about it, it's something that's been discussed at meetings, complaints that nothing's been done, that the security isn't good enough.

He turned into the road where she lived, looked round.

– Funny that we've both ended up here, you and I. In Romerike, I mean.

He said this as though it was fated. A hidden force that wanted them to meet again.

– Drop me off here, no need to drive all the way up.

He dismissed her suggestion with a wave of the hand. – I'll drive you to your door. See you safely inside.

He stopped in front of her entrance, sat there looking up at the block.

– So this is where you live.

– For the time being.

– Finished with family life?

She hesitated. No matter what she answered, it would be wrong.

– You've got two sons, he went on, – but they've been kicked out of the nest a long time ago presumably?

A vague sense of discomfort that he should have remembered them.

– Yes, she said.

– Yes, he repeated, and if she didn't hurry up and get out of the car, other things would be said. About what happened between them, about what didn't happen. Why he had so suddenly stopped contacting her. Back then he had a boss who wouldn't stand for that kind of thing, who exerted an intolerable control over the workplace. Roar had put up with it, he was the adaptable type. She had not grieved for even a single day over the fact that he had dumped her. She could feel his eyes on her, suddenly felt sorry for him, couldn't bring herself to leave. Then the dog was there again, sticking her nose up, sticking her whole head between them and making noises, as though she were jealous.

– You've got quite a few things to think about, said Jennifer as she opened the door.

He watched her. How about a coffee? his gaze asked. How about if I came up with you? It was as though she could see in that gaze everything that had changed in her life, everything that had passed on, burned out. Everything she no longer felt capable of missing. Maybe this is how it's going to be, she thought suddenly. First signs of death.

– I'll call you, she said.

He nodded, still looking at her. The dog did the same, the two sets of eyes not so very different. They probably got on pretty well together.

– The autopsy report, she added, to make sure there was no misunderstanding.

30

AFTER WAITING HALF an hour, Sigurd had had enough. He'd sent three texts that hadn't been answered. He slammed the car door shut behind him, crossed the road, rounded the corner.

Aladdin's Grill was empty. He stepped over to the bar. Steam was billowing from a coffee machine. A burnt chicken on top of a microwave.

– Hello.

The boy emerged through the curtain to what was perhaps a kitchen.

– Katja, said Sigurd.

– You what?

– The girl, the one I was here with just now.

The boy shook his head. – Not here.

– She must be.

He shrugged his shoulders, stood there looking at Sigurd's T-shirt. – Are you an Australian?

Sigurd glanced down at the motif on the chest of the shirt, Ayers Rock with a crescent moon above it.

– Yes, that's where I come from.

A door at the back of the place opened. Katja appeared, seemingly from a back yard.

– Couldn't you wait? she said irritably, and turned to the boy. – Tell Tariq it's cool.

She headed for the entrance.

– Where have you been? Sigurd asked once they were outside on the pavement.

She ignored him. Carried on walking down the street.

– Do you mind giving me some clue about what's going on?

– What's going on?

At the corner of the street he stopped her, his irritation on the verge of turning into something else.

– I got hold of Uncle Mujo, she said, pulling herself free. – He's going to meet me.

– Your uncle?

She blew out her breath impatiently. – Ibro's uncle. You can come along.

– Thanks a lot.

She continued heading towards the car, not looking at him.

– Meeting him has always been a dream of mine, he added as he unlocked the car doors.

The time was approaching eleven when she indicated that he should pull into a building site down by the docks. They waited there for ten minutes. Her phone rang. She took the call. Listened for a few seconds.

– That's right. Norwegian licence plates.

She turned to Sigurd. – Flash your headlights twice.

He did so.

– Drive back out on to the road.

As he was pulling out of the building site, she asked him to stop. A few seconds later he saw a shadow in his wing mirror. Both back doors were opened and two figures jumped in.

– Drive, said one of them.

Sigurd did as he was told, glanced in the rear-view mirror: two men, one middle aged, one young. – Hi, Mujo, he said with a mirthless grin.

– Do I know you? The voice was hoarse and quite light. He had a baseball cap pulled down over his face, Chicago Bulls.

– Don't think so.

– Tell the Norwegian to keep his mouth shut.

Katja elbowed Sigurd in the ribs. – He's my driver, she told the two in the back.

A grunt from behind. Sigurd accelerated and turned the corner by the half-demolished building, continued across a bridge at the end of the road.

– I don't understand it, said Katja. – No one knew what Ibro was planning to do. Only me.

A long silence. In the mirror, Sigurd looked more closely at Mujo: grey moustache, longish grey hair below the cap, eyes irritable under the peak. The young man had short black hair and letters tattooed down the side of his neck. He sat looking out the window.

– Ibro rang Friday night, said Uncle Mujo. – He was in hospital.

Katja turned to him. – He called me too.

Sigurd remembered he still had her phone in his bag. Now wasn't the time to return it and dish up some story about how he'd found it.

– That's where it happened, at the hospital. He was admitted, unconscious.

– What the hell, exclaimed Uncle Mujo. – He could have talked to me.

Katja explained.

– This doesn't add up, growled Uncle Mujo. – They would have finished him off on the spot, they shouldn't have needed to follow him to the hospital.

Sigurd kept his eyes looking straight ahead.

– It was something else, said Katja. – What happened first. Ibro got into a fight with someone. It wasn't them.

– But they knew he was at the hospital.

– They must have seen the ambulance arrive.

– But who called the ambulance?

Katja glanced at Sigurd. Suddenly he had the idea that he had been lured into a trap. One word from her and he was at the mercy of the two in the back. He didn't doubt for a moment that they were carrying weapons.

– They followed it, got inside the hospital and . . .

Katja's voice cracked; she turned away.

Uncle Mujo leaned forward and touched her shoulder. – Difficult times, he said, and his voice had lost something of that rough, hard edge. – Bad times, he added in English.

Katja turned towards him again. – What did he say to you?

Uncle Mujo pulled the peak of his cap lower over his forehead. – That he'd hidden a murder weapon. He said *you* know where it is, Katja. In a house.

– The house in Norway?

– He didn't say, but he talked about you. That if anything happened to him we should look after you.

Silence descended again. Katja's irregular breathing. She was crying soundlessly. It was Uncle Mujo who did what Sigurd couldn't: put a hand to her cheek, brushed away her tears. She leaned towards him, moving her head from side to side as though eating from the comforting hand.

– Where are we going? Sigurd asked.

No one answered. He slowed as the traffic lights in front of them changed to amber, then changed his mind and accelerated. Almost collided with a bus.

– Take it easy, for fuck's sake! Just keep driving, stay in the centre.

Uncle Mujo's arm still around her shoulders.

– Did you say he was unconscious when he was taken to this hospital? Are you sure about that?

Katja sat up straight, and again Sigurd felt the touch of her glance. Like a signal that at any moment she might decide to tell them what had happened. Maybe that was why she had taken him there. To hand him over to the gang for revenge.

– They think I have the gun, she said. – And now they'll be coming after *me*, people who were once Ibro's best friends.

Uncle Mujo leaned back in his seat. – I've spoken to someone.

– Who?

He nodded his head. – Someone in the know.

– What did they say?

– They deny it was them who did it. Say they didn't know Ibro wanted out.

– They're trying to get us confused.

– Exactly. And then they made a suggestion.

– What was that?

He leaned forward again. – Get rid of the Norwegian.

She put her hand on Sigurd's arm.

– What is it now?

– Pull in. Get out and wait. Sting'll drive.

She pointed to the younger man in the back, who still hadn't said a word.

Sigurd stared at her, furious.

– Do as I say.

Somewhere in her voice he heard a threat. He pulled up on to the kerb, opened the door. The young man got out, walked round the car, looked at him with a grin and sat in the driver's seat. An almost irresistible urge to drag him out of there, smash him in the face. – Sting, he murmured sarcastically. Could you get a more ridiculous poseur's name?

Katja opened the window. – Just a few minutes. Don't go too far away.

He stood by the half-demolished building, staring in through what was left of its facade. He had never hated anyone before; it confused him. He paced up and down the block for a while, down towards the building site, back towards the docks. When did I become like this? he groaned to himself.

When the car eventually reappeared, he saw that she was alone. He swung the door open and motioned for her to move over into the passenger seat.

– You don't have a driving licence, he said.

– Oops, guess I forgot.

– What am I doing here? he growled.

– You're helping me.

She reached out, put her hand over his. He removed it.

– Are you sulking?

– No, I am pissed off.

She looked as though she was enjoying herself. – You're jealous.

He turned the cooling system on full, breathed himself calm.

– Finished doing what you had to do? he asked finally.

– Almost. She leaned over towards him. – It'll all work out, Sigurd. We'll go back home tomorrow. And we'll be done with this.

She put her arm around him, her mouth to his neck. Sigurd breathed out hard through clenched teeth.

– Drive down there, she indicated. – There's something I want to show you.

– You're angry with me all the time, she continued as he accelerated out into the four-lane highway.

– Maybe.

– But you're still helping me. Do you realise how much you mean to me?

They drove for a couple of minutes. A construction loomed from their right side, a gigantic concrete block that looked like a prison, impregnable, escape proof.

– Rosengård, she said. – It starts here. Everything starts here.

He'd heard of Rosengård. Riots, burning car tyres, young people throwing stones, with guns in their jacket pockets, police that didn't dare to intervene.

– Turn off here.

He moved into the right-hand lane, then up on to the flyover.

In between the blocks, four or five boys were playing football in the drizzle. None of them looked Swedish. Young people stared at them from a bus shelter.

– Ibro grew up here.

– I guessed.

– He came here alone. Just turned thirteen. He watched as they dragged his father out and shot him in front of their house in the village. His mother and sister were sent to a camp, never came back. Ibro was the only one who got out. He never understood why. Then he ends up here, with relatives. Ten or twelve people sharing a three-room apartment.

– That doesn't necessarily mean you have to become a gangster, Sigurd grunted.

She blew out air in a short blast, perhaps in response to his comment.

– The worst thing about those flats is not that they're small. It's the cockroaches. The children can't sleep, because they crawl across their faces all night. They get asthma from the damp and the mould growing on the walls.

Sigurd shrugged his shoulders. – The parents should be able to do something about that.

– What can the parents do? The authorities leave the running of the place in private hands, and why should *they* waste money on maintenance? The refuse companies don't pick up the rubbish. Once car tyres and a lot of other stuff were burning for a whole day, but the fire brigade never came. All the apartments were filled with smoke. In the end the council had to do something. They daren't risk an all-out war. Now the worst of the slums have been moved somewhere else.

She nodded in the other direction. – Seved, Lindängen. Best way is just move the dirt around.

Sigurd leaned back in his seat. – Okay, I understand that the gangs recruit kids from round here. But everyone has a choice.

She shook her head. – If you stand alone in a place like this, you have no chance. You'll be mowed down, blown away. Kaput.

He continued to argue with her, saying that things were like that even where he came from. You had to form alliances with those who could protect you. Before you were strong enough to break away and stand alone. That was the road he'd taken himself. The road he was still on.

– I told you I was adopted, she said suddenly. – Since then you've asked me about it several times.

He had done. Now he no longer needed to know.

– I lived here for the first four years of my life. A gigantic black hole. I can't remember a thing from any of it.

Probably just as well, he caught himself thinking.

– Maybe I was lucky, maybe not. I grew up a few hundred metres away from here. Might as well have been another planet.

– How did you meet Ibro? he asked.

She thought about it.

– There was a group of us girls who weren't interested in swotting or working out. And we couldn't stand staying at home in the evenings. Couldn't stand being at home at all.

She fell silent for a moment; he could have taken the chance to change the subject.

– We hung out in the city centre, she said finally. – Stayed out the whole night and said we were sleeping over with friends. Starting hanging out in the black clubs.

– Which are?

– Private clubs where you can buy anything and do anything. They never close, and when you go there, it's at your own risk.

– Great place to grow up.

– We thought it was cool. They were dangerous places for fifteen-year-old girls, and that's why we were there. Playing with fire. One night, things got out of control. We were supposed to look out for each other. But the rest disappeared. My head wasn't right, I'd had too much of something I couldn't take. Woke up in a strange room. Some kind of office; at any rate there was a desk. I was lying on it. Two men bending over me. I wanted to get out. Suddenly one of them had a knife. I screamed. He held his hand over my jaw and squeezed my mouth shut. Like that.

She demonstrated the grip.

– Then the door burst open. It was Ibro. I'd met him once before. He got hold of one of the men, the one with the knife, said something to him in a low voice. Then he lifted me off the table and carried me out to a car. Drove around until my head was clear. Then he drove me home.

She was staring straight ahead. – After that he was my protector.

He dropped her off outside a four-star hotel in the centre. Found somewhere to park a few blocks away. When he entered reception, he found her checking in under another name. She had seemed less afraid after the meeting with the two Bosnians in the car, but now she apparently felt it was necessary to use an alias.

Sigurd couldn't persuade himself it was all that dangerous

to wander about in a Swedish town, but didn't say anything about her new identity, not wanting to start quarrelling again. He'd been a complete idiot to head up to Nittedal and break into the house, she told him. But he was no killer; she had clearly made up her mind about that. He avoided any comment about what sort of idiot *she* was for trusting a man like Ibro Hakanovic. About how insanely idiotic it was of her to get involved with someone who was trying to put pressure on a bunch of violent gangsters. Nor did he say anything about the fact that she had kept all this from him.

He stood by the open window in the hotel room, the sounds of traffic far below, a few drops of evening rain touching his neck. Watched her as she lay there scrolling through her phone, hair gathered on one side, the red dress creased so that it just about reached her thighs. And half hidden by the shoulder strap, that little tattoo, exactly like the one her *protector* had had. He took four steps across the room and stood beside her, and she dragged him down, suddenly wide awake, pulled off his trousers and couldn't get him inside her fast enough. She is an emptiness, he thought. The more that goes into her, the emptier she gets. He had never heard her scream so loudly before, and as she collapsed beneath him, he could no longer hold the thought at bay. It had come bubbling up, maybe had been there all the time; now it forced everything else to one side.

It's over, Katja.

31

WITH ONE HAND, Jennifer shielded her eyes from the morning light as she peered at the DNA diagram on the table in front of her.

Lydia had just opened the curtain again after giving a PowerPoint presentation of the diagram. Jennifer had never seen her so excited before. There *was* an aberrant pattern there, in the same gene in all three individuals. And those egg cells in which the membrane had not sealed itself as it should do after fertilisation all came from these same three women. If they could confirm the findings, it would strengthen Lydia's hypothesis about the location of the damage in these rare cases of genetically determined infertility. She seemed convinced that the changes first noticed by the student and for which Jennifer was now being given credit represented a decisive turning point in their research project.

– If we had a bottle of champagne, this would be a suitable occasion for popping it, she said with a quick smile.

Jennifer wasn't feeling in a champagne mood, but she did her best not to put a damper on the enthusiasm in the room. It seemed as though the four other researchers were all more deeply involved in the project than she was. She felt there were too many unanswered questions. Couldn't shake the feeling of working on something that wasn't important enough. Not for her. Not for the world. The predominant cause of female infertility was a fault in the reproductive organs. Blocked fallopian tubes, scarred as a result of chlamydia or other infections. Those who were unable to bear children because of a defect in the membrane of the egg cell couldn't account for more than a tiny fraction – if they even existed at all. It was still illegal to carry out therapy on reproductive cells. But changes in the law were on the way, and Lydia was undoubtedly right in that these would be adjusted continually in accordance with discoveries made through research. For the time being, she seemed most interested in the fact that the results could shed light on other aspects of reproduction, and how cells communicated with each other in general.

Jennifer recalled Knut Reinertsen's comments on the project, and for a desperate moment she had to prevent herself from standing up and announcing that the problem wasn't too few children being born in the world, but too many. That being unable to give birth wasn't an illness but a natural part of life, that each of us had differing fates, and that one of life's obligations was to learn to accept this. Easy for you to think like that, she rebuked herself. You've given birth to two children. And even if you never got the daughter you always wanted, you've been incredibly lucky. You no longer hear the ticking of a clock inside you, but once you would have been prepared to do almost anything to be able to have children. If that need hadn't been as strong as it was, humans as a species would not exist.

– It's so good to have you with us on this, Jenny, said Lydia after the meeting was over.

Jennifer smiled through that cursed blushing. She was approaching fifty; sooner or later it must end. – I'm not exactly indispensable to the project.

– To me you are. And now you've found something that might turn out to be a breakthrough.

– The student did, Jennifer corrected her.

Lydia laughed, quick and dry, and Jennifer felt her antipathy slip away. It was probably not Lydia's intention to remind her of how inadequate she was as a researcher in the service of humanity.

– Have you thought any more about my offer?

She hadn't.

– I think there are others better suited to take on leading roles than me, Lydia. Quite a few who have a lot more to offer.

– But none with your spirit and drive. And ability to see things through to the end.

– I'll give it a little more thought, Jennifer said, interrupting, knowing that her decision had been taken a long time ago.

They walked down the corridor together.

– Knut suggested that we come out to the cabin too this weekend.

It took a couple of seconds for Jennifer to realise what this meant, that she wouldn't be there alone with Zoran. That it meant two whole days with Lydia and Knut Reinertsen.

– Oh that would be nice, she said, not looking at Lydia, with an excuse not to go already worked out in her head. Suggest to Zoran that they go somewhere else.

She got hold of him after lunch. He was dictating journal entries.

– But you're actually quite a sociable person, he remarked.
– You like being around other people.

He knew what she thought of Knut Reinertsen. He had a different opinion, had seen Knut helping out in humanitarian catastrophes, but didn't try to change her mind.

– Let's drop the whole trip, she said, hearing the question mark in it.

– Fine by me, Jenny.

– We can do something else together.

– Indeed we can.

Her phone rang. The lab at the pathological institute.

– We've got a lot out of the material you sent us. Ibro Hakanovic.

Jennifer recognised the voice of the technician she had spoken to the previous day.

– The hair?

– That's more doubtful. But the skin cells you found beneath the fingernails were perfect. Full of information. Though we're not sure where to send our findings.

She gave him Roar Horvath's name, felt the return of that consuming curiosity that had been sadly absent throughout the research team meeting.

– One person, or more than one?

– Just one. Badly scratched on the underside of the arm, I'd guess. We found plenty of blood cells.

Zoran had been looking through his papers while she spoke on the phone. He didn't seem stressed, but as usual had more to do than was possible to fit into a normal working day, even with several hours' overtime.

– I'll call you later, she said to him. Rather that than hang around waiting for him to ring.

– Anything new about Arash? he asked as she stood with her hand on the doorknob.

– They're analysing the shell casing. There's a lot to suggest he was telling the truth.

– I've never doubted it.

– If the DNA results strengthen his case, then I'm guessing they'll have to release him pretty soon.

Zoran nodded slowly.

– Hope it isn't too late, he said, a worried look on his face. – Hope he hasn't been driven beyond what he can endure.

32

SIGURD FETCHED THE car, drove up to the hotel entrance. Katja came out on to the steps. She was wearing a hoody and looked left and right along the road before putting her bag in the back of the car and getting in beside him.

– Yes, we're going to Oslo, she said before he could ask. – There's just one thing I have to deal with first, then we can go home.

He had built up a reservoir of patience, but it was rapidly running out now.

– Let me guess, he said. – You're going to see *Uncle* Mujo.

She yawned. Without make-up, her eyes looked small and swollen. She'd dressed in haste and was wearing a pair of baggy tracksuit bottoms and trainers. She turned and stared out through the rear window.

– Have we got the X-Falange after us? he grunted with a weary glance in the rear-view mirror. A red Saab directly behind them, then a grey van. – Or is it the Y-Falange? What is it that makes you trust guys like that?

She texted someone. He didn't give up, repeated his question.

– I've known Ibro since I was fifteen, Sigurd. Uncle Mujo almost as long.

He didn't think the answer was good enough.

– I know who I can trust, she said, brushing him aside.

Her phone rang. She listened for a few seconds, ended the call.

– Drive back to where we were yesterday.

He did as she said, found a space in the street outside the People's Park, reversed in with a single spin of the steering wheel.

– You can go over there and get something to eat, she said, and pointed across the street to a snack bar.

He scratched his head with both hands.

– I've just eaten, you know that.

– Just think of something. She opened the door. – I'll call you.

– I'll wait five minutes, he said as calmly as he could. – Not a second longer.

She blew out heavily. – What's so fucking weird is that you still don't get it. I've tried to explain it to you, but you don't listen.

– Shut up, he roared suddenly, so close to her face that she jerked backwards. – You go around playing these gang-ster games and I don't get a fucking word of explanation.

– Okay, she said, and blinked a few times. – It won't take more than five minutes. Guaranteed. I'll explain afterwards.

She leaned towards him, kissed him on the cheek. Her hair smelled of straw. He pulled away. He didn't have any clean T-shirts to change into, but at least he'd washed his hair. He sat there watching her until she turned the corner and disappeared. They were going to be spending the whole day in the car. He knew roughly what he had to say, but not yet how. On the far side of this drive, get back to where he was before he met her. Not the same place any more. Start something new.

He glanced at his watch. Due at a Newlife meeting in Oslo in eight hours. Had to correct the bad impression he made last time. He'd learned something from all this, he tried to tell himself, something he could use. Didn't know if that was true.

He tugged on the washer handle, watched the wipers cross the already clean windscreen. The five minutes was up long ago. He opened the door. The sun had broken through, the asphalt was steaming. He threw his jacket inside and locked the door, strolled up past the park. She'd been gone a quarter of an hour. He had no business in this town and never did have. Find her and tell her that, then it would be up to her if she wanted to drive back to Oslo with him or make the trip some other way. If that was where she wanted to go.

As he was approaching Aladdin's Grill, he received a text message. *Finished in a few minutes.* He tapped out an answer. *Not waiting more than two.* A grey van rolled by, stopped a little further ahead. Sigurd stood there watching it, working out another line of text in his head, one that would make it easier for him to say what he had made up his mind to say. At that same moment the door of the café opened and two people came out, both wearing dark coveralls and balaclavas. One of them with a rucksack on his back jumped into the van, the other walked rapidly away along the pavement on the other side and disappeared round the corner.

Sigurd muttered something or other to himself. Time to get out of here. It took a few seconds before the van was out of sight too. He carried on talking to himself, repeating the same thing over and over. Time to get out of here.

Suddenly he crossed the street. The door of Aladdin's Grill was ajar, the blinds drawn; there was a sign with the word *Closed* on it.

He shoved the door.

– Katja?

As soon as he put his head round the door, he smelled faeces. Mingled with it was the smell of cooked meat and barbecue spices, along with a trace of cigarette smoke.

Someone was lying on the floor at the back of the café.

Sigurd took a couple of steps inside. The boy, he thought. His body lay in a contorted pose in the half-open doorway that led out into the back yard. Half of the face was gone, fragments of something white grinning up at him; what was left of the teeth.

He backed away. Heard a sound from the room next to the bar. Running water.

Katja, he murmured, and prodded the door open with his foot.

It took him a few second to recognise who it was. Recognised the Chicago Bulls baseball cap that was still on the head.

Mujo's head was bent backwards over the bowl of the toilet, the throat cut open like a fish's belly, a thick, dark fluid pumping down across the white porcelain. The eyes stared up at Sigurd, a trace of movement in them, a gurgling sound that caused bubbles around the mouth of the wound, and then the eyes whitened and something departed from them.

The next thing he knew, Sigurd was outside on the pavement again. He walked stiffly along the pavement through the piercing light. Music from a window, a kid screeching, a motorcycle starting up and driving off. He didn't start running until he was round the corner, stumbled against a car door, broke a wing mirror. Got to his feet and ran on. Raced across the square, brakes squealing, he twisted out the way. Someone wound down a window and yelled at him.

When he looked up, he saw he was on his way back to the People's Park. He staggered over to the car, fumbled for the keys, thumbed the opener; the lights flashed. Was about to cross the street when he saw him. Standing by the fence a few yards away from the car, in the shadow of a tree. He was wearing dark coveralls in the heat, a cap pulled down low on his forehead. As though he was waiting for him. Sigurd carried on past the car, on to the pavement beyond it, didn't look back. Heard footsteps. Maybe his own. Didn't look back. Heard breathing, maybe his own. Didn't look back.

Then he ran.

Came to the park gates, into the park, stopped at one of the stalls among people waiting their turn to fish for a fluffy toy. Glanced over his shoulder. The man in the coveralls was coming straight towards him. Sigurd backed away, kicked out at something or other. Behind him, a child fell to the ground, a woman swearing. He knocked into a fence, grabbed at the top and jumped over. In below the rails of the big dipper. Someone screamed; he screamed too. Ducked down as one of the carriages swung directly above his head. Crawled across several rails, beneath a power cable, another carriage approaching. He dived out of the way, tumbled on to the open grass, up and into the trees, started climbing the fence facing the road. A hand grabbed his T-shirt and dragged him down. The man who'd been waiting by his car. In his other hand he was holding something that glinted in the sunlight. The eyes beneath the peaked cap, pupils so big Sigurd could see himself in them. He managed to twist free, felt something rip at his hip and move up and knew that it would hurt, that it would bleed. He smelled something and knew that it was coming from him, from his pants, like a signal that the fight was already over.

– Who are you? he howled.

No answer, no movement in the man's face; only the hand moved, and the glinting thing it held. And then everything cleared. Like coming into a room without furniture. A room in which he could move about freely. Sigurd had never been in that room, never experienced time within it, how slowly it passed, and yet he knew how to move in there, first to one side, follow the knife, carry on in an extension of the arc it would carve. Take a step backwards at its final position, then quickly in the opposite direction, then get away before the knife was there. MacCay's voice: *Put your shoulder into it, channel all the force into your knuckles.*

He caught his attacker in the throat, didn't get away before the knife was there, but it didn't cut deep because the hand holding it was no longer in charge, and something new appeared in the wide-open eyes. Sigurd forced himself to look into them, and he no longer saw himself there, but the pain of the other, and when he kicked out at the groin, he knew his aim was good. The man doubled up, didn't drop the knife, but Sigurd kicked it out of his hand and hit him hard twice on the neck, then in the face. He felt himself strike bone, as though his knuckles splintered. He grabbed for the man's head, got hold of the ears, drove his head against the railings, counted how many times, three, four, reached five. This is what it's like to kill, he heard himself think, and only then did he loosen his grip, as though the word *kill* flared down into his fingers, burning them so that they had to let go.

He took a step back. Then three more. A woman ran between the trees dragging a girl with bouncing plaits, the girl holding on tight to a piece of string at the end of which a helium balloon bounced. He saw it glistening in the sharp light; it could well have been a lion, but with a moustache and actually more like an ape. *Don't let go!* he shouted, and the girl did as he said, she held on tight to the string as she was pulled along, and the balloon did not disappear up towards the light clouds.

Outside the gates he limped away, one hand held to the wound in his side, feeling a slight trickling between his fingers. Realised he was going in the wrong direction, turned and headed back the other way, past the main entrance. He heard sirens in the distance, saw a crowd of people gathering; he continued along the fence, moving from shadow to shadow as though that could make him invisible.

He didn't see her until he was back at the car. Leaning back in the passenger seat, not moving. He wrenched open the door, pulled her arm.

She stared at him. – Where have you been?

– I thought, he shouted, struggling to control his voice. – Thought they'd got you too.

He climbed into the driver's seat, started the car, threw it into reverse, braked millimetres from an old woman wheeling a shopping bag, waited for her, reversed again, stalled the engine, started it again.

– Jesus Christ, what's the matter with you, Sigurd?

He straightened the car up and sped towards the junction.

– We're going left, Sigurd. Pull yourself together.

He drove up on to the kerbstones, tried to make a U-turn, heard the screeching of brakes and a chorus of horns, gave up the attempt and carried on in the same direction.

– Mujo, he finally managed to say.

– What about Mujo?

He heard the panic in her voice; maybe it was his own.

– Dead. The boy, too.

– No!

Her scream started a wave of tremors through his body, as though only now did what he had seen become real.

He tried to make a slashing motion across his throat. The car glided over the central line, a trailer coming right at him. He managed to straighten up just in time, accelerated hard.

– Which way? he shouted. – Tell me which way to drive to get the hell out of this fucking town.

– Carry on.

– Carry on where?

– I don't know. Shit, you're lying, right?

He drove straight ahead, over every junction he came to, looking in the rear-view mirror, certain someone must be following them.

– Calm down, said Katja again. She took hold of his T-shirt, realised it was soaked in blood, and screamed. Her screaming turned to sobbing, and then whimpering.

Not until he came to the last roundabout and swung out on to the E6 towards Oslo did she fall silent.

It was two thirty before he thought of checking the time. They had passed Helsingborg. He concentrated on the road ahead, on pulling out in plenty of time before overtaking, on making sure he kept his speed below a hundred and forty. He checked the road behind them, to see if any of the cars he saw stayed with them, got closer, followed them.

The stink from his trousers filled the car. Katja hadn't said a word since leaving Malmö, sat hunched up next to him, the only sound her low whimpering now and then, but she must have noticed the smell too.

He turned off after Halmstead and pulled in at a petrol station.

– Go and buy something I can clean myself with.

She straightened up, looked across at him.

– Have you . . . messed yourself?

He shook his head.

– That guy, he said. The other bloke. He had a knife. I was holding him. He just emptied himself. He gestured in the direction of his trousers. – Get the bag out first, my clothes.

She went to the boot and got him what he asked for. Came back from the forecourt shop with a pack of wet wipes. He cleaned up the seat before taking his clothes and locking himself into the toilet.

When he returned, she was sitting there with her phone in her hand.

– What's happening? he asked, his voice still not back to normal.

She was looking straight ahead, over towards the far side of the motorway, into the landscape of fields, a derelict barn with a hoarding on the side advertising hamburger and chips.

– I'm talking to you.

He grabbed her by the neck and forced her to turn her head until her eyes met his. Empty. It was as though she was still staring into the horizon.

– Who the hell are you calling?

He struggled to control his breathing. It seemed to run on ahead by itself.

– Sting, she said at last.

– The guy who drove my car?

– He saw you. You came running out.

Sigurd realised what she was thinking.

– Sting's asking if you have anything to do with it.

The boy with the burst-open face. Mujo's eyes. The blood pumping in thin jets into the toilet bowl. He blinked hard to drive the images away.

She turned towards him. – Was it you?

He stared down into her eyes, still couldn't engage her attention.

– First you were in the house and you beat Ibro up. And now when Mujo was killed . . .

He couldn't say a word.

– Did you do it?

The question sank into him, reached a base.

– I, he began. Had to search for words, put them together. It took time.

He was balanced on an edge; a breath of wind would be

enough to knock him over. He had an unendurable urge to hit her. If he did, it would take possession of him, nothing would be able to stop him, not until she lay bleeding on the asphalt.

– What you are asking me . . .

He felt something let go inside him, that itch in his chest. His breathing slowed. He felt he had come to some end point, had let everything go and now was lighter than air. It stops here. Or turns. The same room he'd entered when the knife came towards him. Could enter it now. From now on he could enter it whenever he wanted.

– I don't ever want to hear anything like that from you again. Ever.

She looked up. For a few moments she seemed confused. Then she leaned up against him and held on to him. – You're the only one I have, she murmured. – No one else but you.

She had offered to drive; he wouldn't let her. She didn't have a licence. And right now the best thing for him to do was sit behind a steering wheel at a hundred and thirty-nine and let his eyes follow the long lines of the road ahead, the light above the sea on their left, the forests on their right. He felt a throbbing in his side, a wound that ran from his hip to the bottom rib. She'd found a bandage in the first aid kit and bound him with it; it was saturated immediately, but the blood no longer ran. He'd explained what had happened three or four times. She was the one who wanted to hear it again. But no questions about why he'd gone looking for her. That was something he'd asked himself. And maybe she had asked it anyway, wordlessly, after she fell silent and leant in against him, her head pressed against his chest, one hand carefully touching the cut in his side, as though wanting to cure it by the application of a power of some kind that she had no access to.

Near Uddevalla they stopped to fill up with petrol. She used the toilet. From where he stood, he could follow every movement at the other pumps. A goods wagon glided in and a guy about his own age jumped out. He was in poor shape, round shoulders slumped in a tracksuit that was much too tight. He disappeared into the forecourt shop without looking round, and for a moment relief was mingled with something else, a tingling that reached all the way out to his fists. He might even have called it disappointment.

Katja returned, put her arms around him, repeated some of the things she had said earlier: now there's just the two of us. Back on the road again he asked: – What was Mujo supposed to be sorting out for you?

She opened the side window slightly, the wind catching in her hair.

He asked the question again. She adjusted the seat back. – He was going to find out who knew about Ibro not having got rid of the gun like he was supposed to. The proof.

– And?

– He was going to tell them I didn't know anything about it.

– And?

– He made a deal. I've got two things to do. Then I'm out of it.

– Find the gun and hand it over to the person who did the killing?

– Yes. Or make sure it's destroyed.

– And the other thing?

She didn't answer.

– What was the second thing?

– Something I've got to deliver. Sting had it in his car, that's why we weren't in the café. We went out the back way, see? That's what saved me.

He didn't let her distract him.

– Exactly what are you supposed to deliver?

She nodded over her shoulder, towards the boot.

A dark suspicion clouded his mind and he pulled over on to the hard shoulder. He jumped out, walked round to the back of the car, lifted the boot. It felt as though the wound in his side opened up again.

Her little red suitcase was there, and his own sports bag. And two other bags, black nylon, each with a small padlock. He slammed the boot shut, pulled open the passenger door.

– No fucking way!

She got out, stood directly in front of him. Stood like that for a long time, as though looking for something in his eyes.

– All right, she said. – Leave me here.

– What are you talking about?

– You have a choice. I don't.

– And how are you going to get home?

She shrugged. – If you decide to drive on, you don't need to worry about me. It'll be my problem.

He felt the urge to hit her, that thin nose, the half-smiling mouth. She lifted her face to him, as though aware of what was going through his head. He had never hit a girl before, never even been close to it. What's happening to you? he thought.

It was as though the question cleared his mind. He breathed in deeply, released it again as slowly as he could.

– Katja, please.

Her gaze didn't move.

– You know I can't drive off and leave you here. Wake up, for fuck's sake.

He saw something happen in her face; she pressed up against him.

– Wake up, he repeated, but now in the tone he might have used to a child, one that was lost and needed help to find the way back.

He stroked her hair, could feel patches of wetness on the front of his T-shirt.

She had regained her composure by the time they drove on. Began to explain and rationalise, offer alternatives, surprisingly detached, it seemed to him.

– So you don't know what is in these bags we're driving round with?

She shook her head. – I don't ask. I've to find the gun Ibro hid. Deliver some bags. After that they'll leave me alone.

– They cut Ibro and Mujo's throats, and they're going to let you go?

– They'll get their stuff. That's all I can do.

Sigurd bit his lip. – And if they ask you to do other jobs for them?

– We have to see this through, she said calmly. – Or not. And in that case, we know what'll happen to me.

Over the last week he'd done several things he had to get sorted out. He might even be charged and sentenced. But what she was asking of him now was something completely different.

He laid it out for her. The alternative. Go to the police. Hand over the bags, explain what had happened. They wouldn't have anything on her. More on him, actually.

She seemed to be listening, didn't interrupt at least.

Not until he pulled out his phone did she say: – The only thing you haven't thought about, Sigurd, is that I'll disappear.

– Not if you co-operate with the police. You'll get protection.

She gave a loud, forced laugh.

– The police protect me? How? A patrol following me wherever I go for the rest of my life?

– A personal alarm.

Her laugh was even cruder this time, and he could hear himself how unreasonable the suggestion was.

– You've seen how these people deal with things, haven't you? She leaned into him again. – If these bags are found, then I'll take full responsibility. Until the day I die, I'll swear you knew nothing about them.

As though anyone would believe her. That he hadn't a clue what was in his own car.

– On top of that, they have an insurance, she added.

– Insurance?

– The border crossing here is often closed; they don't have the capacity, just do a few random checks.

He pulled into the outside lane, accelerated, over a hundred and forty now.

– And that is an insurance?

– Someone keeps a lookout, up in the forest with binoculars. If the crossing is manned, they send a message. Then we get a call. There's no way we get stopped.

Sigurd increased his speed, a hundred and fifty, fixed his gaze on the far end of the rise.

He guessed before they reached the bridge at Svinesund. He guessed before they passed the sign that marked the precise point at which they entered Norway, guessed before he saw the flashing arrows up on the rising slope. Long before he heard Katja's cry.

– They've tricked us, she yelled.

She grabbed his arm, still shouting, something about how he should turn around, drive back over the bridge, back into Sweden. When she got no response, she bent forward, put her head between her knees.

Sigurd dropped his speed, followed the arrows, pulled over on the right. Only some cars were being stopped, he tried to encourage himself. Most were being waved on. He rolled up to the barrier, wound down the window and looked up at the uniformed policewoman. She bent down and studied his face, and he saw in her eyes that they were not going to be waved on; they would be pulled over.

Another customs officer was standing next to what looked like a garage door, a man, younger than the woman, shaven head, looked like he pumped iron on a daily basis, as though that might have any bearing on what was about to happen. Sigurd pressed the window button, the window closed; he'd forgotten it was already open, wound it down again.

– Where did you start your journey?

It was the woman who asked. He tried to answer, but there was something blocking his throat. He struggled to move the lump lower down.

– Malmö.

– And what were you doing there?

– Visiting family.

For an instant he almost burst out laughing. Family and friends, he almost shouted, we've been visiting Uncle Mujo, the one lying there with his throat cut in Aladdin's Grill, right next to the People's Park. Uncle Mujo's given us a couple of bags to take for him, but we're not to open them, he was very definite about that.

– Been there long?

While the woman continued to ask questions, the muscular guy walked around the car. Sigurd glanced at Katja. She sat staring straight ahead, her skin grey, empty eyed.

– Please step outside and open up for us.

He opened the door a little too quickly; it hit the uniformed woman on the thigh and she jumped back and said something or other. He tried to apologise. A warm wind blew down from the copse in front of him, a summer evening breeze beneath a white-blue sky, and he picked up the smell of pine needles, drew it down with the vague thought that this was the kind of thing he would miss. Suddenly he thought of Trym. Trym up in the barn loft. He's blocking the door with his body, no one is going to be leaving there with a hammer in his hand, no one will run down to the lawn and smash up the blue Renault Mégane, or into the house where his mother has a visitor and smash something else in there.

Sigurd pressed the boot opener, took the five steps back to the rear of the car and raised the door. The muscular guy shone an enormous torch into the recess, as though that was really necessary.

– I think we'll take a look inside your bags, the woman said behind him, and Sigurd nodded, because that was the smart thing to do. He would have done the same thing himself, he thought, almost said so out loud, and maybe he did, because both customs officers looked at him.

Recently he'd been making plans for Trym. Had decided how he would help him. After he'd established a chain of fashion stores in Oslo, he would offer his brother a permanent job in one of them. Wouldn't matter if Trym dropped out, stayed at home in front of his computer instead of going to work; he'd keep the job anyway, and his regular wage, which he could gamble away or do whatever he liked with. He, Sigurd, the kid brother, would be there for him whenever he needed it. He hadn't kept their agreement yesterday, had gone off because Katja called. Trym had been left sitting there waiting, and it was the thought of Trym that was painful as he lifted out his bag, put it on the ground, opened the zip. From now on, Trym would have to manage on his own.

The woman pulled on plastic gloves and started to search the bag. The man did the same with Katja's bag, and even now Sigurd noticed how much he disliked seeing those hairy fists disappearing beneath the tops and the used G-strings, rummaging around in there.

– And now *those* bags, said the woman when she'd finished.

– They're locked, Sigurd told her.

– We can see that.

Sigurd went round to the passenger door, opened it. Katja was still sitting staring straight ahead. She should have done what he was doing, spoken to the customs officers. She was the one responsible for what was in the boot, the one who was supposed to keep him out of it.

She didn't respond when he took hold of her shoulder, and he gave up.

– We don't seem to have the keys, he explained to the female customs officer, and there might have been some movement in the woman's face when he said this. Only now did he notice that she was good-looking, not too many years older than him; he'd always liked the look of women in uniform. Perhaps he was looking for some sign that she liked him too, and was going to say something like *It's a pity you've lost the keys, these things happen, you better just drive on, enjoy the rest of your journey.*

She turned to her male colleague, nodded to him, and he took a few paces to one side, tapped on his phone, gave a brief message, and moments later two officers in uniform were there, one with a dog on a leash.

– We're opening these two bags, said the woman, and they were immediately taken out. One of the recent arrivals produced cutters and snipped the little padlocks open, the echo of the clicks lingering a moment in the evening light.

Sigurd looked for somewhere to park his gaze, found a cloud drifting over the rim of the forest. Could hear Jenny's voice now, saying his name with her heavy accent, always proud when she said it, whether she was talking to him or talking about him.

– What is this? he heard the woman say.

He turned to her. She was holding transparent plastic bags in her hand. Something coloured inside.

– I don't know, he said in a low voice. – That's the truth, I don't know what it is.

One of the new arrivals ripped open the bag with his cutters and let the contents spill out on to the top of Katja's case. It looked like an assortment of socks and boxer shorts.

The woman bent forward and picked something up, held it up in front of Sigurd. A large pale blue garment with greyish-white seams. On the waistband in the same colour the words *Malmö FF*.

It *was* a pair of boxer shorts.

– Why do you keep your old underwear padlocked inside a bag?

He searched in vain for a reasonable answer. – It isn't mine.

– Your girlfriend wears stuff like this?

– Don't think so. Not her style.

The muscular guy gave a forced grin. The others were working on the contents of the second bag, pulled out another four or five plastic bags. Old clothes there too, tops, tights. They put the dog on it, and at the sight of the animal's puzzled reluctance at being asked to stick its nose into a pile of soiled underwear, Sigurd felt a touch of that same relief that had flooded through him earlier in the evening. There was nothing in the world he couldn't handle, nothing that could stop him.

They asked about the bloodstained bandage around his stomach. He explained that he'd fallen off a stepladder. In a garage they were clearing out. After he was dressed again, they showed him into a kind of waiting room. Katja was finished before him, sat in a chair playing with her phone.

He slumped down in the chair next to her, brimming over with what he was going to say to her as soon as he got the chance.

They were searching the car in a nearby building. An hour passed. Katja was curled up, her head on the hard armrest, black hair dangling. But she wasn't asleep and sat bolt upright when the woman in uniform returned, followed by the man with the bulging biceps.

– It took us a while, the woman explained. If that was meant as an apology, Sigurd thought, it was well hidden.

– That's all right, he said, and stood up. – You're only doing your job.

The woman kept her eyes on him. He had a sinking feeling that perhaps they'd found something after all, something behind the interior trim, or in the tank.

– Can we go now?

A second went by, two, three.

– Come here, said the customs guy with a nod to Sigurd. The glaring fluorescent lighting seemed to change colour and drain away. Sigurd took a step that was more like a stagger, held on to the door and stood there, breathing a few times, until the light came back.

The customs officer rolled across the yard, arms dangling out at the sides as though all the bodybuilding meant they no longer fitted the rest of him. The car had been driven out again and was in front of the garage. The man bent and shone his torch up into one of the front wheel cavities.

– See that there?

Sigurd sank to his knees, looked, saw nothing.

– See it? the customs officer asked again. He directed the beam at a small oval object.

– Yes.

– Did you put that there?

Sigurd felt his stomach lurch and had to fight to keep

the contents down. At the last moment, he decided not to answer.

– Let me put the question another way: why are you driving round with a GPS transmitter attached to your car?

His thoughts raced through a list of possible answers.

– Is that illegal?

The customs officer straightened up. – It's very bloody strange.

– I know.

– As bloody strange as driving around with dirty underwear locked in bags to which you don't have keys.

Sigurd managed to collect his thoughts.

– It's the sort of thing people do, he said, surprised at the clarity in his own voice.

This will be our final conversation.

Is that supposed to upset me?

You're the only one who can answer that.

It appears that on at least one occasion you have changed your identity. Was that something your protector helped you with?

I can't tell you that, but I presume you now know what you need to know about me.

In a way. I have a very specific assignment. And now you have agreed to talk to the police.

I've got nothing to say to them.

You've probably got nothing to lose by allowing yourself to be interviewed.

I have everything to lose. A person who stands alone always loses. You know what happened to Ibro Hakanovic.

Do you want to talk about him now? They'll be asking you about this at the interview.

He was supposed to be abducted from the hospital. He was going to get an offer he would be able to live with.

So he wasn't supposed to be killed?

He wasn't supposed to be killed. Something went wrong.

Can you say anything more about what went wrong?

Only that it led to several other things happening that should never have happened.

If it had been your decision?

It would never have happened.

Does that mean that others were in charge of what was happening?

I can't tell you anything about that.

Or was it chance?

What is chance? One thing leads to another. Someone makes a decision, it seems like the right thing to do. But it leads to an avalanche of events that are impossible to predict, impossible to control, for anyone.

From the expert witness's notes, 4 August 2014

PART V

18–19 June 2014

33

Sounds from the inside. Sounds from the outside. He is not dead. Listening out through layer upon layer of sound.

He opened his eyes. Looked up at the air vent high up on the wall. The light coming through it was yellow at its core, surrounded by white. Slowly it grew weaker, browner, and he understood it was night on the outside. He returned to his listening, inward now. The sounds opened up. He sank into something that must be another room. Marita spoke to him, but he stayed silent, didn't want to call her back. His father was there too, in his chair, his back turned. He said nothing, was still waiting for an answer, the one Arash should have given him long ago.

The door was unlocked. Opened slightly, then wide. Two uniformed men standing there.

– Come with us, said one of them.

Arash remained seated on the floor. They came in, took hold of him by the arms, pulled him to his feet. He let them do it.

– You're to be interrogated.

The room he was taken to was greyish white. Three chairs, a table, no windows. A jigsaw puzzle on a stool in the corner, a fluffy brown monkey. As though a child had been sitting there playing.

Two other men entered. They were not in uniform. They shook his hand, said their names clearly, no way of knowing if these were their real names. They were from the NCIS, one of them added. Both looked directly at him, neither friendly nor hostile.

– You can look at me as long as you like.

Smiles that appeared and vanished again.

– That's okay, Arash. Everything will be fine.

– For me?

– For you too.

– Is good for me the same as good for you?

– Good question.

– We've heard that you're an intelligent guy.

– Is it good for you if I'm an intelligent guy?

– It's good for us. Very good. Everything we say in here is going to be recorded. The man pointed to an object resembling a mushroom up on the ceiling.

– And filmed, added the other.

– Who's going to see this film?

– Those of us investigating this case.

– Nobody else?

– Nobody else.

Arash wanted to go on asking them questions. If he asked questions the whole time, sooner or later he would know what he needed to know. And he could get out of this without losing anything. If there was a way out. *The surest sign.*

– What did you say, Arash?

– Did I say something?

– You said something about a sign.

– What did I say about a sign?

The two exchanged looks. Quick looks. He was doing all right. *Silence is suddenly born into colours.* So not in the order the words were written down. That was another way of reading Rumi, take it apart, line by line, put it back together in a different order. It would point another way then. That was what he should have talked to his father about. Now he would have to find out for himself.

– Your lawyer will be here in a few minutes. He's been delayed; we'll start without him, if that's all right by you.

– Is that all right for you?

– It's all right for us.

– Where is Ina Sundal?

– Who is she?

– Don't you know the people who work here?

Again they exchanged looks.

– Was she present when you were interviewed previously?

– The question is, can she be here now? Until the lawyer arrives?

One of them stood up, left the room. Minutes passed. Then he returned with her. He was carrying a chair. It made the room more crowded but easier to be in.

– Hi, Arash.

She seemed uncertain but smiled at him anyway. Wearing jeans and a pale yellow blouse. Ina Sundal also brought other colours with her that weren't visible. The light in the room changed after she came in.

– Are you well, Ina Sundal?

She nodded, and he understood that she was going to be present but not say anything. He laughed, because now it would be a different conversation. Possible to answer questions, not just ask them.

– We want to ask you about Ibro Hakanovic, the man who was murdered at the hospital.

– I know who Ibro Hakanovic is.

– You said previously you didn't know him.

– I know who he is.

– Did you know him before the evening when he was admitted?

He looked at Ina Sundal. She had asked the same thing, the following night. She nodded again, faintly; no one else but him could have detected it.

– I had never seen Ibro Hakanovic before that evening.

He leaned forward, looked from one to the other of the two men. – Is Ibro Hakanovic dead?

– He is dead.

– Where is he?

– You mean his body?

– Aren't *you* talking about his body?

The men smiled. Ina Sundal didn't.

– He's probably at some hospital or other.

– In the mortuary?

– Why is it important for you to know this?

– I want to know that he's dead. Can you prove it to me?

They didn't look at each other now, were careful not to. This told him that they were approaching something they thought was important. He held his breath for a few seconds. When he didn't breathe, something happened in his thoughts, as though he knew in advance what they were going to ask him about.

– We know a great deal about what has happened over the last few days, Arash. And we know that what you have told us is for the most part true. But we still need a few pieces filling in before we have the complete picture. That's where we need your help.

That was well said. They needed him.

– You need me. Do I need you?

One of the men nodded firmly. – We can't rule out that you're being threatened by someone. If so, then you need protection.

Arash glanced across at Ina Sundal again. It was what she thought too, he could see that. The light from her blouse had deepened, throwing a glint of dark gold across one cheek.

– Have you ever been to Malmö?

– Malmö is a city in the south of Sweden.

– Correct. Have you been there?

He had been in Copenhagen. Took the plane there to Oslo.

– Never.

– Do you know anyone there?

He did not. And yet he waited before answering. Had to show he was taking the questions they asked him seriously.

– Not to my knowledge.

A thought occurred to him. – Was Ibro Hakanovic from Malmö?

– Yes. Do any of your friends know Malmö?

– I don't know.

– Of course not, Arash. That was a tough question. But to the best of your knowledge, do any of your friends have any connection at all with Malmö?

– Not to the best of my knowledge.

This was a good conversation. The questions were easy to answer. It helped when the questions had one right answer and all the others were wrong. More questions about Malmö. Let's have them. And then about the forest. And he was ready for them too. Was he followed by one or two people? Did he hear people talking? How many shots were fired? What did the person following him look like? More difficult that one, several possible answers. He exerted himself, and Ina Sundal watched him. The black hood, which he first saw reflected in the waters of the stream, for a moment he had thought it was a woman wearing niqab. But the hood was the type people called a balaclava. And the dark clothing was a coverall. Gloves. Something odd about the way the person in black walked.

– Odd how?

He thought about this. Went back in his mind to the bracken by the boulders. The follower bending, peering into the little cave he had almost crept into.

– The person in black had a limp. Not much of one.
– Which leg?

He closed his eyes. – The left. Something else, too. The gun was held in the left hand.

Suddenly he saw himself through the eyes of his pursuer. How Arash emerges from hiding among the bracken, the light from the evening sky falling and falling between the trees. In the middle of this light, a track down a slope. Turns into a narrow path.

Ina Sundal was still looking at him. He tried to hear something she wasn't saying. Still a long way to go, Arash. But you just might have found a way out.

34

Before Jennifer was properly inside the door, the dog was greeting her.

– Pepsi, said Roar Horvath sharply, not that it took any notice, desperately anxious as it was to get a sniff between her legs. He grabbed hold of the loose skin around its neck and tossed the dog out of the way.

– Sorry, Jenny. She's not exactly the perfectly trained dog.

– Don't worry.

The animal whined and peered up at her with an injured look.

– They did their level best to spoil her where she was before. Dan-Levi was a thoroughly good human being. Far too nice a person to train a dog.

The office looked out over the river and the headland. It was simply furnished: a couple of shelves with folders, beige walls, beige curtains, a colour Jennifer had never liked. Four or five empty chewing-tobacco packets were visible in the rubbish bin. He followed her gaze and with one foot shoved it under his desk, at the same time offering her the visitor's chair with its rough cover, which was beige too; at least it harmonised with the general sterility of the room.

– Thank you for coming in at such short notice. I realise you're very busy.

She was. Behind with her everyday routines, behind with her research work.

– I'm sure you've got plenty to do yourself, she answered.

He waved dismissively. – Don't worry about that. I'm glad to see you. A lot can be done over the net. But it can never take the place of personal contact.

She felt herself blushing, made up her mind that before she left the office this time she would make it clear, once and for all, that he had no reason at all to read anything personal into these meetings of theirs.

He pulled his office chair out on to the floor, sat down opposite her. – I've asked you to come for several reasons, Jenny.

– I can't wait to hear them.

He turned, removed some photographs from a large brown envelope and placed them on the desk. She recognised them as being from the two most recent autopsies.

– You've indicated that there are a great many similarities here.

She nodded. – The same weapon may have been used. The cut made in the same way, probably by someone left-handed, though the one that killed Marita Dahl is longer, so that the large veins on the left have been severed.

– Take a look at this.

He laid a picture on the table, looking like a bridge player who'd been sitting waiting with a high card in his hand. – A new victim.

She saw it at once. The cut across the throat slanting down to the left, almost certainly done from behind, rapidly and with the left hand.

The man in the photograph was laid out on a zinc table. He was in his fifties or sixties. The eyes stared out blankly past the photographer.

She looked at Roar Horvath. – Where was this taken?

– The pathological institute in Lund. The victim is Mujo Hakanovic, Ibro Hakanovic's uncle. Killed yesterday in a kebab shop in the centre of Malmö. Along with a fifteen-year-old boy who worked there.

She felt a mixture of excitement and relief.

– So, gang related, she said.

– That hypothesis is strengthened. Malmö police have good contacts there. Three months ago, a man named Vuk Pashar was killed in a bar in the middle of town. He was a member of the so-called V-Falange. They're involved in a long-standing war with the R-Falange, of which Ibro Hakanovic was a member. The killing of Vuk Pashar is believed to have been in revenge for another murder, that of Hasan Arapovic, a close friend of Hakanovic.

– Sounds like a nice cosy world.

Roar spread other pictures of the victim out across the desk. – They've had around twenty murders related to these gangs since 2005 down there. Only a couple of those cases are regarded as being closed, and even those have left a lot of questions unanswered.

– Probably not easy to get people to come forward.

– Anyone who breaks the code of silence lives the rest of their life with a death-sentence hanging over them.

– So Ibro Hakanovic's murder was a revenge killing?

– It's not unlikely. But there may also be other explanations. He leaned back in his chair. – One of the informants claims that Ibro planned to start up on his own.

– Self-employment.

– Exactly. He worked for years as an enforcer. He might have come to Norway to start his own drug-smuggling network. There's talk of cocaine taking a new route to Oslo via Lithuania and Stockholm. The old Copenhagen–Malmö route is so well known, and it's swarming with undercover operatives, take my word for it.

– This guy was going behind someone's back. And so one of his own took him out.

– Possibly. But not definitely. Practically all the murders in recent years have been carried out using firearms. Even the few that weren't don't resemble this. He nodded at the pictures on the desk. – Could be we're dealing with a newly formed gang. Maybe someone Ibro Hakanovic started working with. Or else he's strayed on to their patch. Directly before the bodies were found, the police were called to a disturbance in a nearby park, a knife fight. There could be a connection.

– They don't know?

– By the time they arrived, those involved were gone. Just a few splashes of blood left.

Jennifer flicked her hair back. – All of this strengthens Arash's case.

Roar Horvath rubbed his cheeks with both hands. – That's in no small measure due to you, Jenny. It seems highly probable that someone up there in the forest took a shot at him.

– After killing Marita Dahl. Might *she* have any connection with these Malmö gangs?

– We're following that up. So far we've found nothing to indicate that is the case.

Roar Horvath sat looking at her. Jennifer crossed one leg over the other, looked out the window.

– I was lying there thinking last night, she said, realising she had to choose her words with care. – If Marita Dahl had her throat cut by someone who knew exactly how Ibro Hakanovic was killed . . .

– I can see where you're going.

– Arash was interrogated here on Friday night. If someone who works here had access to that interrogation . . . I'm guessing, of course, but Arash might have mentioned something about Marita. Maybe this policeman read the report.

– Naturally we have considered that.

– Could be you're extra-cautious when you're dealing with a colleague. That would be only natural. Doctors protect each other, it's pure instinct. Policemen too. It's inevitable in professions exposed to risk.

Still a pang in her chest every time she thought of her meeting with that policeman by the stream in the forest.

– Does Dahl have an alibi?

Roar Horvath scratched the side of his neck with his index finger. She was deep inside investigator territory and wasn't expecting an answer, but he said: – He was at a shooting-club meet up in Nes.

– Well, that isn't far away.

– He's been interviewed at length. Every detail of his account will be checked and double checked. Don't worry about it, Jenny.

– Is he left handed?

Roar Horvath spread his hands, and she didn't pursue it.

– What are you going to do with Arash? she asked instead.

– The charges will probably be dropped in the course of the day.

– Are you going to release him straight back on to the streets?

– We're still deciding what to do.

– He's been in close proximity to two murders. He might be in danger. He saw the person who killed Marita Dahl.

Roar Horvath thought about this. – Masked, if we believe what he says. But there is another possibility here.

Jennifer nodded. – It could be Marita was just in the wrong place at the wrong time.

– You lay awake a long time last night, I can see that. You've really been thinking about this.

Again she blushed. – Well, Arash spoke to Ibro Hakanovic at the hospital. He might have found something that . . . He should definitely have protection.

– We'll try to get him admitted to a psychiatric wing. Whatever else, he needs treatment.

The sudden concern didn't sound convincing.

– Damn, I forgot the coffee, he said.

– Don't worry about it. I won't be staying long.

There was no stopping him; he was already on his feet. Pepsi jumped up and followed him. With a mixture of hand signals and verbal threats he persuaded the dog to lie down by the window again.

– She can't bear being left on her own, he sighed. – Usually my mother looks after her during the day, but she's going away.

He'd mentioned something about moving back into his childhood home. Back to Mum, thought Jennifer, and felt an unexpected surge of sadness.

– If I leave her at home, there's not a single chair left in one piece, chewed to bits, stuffing all over the place. Not to mention shoes. She's a shoe fetishist.

– This is your mother you're talking about?

He laughed loudly as he disappeared out into the corridor. He wasn't gone more than twenty seconds. The coffee didn't look any worse than what she herself usually served at work. He carried a plate of biscuits, too. All that's missing is a glass of wine, she thought with a shiver.

– And now the other reason I asked you to come in, he said, and it occurred to her that it might be about that glass of wine. – We need to go through that evening at the hospital one more time.

– Sounds like a good idea, she said, relieved.

– Don't you think it's odd that no one saw the bed with Hakanovic in it being taken down to the basement?

– Apparently it was the usual hell on earth that evening. People running round in all directions.

– I realise that. But we need to check everything on the

timeline, who the patient was in contact with, whether anyone saw or heard anything we don't know about.

She knew what he was going to ask her about.

– In which case someone needs to go through the journals and all that. Confidential material. I thought you might be in a position to help us there.

– So that's why you're spoiling me like this, she said, glancing at the mug of coffee and the plate of biscuits.

– Of course. No such thing as a free lunch, he added.

She had to laugh. Knew at once that she would say yes. – I'll go through the journal notes. If the hospital authorities allow it.

– Brilliant, he exclaimed.

– I can also talk to the people who were on duty that evening. Not question them, just find out if there's anything related to the journals.

– I don't know how many times I've told you this, Jenny. The police force missed out on a first-rate detective in you. It's good that we can make use of you now and then.

She wished there had been a little more irony in his voice. He *had* changed, it struck her. Or pretended to have. Once she had been convinced that at heart people didn't change. But she had to admit that she had done so herself. And maybe it was everything she no longer was, and didn't want to be reminded of, that became so oppressive when Roar Horvath looked at her. Of any feelings she might have had for him, only the embarrassing ones remained.

– Actually there was something I wanted to show you, he said suddenly. – Some video sent to us from Malmö. Including footage from a CCTV camera close to the crime scene.

He leaned over the desk, switched on the computer. – Take a look at this.

She stood up, fished her glasses out of her handbag and

plonked them on the bridge of her nose, aware of how little they suited her.

A black-and-white image appeared on the screen. He pressed a key and the image began to move.

– The killing happened mid-morning. Not as many people around as later in the day. That makes it easier to sort out whatever might be relevant.

The film cut between several camera angles. People passing by wearing summer clothing. An elderly woman with a shopping trolley, a young woman with two kids in tow. A tallish figure, seen from behind, dark coveralls, head hooded in a balaclava.

– Not your average morning outfit, said Jennifer as she leaned closer to the screen.

– Notice the way he walks.

He ran the film again, this time in slow motion, and then again at normal speed.

– Slight limp in the left leg, said Jennifer.

– That's what we've been wondering about. What can you tell us about the possible causes of that?

She studied the sequence a couple more times. – She isn't dragging her foot.

– She?

Jennifer frowned. – Isn't that a woman?

– That's what we think. Roar Horvath pointed to a document on the desk. – The skin cells under Ibro Hakanovic's nails are from a woman.

– Really?

– According to the DNA. Double X, which is what you have and I don't.

– Well, I presume so, said Jennifer, deep in thought. – Until proven otherwise. But he might have scratched someone prior to being admitted to hospital.

– All the signs are that he scratched the person who killed him. Possibly as his throat was being cut.

He fell silent, which annoyed her. It was as though he was hoping to excite her curiosity.

– We sent the profile to Malmö.

– And they found a match?

– Not there, but they've been on to Europol and they have two different crime scenes with matching DNA. Hamburg and Cologne. We're talking about four murders around the turn of the century.

– None solved?

– Contract killings. Professionals.

– Who nevertheless leave evidence behind?

He shrugged. – If you kill enough people, that's probably unavoidable.

– Arash is innocent.

She said it as though she had believed it all along.

Roar Horvath thought about it. – In some way or other he is involved. But for the time being we don't know how.

Once again he brought the figure up on the screen, the head and back, the five-second walk before it disappeared around a corner. Then he fast-forwarded, paused. Another camera. The person in the coveralls approaching.

– That's her, said Jenny.

The person was no longer wearing a balaclava but now had a cap pulled down low over the forehead.

– No doubt about it.

– You need to ask an orthopaedic surgeon or a neurologist about that limp, but my guess would be that the person has a hip injury. Jennifer pointed. – The way the pelvis jerks upwards.

She took a couple of paces towards the door, demonstrating what she meant. – It doesn't look like paralysis.

– Fresh injury?

Jennifer had to smile. – You're looking for half-educated guesses, I can see that. But no, she's probably had that for a while. It takes time to learn to walk as fluently as that with a hip injury.

The film continued. As Roar Horvath was exiting it, Jennifer exclaimed: – What's that?

He opened the file again, navigated back through it.

– They sent us almost an hour, from three different cameras.

Jennifer leaned forward and stared at the screen. The young man wearing a T-shirt and knee-length shorts appeared and hurried by, his face half turned away. It took just a couple of seconds.

Roar Horvath ran the sequence again. – Someone you know?

That powerful build, the way of running, the short haircut. She knew it before Roar Horvath paused the film and zoomed in, before she could make out the picture of Ayers Rock on the front of the T-shirt.

She forced herself to shake her head. – He looked like someone . . . It isn't him.

But that was exactly who it was. Suddenly the smell of Roar Horvath's aftershave became so oppressive she had to turn away.

– I've got a lunch appointment, she said, more quickly than she ought to have. – I'll go through those journals as soon as I can, be in touch.

– Jenny, there's something I've been thinking about.

She looked at her watch, put her hand on the doorknob.

– One of these days, maybe we could go out for a drink.

– No thanks, she said, much too loudly, her voice somewhere between a groan and a yell.

She went out into the corridor, on down the stairs, out

through reception, four or five people waiting there. She could still see that image of Sigurd as it flickered by, wearing the T-shirt she had given him, the one she'd been so proud to see him wearing.

Roar Horvath followed her. She stopped outside in the car park.

– I never managed to tell you, Jenny. What happened that time. It wasn't very nice of me.

He'd dumped her. These things happened. She was upset for three days. Then relieved.

– Think about it, he said. – We could talk. That's all.

– All right, she said. – I'll think about it.

35

KATJA LAY ON the bed, eyes closed, her face in the pale light from the window glistening with sweat. She might have been asleep, but she tossed uneasily, whimpering now and then. Sigurd turned away, peered out through a gap between the curtains, pressed his hand against his damp bandage. On the drive back from Svinesund she hadn't given a proper answer to any of his questions. Had talked incoherently about people he didn't know, wailed, wept, pleaded with him, as though she thought he might throw her out of the car.

Late that night they had taken a room at a hotel near Bislett stadium. The car was up at Fagerborg, the GPS transmitter transferred to the wheel arch of a car with Polish number plates. It had pulled into a petrol station near Sarpsborg, coming from the north and heading south. It would be some time before their pursuers realised. Sigurd had no idea what to do with that time. He stood by the window and sifted through his thoughts. Was still standing there when she said his name in the half-dark.

– You didn't leave?

– No, he answered. – I didn't leave.

She lifted her arm, as though there was no strength in it. He went over, stood beside the bed.

– I've got you, she said as she took hold of his hand. – Do you know?

– Know what?

– What you mean to me?

He thought of something. – Your phone. I found it.

He pulled away, opened the side pocket of his bag, handed it to her.

She looked at it. – You knew where it was all the time, didn't you?

He gave a non-committal grunt, but she let it drop.

When he came back from the toilet, she was still lying there looking at it.

– He called me, she said quietly. – Ibro called me and left a message.

– Is that unusual?

– He called me from the hospital.

– You told me that.

– He called me on this phone, too. She waved the one Sigurd had hidden. – Afterwards.

She picked up the new one, looked from one screen to the other.

– I presume you told him that phone was missing?

She nodded.

– Then why would he ring you on that one?

– I don't know.

– What does he say?

She glanced up at him,

– I can't bear to listen. I'm deleting this message. She started to fiddle with the keys.

– Christ, you mustn't do that.

He grabbed it off her. Her pupils expanded; she lowered her head as though she was about to go for him, then she collapsed.

Sigurd scrolled down the list. What she said was right: a call from Ibro on Saturday, two minutes past midnight. The call on the new phone was more than an hour and a half earlier.

He called the answering machine: fourteen new messages. The first, from Vanessa, he clicked past. The next three as well.

The fifth message was from Ibro. Sigurd put the phone on speaker.

Katja.

She gave a start at the sound of the voice, stared at it as though it were communicating from the beyond. Sigurd squatted by the bed. She bit her lip; he could see she was struggling to hold back the tears.

Katja . . . something's happened.

The voice sounded drowsy. Not just drowsy; he had to be drunk, or stoned. So out of it he was calling her on a phone she no longer had.

But you mustn't let them—

Katja shut off the recording. – I don't want to hear any more.

– What do you mean?

– Surely you understand. He's dead.

– Hell, Katja, maybe he's saying something about what happened.

– I know who they are.

Sigurd eased on to the side of the bed, wincing with pain. – If he gives the names, the police will have to do something.

– You listen, she mumbled.

He navigated back to the message.

You're the only one who knows where the proof is . . . I can prove . . . Katja, you must fetch them. She can't—

Katja covered her face with her hands. – Turn it off.

Sigurd shushed her. The voice grew even more slurred. Again something about proof, and some names. One of them repeated; it sounded like Ludmilla something or other. Golobova maybe. And then Katja's name, repeated several times; it sounded like a prayer, directed at her. She curled into a ball, squeezed the pillow as though it were a child she was protecting, and at that moment he could have stroked her hair, lain on the bed beside her and held her tight. But he didn't lift his hand; instead, he turned away.

Suddenly Ibro Hakanovic's voice changed, becoming louder and clearer. There was another voice there too, further off, but clear and even deeper. *Put down that phone,* it seemed to be saying. Then something else in a foreign language. Ibro answered in what sounded like the same language; he sounded angry, or afraid.

Take the phone, said a third voice, a woman's voice, followed by a series of dull sounds, a loud bang, then Ibro, distantly: *You don't work here. Who the hell are you? What are you doing with that knife?* Another bang, then a scream.

– Fuck, shouted Sigurd, pain shooting down his back and into the wound in his side. – Now they're killing him.

Gurgling sounds from the phone, the last remnants of a human voice drowning. Katja clung to him, her whole body trembling. He put his arms around her shoulders to calm her. It didn't help, and that only increased his own distress.

He stood by the window, watching the street below. Stood there and heard the shower running. Was still standing there half an hour later when it was turned off. Finally he knocked on the door. No answer. He didn't give up, knocked again and again until she opened it.

She was bent over, sitting on the toilet seat, naked. Water from her hair formed a puddle on the floor. He put a finger under her chin and lifted it so he could see her face. Two wide red stripes running down each cheek. Blood dripping from them. More stripes on her throat, and on her chest.

– What the hell are you doing?

She looked at him, her pupils like pinheads. – Please, she murmured. – Don't hit me.

He let go of her. – What are you talking about?

– You're angry. You hate me.

Perhaps he was angry, or perhaps it had passed. He didn't know.

– Katja, he said in confusion, and placed a hand on her cheek.

– You mustn't go, she whispered, rubbing her face against the flat of his hand.

She was trying to tell him something, or she was lying without knowing it herself. Abruptly he wanted her; it forced its way through the maze of thoughts. With one hand she pulled off his boxers, and when he pushed his way into her, she screamed and bit his neck.

Afterwards he sat on the floor, the cold from the tiles moving up through the soles of his feet and his backside. She still sat on the toilet seat, mumbling something or other, crying perhaps. He couldn't bear to look at her.

– We need to think, he said. The bandage had been torn off and his wound was throbbing. – We've got to work something out. We have to talk to someone.

The sound of his phone out in the hotel room; he let it ring and ring.

It was after four when he returned to the room with a bag of food from Deli de Luca. Found her naked on the floor in the half-dark beneath the window, water trickling from her hair, as though she'd just taken another shower. He broke off a piece of bread, put a cheese slice on it, he'd bought a salad too, held it out to her. He couldn't remember the last time he'd seen her eat.

– We need to think, he said again. – Why would Mujo trick you?

She raised her head and leaned it against the wall, eyes still closed.

– Why did he fill the bags with old underwear?

– Do you think it was *me* who did that? she exclaimed, her voice suddenly clear.

– Stop it, Katja.

– You hate me, she shouted, and curled up into a ball again.

She isn't well, he thought, she's sick, and you haven't understood a thing.

– You're in trouble, he said as calmly as he could. – *We* are in trouble. And you're going to have to tell me everything you know. I don't want to end up like Mujo, in a fucking toilet with my head half sliced off. And you don't either.

She shrugged. – You think you can stop them?

– I can.

– If you'd known they put that transmitter on your car, Mujo would still be alive.

– What?

– It was your car told them where we were, wasn't it? That was how they found us.

He almost burst out laughing, but it stuck in his throat. His phone began vibrating again. Jenny. Calling for the fifth time. He put one finger on the accept call key, but changed his mind. Keep his mother out of this. Go to the police, tell them what he knew. He'd hit a guy with a golf club, but it was in a fight, and that wasn't what killed him. He'd been nearby when two men were killed and he'd left the scene of the crime. He'd defended himself against a knife attack in a park in Malmö. Had tried to smuggle two bags of ragged underwear and socks across the border. He could sort it out, continue with his life. And Katja? She wasn't part of that continuation. He still didn't know how he was going to say it to her.

– I'm going down to the police station. Best if you come with me.

She shook her head.

– I'll take your phone with me, he went on. – Listening to that message from Ibro, I understand why these people are after you. He's almost asking them to do it.

Abruptly she sat upright. – Pull yourself together, she bellowed, so loud that it made him jump.

– Okay then, you stay here.

– How stupid can you be? It isn't you they're after, and you know it. You can walk out of here whenever you like. You're a fucking tourist in my world, a fucking tourist on an ego trip.

Her eyes were consumed with anger, hate even. He didn't know which it was, but it was contagious, and again he felt the insane desire to hit her.

A faint smile appeared on her lips. – Go on, do it.

He slumped down into a chair, took hold of his own arms as though to control them. I'm in her world, he thought, this is what it's like to be her. Didn't know where that thought came from, but at once it made him feel calm.

– You're right, Katja. This is something I don't understand.

Maybe it was the way he said it that changed her. The anger drained from her eyes, and they flooded over.

– Sorry, she said, burying her face in her hands.

– It's all right. I'm the one who should apologise.

Impossible to mean this, of course, but he repeated it.

– You're all I have, she murmured, holding on to him. – Do you realise that? No one else but you, Sigurd.

She took a few bites of the sandwich he offered her. A good sign, he thought. She ate more, ate from his hand; that was what she wanted, lying on the rug, still naked, eating the mouthfuls he held up to her, like a little animal he had tamed. Outside it had clouded over. A brown dusky light through the gap in the curtains that rubbed out the shapes of things until they seemed to dissolve into each other.

– We must do something, he said yet again. – We can't stay in this room for the rest of our lives.

– The rest of our lives, she repeated, like an echo.

– We have to go to the police.

She shook her head. – The people who killed Ibro have to have that gun. The evidence. Maybe then they'll leave me alone.

– But you don't know what he did with it.

– I know where I ought to look.

– You mean that house in Nittedal?

– Ibro had other things hidden there, in a cupboard. And we need to deliver the bags, too.

– A few faded pairs of underpants? Please don't joke with me.

– You don't know them. That was a test. If they don't get those bags, they'll think I've tried to double-cross them.

His thoughts began to revolve again, as though they were in orbit around her. That was what he had been trying to do ever since that first evening at Togo, trying over and over again to circle her in. Each time he thought he had, he found she wasn't inside the circle but somewhere else. Now he couldn't bear the thought that he might have managed to find her.

– You were with him, he said, and it was a relief to say it straight out, as a way in to what he had to tell her. – You were with Ibro Hakanovic while you were living with me. He said it as though he were talking about a rental agreement.

She shook her head for a long time. – It's not like you think.

– I don't think anything different from what you've told me.

– We weren't together. Not like that. Ibro couldn't do it.

Sigurd snorted, but all that emerged was a puff of air.

– He had an injury. Was almost beaten to death when he was fifteen. After that, he couldn't.

– And you expect me to believe that?

– It's the truth.

– Why did you say you were a couple?

A trace of a smile. – You were so jealous.

– And you wanted me to be?

– I wanted it to be us two, no one else. That's all I want, Sigurd.

I have to get out, he thought, and stood up.

36

THE RING!

Arash woke in the half-dark, felt with his left hand. There it was, on his longest finger.

He sat up. There was a strong smell of paint in the room. The curtains brown, yellowish walls. They had repeatedly said that it was safe to sleep here. Finally he had relented, climbed into the bed and vanished into something dreamless and grey as the evening sky outside.

He looked at his finger. Held it up in the strip of light, the gold winking, and when he turned his hand, this golden glow rose and fell, as though it was not a reflection but came from somewhere inside the ring itself. Around it his fingers were covered by a stain that stretched across most of the back of his hand. He scraped at it with his nail. Something sticky.

Abruptly he got up, opened the door to the bathroom, turned on the tap, rubbed at the stain, soaped it, rubbed again. It wouldn't come off. In a few quick movements he tore off his clothes and examined his body in the sharp light of the lamp above the basin. Cuts and scratches on his thighs and stomach, but no more blood.

He removed the ring, washed it with soap, rubbed it dry, washed it again. It was Ina Sundal who had brought it to him as he sat waiting in the car, squashed between two policemen. She came running across the yard in front of the police station, handed it to him through the window, along with his ID and his hospital keycard.

There was a knock on the door to his room; he heard it open. They did it that way here, knocked on the door and walked right in, or walked right in and then knocked. He pulled on his underpants. Someone said his name. The bathroom door was flung open.

– Is that where you are, Arash?

– Yes, here is where I am.

The same nurse who had talked to him before he went to sleep, a man in his thirties, stocky and spotty, enormous fists.

– You've been sleeping.

– I have been sleeping. Have *you* been sleeping?

The nurse gave a quick grin. – That's not what I'm paid for.

Arash looked down at the floor. Should have asked this man what he *was* paid for, who paid him, who *really* paid him. Watch how he reacted. Because he'd slept now, not for too long maybe, but his mind had started working again, and his thoughts were coherent in a way he was able to control.

– Your name is Raino.

– Wow, you picked that up, did you?

Arash had picked up everything that was happening. Hadn't been in a state to say much, couldn't answer all the questions they'd asked when he arrived here, but he had registered every word that was said to him, recorded every face, name, smell and sound.

Suddenly there was a loud noise from the corridor, repeated blasts, an alarm. The little box attached to Raino's belt started blinking. He looked at it. – Be right back, he said quickly, turned and disappeared out.

Running footsteps outside. Arash peeked out the door.

Seven or eight people had gathered at the end of the corridor. Loud voices from within a room down there. Someone started to howl wordlessly. Arash closed the door, slumped down on to the bed. Sat there staring at the floor, looking for a pattern in the linoleum, something to hold on to.

He jumped up as the door was opened again. This time Raino didn't knock.

– Sorry about that.

– Sorry about what?

– The alarm. We have to assemble whenever it goes off. Did it frighten you?

– Maybe.

– Everything's okay now. Under control.

Arash scratched his head with both hands. – Can I leave now?

Raino pulled the curtain wide open. It was evening, but grey light flooded the room, filling every corner. A wall on the far side became visible, another wing of the building. Down below, a lawn, some chairs arranged on it, but no one in sight.

– You'll probably have to stay here a while, Arash.

– How long is a while?

– That isn't up to me. But you were in pretty bad shape when you came here.

– Bad shape?

Raino played with his keys; they dangled from a chain of glinting silvery links.

– Think you've been having trouble keeping your thoughts in order. No wonder really. You've been through a lot.

Arash tried to look him in the eye.

– Am I in bad shape?

– A doctor will be round to see you later.

– Which doctor?

– Don't know. But he'll be here.

– So I have to sit here and wait for a doctor?

– I guess you do.

– I have to go out.

The nurse stood there, his face expressionless.

– I need to take a walk, Raino, that's what I'm trying to say.

– Go out for a walk?

As though the nurse didn't know what that meant. – I think that'll be a little difficult.

– Why is that difficult, Raino?

Raino drummed three fingers against the wall.

– I'd have to check with the staff nurse. She'll be here early tomorrow morning. The police think you ought to stay here, for the time being.

– Am I a prisoner here?

– No, you're not. It's a question of your own safety. They have guards sitting outside.

– Policemen?

– A couple of them out in the corridor, keeping a lookout.

– Keeping a lookout on what?

– On you. To make sure nothing happens to you.

He fell silent. Arash waited for him to go on.

– I'll find out if it's okay for you to get a bit of fresh air this evening, Arash. The policemen might as well take a stroll with you. They aren't really being paid just to sit there staring at the wall.

Arash studied him, disguising his interest. The nurse was like a carved granite block, but there was an uncertainty in his eyes.

– I'm off duty soon. I'll have a word with the woman who'll be taking care of you after me.

The woman who'll be taking care of you after me. Arash tried to stop his thoughts moving further down that road. – Things mean what they mean, he muttered.

Raino turned on his way out the door. – Did you say something?

– The police know it wasn't me. What happened to Marita.

Immediately he saw Marita's eyes. He turned, but they were staring at him from the other wall too, blood gushing from the gaping neck, down over the shoulder, over his hand, into the stream.

– Have they caught him? Have they caught the person who killed Marita?

– I don't know, Arash. But that's not something you should be worrying too much about right now.

– Can I talk to Ina Sundal?

Raino's hand was on the doorknob. – I'm going to get your medication.

The chain with its three keys was still on the table. Two seconds later the nurse was back, looked around the room, saw them. – Best not forget these. He grinned, looking relieved. – Don't you agree?

The man who visited him later with Raino had curly grey hair at the sides of his head and was bald on top. He was shorter than Arash, with a roundish face. His square glasses had green frames and made his eyes shrink.

– Knut Reinertsen. I'm a doctor and a psychiatrist.

He held out his hand. Arash took it, knew that was the right thing to do. – Hello, Knut Reinertsen. And what do they pay *you* to do?

Probably not the right thing to say. He tried to smile it off.

Knut Reinertsen smiled back at him. – You might well ask. I don't even work here. He pointed to the chair by the window. – Would you like to take a seat?

Arash didn't want to. – Who *do* you work for?

The man who called himself Knut Reinertsen sat on the

edge of the bed. – I do a bit here and a bit there. Work mostly for myself. And do research.

– Are you going to do research on me?

Raino laughed, as though the question surprised him, but Knut Reinertsen didn't look the least bit surprised.

– Is he your man? Arash pointed at Raino.

– No, said Knut Reinertsen. – He works here. I don't, but I was asked to come along and have a chat with you.

– Have a chat.

– Meaning a conversation. I've met a number of people who've had some very difficult experiences. Been involved in wars, tortured. I want to find out the best way we can help you.

Arash liked what he said. Mostly for the way he said it. As though it wasn't something that was all that important. Not something that had to be proved or disproved. A chat, and that would be it. Maybe something would come of it, maybe not.

– Do you know what I have experienced?

– Only some of it. I've read your admission papers. We also have a mutual friend.

– Which friend?

– Zoran Vasic.

It was as though Arash already knew this.

– Did he send you?

– He doesn't have the authority to do that. But he did want me to talk to you.

– How long have you known Zoran?

– More than ten years.

Something happened in the room. A shadow glided across the opposite wall, but the light outside was still the same grey.

– Can we talk alone?

Knut Reinertsen nodded to Raino, who was standing at the precise point where the shadow had stopped.

– Please, wait outside for a few moments, he said, and the nurse immediately did as he was told. When he stepped out, he took the shadow with him. He left the door ajar.

– Why am I here? asked Arash.

Knut Reinertsen looked at him. – The people who have talked to you think you need help. And protection.

– Do I need protection?

– In the opinion of the police.

– Do I need help?

– I think I probably agree with those who say you do.

– Can *you* help me?

Knut Reinertsen appeared to be thinking about the question. He took his time. He had enough of it. He used that time to find his answer. Anyone else besides Knut Reinertsen might have just said anything at all without really meaning it.

– I can try, Arash. If you want me to.

Arash thought it over. He too took his time, as though he and the other man shared the same quantity of time. He wanted to wait before replying, even though he knew the answer the moment Knut Reinertsen entered the room. He was Zoran's friend.

– I found something written.

Knut Reinertsen said nothing, appeared to be waiting.

– On a mirror. In a cabin in the forest. Written in Farsi. He stopped.

– I heard about that, said Knut Reinertsen.

Arash stared at him for a moment, and for an instant, certain possibilities arose that he did not wish to think about. Then he found an explanation.

– You've spoken to that other doctor. Jennifer.

Knut Reinertsen nodded. – She told me about the poem. It made an impression on her.

– And Zoran?

– He heard it too.

– Heard it?

Knut Reinertsen put his hands together in front of him, laid them on his stomach. They lay there peacefully, like intertwined sleeping lemurs.

– Of course, Jennifer couldn't remove anything from the cell you were in. But when she told Zoran about it, he looked it up on the net. We all looked at it together. It was written by Rumi, several hundred years ago.

Knut Reinertsen said this as though he was very familiar with Rumi.

– How could I have come across this on a mirror in a cabin in the middle of the forest?

There was no answer.

– Do *you* believe it could have happened that way?

– I believe that is how you experienced it, Arash. Precisely the way you describe it.

– But not that it actually happened?

– The likelihood is probably remote.

Arash looked out of the window. He shouldn't have spoken about it to this man after all.

– If it really did happen, someone must have known that you would be coming to precisely that cabin, at precisely that moment in time. Someone must have known that you would be fleeing through the forest, on exactly the same route as the one you took.

Arash observed his face as he was saying this. The eyes mostly, the movement of his gaze. And the mouth, the way it moved. As if it was in these movements that he would find the answer to whether Knut Reinertsen could be trusted or not.

– I think this happened in your thoughts. And in one sense that makes what you experienced in the cabin even more important than if it had really happened.

Arash decided he would have to think this through.

– Can you remember when you read this poem for the first time?

Bring it all together again, everything that had been torn apart. But the pieces no longer fitted.

– Yes, Knut Reinertsen. I remember.

He's sitting at the desk in his room, doing his homework. It is afternoon. His father has returned; he hears the footsteps on the stairs, muted, leather soles on stone. Then he's standing there, in the room.

I've got something for you.

Arash looks up. His father is holding something in his hands, a book. It isn't his birthday, or a festive occasion. He never gets presents for no reason.

Rumi?

He feels puzzled rather than pleased.

His father places a hand on his shoulder.

You're not a boy who's easy to handle. But you are my boy.

No further explanation.

Arash sits there holding the book. Feels how heavy it is. Had no time to formulate any expectations before his father gave it to him, so he feels no disappointment. Rumi's poems are the kind of thing they read at school. They're old. Full of dead words.

Finally he opens it at random. Reads what's written on the page.

This was what he told Knut Reinertsen now. A man about the same age as his own father. A man who had known Zoran for more than ten years. He still didn't know if it was wise to tell this man things, but he had started doing so, and the story just went on by itself until he fell silent.

But there was more.

He wasn't allowed to have books in Evin prison, but this poem was something he had inside him, and they couldn't take it away from him. He recited it to himself every evening in the darkness of his cell. Imagined he was reading it to a large audience. They had travelled from all over the country to hear him speak, to hear his voice, because everybody on the other side of the prison walls had heard of him, he hadn't been forgotten, and he would be returning to them. And he recited the poem to himself when they took him down into the basement and fastened the electrodes to his nipples, and when they took him out into the courtyard and put the gun to his head and pulled the trigger.

Knut Reinertsen had removed his glasses. His eyes were now large and pale blue and full of sorrow.

– Thank you for sharing this with me, Arash.

He sat there for a long time in silence. Then he got up from the edge of the bed.

– I'd like to come back tomorrow. If that's all right by you.

Arash looked out of the window. He would not be there tomorrow.

– Ibro Hakanovic is dead.

There was still a question wrapped in what he said.

Knut Reinertsen nodded. – Yes, he is.

– And Marita.

– She is dead too.

Arash held his hand up in front of him.

– See this stain? He pointed at the sticky substance he had been unable to wash away. Knut Reinertsen bent towards him, studied the hand without touching it.

– This is her blood. She took the ring with her when she died. It has been there with her, on the other side. Now it's back here again with me. I should have gone there too. Followed it.

Stillness in the room. But time still moving. *Walk out like someone suddenly born into colour.*

Afterwards, Knut Reinertsen said: – Someone wants you dead, Arash. But not you.

He had understood, without Arash having to say it. It made it possible to tell him more, perhaps tell him everything.

– I saw myself lying there that day in the woods.

Knut Reinertsen sat down on the side of the bed again, waited. The lemur hands in his lap.

– I saw myself through the eyes of the person in black. I saw myself getting up and heading into the forest. Can you tell me that, Knut Reinertsen? Does death have eyes through which it can see?

– I don't know that, Arash.

– That is what I have to find out. Where are you when you see yourself through the eyes of death?

37

JENNIFER RANG THE doorbell for a second time, heard the buzz inside the flat. It sounded angry, and angry was probably what she was. More anxious than angry; it had been almost five hours now since she had first tried to ring him. It wasn't uncommon for her to have trouble getting hold of Sigurd. Days could go by sometimes without her hearing from him. His phone battery was flat, or he was busy with something or other and didn't want to be disturbed.

But this was different.

She pressed her ear close. Heard what might have been a sound inside. Without thinking, she tried the door. It glided open.

– Sigurd? You home?

An odd thought, that he might have been sitting there and heard the doorbell and not opened up. She looked in the living room. The sofa and chairs all over the place, as though someone had started rearranging the furniture but had not had time to finish. In the bedroom, the wardrobe doors wide open, the bedclothes on the floor. Sigurd had always liked things tidy, was almost pedantic about it. That was hardly the case with that woman who'd moved in with him. Even in her thoughts she was *that woman*.

There was a click from the front door.

– Sigurd?

She looked out. No one there. Opened it. Footsteps on the stairs, going down.

– Sigurd, she repeated. The footsteps halted. She leaned over the railing, thought she could hear someone panting. Again the footsteps going down, the street door opening then closing.

Her thoughts had been building throughout the day; now it was as though they had broken free and were colliding with each other. Sigurd had gone to Malmö to help that woman. All his questions about what had happened at the hospital that evening. Sigurd on the CCTV camera right by the crime scene. Because she hadn't doubted for a second that it was him.

There were possible explanations. Chance, coincidence.

This is something else, she said to herself again as she stepped out into the light, close evening. She became aware of a figure at the end of the block, walking away. Stopped and studied her. Because it was a woman. Dark jacket, quite tall, dragging her left leg slightly. Looked to be holding a phone to her ear.

– Hey, she shouted, and set off after her, trotting in her high heels. The woman turned the corner, and by the time Jennifer got there, she was gone.

– Get a grip, she warned herself.

As she was opening the car door, Sigurd rang.

– Where the hell have you been? she shouted into the phone, realising at once how wrong it sounded. – Sorry, I'm in a bit of a state.

– I see you rang, he said quietly, as though he was in a room with someone who mustn't be disturbed. – I've been very busy.

– I need to talk to you.

He didn't answer for a few seconds. – Sorry about Trym. I just had a bit too much going on. I'll do it as soon as I have time. Sorry. Really.

– I need to talk to you, she said again. – It's not about Trym. Where are you?

It sounded as though he hesitated. – At home.

– I've just been there, half a minute ago.

– Well, actually, not quite home.

– Are you in Oslo?

– Yes.

– Tell me where we can meet.

– You don't mean now?

– Now.

She emptied her cup and ordered a refill. Shouldn't be drinking coffee at this time of day. But there were other things to worry about.

Then he was standing in the barroom doorway.

She was on her feet, round the table. He bent and gave her a hug, sank into a chair, looked around for a waiter, avoided meeting her eyes as he usually did. He always looked people in the eye when he spoke to them or listened to them. It was something he had learned from her.

– Hi, she said, and waved her hand, attracting his attention.

– Hi.

– You know what I want to talk to you about?

– No.

She waited until the waiter had served them coffee and mineral water.

– You've been in Malmö.

– I told you that.

– You were in a street where two people were killed; you were there at exactly the same time as it happened.

He jumped in his chair, grabbed the water bottle, filled his glass, sat there picking at the label.

– How did you know that? he asked finally.

She explained.

– And you haven't answered your phone all day. So no wonder I'm worried.

Suddenly she felt out of breath, had to put down her coffee cup. Still waiting for him to say that she had got it all wrong. It wasn't what she thought, she was wrong about the whole thing. He didn't.

– You're involved in this somehow, she groaned. She felt like screaming.

He sat there studying the half-peeled label.

– Say something, she almost shouted.

He ran his fingers through his short hair, scratched his head. – There was a lot of trouble. Someone we knew was killed. And then we left.

– And all because of this Katja, she said as calmly as she could. He looked straight at her, eyes full of anger, and for a moment she thought he was going to start shouting at her.

He lowered his head again. She forced herself not to put her arms around him; he had never liked that. Never went to Ivar or herself for comfort, preferred to deal with it alone until it passed.

She reached out a hand and stroked his forehead. – You can tell me, Sigurd.

He nodded a couple of times.

– What's going on with Katja?

– She needs help. And I'm the one who has to help her. I started it all.

He leaned back in his chair, drank from the bottle.

– I had a fight with this guy. Knocked him down. He ended up in hospital.

Jennifer stared at him. – You're not talking about the Bosnian? Ibro Hakanovic?

He looked out at the empty street, said nothing, but she didn't give up until she had got most of the story out of him. And of course, it was all about Katja.

– Why are people from this gang after her?

No answer.

– Listen, Sigurd. I'm your mother.

He gave a quick smile, hard to interpret.

– I'll do anything for you.

– Really?

– You know that. But you must tell me the whole story.

– I've told you all you need to know.

– No you haven't.

Suddenly she thought of something.

– Do you know who these people are?

He shook his head.

– But you say you saw the ones who killed this uncle.

– A couple of them.

– Describe them.

He ran a hand through his hair. – One powerfully built, overalls, maybe Bosnian as well.

– And the other?

– Don't know. Thinner, quite tall.

– With a limp?

– I didn't notice that.

– Could it be a woman?

– Maybe.

– When I was up at your place just now . . .

She told him she'd been inside his flat, about the front door slamming. She knew now it wasn't the wind, that the person she'd seen in the street outside had some connection with all this.

He listened, eyes wide. Suddenly he jumped to his feet, went over to the door, out on to the pavement, looked up the street, then the other way, came back to the table.

– Did anyone follow you?

– Sigurd, sit down. I'm not letting you leave here until you've told me everything.

– Did anyone follow you? he repeated, a note in his voice she had never heard before.

– They can't have done.

– Do you *know* that?

She couldn't know for certain, but he sat down, again scraped through his hair with both hands.

– Ibro had proof that someone in the gang had committed a murder. He had the gun that was used. It's hidden somewhere. And for some reason these people think Katja knows where it is.

– Is that it?

– Isn't that enough?

Jennifer drummed her fingers on the table.

– We have to go to the police, she said firmly.

– No.

– What do you mean?

– They'll kill her.

– And what about you?

He shrugged his shoulders. As though the predicament he was in didn't matter, as long as Katja was all right.

– If you won't go to the police, I will.

Again he flared up. – If you do, I'll never speak to you again.

– You don't mean that.

He stood by the table, peering intently at her, seemed to be weighing up something or other.

– Does the registration number CF three zero five four three mean anything to you?

She shook her head.

– Renault Mégane. Blue.

Still no idea where he was going with this.

– Father away somewhere, we were at school. And you had a *visitor*. Have I ever asked you about that? Demanded to know who it was?

He turned, headed for the door. She ran after him, held him back.

– Sigurd, she pleaded. – Please.

She heard her own voice breaking, and maybe that was what made him turn round. She tried to wrap her arms around him; he groaned and pulled himself free.

– You're in pain, she exclaimed, and had already lifted his jacket to reveal the bloodstained T-shirt underneath.

Zoran was still up. Muted sounds of piano music from the living room as she let herself in. It was past midnight.

He turned the sound down as she entered the room.

– Did you meet him?

– I should never have let him leave there.

He stood up and held her. – You're trembling, he said.

– I should have made him come with me. Driven straight to the police station.

Zoran went out to the kitchen, came back with a glass with something brown in it. It was strong, burned right through her, then the churning began again.

She opened her bag, took out her phone.

– I'm calling the police.

Zoran laid a hand on her arm. – Maybe you'd better tell Sigurd first. So he won't think you're stabbing him in the back.

She let go of the phone, grabbed the glass and forced another mouthful down.

– Bloody bitch, she said in English.

She was furious now. Cursed Katja, reeling off the crudest profanities she could think of.

Afterwards, she lay on the sofa with her head in Zoran's lap.

– You say they've booked into a hotel in town. There's not much chance of their being traced tonight. If someone really is after them.

– Is that a chance I can take?

He ran a finger over her forehead, tracing the hairline, the rim of the ear, the outline of the face. Images flooding her mind. The boys running out into the yard. But there's no blue car there, not in the images she allows herself to see.

Suddenly she thought of something.

– Arash.

She looked up into his eyes.

– Remember what I told you? What he heard Ibro Hakanovic talking about at the hospital? Something about a cat and a car crash.

Zoran carefully raised her head, prised himself free, stood up. – I don't recall you telling me that.

– About a cat that didn't die in a car crash? Jennifer sat up, pushed her hair back behind her ears, tried to hold it there. – I heard him wrong. It was his accent. I thought he was talking about a cat, but he was talking about Katja.

– Has she been in a car crash?

– I've no idea.

– You think this is important?

She followed him out into the kitchen, rested her head against his chest, exhausted but unable to calm herself.

– I don't trust her. Not for one second. She knows more than she's telling Sigurd.

The glow from the liquor she had been drinking was gone now, and she felt cold again.

– We'll get to the bottom of this, Jenny.

She closed her eyes, raised her hand and found the heartbeat beneath his shirt, strong and steady. A clock that must never run down.

38

She wasn't there.

Sigurd noticed as soon as he opened the door to their hotel room. Her things, the open suitcase, the dress draped over the lid, one cup of a black bra sticking out from beneath a chair. He looked in the bathroom. Looked under the bed and in the wardrobe. Searched for a message on the table, on the floor, in the drawer of the bedside table, under the pillow, in the pile of bedclothes.

He grabbed his phone, got straight through to her voice-mail.

– Katja, for Chrissake, where are you?

He stood there fiddling with the screen. Crossed to the window, opened it to the sounds of the city. No one in sight on the street below. A car came round the corner.

– Oslo police.

Without thinking, he had hit the emergency number. The voice repeated that he was through to the police.

– I've got something to report, he muttered finally.

– I can't hear you. Speak louder.

Then he caught sight of her. Walking up the pavement on the other side. He hung up, was about to shout down to her, caught himself in time.

A minute later, she was in the doorway. He forced himself to remain sitting on the edge of the bed.

– Where have you been?

She didn't answer, pulled off her thin jacket, put something down in her suitcase; it looked like a bag from the chemist's.

– Fucking hell, Katja.

– Don't speak to me like that, she retorted.

He could hear she was on something. Her voice was lighter. She smiled to herself, not from happiness but from a sick energy. He had seen her like this a couple of times before.

– Is this a good time to be getting high?

– Shut up, she growled.

Then he was standing over her. – What the hell do you think you're doing? he bellowed into her face.

– Not going to hit me?

She looked him in the eye. Hers were big and wide open. He dropped his hand, sank down beside her.

– You are hopeless, he muttered.

– Am I? She turned to him. – Am I the one who's hopeless? All you can do is run off to talk to Mummy. I'm the one who's left to sort this shit out.

He looked at her in surprise. Sensed her reaction had something to do with Jenny.

– In the first place, this is *your* shit.

– What did you say?

– Your shit, he repeated.

She slapped him; he felt a stinging from his chin up along his hairline and back across the top of his skull. The pain got him back on his feet.

– You never do anything, she hissed. – All you can do is talk.

He was on the edge. One more step and he would hit back. And then anything could happen. Suddenly he saw Trym, alone in the barn loft. Still with his back to that rickety door, blocking it with his body.

He backed away from her, leaned against the wall, suddenly

relieved, as though he had passed a test. Now it was possible to say what had to be said. And then leave her. If he'd hit her, he would be trapped.

– Ibro Hakanovic, he said, quite calmly. It was somewhere to begin. – He was the type that does things. Drug smuggling and murder. Doesn't matter what it is, as long as you *do* something.

– And what do you know about Ibro?

Sigurd pulled the chair out into the room, sat on his fists to keep them under control.

– You get everything on a plate, she said. – Mummy and Daddy take care of it all. You have no idea what other people have been through. You know nothing about Ibro, so please shut up about him.

He laughed, his laughter too cold, too high pitched. – I'm not particularly interested in the guy.

She stood up, looked out on to the street.

– Don't show yourself at the window.

With a quick jerk she closed the curtain. – Can you imagine what it's like to be held prisoner in a camp? Your mother and your sister raped. Over and over again. You're twelve years old and you're forced to watch. You know what that twelve-year-old thinks?

This wasn't what Sigurd wanted to talk about.

– He thinks it's his fault, she answered herself. – That he should have protected them. That was what Ibro did for the rest of his life, do you understand? He protected people. You are so fucking full of contempt for people you don't know anything about.

She went into the toilet, busy in there for a while, flushed.

Sigurd tried to hold on to what he had made up his mind to say. Tell her. Then take her with him to the police. Leave it to them to look after her, send her somewhere where no one knew who she was. New name, new appearance.

By the time she returned, he still wasn't ready to say what had to be said.

– And how do you know it's true? he asked.

– What?

– This about Ibro.

She took off her dress, lay down naked on the bed.

– He had documentation.

– What kind of documentation?

– Diaries, court papers, newspaper cuttings. I've seen some of it. He carried it about with him everywhere.

– But the people who raped and stuff like that were caught, Sigurd objected. – There were court cases for years afterwards. The war criminals were brought to justice.

She gave an overbearing smile.

– The really bad ones always get away. The ones who were supposed to punish the criminals ended up hiding them. That was what Ibro wanted to do with his life. Make sure those fucking killers got what they deserved.

So that's why he started smuggling drugs? Sigurd thought of asking but didn't.

– Ibro was afraid. He believed what happened back then could happen again, at any time. That the people who killed his family could come after him. That's what happens to you when you get damaged as a child.

– Okay, I understand all that.

– So that's why he hid things. Only showed them to people he trusted. Talked to me about it. I managed to persuade him to get a hold of himself when it got to be too much.

Suddenly a sound out in the corridor, footsteps on the carpet, stopping outside. Sigurd jumped to his feet.

– What is it?

He hushed her, padded across the floor, put his ear to the door. In that same instant, someone knocked, thunder pealing through his head.

– Get your clothes on, he whispered.

She looked at him in fright, grabbed her nightgown from the chair and covered herself with it.

He switched off the light, crossed to the window, opened it. They were two floors up, above a little patch of lawn next to the wall. Four cars parked on the far side of the road. He couldn't see anyone inside them. There was another knock, louder this time, and he thought he could hear a voice outside.

He sprang back to the door again. Indicated to Katja that she should get ready to jump out the window.

– Who is it?

A male voice said something or other. Sigurd got his phone from the bedside table, tapped in the emergency number, held it ready.

– I've called the police, he said into the crack. – They'll be here in thirty seconds.

– Sigurd, he heard. – I have to talk to you.

A few moments passed before it dawned on him who it was.

He pulled his shirt over his wounds. Waited until Katja had her nightgown on.

– You're getting us really worried, said Zoran when Sigurd opened the door slightly.

– What do you want? he asked, even though he already knew.

– Jenny . . . Zoran began.

– Did she say where I was?

– She didn't tell anyone else. She's sick with worry.

Sigurd put his head out into the corridor, checked there was no one else there. – So she sends you.

– So she sends me. Zoran nodded. – Can I come in for a few minutes?

Sigurd let him in. – And you're not being followed by anyone?

– CIA. That's all.

– Sit down, growled Sigurd, not laughing. He pointed to the chair by the desk.

– Hi, Katja, said Zoran, moving the clothes lying on it.

She took them from him, tossed them into her suitcase.

– How did you get into the hotel? Sigurd wanted to know.

– I booked in.

– Your own room?

Zoran fished something from his jacket pocket, waved a keycard. – The next floor. It was the only way to get in touch with you without causing a lot of unnecessary bother.

Sigurd didn't know if he liked Zoran, but there was something about his manner that was calming. Looking across at Katja on the bed, he could see that she reacted the same way.

– Mother's emissary, he said acidly. – An honourable posting.

– I'm not too concerned about honour, answered Zoran. – I wanted to see if there was anything I could do for you. Check that wound, for instance. He said it in a completely matter-of-fact way, as though offering to change a punctured tyre.

– And what else can you do for us?

Zoran scratched his unshaven chin. – Listen to what you have to say. Maybe give you some advice. If not, then I'll keep my mouth shut.

– What has Jenny told you?

– She tells me most things. It pains me when she's afraid. He pointed to his chest. – That's the way we are.

He nodded towards the bathroom. – Let's look at that stab wound first.

The gashes opened up again as Sigurd pulled off the bandage.

– Sit down on the toilet.

Zoran bent over him, examined the cut closely.

– When did this happen?

Sigurd glanced at his watch. – Seventeen or eighteen hours ago.

– It can still be stitched, but we'll have to wait a couple of days. You'll need a tetanus jab, and you must be careful to keep it clean and moist.

– If not?

– Then you'll be walking around with a scar like a war hero.

– Fine, as long as I don't have to go to A and E now. That's not an option.

Katja came in with a packet in one hand containing plasters and dressings, and some disinfectant in the other. Sigurd noted that the agitated look was gone from her eyes.

– Great, Zoran said to her. – You could have been a surgical nurse.

For an instant or two he seemed to be looking at the scratches on her cheeks.

– Is that what you were doing in town? Sigurd asked quickly. – Going to the chemist's?

She gave him a small smile. – I care about you. Haven't you realised that yet, Sigurd Woods?

After changing the bandages, Zoran washed his hands in the sink. Back in the room, he said: – I'll write you a prescription for antibiotics. But you're going to have to tell the police what you know soon.

He glanced at Katja. – What *both* of you know, he

corrected himself. – If you don't, Jenny's going to talk to them.

– Christ, she's my mother.

Zoran nodded. – That's why.

– We know what you mean, said Katja. She was sitting with her legs drawn up underneath her, wearing nothing but the flimsy nightdress. – We're happy you want to help us, she said, not taking her eyes off him.

Zoran appeared to be thinking.

– Have you ever been in a car crash? he asked suddenly.

Katja stretched her legs out in front of her. – Why do you ask?

– Something Ibro Hakanovic said at the hospital. That he had to talk to you about a car accident. That you weren't dead after all.

Her eyebrows arched. – Did Ibro say that? She got up, crossed again to the window.

– What did he mean? asked Zoran.

She turned and looked at him, suddenly more distant again, as though she were moving between memories. – Don't know, she said finally. – But you're right. We have to get this sorted out. We just need a few hours, then it will all be over.

– The police?

– I'll go to the police later today. Or Sigurd will.

Zoran looked at her for a long moment.

– You two know what you're doing?

Sigurd didn't answer.

– We know what we're doing, Katja said.

As Zoran was opening the door, Sigurd stopped him.

– Can I ask you something?

Zoran turned, half a head taller than him. – You know you can.

– We've got a voicemail message Ibro left for Katja. We can hear him being killed. Do you understand Bosnian?

– Bosnian and Serbian are the same language.

– Can you listen to it for us?

Sigurd held his hand out to Katja. She hesitated a few seconds before she picked up her phone, tapped in the code and handed it to him, left it to Sigurd to navigate to the message. He found it and passed the phone on to Zoran.

Zoran stood by the bathroom door, a thin strip of light from within crossing the cropped grey hair. It moved as he listened. Something changed in his face too. Starting at the forehead and spreading down his cheeks.

– I don't understand . . .

He tapped the screen, held the phone to his ear again. A different reaction this time; he nodded a couple of times, as though it were he Ibro Hakanovic was talking to.

– Can I take this with me? He looked at Sigurd.

– Don't see why not. At least the SIM card.

– No he can't, said Katja.

Sigurd stood in front of her. – Well, you've got the other phone.

– Mind your own business.

She pushed him aside, walked over to Zoran, took the phone from him. – I have to look after it.

Look after Ibro's voice, thought Sigurd. A tiny shrine where she can visit him.

– Has anyone else heard this? Zoran wanted to know.

– Why?

– What he's saying, I need to hear it again. He held out his hand.

Katja seemed to think about it, then gave the phone back to him. Zoran took a card from his pocket, a ballpoint pen. Clamped the phone between his ear and his shoulder and took notes as he listened for a third time.

– Then you'll be staying here.

It sounded more like a decision than a question.

– For the time being.

He turned, his hand on the doorknob.

– Jenny or I will call you at regular intervals, Sigurd. And you must answer. If not, the police will be here within three minutes. I'm serious.

Sigurd thought about it, half reluctant, part relieved. He picked up the bloodstained bandage, rolled it up and tossed it into the waste basket.

– I'll answer, he said. – Thank you for taking the trouble, he added.

Zoran nodded briefly and went out.

Afterwards, they sat beside each other below the window, half-naked bodies in the light from the night sky. Her breathing came more easily now, a deep sound he could feel through the hand that was touching her back. It occurred to him that it was he who kept her breath going. If he let go of her, she wouldn't be able to go on.

– Why did you ask him to listen to the voicemail? she asked suddenly.

He hesitated before answering. – Just a thought. In case what happened to Ibro had nothing to do with the gun or the gangs in Malmö.

She snuggled up to him, her cheek against his.

– Do you care about me, Sigurd?

Time to say it. No bullshit about still being friends. Do what had to be done, make sure she was somewhere safe. Then separate ways. Never meet again.

– Sure.

He pulled free. Something in her eyes, something that was always there during the early days.

– Pack your things, he said. – We'll go to another hotel.

– Why?

– Someone knows we're here. He stood up. – You've been out. So have I.

– Wouldn't they have been here long ago?

– We're leaving, he decided. He went into the toilet, emptied his bladder even though there wasn't much there. Washed himself with a cloth, cleaned away the pus that had seeped through the bandage. Tossed the cloth into the bin. Caught sight of the tip of something lying there. He lifted the paper that was obscuring the rest of it.

A small white stick at the bottom of the waste bin.

He picked it up between thumb and index finger. Knew at once what it was. It resembled a pen, but with a small window. Inside this light blue window, clearly visible, a plus sign.

Still holding it between the tips of his fingers, his hand out from his body, he went back into the room. Dropped it on the bed, right in front of her face. He couldn't say a word.

She sat bolt upright, wrapped her arms around her knees.

– I won't do it.

With her face buried between her legs, she began to rock back and forth.

– You hear what I say? There's no way I'll get rid of it. No way.

He slipped down the wall until he was sitting on the floor; it made the pain in his side worse. He needed that pain now.

39

ARASH HEARS WATER running. He crawls out of the hole below the boulders. As he emerges, it turns into a grave chamber. Someone moaning; the moaning spreads, as though the sound is flooding from the trees. He heads into the forest. She's still lying there by the stream. He bends over it; a face comes floating up through the liquid mirror.

He awoke with a start, stood in the middle of the floor in the bare room. For a few more seconds he continued to see that face, before it vanished.

In the bathroom, he washed his hands. Still that sticky substance on the back of one hand, impossible to get rid of it.

There was no towel. To get one he would have to talk to a nurse. No problem in thinking that through. The thoughts took hold, formed a chain, no longer piled up on top of each other and strained in all directions.

Two things he knew. He had to go back up there again, the place where he'd found Marita. Where the face in the water came into view.

And he needed to talk to Zoran, that was the other thing.

It wasn't Marita they were after up there in the forest, Arash. You know that.

Yes, I know that.

It was *you* they wanted to kill.

I understand that now.

There could be no witnesses to what was going to happen. Marita was killed because she was with you.

He saw himself lying on the headland by the water.

Because they dealt with her first, I had time to get away. I am alive because she is dead.

That was what he had to talk to Zoran about. Someone had tracked him down, followed him.

Why?

If he thought back, minute by minute, he would sooner or later find the answer. Ferhat the Kurd, sitting in his flat day after day, waiting for something. Was it the Iranian security services who had contacted him? And everyone he had seen in Lillestrøm when he was with Marita. He recalled the man he had followed and threatened with a butter knife. He looked like Ibro Hakanovic, but it couldn't have been him. A woman in red had passed, on her way to the station, and another woman, with a limp. The person in black in the forest had a limp too. He squeezed his eyes shut, tried to conjure up the figure again, see if it was the same leg.

He sat on the edge of the bed, rested his forehead in his hands. Could not work it out, where the connections were and what was just chance.

Ibro Hakanovic told me something that evening, he should have said to Zoran. *Is that why all this happened?*

What did he tell you?

He thought about it.

That is what I don't understand, Zoran.

He pulled back the curtain, clouds lifting, a wide chasm of blue across the sky. He struggled not to disappear up into it.

Later he went out into the corridor. No one in sight, no sounds of people. Everyone's gone, he thought, and headed towards the exit. The door glided open. Raino stood there.

– Hi, Arash. Sleep well?

– I have slept well. Have you?

Raino grinned. – I'll sleep when I get old.

Arash grinned too. – Can I take a shower? he asked.

– Glad you noticed it yourself. Raino nodded. – You're making progress. I'll bring you some fresh towels and something to wear.

But when he entered the room, he wasn't carrying clothing. Not towels, either. He held a telephone, which he handed to Arash.

– For you.

Arash took it. It was Knut Reinertsen.

– I won't be able to see you today as arranged. Something's come up. I'm very sorry about it.

– So am I, Knut Reinertsen.

Arash felt that he meant it.

– I want us to continue our conversation, Arash, as soon as possible. But unfortunately not today.

He could tell from Knut Reinertsen's voice that he was very busy, so it was most likely true that something had come up. But still he'd taken the trouble to call himself.

– While I've got you on the line, can you answer one question for me?

Arash thought about it. – You'll have to ask it first.

– I agree. It's about what happened at the hospital the evening the patient was killed.

While he listened to what Knut Reinertsen was asking about, Arash glanced over at Raino, who was still standing there playing with his keys.

– And you are quite certain about this? Knut Reinertsen said after Arash had answered the same question for the second time.

Arash closed his eyes and went through the situation again.
– I am quite certain.

– Have the police asked you about this?

He had had so many questions about that evening, but couldn't remember if this was one of them, and he said so to Knut Reinertsen.

– Now for that shower, said Raino after he got his phone back.

Arash stood for a long time watching the shower without walking into the stream. Easier to think to the sound of splashing water. Keep the thoughts separate, arrange them in their proper place. Rumi's poem written on the mirror in the cabin. It might have been a dream. Why was Knut Reinertsen so interested in that? And why did he call to ask him about the night Ibro Hakanovic died? Knut Reinertsen said he would be back. Suddenly Arash didn't know whether he wanted to talk to him again.

Clean clothes laid out on the bed. Dark blue tracksuit, red stripes down the arms and legs. Trainers in a box on the floor. They looked new, too.

– Where does all this come from? he asked Raino.

– You've got some good helpers, Arash. People like you.

It was obvious he didn't want to say it was Zoran who had arranged for the clothes.

Raino went into the bathroom, emerged with the towels.

– Have you used these? They're practically dry.

– I have used them.

– Okay. Breakfast?

– Can I eat here in my room?

– Room service? I'm sure that can be arranged. Juice? Bread? Ham and cheese? Nobody said anything about you wanting halal.

After he'd gone, Arash remained seated on the bed. For a moment, he saw a connecting thread to Knut Reinertsen; it ran off into the shadows. Someone was standing there holding it. Who are you working for, Knut Reinertsen?

Knut Reinertsen hadn't answered that question.

The food didn't arrive. He was thirsty, but apart from that he would be fine. He put on the shoes, walked into the bathroom. They fitted him, light and comfortable.

On the rim of the basin, a glinting silver chain with three keys attached to one link.

In a flash he saw the connection. The new clothes. The shoes. The keys left out for him. He shoved them into his pocket, where his own keycard was, let the water run until it was cold, drank, positioned himself by the wardrobe.

A few minutes passed before Raino appeared. His eyes searched the room. Arash watched him, leaning against the wardrobe door, all his muscles tensed.

– You haven't seen—

The nurse interrupted himself. As he entered the bathroom, Arash slipped out into the corridor. He'd made up his mind it was the biggest key, pushed it into the hole and locked, heard Raino shouting something or other inside. He walked quickly to the end of the corridor, rounded the corner, opened a door.

A woman was sitting in a chair by the window. She turned towards him. She was elegantly dressed, dark jacket with narrow stripes, skirt in the same pattern, gloved hands.

– Are you here to help me?

She stood up. Arash didn't know how to answer.

– Do you understand what that means? the woman went on. – That someone is in a position to help me?

Her eyes seemed to go hazy. She stood there, studying him.

– You are a good person, she said finally, in a voice that seemed wrapped in that same haze.

The alarm began to sound. Running footsteps outside.

Arash held a finger to his lips to say that what was happening out there had to do with him. The woman crossed the floor, laid a gloved hand on his arm. – You need a shower, she informed him in a low voice. – But you are a good person.

As Arash let himself out, he heard shouting from the corner where his room was. As calmly as he could, he headed for the door that led out of the crisis unit, chose the same key and let himself into the dining room. Someone sat eating at one of the tables. A young girl approached him.

– Don't go, she said, grabbing him by the arm.

He didn't know if she was a nurse or a patient, shook her off. She sat down on the floor and hid her face in her hands but said no more, and he carried on through the room, past an office door, someone inside talking very loudly on the phone. He knew where the main exit was; the same key, he didn't need any of the others. There was a connection, he thought again, the clothes, the shoes, the key. But it was one of the others that fitted.

In the corridor outside the psychiatric wing a policeman sat reading a newspaper. Arash permitted himself a nod. The man gave him a searching look, as though he was trying to remember something, but didn't shout until Arash was halfway down the stairs.

He speeded up, let himself into the basement with the keycard. Not the main entrance, he thought, and darted round the corner on the left. He knew every single corridor in this block, every staircase, and as he jogged off in the direction of the exit by the A&E, he burst out laughing at the thought of those in helpless pursuit of him.

40

JENNIFER HAD BEEN sleeping for half an hour. Not sleeping, but slipping in and out of a state in which images and thoughts mingled together beyond her control. Sigurd comes in and shouts something or other about a blue car, then goes out again. Something else crops up too, something to do with Arash; she hears him say her name and then something she can't make out.

When she opened her eyes to sunlight streaming in through a tiny hole in the roller blind, his voice was gone.

She sat up, grabbed her phone from the bedside table, called Sigurd, got straight through to his voicemail.

In the kitchen, she opened the fridge, closed it again, made do with a cup of coffee, couldn't face the thought of food.

In the course of the night her sinuses had become blocked and her face started to throb. She sprayed each nostril twice. Something is terribly wrong, she murmured. Why don't I go to the police? – Zoran, she said aloud, and picked up her phone again. At that moment he rang. She noticed that she was angry. Not at him, but she had nowhere to get rid of her anger.

He got her to sit down. He told her what had happened, that he had been to the hotel, and yes, Katja was there too, and the moment that name came up, Jenny's anger found a focus at last. That woman, who had broken into Sigurd's life and was using him, was about to destroy everything for him. Everything that had happened was because of her.

It helped to say this to Zoran. He didn't comment, just let her carry on until she calmed down.

— I'm going to the police, she said, not because she had made up her mind to, but because she had to know what he thought.

He didn't comment on this either.

— Shall I call them now?

— I don't know, Jenny. Sigurd says he's going to do it himself, in a few hours' time.

— And she's stopping him?

Zoran didn't answer at once. — He realises that he has to tell them what he knows, he said finally. — I think we should let him have the few hours he needs. I can go back again after lunch. I've got an operation now, but that shouldn't take long.

His concern even extended to Sigurd, as well as everything else that really mattered to her. Don't hang up, she thought, but he was gone already. Then she remembered what she should have asked him about. Arash had said that Ibro Hakanovic seemed to be sedated; his speech was slurred and his pupils constricted. But when she went through his admission papers, she couldn't see that he had been given anything stronger than paracetamol.

She was about to call Zoran back, but changed her mind and decided to wait until she had checked again.

The air outside was close. The heat like a damp film across her skin. Her whole face was throbbing, but it helped to be in motion. Four-minute walk to the hospital. Three minutes through the lobby, the lift, the corridors, to her office. One minute to boot up the computer.

Admission tests carried out on Ibro Hakanovic showed no signs of narcotics or other medications. She picked up the phone, explained to the person on duty at the Department of Forensic Toxicology who she was, why she needed the post-mortem blood analysis and why it was urgent. Those two words 'murder investigation' always made an impression. The person on duty promised to check, even though it wasn't his field.

Five minutes later, he called back.

– The samples from the deceased have been analysed, he said. – You'll get a copy of the results in a day or two.

She explained again why she needed it immediately. He had long ago accepted her argument, and his protests were simply for the sake of form, to let her know she couldn't ring at all hours of the day and night and expect answers to things she had on her mind.

– Shall I read out all the findings?

She drummed her fingers on the desktop. – I'm most interested in narcotics and medications. The tests from admission were clean, and I need to make a comparison.

She could hear him tapping on a keyboard.

– We did find something, he said finally.

– What?

– Morphine.

She shot to her feet, brushed her hair from her forehead, grabbed a pen.

– Amount?

The amount was read out at the other end. Even without checking the reference, she knew the levels were high.

She noted down the rest of the findings, the electrolytes, the haemoglobin and everything else she had asked them to analyse, registering as she went along that none of them were abnormal. Even remembered to thank the guy for taking the trouble to help her out in the middle of a busy watch, though she had no reason at all for thinking it was.

Seconds after she rang the bell, a figure appeared up in the window of the front room. She recognised the round face.

– Can I have a word with you? she said when he came out on to the balcony.

The junior doctor peered down at her in the bright light. He was wearing large spectacles and his hair was twisted up in a thin peak. – About what?

When he came down and let her in, he was holding a baby in a blanket to his shoulder.

– Didn't see who it was at first, he said apologetically.

– I tried to call you.

He sighed. – Supposed to be off free. All the way until two o'clock.

He went ahead up the stairs. – Free and free. Bit of an exaggeration to say free when you've got two sick kids. It's my shift. At home, I mean. An afternoon in the operating theatre is a lot more relaxing.

– Sorry. But this is important.

Only now did he hold out his free hand. – Finn Olav, but I guess you remember. He pointed to the bundle. – Don't let this fool you. The infant lay with its head resting against his shoulder and looked quite contented. – He starts screaming the moment I try to put him down.

Finn Olav indicated that she should go into the room first.

– He's kept it up all night. Have a seat.

She sat on one of the straight-backed chairs by the dining table. – It's about the patient who was murdered.

– The patient? For a moment there I was worried it might be something to do with Zoran.

She looked up at him. – Zoran, why him?

Finn Olav carried on pacing up and down with the bundled infant held to his shoulder. – Well, I know you and he have—

– You examined the patient when he was admitted, she interrupted.

– Correct.

– According to the papers, you didn't give him any medication apart from paracetamol.

– Correct.

– And yet he had a high concentration of morphine in his blood when he died.

Finn Olav stopped so abruptly that the baby's eyes opened.

– That's nonsense. Guaranteed one hundred and ten per cent.

– The test results show that you're wrong, she insisted. – No matter how many per cent certain you are.

He shook his head. The infant wriggled.

– He didn't get so much as a single nano-gram of morphine from me.

– And not from anyone else either?

He rolled his eyes. – The man had been unconscious, probably a minor injury to the head. It was necessary that he be observed without being under the influence of strong painkillers. That's kindergarten stuff.

She knew that too.

– If necessary, he could be given another paracetamol. Nothing stronger, and certainly not without contacting me first.

– Did you discuss it with anyone?

He shook his head. – Would I bother anyone on call with something like that? I rang Zoran to get the okay for the admission. Zoran had seen the patient in the corridor at the emergency unit. There was no need for him to come down from the operating theatre for something like that. After all, I've had almost four years' experience in the unit. He held up four fingers, gave them a little wave.

– Could the nurses have given him something without your permission?

– If so, then they need stringing up. And I shall personally make sure that whoever did it is boiled alive first.

He appeared to be thinking about it. – These are experienced people, after all. I know some of the nurses can start to get ideas, boss people around and carry on as if they had ten years at university rather than three years at nursing college. But none of them are *that* stupid.

The little boy began whimpering. Finn Olav bounced him up and down, not that it seemed to do much good. – And he hadn't taken anything before he was admitted?

– The admission tests show no trace of morphine.

– What does it say in his journal?

She took several deep breaths, suddenly dizzied by the bouncing of the baby, as though it were her who was being lifted up and down like that.

– Nothing about painkillers, she said.

Finn Olav tut-tutted and shook his head. – Bit of a cock-up. And then not entering it in the journal.

He whistled; it might have been the opening bars of Beethoven's Fifth, though rather than being despondent, he seemed to be deriving a curious enjoyment from the situation.

– *If* it was a cock-up, Jennifer murmured.

When she emerged from the lift on the fifth floor, Lydia was standing there.

– I was just looking for you, she exclaimed. – You look pale.

Jennifer leaned against the wall for support.

– Didn't get much sleep. My sinuses are blocked. Nothing serious.

Lydia linked arms with her, walked her down the corridor, opened the door to Jennifer's office.

– Sit down on the sofa, she said after she closed the door.

She filled a mug with water, put it in front of Jennifer.

– You wanted to talk to me?

Lydia nodded. – I need to check some of our results again. There's something that doesn't add up. Rather odd.

Jennifer nodded at her computer. Right at this moment, there were few things that meant less to her than the research project.

She tried to pull herself together. – It's on. I'll find the images for you.

Lydia raised a hand. – It can wait. You're driving yourself too hard. She gave her a professional look. – You'd better go home and rest, she said firmly. – We're going to the cabin tonight. By the time you arrive tomorrow, everything will be ready.

Jennifer couldn't face telling her the truth, that this was about the last thing she wanted to do.

– Table laid and spiders' webs removed.

Lydia said it with a smile, probably recalling the arachnophobia Jennifer had once offered as the reason why she had left her homeland.

Just then the phone rang. Roar Horvath.

– I have to take this.

Jennifer got to her feet, still unsteady. She should have contacted him long ago. Told him her own son was involved in some way or other and that she needed to give a statement. She should have offered her profound apologies for not having told him at once. Withdrawn from any further active involvement in the investigation.

– I was actually just about to call you, she said after Lydia had let herself out, and at least it wasn't a very big lie.

– What did you want to talk to me about? His voice sounded sharp, and it occurred to her that he might have already found out about Sigurd.

– Something I discovered as I was going through the test

results, she said quickly. – Ibro Hakanovic was given a large dose of morphine at the hospital, but there's no record of it in his journal.

Brief pause.

– And that means?

– Hard to say. Someone might have given it to him as the result of a misunderstanding and said nothing in the hope that the mistake wouldn't be found out.

– Or?

She thought about it, even though she'd already considered the possibility several times over the last few minutes.

– Or someone gave it to him for reasons other than medical.

– Trying to kill him?

– Hardly, the dose wasn't big enough. But the aim might have been to slow him down.

She thought of something. – Arash said he knew the patient had been given morphine. I think he said it was injected. I'm pretty sure that's what he meant.

– Injected by whom?

– He didn't say. Maybe it's in his interrogation report.

– That could be checked.

– Or you could ask him now.

– No, we can't.

– Why not?

He didn't answer. Instead he said: – I hear you're very friendly with one of the surgeons over there.

She felt her face burning up. And then anger.

– And if I am, what relevance does that have?

– Relevance to what?

– For the case.

– You've had access to a lot of privileged information. I've shared this with you on the understanding that you have no personal involvement with any of those connected to the case.

She hurried out into the corridor. The research student was standing there, trying to say something or other to her, something about the computer. Jennifer waved her away with her free hand.

– And now you've heard that I do, in fact, have such an *involvement*? she said to Roar Horvath.

He made a guttural sound, of uncertain meaning, but it wasn't pretty.

– This surgeon is apparently friendly with Arash Rahimi. And you knew that.

She didn't respond.

– The point is, Roar Horvath went on, – that information was given to you in strictest confidence, and what we're finding now is that there is one hell of a mess of interconnected stuff here. Had I known about this, my approach to you would have been different.

She stopped at the lift, her anger suddenly gone, dreading like a child what she was about to say, what still remained unsaid.

– Sorry, she said weakly. – I didn't mean to cause trouble for you.

Again that guttural noise from the other end.

She opened her mouth to tell him that her association with those involved in the case went much, much deeper than he thought.

– I did the job I was asked to do, she began.

– You have done a great deal more, Roar Horvath growled. – You've really fucked things up and made a right hash of things, and now I have to get out there and sort it out.

She tried to imagine where *out there* might be.

– I can explain—

– I just hope you can, he interrupted. – Because it won't be to me.

He hung up. It was past nine o'clock; the departmental meeting had started long ago. She was never absent without leaving a message. The phone was still in her hand. She ought to call Roar Horvath again. He had to be told about Sigurd. And about Katja and the connection with Ibro Hakanovic, about the woman with a limp, who might well be in Oslo, hunting down her son.

Instead she called Sigurd. When she got no answer, she tried the hotel. They claimed to have no record of anyone with that name there.

– He arrived yesterday, she explained. – Blond, well-built young man, good-looking. With a dark woman. She speaks Swedish.

Short pause.

– Who is this?

– This is his mother.

A sound that might have been a snigger.

– They aren't here now.

– Yes they are.

– They checked out fifteen minutes ago.

41

Back seat of a taxi. Katja with her head pressed against his chest, clammy hands under his T-shirt. Sigurd felt as though she wanted to crawl inside him. He sat up straight, released himself from the pressure of her body.

– I'm glad, she said suddenly.

He didn't know what she was referring to and didn't respond.

– *You* aren't, though. Think I can't tell?

He glanced up at the rear-view mirror, the driver's eyes following the traffic in the road ahead.

– Maybe you'll be happy about it. One day.

He wouldn't be. She would never have a place in his life. That was what he ought to say to her, use those very words. But first help her out of this mess she'd got herself into.

– When I'm with you, she said, her voice so low he could pretend he hadn't heard. – I don't know. I know almost nothing. But when I'm with you, I know who I am.

He looked out at Ullevål stadium, fixed his gaze on one of the floodlights.

– Since I met you, everything's changed, Sigurd. I can get away from all the crap. Once and for all.

Her phone rang.

– Shouldn't you take that? he asked when she made no move to do so.

– Why should I?

He grabbed it out of her bag.

– It's Sting, he said. – We need to hear what this is, okay?

He swiped the answer icon, held the phone to her ear.

There was a mumbled conversation, monosyllabic words, reluctant, or frightened, or indifferent. He grew even more irritated.

– Any news from Gangland? he said as soon as she put the phone back into her bag. He hadn't intended to adopt that tone, but couldn't stop himself. – Has your friend found out what happened down there? he asked in a more neutral voice.

She leaned her head against his chest again. – Everyone he's talked to denies all knowledge of it. Mujo and the boy.

– You've got to tell me everything this Sting guy said.

She wriggled a little. – He's had a meeting with some of the guys in the same gang as Ibro. If they get this gun, they'll leave me alone. Or if I get rid of it myself once and for all.

– And if it should ever somehow re-emerge?

– Well, what do you think would happen?

Again he tried to imagine it.

– Helping them get rid of crucial evidence in a murder case doesn't bother you?

She scraped a nail across her cheek; a tiny drop of blood appeared in one of the cuts. – I can't think like that. Not if I'm going to get out of this.

He thought of something. – Give me the other phone. The one with the message from Ibro.

She did as he said. He navigated to it.

You're the only one who knows where the proof is . . . I can prove . . . Katja, you must fetch them.

He played it again a couple of time. Should have asked Zoran what was being said in Bosnian. Wondered whether to call him.

– He says pick *them* up. *Them*. Is there more than one gun?

– No.

– Do you know someone called Ludmilla Golobova or something like that?

She shook her head.

– He mentions the name several times. Or something that sounds like that. Think.

– Don't you understand? I'm thinking all the time.

– You said something about Ibro's mother. When we were at the hotel.

She peered up at him, her eyes glazed.

– What about her?

– You said she was dead.

Katja changed position slightly. – She was killed when she refused to leave her daughter. In the camp where they were held prisoner. They were carrying out experiments there.

– Experiments? On the prisoners?

She didn't answer.

– They weren't in a fucking Nazi concentration camp, Sigurd protested. He saw the flash of anger in her eyes.

– Okay. He clenched his fists, relaxed them again. – It just sounds a bit . . . extreme.

– It *is* extreme.

They turned off the ring road. Sigurd explained where the hotel was; the driver looked at him in the mirror.

– I know, he said.

Sigurd looked away. Just then a phone rang, his own this time.

– Haven't you spoken to them yet? Jenny said, her voice full of reproach.

– To who?

– You were going to go to the police. We made an agreement—

– Listen, he interrupted her, and she fell silent, but he didn't know what to say.

– You have really got to wake up now, she said suddenly.

– What's the matter with you? he replied angrily.

He heard her take several deep breaths before she responded.

– We are talking about four murders, Sigurd. You possess information that is important to the investigation. And this gang could be after you too.

– It's not like you think, he protested.

– And how do I think?

– You think Katja has done something that—

– That's what you said.

He felt as if he was about to take a huge gamble. – It's possible Ibro was killed because of something that happened years ago.

– Don't be ridiculous.

– His mother and sister were killed in Bosnia.

– What are you talking about?

– They were held in a camp. Apparently experiments were being done on the prisoners. Ibro spoke to Katja about it a lot. He was gathering evidence. Someone might have found out. Followed him to the hospital.

He heard a sound at the other end, as though she had dropped the phone on the floor. A few seconds later, she was back on the line.

– And why do you believe these stories? There was still anger in her voice. He could never handle it, always ended up doing something to get her sounding normal again.

– The people Katja knows in Malmö say they don't understand any of what's happened.

– And what does that prove?

– There's something else. Ibro left a voice message on Katja's phone. I think maybe he refers to it there. This thing that happened in Bosnia.

– And you have access to this message?

Sigurd explained. She cut him off.

– If he's speaking Bosnian, how do you know what he's saying?

– Only some of it is in Bosnian.

He had another thought.

– In the café, you asked me about a woman with a limp. Could her name be Ludmilla Golobova or something like that? I think he mentions that name several times.

– I don't know, Sigurd. If you bring the phone here, I'll get Zoran to listen to the message.

– Zoran has already heard it.

– He has?

– Last night, when he was with us.

– And?

– And what?

– What did he think?

– Nothing special. He asked if he could take the phone with him.

– I'll call you back, she groaned. – And I want you to answer at once.

They pulled up in front of the hotel. He got Katja to sit up.

– Wait here. He nodded to the driver, opened the boot, took out the bags, walked in with Katja.

– I think you're wrong about what Ibro was trying to say, she told him as they stood in the hotel reception.

– Maybe, he answered, relieved that she seemed to have woken up a bit.

– I need to get up there and find that gun.

He shook his head. – *I'll* do that. You wait here.

She stared at him. – That's not going to happen. You're not to go there. Ever.

The look she gave him reminded him of when they first

met. As though it might after all be possible to live with
her. The thought was there for a second, maybe two. And
then gone, and again that feeling of being stifled. Something's
wrong with me, he thought. I'll never be able share my life
with anyone.

— I don't have any choice, he said, and that was what it
felt like. If I'm to be able to leave you, he added to himself,
then I must do this for you. And then we're even.

As though it was all about an unpaid bill.

42

A FEW MONTHS previously, Arash had seen an advert on TV for trainers. Running turned into a state that required no energy from the runner, all the energy coming from the soles of the shoes. That was how it felt now. As though his new shoes sucked up power through the farm track and ran it through his body. A tractor stood out in the yard with its engine running, but he didn't see anyone there. He jogged on between the fields and up to the forest track, into the smell of the corn, of cow muck and yellow flowers he didn't know the name of.

Suddenly he stopped. Not because he was tired, though he was breathing deep in his chest. He stood there and listened. A slight wind in the spruce trees, almost in rhythm with his own breath. The sound of a tractor, far away now. In the sky above, a plane dragged its tail of white foam through the blue.

The birds.

They sounded different. He was able to distinguish the various notes. Some as thin as needle points, others long, dark threads. But they wanted nothing of him. It was nothing more than birdsong, and it hurt to know that. No one saw him, no one knew he was here; from now on, he was on his own.

On the headland where they had bathed, he stopped and looked out. A breeze had risen, small ruffles on the black surface of the water. A length of security tape still dangling there. He ducked under it, found the path between the trees, followed it up beside the stream. Came to the fallen pine, started across to the other side, slipped on a rotten branch, one foot dangling in the water, his shoe soaked so that it squished with every step he took as he walked on through the trees. He had to look for a while before he found the bog and the little slope he had climbed up. Again he stopped to listen out. Nothing but the wind and the birds. The sun was high, but the clouds were rushing in from all sides, and as the light greyed, a few drops of rain fell in his hair. He scuttled down the other side, landing right next to the boulders, crept in below them. He stayed in that little shelter for a long time, looking out at the rain, at the drops that placed themselves one by one on the fern leaves.

He closed his eyes. Imagined it had been here he hid during his flight. Imagined the person in black suddenly appearing at the edge of the clearing, heard the approaching steps. A branch snapping. He started, lay motionless until he had regained his composure.

When he looked up, there was no one. He got up, stood where his pursuer had stood, stepped slowly over to the place where he had lain hidden, stood there until at last he could see Arash stand up. The head visible first, then the chest, the hips, the dangling genitals in the bracken. Arms outstretched, as though begging for his life.

I see you, Arash. You can go now.

The naked body turns and disappears between the trees.

By the time he arrived back at the fallen pine trunk, the rain was heavier. He raised his face and stuck out his tongue. At that moment he felt an overpowering thirst. He fell to his knees and, bending his face, lapped at the surface of the water. It tasted of earth and metal.

Looking into the liquid mirror, he could see the face from his dream, the bony, chalk-white outline around the empty eyes. His own appeared behind it, as though it rose towards him from the bottom of the stream, the eyes still indistinct. But it *is* you, he murmured.

– You shouldn't drink that water.

He whirled round, got to his feet, for a moment shot through with what had made him flee. Then he realised that the man standing on the other side of the stream was wearing a uniform, and a cap with a police badge on it.

– Dead animals, the policeman explained. – And all the dogs that run around up here and shit.

Arash dried around his mouth. – I guess I'll live.

The policeman shook his head slowly. – Where you come from, you're probably not used to clean water.

Arash had to laugh, and it felt good. – We mostly drink sewage, he said.

The other did not laugh.

– Out jogging?

He considered the question. He was out, and he had run most of the way.

– Yes, I am out jogging.

– Didn't you see that this whole area has been cordoned off?

– I saw the tape, Arash replied. – But presumably there's no law against being here.

Now the policeman parted his lips, revealing sharp teeth beneath his greying moustache. – What do you think the tape is for?

Arash looked around. – Something happened here.

The policeman took a step closer. – Yes, he said. – *Something* did happen, right where we're standing.

– Is that why you're here? Arash wanted to know.

– I see you don't read the newspaper, the policeman said. – They're still writing about it. But not the details. Not how they found her. Not who she was, because they don't know that. Her name, yes. Her age. Where she came from. But not who she was. *Have* you read about it in the papers?

His tone reminded Arash of the interrogations he'd been through.

– Not much.

– Because presumably you're not wandering about here because you want to know what the scene of a murder looks like. The policeman's eyes narrowed. – The throat cut, the blood jetting into the stream. That's not what you're after, is it? Imagining what happened here, what it was like for her to look into the eyes of her killer.

He was evidently not interested in Arash's answer, because he carried on talking, never looking away from him.

– They say she wasn't raped. Naked woman in the forest, cut open with a knife. Clothes found down by the lake. They arrested a guy who was up here with her. They let him go. No proof, that's what they're saying now. Alone with her, here in the depths of the forest, off he runs. Insane foreigner. And they don't have any proof. Or they believe his story. See where I'm going?

Arash had to look away.

– Where you come from, they don't muck about if someone's had it away with someone they shouldn't, do they?

– What does that mean, *had it away?*

The policeman gave a quick laugh.

– If a woman goes with a man who isn't the man she's married to, she gets sentenced to be stoned, isn't that right? The bloke she's with, too. Or the family deal with it. Imagine if that was what happened here. He pulled the peak of his cap down lower. – Only a person who's deaf and blind could fail to notice when something like that happens right under his nose. You don't need to sneak a look at the interrogation reports to know it. He spat into the stream. – What do you think would have happened if he'd left that shooting club meeting without telling anyone? It's not much more than an hour's drive away. What do you think? If he'd come home and found them at it? He made a gesture, drawing his finger sideways across his throat. – Both of them. But if they weren't fucking well there, if they've slipped off into the forest somewhere and he can't find them, what then?

Arash might have turned and run, as fast as he could. Something told him not to do that. It's you who's the snake now, Arash. You mustn't move.

– She's all right where she is now, said the policeman. – It's more than she deserved. It's about the ones left behind, isn't it?

Arash didn't move a muscle.

– Imagine if it was you who was waiting in the evenings. You carry on laying the table and making dinner for her. As though she'll be coming back from that walk.

He took a step closer to Arash, staring at him, his eyes burning Arash's cheeks. He said something or other, Arash didn't hear what it was, forced himself to look across at him, into the narrow bloodshot eyes.

– Go now, the man repeated. – Get out of here. Don't let me ever see you again.

The third time he rang, Zoran answered.

– Are you all right?

Arash was panting. – Been running.

– Where are you?

Arash looked around, even though he knew where he was.

– A shopping centre.

– In Lørenskog?

– Metro. Borrowed a phone in a shop. Cubus. Thanks for the clothes and the shoes.

– I was going to visit you, Arash. Why did you have to run off? You were safe where you were.

Arash slumped down on to a stool in a changing room. The sound of Zoran's voice calmed him.

– Knut Reinertsen, he said. – He says he knows you.

– That's right.

– Is he working for someone?

– I asked him to have a chat with you. You can trust him.

– He asked me some odd things. About Ibro Hakanovic.

– Arash, listen to me. You know I want to help you?

He knew that.

– You must do as I say now. You must come to my flat. As quickly as you can. It's safe here. This will soon be over.

– Yes, replied Arash. – If you say so.

– Stay away from people. Don't talk to anyone about what's happened. If anyone asks you about Ibro Hakanovic, don't say anything. Not until I've talked to you.

And then he understood.

– It's the morphine, isn't it? That Ibro Hakanovic was given.

Zoran didn't answer.

– That's why all this is happening.

– I'll explain when you get here, Arash. And then you'll have nothing to be afraid of any more.

43

JENNIFER THREW OFF her white coat, hurried down the stairs to the radiology department, opened the door to the meeting room a fraction. One of the radiologists was showing pictures to the surgeons. Zoran wasn't there.

Two minutes later, she was standing at reception in his department.

– I'd like to speak to Zoran Vasic.

The secretary tapped some keys, looked at the screen.

– He's gone for the day.

– That can't be right. Jennifer shook her head, unleashing a blinding pain into her sinuses. – Doesn't he have an operation straight after lunch?

More tapping of keys. – It appears he's made a swap.

Back in pathology, she let herself into her office. Should have gone home, taken another paracetamol, had a lie-down. The thought of doing nothing was distressing.

She booted up her machine, clicked on to the research project, had half a mind to find out what Lydia was talking about, that something didn't add up, but got instead an error message saying the program could not be accessed and turned the machine off again, got up out of her chair. She stood at the window, staring out for several minutes. Trying to sort out her thoughts, look at her alternatives. She knew what she should do, but not in what order. Call Roar Horvath. Talk to Zoran first. Before anything, call Sigurd again. She was the one who had to help him out of this mess. Don't put a foot wrong, she mumbled to herself. You mustn't ruin everything. The blue car. What did he mean, saying she had a visitor at the farm? As though she didn't know. She tapped her fingers on her cheekbone and felt the pus building up inside. Sean's car was blue, could well have been a Renault, she'd been in it many times. She had told him he was never to visit her at the farm, but he ignored rules and regulations like that. And when he did arrive, she'd been unable to get him to leave; he had that effect on her, he paralysed her will. It had happened twice, with Ivar at work and the boys at school. But now it turned out they hadn't been at school after all. She pinched the side of her neck so hard that it made her gasp.

The door behind her opened.

– I thought you'd gone home sick, Jenny.

Zoran stood in the middle of the floor.

– Something I had to finish first.

– I hear you were asking for me.

– She is destroying him.

He stroked her neck. – You mean Katja?

She nodded.

– She's unscrupulous and unstable.

It wasn't Katja she ought to be talking to him about. She half turned and looked up at him. He looked worried too, his forehead a sea of wrinkles.

– They've left that hotel.

He gave a start. – I told him to stay put. Where are they?

– Another hotel.

– Do you know which one?

She shook her head.

– You ought to find out.

– I've talked to the police, she said, and could feel how heavy her own breathing was.

The frown on his forehead deepened. — Did you tell them about Sigurd?

— I couldn't bring myself to.

She related what Roar Horvath had said, that she had abused his trust.

Zoran's eyes changed, growing narrower and darker. — We haven't done anything wrong, Jenny.

Of course they hadn't.

— You listened to a voicemail recording, she said. — Ibro Hakanovic.

He gave a slight nod.

— Why didn't you mention that?

He took hold of her shoulders. It felt as though he were stopping her from falling over. — You have enough to worry about.

— Sigurd thinks there's something important in that message.

— We'll have to see, he said.

She felt a huge weight in her face, as though her sinuses had filled up and were constricting. The whole of her upper jaw throbbed.

— You never talk about yourself, she said suddenly.

— Don't I?

— I'd so much like to know more, see more, share more. You came from a place, from a whole life, before I met you.

He wagged his head a couple of times.

— Didn't we agree not to dig into each other's past?

They had indeed. It was liberating when they met. Start afresh, no need to account for all the faults and mistakes.

— What do you want to know, Jenny?

She picked up her bag, put it down again. — For example, you have a daughter. You never talk about her. She ran a hand across her forehead; it was cold and damp. — I always wanted a daughter.

– I know that.

– Yes, because you know so much more about me than I do about you.

It sounded like an accusation. He looked out of the window, an ambulance helicopter flying above the blocks, heading northwards.

– There isn't a lot to tell, Jenny. She fell ill once. The way children do. Usually it's something trivial, but not this time. I should have realised, but I left it too late. That's what happens when the father's a doctor. It left her damaged for life. No one said anything, but everyone blamed me. And they were right to.

He removed the arm that had been holding her. She slumped slightly.

– I have you, she said.

– You have me.

– Do you promise?

He was smiling now, but looked sadder than she could ever recall seeing him before. – Promise.

She went out with him, took out her keycard.

– Are you on your way home?

He nodded.

– Can I . . .

– Not now. There's something I have to do.

– Can't it wait?

– No, it can't wait.

She opened her mouth, couldn't let him go without asking.

He placed a finger over her lips. – Later, Jenny. I'll come over. We'll talk more about it this evening.

She held him back by the arm. – You said you hadn't seen Ibro Hakanovic.

He rubbed his temple. A short grey hair came loose and drifted on to his shoulder.

– The junior doctor claims you spoke to him in reception.

He wrinkled his brow, as though trying to remember.

– I didn't *speak* to the patient. I took a look at him as I was passing. Ascertained that he was conscious. Why are you asking me this, Jenny?

He freed himself from her grip. The corridor swayed up and down, like a boat deck. She took hold of his arm again, gripping hard.

– Forget it, she said. – It isn't important.

44

Sigurd got the taxi driver to drop him by the petrol station, walked the rest of the way. After a while, a car passed coming from the other direction. He turned up his collar, looked away. He was there to help Katja get rid of a weapon used in a murder committed in a Malmö bar. Then it would be over. But not with her. If she meant what she said, he would stay attached to her for the rest of his life. He brushed the thought aside, imagined himself putting it in a drawer and then closing it. Maybe open it later, when he was able to think more clearly.

He straightened up, started to walk faster. Two cars parked outside one of the garages he passed. But the house where Ibro Hakanovic had been staying still looked deserted, the police tape gone now. He rang the bell, waited for a minute before making a circuit around the house. The cellar door was locked now, but he'd bought a hammer on the way, the smallest one they had. A cellar window was the obvious choice. He struck at it three times before it broke, stuck his hand through the hole and flipped up the catch, wriggled through and down on to the stone floor among the shards of broken glass.

He looked into the kitchen. Dirty dishes in the sink, some glasses, a couple of beer bottles, a dried-out plant. Couldn't see anything that looked different. According to Katja, the owners of the house would be back sometime in the summer.

On a sheet of paper she'd drawn where he should look.

It was obvious she knew the house inside out, but he'd avoided saying anything about that. But she confused left and right; the bathroom wasn't where she had put it on her drawing. He oriented himself, opened the doors to all the rooms on the first floor. Three were bedrooms. One was clearly a girl's, pink wallpaper, pictures of dogs and a bed full of cuddly toys. The next one was larger, with a double bed beneath a window facing out on to the fields. The bed was made, but the blanket left in an untidy heap. This was where Ibro Hakanovic had slept at night. Alone, or with her. Ibro couldn't have her. Not the way he could. According to her. He pulled a face and felt it freeze into place.

The third bedroom looked unused. Katja had called it a guest room. The curtain half closed, a thick layer of dust on the desk. He returned to the room with the double bed. In the wardrobe, she'd said. What kind of idiot hid things in a wardrobe, the first place anyone would look? But no one had been there and pulled the contents out. If a gang leader in Malmö thought Ibro had hidden evidence that could put him away for life, he would have sent someone up here and turned the house inside out.

He opened the cupboard. It was full of towels, bedlinen, T-shirts and shirts. Women's panties, quite large. He quickly searched through it. Then again, more systematically. Finally he tried to call her. A few minutes later, she rang back.

– I was in the bathroom, she apologised.

He told her where he'd looked.

– It's the other room, Sigurd.

– There are three bedrooms here, he growled.

– The smallest one.

– The child's room?

– Yes, I told you that.

That was not what she had said. He went back in there.

– The second or third shelf.

He thought he heard a car, hurried to the guest-room window, couldn't see anything on the road. Back in the child's room, he carried on searching behind the shelves.

– There's no loose plank here.

– Then try one of the others.

He could feel his anger building but just gave a grunt. It sounded like a bark. He reached up and pulled down the things from the top shelf, boxes with old games. Whac-A-Mole and Spooky Stairs. Monopoly, which slipped from his hands and fell to the floor, the pieces and notes scattered all over the carpet, along with a pile of CDs.

– Is there a hiding place there?

He tapped; it sounded hollow. He picked up a broken CD case, wedged it into a gap in the wall at the back of the cupboard and levered. The plank moved. He put down the phone, found another CD case, levered with both hands. The plank came loose; he pulled it out and felt inside. Took out a folder full of paper, mostly old newspaper cuttings. He clambered up on to the bottom shelf, got his whole hand inside, felt all around the space before jumping down and picking up the phone again.

– There's no gun here.

– There has to be!

– Come and check for yourself, he snapped.

– Is there nothing there?

– A folder.

He picked it up, opened it.

– Newspaper cuttings, notes, printouts. Looks to be in Bosnian.

– All that old stuff, she groaned.

– What are you talking about?

– Ibro's documentation. About what happened to his mother and his sister.

– I'll take it with me.

– It's the gun we need, Sigurd.

– Don't you understand, it's not here. You've been tricked. He lied to you.

He piled the games and the other stuff back on to the shelves. Sat down on the bed, brushed aside some of the fluffy toys. In a flash of annoyance, he grabbed the largest of them, a stuffed Eeyore, and tossed the donkey at the wall on the far side of the room. It hit the ground with a dull thud.

– I need to talk to Sting. If you don't find anything—

– Wait, he said, and picked the toy up again. – He wasn't stupid enough to hide it in here, was he?

Eeyore had a seam along his underbelly; a couple of the stitches had come loose. Sigurd tore them apart, ripped open the whole stomach, plunged his fist inside, pulled out a plastic bag.

– Sigurd, what is it?

He turned the bag inside out without touching the contents, something wrapped in a stained piece of cloth.

– Found it, he told her. – It's wrapped inside a towel that looks to be covered in blood.

– I knew it, she shouted. – What are you going to do now?

– Get out of here.

Suddenly it felt like a matter of urgency. He packed the gun back inside the plastic bag, grabbed up the folder with the cuttings and notes, left the room and made his way downstairs as calmly as he could.

– Everything'll be all right now, Sigurd. Everything will be okay.

He could hear she was close to tears, and suddenly pitied her. Mostly because of what he had not yet managed to say to her.

In the hallway, he wedged the folder down the back of

his trousers. Two or three cuttings fell out. As he picked them up, one caught his eye. Something about an accident, a large photo of the squashed wreck of a car. Two smaller photos showed a man and a woman. He stood there looking at them for a few seconds before pushing open the kitchen door. He put the folder on the bench beneath the window and studied the pictures more closely. Several of the other cuttings appeared to be about the same accident. They were dated October 1995.

45

KATJA WAS STILL talking to him, something about how often she thought about that first evening they were together.

– Do you understand, Sigurd? she said again. – I knew, the moment I laid eyes on you—

– Zoran asked you about something, he interrupted before she could say what it was she had known that moment. – When he was in the hotel room. As he was leaving. He asked you about a car crash.

– Did he?

– Ibro had said something about it at the hospital.

– I don't know anything about it. Why would I lie about a car crash?

Why did she lie at all?

– That's not what this is about, he said firmly. – What else do you know about what you were talking about earlier, about those experiments in Bosnia?

– But you said you didn't believe any of it.

– That's not what I said. What did Ibro tell you?

– His mother and sister were killed. Those bastards cut people's organs out.

– Who did?

– The doctors.

– You mean all the doctors were psychopaths, something like that?

– Some of them were. There was one especially that Ibro

hated. A doctor who was supposed to be helping them. Who turned out to be the worst of them all.

Sigurd flipped on through the folder. – Did he say anything else about this doctor?

– Can't remember. I didn't want to hear about all the shit he'd been through. I'm finished with that stuff. Everything's going to be different now.

Sigurd spread several other cuttings out across the table, leaned over them, looking from one picture to the next.

– I'll call you later, he said suddenly. – And you stay in the hotel room, you got that?

He hung up and found *Jenny* on his contacts list.

Jennifer let herself in. Couldn't even face unfastening her sandals, took two paracetamol, slumped down on the sofa, head on the armrest, jiggled a pillow under her neck. It was past twelve, the sun was at its highest; she wished it could be turned off, darkness at last.

She felt at once that the paracetamol weren't going to work. She had a packet of co-codamol in the bathroom. Lay there summoning the strength to get up and fetch them. Dozed, woke from her slumber with a jolt, because she mustn't sleep, sat up, called Roar Horvath's number. Not sure how much to tell him. Start with what Sigurd had said. Maybe this Malmö connection had set them off on the wrong trail. Maybe Ibro Hakanovic and his uncle were killed for another reason. The phone kept ringing. Still no answer. She felt even more desperate. She must tell Roar Horvath that they had to search for something else, something lying in the shadow of what they were looking at.

Three, four rings. Another call came in; she looked at the display.

– Sigurd, are you there?

He was. Spoke in a low voice.

– Are you still at the hotel?

– No.

– Sigurd, I've rung the police. I'll try again in a minute. Then I'll tell them everything—

– Zoran asked Katja about a car accident, he interrupted her.

– Do you hear what I'm saying? she shouted. – Go to the police at once.

– I'm sitting here looking at some old newspaper cuttings Ibro Hakanovic collected. And copies of articles.

– Where are you?

– In the house where Ibro was living.

– In Nittedal?

– He had these cuttings in a hiding place behind a cupboard. Several of them are about a car crash. There are pictures of what appear to be the victims.

She slipped back down on to the sofa. – Can you read what it says?

– It's Bosnian, or Serbian, or something like that.

She forced herself to ask: – And the other papers?

– Don't know. Some from the war back then. At least from the nineties, judging by the dates.

She could hear him flipping over pages.

– And something from a hospital.

– Hospital?

– Picture of some doctors. Looks like they're in an office. He lowered his voice even more. – Five people in white coats.

Something heavy spread through her, all the way out to her fingers. She felt as though she'd never be able to stand up again.

– Here's more about the car crash.

– That picture . . . the doctors.

– Yes?

– Is there anyone you recognise?

Long silence from the other end. She could see him in her mind's eye, bending over the page of a newspaper.

– It's not very clear, he answered. – Three men and two women.

– Read the names for me, she said quietly. – Slowly.

– Slava Kurtic, he began. – Dragan Michailovic, Ludmilla Golubeva. Fucking hell, that's . . .

– What is it?

– Wait, he whispered. – I think someone's coming.

– Sigurd, she shouted into the phone.

– You mustn't shout, he whispered. – Call you later.

– Don't hang up! Do you hear?

He couldn't hear. He was gone already.

She got to her feet, stood staring in front of her. Ten seconds, maybe fifteen or twenty. Then she called back. Answer, she muttered, pacing up and down the room, you must answer. Tried another five or six times before finding Roar Horvath's number. She tasted blood from where she'd bitten her lip.

She jumped when she heard Roar's voice.

– I've got something to tell you, she began. Something to confess, she might as well have said, because that was what she was doing now. Should have done it a long time ago.

A few seconds silence on the phone once she'd finished what she had to say. She waited for Roar Horvath's anger to flood over; she deserved it.

– He's your son, he said in a subdued voice.

– You must find him.

– In a house in Nittedal?

– Where Ibro Hakanovic was attacked. The same place.

Again silence for a few seconds.

– I'll get on to the sheriff up there.

She felt a surge of gratitude. Crossed to the window, the

sun still high, the sky full of white fluff. The air looked damp. She could feel the sweat running under her arms.

– There's more.

– Let's have it.

A winter or two was back in his voice. As though he had almost used up the goodwill he had mobilised.

– I think Ibro Hakanovic was murdered at the hospital because of something that happened years ago. During the war in Bosnia.

– That's not a new idea. We're working on several fronts.

– His sister and mother were victims of the mass rapes.

– Like so many others.

– More than that. It sounds as if they were subjected to some kind of medical experiment. Ibro Hakanovic had a collection of documents.

– How do you know this?

She told him what Sigurd had said.

– I think Ibro Hakanovic was killed on that particular evening because he was admitted to the hospital. He met someone there. Someone he recognised.

– And who might that have been?

She looked out into the sharp light. Her eyes coated over with a burning film, and everything out there started to swim.

– I don't know, she whispered, and at that moment, it was as though the day darkened around her.

Sigurd peered out from behind the curtain. There was a car outside now, by the side of the road further up towards the forest, a silver-grey SUV of some kind. Then he heard the sound in the hallway, the humming of a drill. He dropped the pile of newspaper cuttings on the draining board, the page with the group picture uppermost. He was certain now that he recognised one of the doctors, the same one as in the pictures from the car crash. On the bench his phone blinked and vibrated; as he reached for it, the door flew open. The man who burst in was wearing dark overalls, a scarf around his head.

– Don't touch that phone, he said in broken Norwegian as he came towards Sigurd holding a crowbar. He had a large plaster on his forehead, a swelling covering one cheek. It didn't take Sigurd more than a second to recognise who it was: the man who'd cut him with a knife in Malmö. He reached out a hand to the bench, grabbed the bag with the gun, fished it out, turned to his attacker and aimed it at his face.

– This time I'll kill you, he shouted.

The bloodstained towel in which the gun was wrapped had stuck to the trigger guard, and he tugged it loose.

The man shook his head, as though he was trying to look sad.

– Put it down, he said. – We're not going to harm you.

It dawned on Sigurd, far too slowly, that the man was talking about *we*. As the realisation hit, he heard a sound from behind. Didn't hear it so much as saw it, the shadow entering from the front room. He spun round, took a step to one side, tried to hold the gun firmly in a two-handed grip. The thing that struck him seemed surprisingly soft, but he knew the softness would be followed by a wave of pain. He steadied himself against the stove. A high-pitched noise in his ears, rising and rising. He was out before the wave of pain had reached its full height.

His own vomiting woke him up. His hands were taped together behind his back.

There were two of them, the one in the overalls leaning against the worktop. The other, wearing a dark jacket and a cap, sat on a chair. The one in the overalls turned on the tap, filled something with water. The next moment, his head and neck were soaked.

– Stand up.

The kick in his ribs sent him tumbling into the cupboard; his face ended in the pool of his own vomit. He sensed the man was getting ready to kick him again. Abruptly the other stood up, went in front of him, said something or other. A female voice.

Sigurd drew up his legs and tipped over on his side. Felt himself grabbed by both arms, jerked to his feet, slammed down on to a chair.

– Now you're going to help us, said the woman. She took off her cap. – If you do, everything will be all right.

Her Norwegian was almost perfect, the stresses fractionally displaced in a couple of words.

– Don't know anything, Sigurd mumbled.

The man in the overalls grinned so broadly that the cut on his cheek opened along its edges. His eyes were large and bulging.

– Take your time, he suggested, in more broken Norwegian. – We're in no hurry. You're the one who's short of time.

– The police are on their way, Sigurd mumbled, couldn't think of anything better to say.

The woman sat down again. She had a long face, a scar visible along her hairline, as though someone had tried to scalp her. She looked to be over forty and might once have been attractive, in a strange, equine way. She sat with a mobile phone in her hand. Sigurd saw that it was his.

– Jenny, said the woman, looking at the display. – It was your mother trying to get through to you. She put it down. – That's a shame, because you're going to be tied up for a while.

Sigurd tried to answer, but his tongue felt as though it was stuck to the roof of his mouth.

The man opened the drawer, took out a breadknife, held it to the window, studied the edge in the light. The woman, still seated, said something in a foreign language. Two sentences that sounded like an order. And suddenly the man was over him, grabbed him by the hair, bent his head back, exposing his neck, the blade pressing against his throat.

– Where is the girl? said the woman.

Sigurd made a gasping sound. The grip loosened.

– What girl? he said hoarsely.

The knife was there again, edge against the bulge of his Adam's apple. – You're the one who's short of time, Overalls said again.

– The gun, Sigurd stammered, nodding to where it still lay on the floor. – The one you're looking for.

Overall's laughter was like a cooing, and Sigurd knew that this wasn't about the gun. But he needed the seconds he gained by talking about it. No idea how he was going to use them, only that he mustn't say anything about Katja.

The woman suddenly said something or other in her foreign language. Sounded like she was handing down a sentence.

– Your girlfriend. Overalls pushed his face right into Sigurd's, breathing the stink of cooked asparagus all over him. – Don't say you don't know what we're talking about. You haven't got time for that.

Sigurd swallowed. The knife edge pressed harder into his throat, opened a nick in the skin.

– Katja. It just came out of him; he didn't want to say her name, but now it had been said.

– Katja, the woman repeated. – Right, then. The thing now is to find her.

– She isn't here, whispered Sigurd, the blood beginning to trickle down into the hollow of his neck.

– We know that, the woman said calmly. – Don't keep telling us things we already now. You'll regret it.

– Katja doesn't know anything about this, Sigurd managed to get out. – She doesn't know anything about what went on in Bosnia.

The woman smiled, teeth white and even; they didn't look real. – Protecting your girlfriend. I like that.

Abruptly she bent forward and held something up to him, the newspaper cutting about the car crash.

– And what are you doing with this if your girlfriend doesn't know anything about it?

– She . . . thinks this is about something else. She thinks a gang in Malmö is after her.

The woman winked at Overalls. – He's a good liar. She turned back to Sigurd. – Bad luck for you that we heard what the Bosnian said to her on the phone.

– Katja doesn't understand what he meant, he tried again.

The woman took the knife from the man's hand, tossed it into the sink.

– This is for cakes, she said, pulling a shaft out of her pocket. She held it in front of Sigurd's face. It was made of dark brown wood, with close-set grooves in it. She pressed a button. There was a brief swishing sound and a blade shot out, like a lizard's tongue.

– Where is Katja?

Sigurd knew he had to answer immediately.

– Malmö, he shouted.

– Shall we believe that?

– She stayed behind in Malmö!

The woman gestured with her hand. Without releasing his hold on Sigurd's hair, the man dragged him to his feet and pushed him towards the door.

– We're going to take a ride, said the woman. – We want to meet Katja.

– Nice lady, Overalls said, smacking his lips. He waited while the woman picked up the gun and the folder with the cuttings and went out ahead of them. She was wearing highly polished pointed bootees. Her feet looked as long as her face. She limped, dragging the left leg.

– Maybe you'll go out for a meal tonight, Overalls suggested. – We know a good restaurant in Malmö.

That cooing laughter. Like a wood pigeon.

Sigurd was bundled into the back seat, with the woman next to him. A drop of blood ran down inside his shirt. Overalls started the engine. In the distance, a siren. Two sirens. Colliding sounds, out of synch. Overalls' eyes in the mirror, catching the woman's. Then he reversed and sped away.

A cloud of dust appeared a few hundred metres further down the road. A police car emerging from it. The two exchanged a few words.

– You must stop, said Sigurd as loudly as he could. – They know I'm here.

The woman turned and punched him in the mouth. The light outside became opaque. Nausea shot through him once more, he slumped over on his side. Another punch, this time to the kidneys. He tried to twist away, the punches kept coming, waves of pain, deeper than any he had felt before, until everything went dark.

His head bumping against the side window. Somewhere far away, the two of them talking, their voices wrapped in glass wool. He opened his eyes, saw the police car approaching. It stopped, a man got out, uniformed, signalled to them.

The car jerked violently as it accelerated forwards. They hit the police car. Sigurd heard a shout mingled with the sound of metal buckling, the SUV bounced and skidded, momentarily down in the ditch before it righted itself and screeched on down the road.

The vibrations in the car made his forehead drum against the damp window. The sound of tyres gripping the asphalt, the nauseating smell of new plastic from the seat. Beside him the woman was speaking in a foreign language that he thought was probably Polish or Russian. Sounded as if she was quarrelling with someone. Suddenly she leaned forward, said something or other to the driver. Immediately afterwards he left the motorway and continued east, accelerating to a hundred and forty. In the distance, the sound of sirens. Abruptly he braked, turned into a lane, stopped, reversed on to a gravel track. The woman looked out of the window on both sides. They stopped at a grove of trees she pointed to. She unwrapped the cloth around the gun Sigurd had found, took out the clip, examined it, snapped it back into place, took aim between the trees. Something funny about the way she held the weapon, thought Sigurd. She must be left handed, as though *that* mattered. With a quick word to the driver, she jumped out, limped off in the direction of a small group of houses. A car approached, a red station wagon. The woman stepped out into the road and waved. It flashed its lights and slowed down.

– Don't stop, muttered Sigurd, as though the person in the car could hear him. – Don't stop, he shouted.

Through a film of damp he saw the woman up ahead. She pulled the gun out of the back of her waistband and pushed it through the car window. Sigurd could see a jolt pass through the body behind the wheel. The woman pushed the body to one side and got in, turned the car around and drove back up the track. They followed, past the group of houses, up a forest track. After a while, she pulled into an overtaking bay and they stopped beside her. Overalls got out, dragged a bundle out of the other car and across to his, jammed it into the back seat next to Sigurd. Staring eyes, a woman with brownish hair, grey at the roots in the sharp light, a hole the size of a coin in her forehead. Something brown oozing from it. Sigurd bent his head between his knees and vomited. The head of the dead body slumped against his shoulder.

Overalls backed the car up into the trees and stopped. The back door was flung open, the woman threw the gun on to the floor, shoved it under the seat.

– Out, she shouted, grabbing Sigurd by the collar of his shirt.

He landed with his face in the dry clay, dragged himself upright, felt bits of broken teeth in the slime on his lips. The woman thrust him in front of her, over towards the other car, a Toyota. He was pushed into the back seat, into a stench of mouldy plush. A few seconds later, smoke began rising from the SUV. As Overalls came running towards them, a fireball flared between the trees.

The woman drove now. They rejoined the motorway, heading east. A blue light approaching the other way. Sigurd tried to sit up; another punch to the head. Overalls staring at him over the seat back.

– You move once more and we'll push you out and drive over you.

Arash took the escalator to the floor where the exit was. Zoran had said he had to come as quickly as he could. But he was still thirsty, found a door with the word *Toilet* on it, let himself in and locked it, turned on the tap, let the water run, filling his hands, filling his mouth, drinking until his stomach began to hurt, rubbing water into the skin of his face. Afterwards he dried himself with paper towels, examined himself in the mirror. His hair was sticking out at the sides, hanging over his forehead in a greasy curl, his beard as wild as forest under-growth. Stood there looking into his own eyes, the black expanding and contracting. He didn't look away; the face in the mirror changed, but it was always his.

He chose the route across the long stretch of flat ground by the old church, came to a little bridge. He'd run off. They tried to catch him. He had a feeling that something was urgent, and yet he stopped and stared down into the murky water, greeny-brown and shallow. An ambulance helicopter took off from the hospital. He looked up as it glided over the church steeple, on above the river flats until it disap-peared behind the hill, above the forest he had run through a few days previously. That day he could have carried on running, he thought, deeper and deeper inside.

That wasn't where he was going.

Turn back. Not knowing what to. He was on his way home. He had no home.

Jennifer hurried past the bus shelter, crossed the road at the roundabout. She wouldn't ask Zoran about anything, just put the pieces on the table in front of him, not try to fit them together. Ibro Hakanovic had recognised someone at the hospital. Someone gave him morphine. Arash saw it, that was why they tried to kill him. Marita Dahl became an accidental victim. Dead because she was with Arash.

Now they were after Sigurd. Her Sigurd. She took out her phone, called him again as she let herself into Zoran's block. There was a smell of basements and newly washed clothes. A pushchair by the stairs; she had to move it to get past. Stopped on the second floor and stood outside Zoran's door, struggling for breath, her back sticky with sweat. Please, she prayed inwardly, but without knowing what she was praying for.

The sharp sound of the bell penetrated through his flat and died away. Thought she heard a sound in there. Could be from one of the other flats. She rang the bell again. Put her ear to the door. A faint scraping sound. Suddenly she saw an image of Sigurd.

I can't handle this, she muttered, fumbling for the key, letting herself in.

Dark in the hallway. The door to the front room shut. She opened it slightly.

– Zoran?

She didn't want to go in there, wanted this to stop here, without her needing to know any more.

No one in the living room. No one in the bedroom. She tried the bathroom door. It was locked.

– Zoran?

She knocked, cautiously.

– I must talk to you. Before I talk to anyone else.

Not a sound from inside. She knocked again.

– I need to ask you about what happened back then. In Bosnia.

No answer.

– Come out when you're ready.

She stood in the living room, looking out the window. The light that slowly rose and fell, that never disappeared. The moment when she had decided to come to this country: she had met Ivar on holiday in another mountainous country, much further south in Europe. She had sat looking into the open fire on the evening her decision had been made. If she'd been able to see her story there in the embers, everything that would happen to her, all the dead ends . . . Everything was a dead end. She jerked the curtain closed.

The kitchen door was ajar. She pushed at it, something blocking it. When she pushed harder, a shoe came into view, part of a trouser leg.

She leaned all her weight against the door. Got it open enough to put her head round.

He lay on his stomach. Bleeding from his face, a pool of blood below his cheek.

She forced her way in through the opening, fell to her knees, shook him, got him over on his side. He had his reading glasses on, one of the lenses broken. The eyes closed, the skin pale blue.

– Zoran, she whispered, her hand on his neck, looking for a pulse.

Then a sound from the door behind her. She turned, looking up into those grey eyes, one of them squinting off in another direction; she had never been able to work out which one was looking at her.

They drove more slowly now, not much above the speed limit. Sigurd tried to keep track of the signs they passed, repeated the names inside himself, something to hold on to. The sound of a helicopter hammering above them, then disappearing. They passed Kongsvinger, going south, turned off suddenly and followed small country roads that led through forest. Sunlight between the trees, the landscape opening up towards the shores of a lake, closing again.

They pulled in at a petrol station. Overalls got out, filled the tank. When he returned, the woman moved to the back seat.

She took out a phone. Sigurd saw that it was his.

– You're going to talk to Katja, the woman told him.

Sigurd said nothing. Overalls started the engine and they drove on.

– What's your code?

He was still holding back answers he could have given. The woman grabbed him by the hair.

– You are alive, she said. – You should be grateful to me for that.

Suddenly she had a gun in her hand and was pressing the barrel against his throat, this one longer and bigger than the other, the one she had thrown into the car they set on fire.

– Four five four three, he stammered.

She tapped in the numbers.

– Now I'm calling Katja. You're going to ask her to meet us. Got that?

He nodded.

– And she's to give us the phone with the message on it. You know the one I'm talking about.

The phone rang a few times. Then Katja's voice, coming over the speaker. – Sigurd, she said. – Have you got the gun?

He swallowed, tried to see again that burning SUV. – It's all taken care of.

– Taken care of?

– No bloodstains on it. Burned.

The words got stuck between his swollen lips.

– Are you sure?

– Yes.

– Where are you?

– In a car. He made an effort to speak clearly. – Not the gun they were looking for. That prison camp you talked about . . .

The woman dug into his side.

– Don't go anywhere, he said loudly. – See you when I get there.

He pressed his face against the car window.

– You must stay exactly where you are, he said.

– We'll manage it, Sigurd, no matter what happens.

He couldn't let her go on believing that. He'd helped her; they were even now.

Then she said those three words. Had never said them to him before.

– Not that, he mumbled. – I don't want to hear you say stuff like that.

The woman ended the call.

– She didn't say where she was, Overalls growled.

Silence in the car.

– She's in Malmö, Sigurd managed to say. – Close to Malmö. A summer cabin by the sea.

– Call her and check.

– Then she'll know something's wrong, the woman said. – She'll hide.

A few moments later she added: – I don't think he'd dare trick us. She bent over Sigurd. – You'll call her again in a little while. Arrange where to meet.

Sigurd felt his stomach heave again, a spasm that bulged up through his chest, as though his insides were being sucked out of him. – It won't work, he groaned.

The woman hit him, just above the cheekbone.

– You do as we tell you, she barked in his ear. – When we don't tell you to speak, you keep your mouth shut.

Jennifer backed away, knocked into the kitchen table, so hard that the computer on it woke up out of hibernation mode. – What's happened?

Lydia in the doorway, fiddling with something in her jacket pocket.

– Nothing dangerous.

She was holding something that looked like a gun in her hand.

Jennifer continued to stare at her. – What have you done to him?

– Just an electric shock. I had to defend myself.

– Can't you see he's bleeding?

– A cut on his cheek. His glasses broke when he fell.

Jennifer bent and shook Zoran. As she raised his head, he opened his eyes.

– Jenny, he stammered.

– Lie still, I'll call an ambulance.

She helped him up into a sitting position. Blood ran from a cut below his eye. She removed a shard of glass that was sticking out of it.

– Look out, he muttered.

When she got to her feet, Lydia was still standing there with the stun gun in her hand.

– I don't understand, said Jennifer.

Zoran tried to stand up, slumped down again. – The computer.

Jennifer turned and looked at it.

– It's her, said Zoran, his voice a little stronger.

A list of names on the screen. Picture of a group of men and women in white coats outside a hospital entrance.

– It's her, he said again. – In the picture . . . A hospital in Bosnia. Her name then was Ludmilla Golubeva. He raised his hand, as though he was trying to point to Lydia. – Ibro Hakanovic recognised her.

Lydia waved the stun gun. – He's lying, Jenny. You mustn't believe his lies.

Jennifer looked at him. – You heard that voicemail message last night. Why didn't you say anything?

He blinked a few times, as though he'd got something in his eyes. – Had to be sure first.

– He's making things up, Lydia protested. She took another step into the room. – He has strange notions. Look at me, Jenny. Do you believe I killed that patient? A man over one metre ninety?

Jennifer shook her head. – Hired killers did it. Someone brought them in.

Lydia gave a brief laugh. – And I'm supposed to be someone who can get professional assassins to turn up for me whenever I need them? Do you really think I'm that important?

Zoran put one hand on his chest, the other underneath him, got to his feet.

– The research project, he said, breathing heavily. – That's why, Jenny. Everything that's happened . . .

– Just keep still, Jennifer ordered him.

He supported himself against the kitchen table, clicked the mouse.

– A colleague in Bosnia sent me this.

A photograph appeared on the screen, a crashed car. Next to it a picture of a woman, unclear, but Jennifer could see who it was.

– Zoran, please.

A crookedness spreading over his face. Starting at the eyes, moving down, as though half of the face was dying.

– The research, he lisped.

She tried to support the heavy body as it collapsed against her, was dragged to the ground with him, twisted loose and got to her knees. When she managed to put two fingers to his neck, the pulse was weak and irregular, one beat missing, then several in quick succession.

– Damn, she muttered, fumbling to get the phone out of her jacket pocket.

Lydia grabbed her by the wrist. – If you ring from that phone, someone will die.

Jennifer pushed her aside. Her thoughts were loose scraps floating around her; she couldn't get hold of them but knew that something terrible was about to happen.

– Do you hear me, Jenny? If you ring, your boy will die.

– No, she shouted. – You're lying again.

Lydia looked sad, a lock of grey hair hanging over her

eyes. – I'm not lying. They have Sigurd. They have your son in a car.

Jennifer tapped in the emergency response number.

– I can stop them, Lydia said quietly, as though imparting a secret. – I've been protecting him all this time. Give me your phone.

– Oh my God, Jennifer groaned. – Dear God in heaven.

– Give me the phone, said Lydia again. – I'll call them and tell them to let Sigurd go. Your son, Jenny. And then I'll leave here.

Jennifer blinked in confusion. – Zoran needs help. Immediately.

– You'll have to choose. If you want Sigurd to live . . .

– I don't believe you! she screamed.

Lydia took another step closer. Her whole face was twitching. – Will you believe me if I let you talk to him?

She took the phone from Jennifer's hand.

A wall of water in front of them, the worn wipers unable to swish it away, rivers cascading down the car windows. Overalls had to drop his speed. When the rain eased off a bit, Sigurd made out a sign with Strömstad on it. They turned off directly after that. A few minutes later, they rolled into the little town. Overalls spoke on the phone. Seemed to be explaining something or other. Drove into an area down by the waterfront, behind what looked like a storage depot.

– Now follow me, said the woman. – Walk properly and keep your mouth shut.

She opened the door for Sigurd, shoved him out. It was still raining, quiet and warm. She held him by the arm, led him over to a BMW standing there, the same model as his own. He looked around. No one in sight, no one to call out to.

She sat beside him in the back seat. There was a smell of vomit, mingled with animal sweat. It could be his own. The woman seemed not to notice.

Overalls disappeared round the corner in the Toyota. Moments later he came hurrying back, hopped in behind the wheel.

The E6 heading south; Sigurd recognised the road. It was as though he remembered every turn and every slope.

First to see the bridge lives. The loser dies.

Can't you find a different prize?

Trym doesn't want to. Live or die, that's what it's all about.

Again the phone in the front rang. Overalls handed it to the woman. She listened for a while. Said something, her voice agitated. Listened again, just a few seconds this time, then began speaking at a furious pace, sounded as if she was telling someone off. Sigurd lay there and felt relieved that this time it wasn't him, that someone else was being subjected to this flood of rage.

Suddenly she held the phone to his ear.

– Who is this?

Jenny's voice. She was afraid. The way her voice sounded when she was getting into one of the gondolas on the big dipper. She had never liked heights. But he and Trym were able to persuade her. It had to be her. Ivar had had an infection of the vestibular nerve and could never ride with them.

– It's me.

– Sigurd? My God. Where are you?

– In a car.

A few seconds' pause.

– Is there . . . Have they hurt you?

– I'll be all right.

– You will be all right. You hear me!

– The bridge, he said. – The one that looks like a ship. That's where we're going.

– What bridge? shouted Jenny as the woman grabbed the phone and cut the connection.

Overalls asked about something or other. Again she started to rage. Sigurd leaned as far away from her as he could.

– They want us to let you go, she shouted in Norwegian.

He didn't know if he had heard correctly.

– They want us to let you out. Idiots!

He groaned, and it was as though that slight movement caused his throat to close up. He could hardly breathe.

– Someone has been praying to God for you, she hissed in his ear. – Think that might help you?

Arash followed the footpath round the hospital, emerging by the block where Zoran lived. Didn't walk through the residential area, kept off the road where he might meet someone who knew him. That was what Zoran had asked him to do.

At the edge of the small patch of grass, he stopped and looked up, located Zoran's flat on the second floor. A movement in the curtain up there; for an instant a face came into view, then the curtain was closed. His body tensed, his thoughts racing. That was the face he had seen in the examination room that evening. The doctor who had stood behind Ibro Hakanovic, talking to him as she injected something into his drip.

Arash tore himself away and started walking towards the end of the block, rounded the corner. Speeded up. The door to the third entrance was wedged open with a wooden block. Inside, he squeezed past an empty pushchair.

In that same instant, footsteps on the stairs. He turned back, moved the pushchair.

She came running down. The doctor from the emergency unit.

– It's you, he said.

One eye squinted out sideways; for a second or two, it stared at him. He raised a hand, as though he had thought of stopping her. Her mouth made a hissing sound and she brushed his arm aside.

He stood there watching her as the outside door glided shut.

A few seconds later he was ringing on Zoran's doorbell. After three rings, he tried knocking. Then, like an answer, he heard banging sounds from inside.

– Zoran, he called into the crack.

The knocking became more distinct. He put his ear to the crack, could hear someone shouting.

– Wait, he shouted back. – I'll go and get a key.

Sigurd sees Katja in his mind's eye. She's lying on the bed, the whole of her face bathed in the afternoon light that falls from the window.

I don't want to hear you say that, he repeats.

But she says it once more, those three words.

It'll pass, he protests. *It always passes.*

She slowly shakes her head, a smile around her lips. He can never make her smile that way. Nor anyone else. Then her face dissolves into light, and all that's left of her are the words, like an echo.

I love you, Sigurd Woods. No matter what you do.

He thought he saw Gothenburg 108 on a sign. The rain had stopped. There was something about the movement of the brown clouds. Then the warning arrows were there, detour, cones and flashing lights. Overalls said something to the woman. She shook her head, remained silent. He said it again; it sounded like a question. Then she pointed, and he followed the line of cars leaving the motorway.

The car in front had Norwegian number plates and three

kayaks on the roof. It moved forward a few metres; they jerked along behind it. Further ahead, a roadblock. The two of them discussing something in low voices, the woman pressed up against Sigurd. It was her sweat he had smelled; it penetrated his insides, the smell of meat gone bad.

Sigurd gets to choose, since he won.

Sigurd looks at the two balloons for a while. They're pink, with rabbit ears. About to point to one of them, let Trym have the lion that shines gold and silver in the summer sun.

Three police cars a little further ahead, one of them blocking the road. Four uniformed policemen in yellow jackets, one holding an automatic. Silence inside the car. Sigurd could no longer feel his fingers. His wrists were two throbbing bundles. The woman covered him with a blanket, wrapped him in it. The smell of her sweat even stronger now, mixed with the vomit from the seats, and again he had trouble breathing. – You know what to do, she whispered in his ear. – Not a single fucking thing.

He felt the barrel of the gun in the hollow of his neck.

– Shut your mouth, don't move your lips.

Like some wounded animal he lay beneath the thick blanket, closed his eyes, saw nothing, opened them, saw nothing. The car crawled forward, stopped, moved another few metres, stopped.

He heard the window glide down.

Overalls' voice: – What's going on?

Could drag himself away now, throw off the blanket. Manage to call out before she fired.

The beam of a torch coming through the blanket.

– Pull in to the side here.

Overalls got the car moving, it gave a leap as he put his foot down. Someone shouted, the shout cut off by the racing of the engine, a loud noise as they ran into something, then reversed, turned and drove off in another direction. A booming sound in his ear, the gun going off, another quick turn, then a crashing up through the gearbox, his face thrown against the back of the seat. Sirens behind them, getting closer, then fading. He lay with his face squashed against the leather of the seat, the woman's fist pressing into his back. She screamed something to the driver; his foot went down even harder.

Slowly the skies seemed to clear. Light through the grey, the sun waiting, everything that had yet to happen waiting out there. In the darkness beneath the blanket he imagined the road, the hill up between the cuttings, had studied them so many times, layer upon layer of stone in shades of grey, but with one layer of pink that glistened in the low evening sun. He used to think of it as a wedge in the cutting, an opening in the rock, a gateway to something on the other side. All the places he would never get to see.

Silence in the car once more. Only the sound of the engine and the tyres on the wet asphalt. And somewhere above them, a helicopter.

I'll see the bridge first.

He could see the landscape just the way it had looked that time in the evening sun.

Wanna bet?

What's the point, you always cheat.

No I don't.

The mast with the blinking red light appears. From there he can start to count, knows exactly when to shout out that he can see the bridge, just before the white towers and the cables come into view. Trym can never catch him out.

You're right, Trym, I cheated. I've always cheated.

Around the corner is the bridge, like a ship in the evening sun, ready to set sail.

You'll both get a helium balloon when we reach Liseberg, says Ivar.

What's the point of betting, if everyone wins?

An explosion beneath his ear, and the car started to spin as the air rushed from the tyres, spinning faster and faster in a spiral. The woman screamed, as though it was still an option to give orders, as though it was the car she was trying to command with her scream.

Sigurd stretches out a hand, chooses the lion balloon in silver and gold. Runs off with it across the grass. I'll let go of it. I'll let go of it deliberately. That's what I'll do.

I want it to disappear.

EPILOGUE

In other words, it is very important to have a clear understanding of what is at stake in this matter. As we know, the woman we are discussing here, Lydia Reinertsen, formerly Ludmilla Golubeva, is a Russian citizen. After she sought refuge in the Russian Embassy on 19 June, there have been initiatives on several levels to have her interviewed by the Norwegian police. At an early stage in proceedings, the Foreign Department was involved. Formal charges were made against the woman, and the material evidence presented to the Russian authorities can only be described as conclusive, leaving little room for doubt that she has been involved in serious criminal activities, several of which have resulted in deaths. So far all attempts to have her extradited have failed. She is claiming diplomatic immunity, and maintains that in the light of the extensive media interest in her case and the atmosphere this has created around it, she would find it impossible to get a fair and unprejudiced trial in a Norwegian court of law. The Russian authorities are not prepared to contest this claim, and there are no indications that they intend to hand her over. However, agreement has been reached with the embassy for a Norwegian forensic psychiatrist to conduct a series of four meetings of specific duration with Lydia Reinertsen, on the grounds that the woman has suffered an apparently extreme psychological response to the events, and to the charges against her. These psychiatric consultations have been conducted as planned, and at a meeting with top-level Russian representatives early today, plans for a preliminary police interview with Golubeva on Russian diplomatic territory were discussed. We have reason to believe that this is a first step towards allowing the Norwegian police to conduct formal interviews with the suspect. From a Police Security Service memorandum, 4 August 2104

You say you are fully aware of the charges being made against you?

I've followed the case. Newspapers and TV. And on the internet.

What are your grounds for believing you will not receive a fair trial in the Norwegian courts?

Because this has become a political case.

We can assure you that we shall stick to the facts in this conversation and keep politics out of it. Let's start by recapitulating some of what the investigation has so far revealed. You are of course at liberty to correct and supplement these findings as we go along.

(Accused confers with her lawyer. Interview suspended for two minutes.)

On 13 June, you were on duty in the gynaecological department of Akershus University Hospital. Is that correct?

I have already said I do not propose to comment on any of your claims.

At 22.10 that evening, a patient named Ibro Hakanovic was admitted to the hospital's emergency unit after being attacked in a fight. Following an examination, it was decided that he be admitted to a surgical ward. In the meantime, he was moved to another examination room. In this room, one of your patients had just undergone treatment. You entered the room to see this patient, who was no longer there. This is how you found yourself standing next to Ibro Hakanovic's bed. He at once recognised you, having previously met you on several occasions at a reception centre for traumatised women in the town of Kladanica, in Bosnia, in February 1993. At that time your name was Ludmilla Golubeva, and you were working at a women's clinic in the town. At the same time you were participating in a programme designed to limit the fertility of female members of the Muslim population of Bosnia.

This is a lie.

We are familiar with a number of scholarly articles on the subject written by you and published in Serbian journals. We also have a number of statements from witnesses identifying you as a member of a team carrying out operations of a so-called experimental nature on Bosnian women. As a result of these operations, a number of women died, among them Iram Hakanovic, the sister of Ibro Hakanovic.

I refuse to sit here and listen to this.

(Interview suspended for fifteen minutes. After conferring with her lawyer, the accused returns to the room.)

Then we shall continue. In the days before the negotiated ceasefire in Bosnia, a female doctor with the same name as yours – that is, Ludmilla Golubeva – was allegedly killed in a road accident in the south of Serbia. She appears in photographs in newspaper reports and bears a striking resemblance to you. We believe that as the war in Bosnia drew to a close, you were given assistance to disappear, and reappear in St Petersburg, now under the name of Lidija Petrova. According to your papers, you were born in Novgorod and studied in Moscow and St Petersburg, where you were living until you met the Norwegian psychiatrist Knut Reinertsen. You married him and moved to Norway. Whereas the allegedly deceased Ludmilla Golubeva grew up in a small village in Bakorstostan in the former Soviet Union and studied medicine in Belgrade in the former Yugoslavia. We can prove with some certainty that Lidija Petrova, later Lydia Reinertsen, and Ludmilla Golubeva are one and the same person. This would also seem to be confirmed by a childhood story you told the forensic psychiatrist with whom you spoke last week.

I was in a terrible state that day. I might have said anything.

Then let us move on. We have here a list of numbers you called from your phone. One of these is to a phone found in the car in which Sigurd Woods Plåterud was abducted.

I knew that he was Jenny's son. I didn't want anything to happen to him.

You know who owned that phone?

No comment.

It appears to have belonged to a woman living in Oslo, married to a driver at the Russian Embassy. She spoke fluent Norwegian, as well as several other languages.

I know nothing about her.

How is it that you had that number and were able to ring her in the middle of a hostage-taking situation?

There's no need for me to answer that.

This same woman can be traced to at least two places in Germany in which murders were committed.

I know nothing about that. You'll have to ask her.

As you know, it is too late for that. Let us instead return to the evening of 13 June, earlier this year, at the hospital. We have a witness who came into the examination room, one of the porters. He saw you inject something into the saline drip to which Ibro Hakanovic was connected. Our investigations show that this must have been a large dose of morphine. You have earlier explained that this was done so that Hakanovic could be removed from the hospital without being hurt. If your motive was to treat him as gently and considerately as possible, then surely professional killers were not the optimal choice of collaborators?

I had no idea who was coming to fetch the patient.

And yet you had the telephone number of one of them?

I have withdrawn my previous statement. I was being pressurised.

Most of what you have told us can be documented. And we have formed a detailed picture of the subsequent chain of events. The murder of Ibro Hakanovic solved one problem, but two new ones arose.

Are you trying to get me to join in this guessing game?

The porter who had seen you giving the morphine to Hakanovic had to be eliminated. It did not go according to plan. The woman he was with that day was killed, but he got away.

I'm tired of all these accusations.

In the second place, you and your helpers had to get rid of a friend of Hakanovic's. He called her from the hospital and left a message on her voicemail. The perpetrators had reason to believe that she was in possession of documents that would incriminate you.

Why should I have to sit here and listen to this?

Because we still have a number of unanswered questions. We'll have answers to some of them over the next few days. The others may prove a little more difficult. The simplest solution would be if you helped us.

I have no reason to help you.

We have asked ourselves why an operation of this magnitude was mounted in order to cover up for you. Yes, you risk being accused of war crimes, but we're talking about offences that took place over twenty years ago and that will be difficult to prove.

That just shows how insubstantial your case is.

That's probably not true. The evidence connecting you to the murder cases we're investigating is incontrovertible. The question is, who is behind it all? Who has the means to mount an operation on this scale? And above all, who has a strong enough motive? It may well be in your own best interests if you can give us some answers.

What do you know about it? You have no idea what you're talking about. You have no idea what will happen if I reveal even a fraction of what I actually know.

(Interrupted by her lawyer. Interview terminated.)
Interview report, 10 August 2014

This was the third time Jennifer had been interviewed. Or the fourth. She couldn't bear the effort it took thinking back to tell them apart.

She had slept more over these past few summer weeks than for a long time. Not at night, when she twisted and turned or got up and wandered like a sleepwalker around the little flat, from room to room. She slept during the days. Usually sitting in a chair, bathed in the summer light that never ceased streaming down over her. She had abandoned all hope of protecting herself against it.

But there was something different about the interview this time. It wasn't to take place in Lillestrøm, like the first one, or in the offices of the NCIS in Bryn, like the second. The woman who called asked her to attend at the headquarters of the Police Security Service in Nydalen. Jennifer gathered whatever strength she had, readied herself to go through the sequence of events yet again. Of course she understood why it was necessary to uncover all the details, to clear up as far as possible anything that might cast doubt on the story they were painstakingly piecing together. And with her rational side she understood that she had to do what she could to assist in this. But not even the most detailed recounting of what she knew could change what had happened. And that was all she really wanted.

She drove herself in. Shouldn't have. Not in her state, with her body pumped full of sedatives. But she took the car, and no one thought of asking her if that was a good idea.

The first part of the interview was like the previous ones. What happened that day she entered Zoran's flat, how she got in, how she found Zoran. The woman asking the questions was wearing a dark grey trouser suit. She was about Jennifer's own age, maybe a few years younger, her hair cut short and streaked with grey.

After a while, a man took over. He sat in the chair furthest from the window, wearing a grey suit too, as though the pair of them had agreed on matching outfits. The interview took a different direction. He asked about other things. Why it was she had come to Norway, the jobs she'd had, what aspects of medicine interested her in particular. Her impression was that he had a specific reason for asking these questions, but she let him get on with it.

– How long have you been involved in the research being conducted by Lydia Reinertsen?

– About a year.

– You've played a central part in the project.

That wasn't correct; her feeling the whole time had been that she was working on the periphery.

– But you were one of the group leaders.

– Lydia wanted me to take on more of the administrative duties.

– Did you have full knowledge of what the others in the group were doing?

– Not at all.

– Would you say it is normal for a leader not to know the potential uses to which a project might be put?

Jennifer shook her head slowly. – I don't understand the question.

– Who have you communicated with about the work?

– Communicated?

– Who have you shared the information with?

– No one apart from those working on the project. I was supposed to be co-writer of an article on some of the findings. It never got to that stage.

– So you have not sent data from this research to anyone outside the group?

She felt herself waking up slightly.

– What are you asking me?

The woman poured her more coffee.

– We'll be open with you, Jennifer, she said.

– Open? About what?

– We've examined the computer in your office. Large quantities of data have been extracted from it. A number of files transferred to external hard disks.

Jennifer blinked in confusion. – What does that imply?

The woman leaned across the table, as though about to share a confidence.

– We believe that this research project has an open side,

to which the majority of the researchers have contributed in good faith.

– But?

– But that it had another side too, one that not everyone knew about.

– Has Lydia been fabricating the results?

– That we don't know. But this is about something more than a simple falsifying of results.

Jennifer felt her jaw drop. – You're going to have to help me out here.

The man in the grey suit began to explain. It occurred to her that even his facial expressions were like the woman's, as though they were brother and sister, or a married couple who had lived together for years. She recognised that this was the way her mind had been working in the weeks since it all happened. People became similar, hard to tell apart, as though they glided around her in a mist, different editions of the same person, without inner lives.

– The goal of this research was to discover the genetic causes of childlessness. That is apparent from the project application.

Jennifer nodded. – The possibility of helping some childless couples in the future.

– But not many.

– In the great majority of cases, the causes of the childlessness are elsewhere than in the genes.

The man continued.

– We have reason to believe that findings that emerged during the process were communicated to recipients who had things in mind other than helping childless couples.

Jennifer looked at his expressionless face. – And what might those be?

– Lydia Reinertsen is accused of having carried out the sterilisation of women in Bosnia.

Jennifer had gathered this much in the whirlwind of speculation and suspicion blowing about over the past few weeks.

– The women were apparently ignorant of what was being done to them. Some of the operations were conducted under highly dangerous circumstances. Lydia Reinertsen has written about sterilisation programmes in a publication that promoted ethnic cleansing.

– The research project we were engaged in was about the opposite of sterilisation, Jennifer protested. But she began to have some idea of where they were heading with these questions. – Wasn't it?

The two of them looked at her for a few moments.

– We asked a couple of geneticists to examine as much of the material from the research as survives, the woman said finally. – Their view is that if egg cells can be changed in such a way as to make them easier to fertilise, they can also be affected in the opposite way. Once the code has been discovered and the mechanisms understood. But this is something you know more about than we do.

Jennifer struggled to gather her thoughts.

– Are you talking about finding genetic mechanisms that can *obstruct* fertilisation?

The woman glanced out of the window. – We're not excluding that someone out there is working on precisely that.

Jennifer sat up straight in her chair. She felt as though parts of her brain that had been in hibernation over the summer weeks were being prodded into life.

– But that's absurd. Could Lydia have been involved in something like that?

She grabbed her coffee, swallowed it down. Suddenly it was very important to be awake.

– We've been looking for the missing link in this case.

Something that would explain why so many resources were invested in trying to keep Lydia Reinertsen's former identity a secret. At any cost, it seems, someone was determined to prevent close examination of her past. Because that could put us on the trail of something much bigger than what went on in Bosnia. That is why less than ninety minutes passed between the time Ibro Hakanovic recognised her in the emergency unit at the hospital and the arrival of the professional killers who took him out.

The man was silent for a few moments before going on, as though he too were waiting for her to wake up.

– The indications are that we're dealing with someone with access to a great deal of money. And who sees the possibility of considerable profits. If a vaccine is developed that can prevent pregnancy occurring, what do you suppose that would be worth to people who think they have reason enough to use it?

The postbox hadn't been opened for several weeks. A few papers protruded from its mouth, and when Jennifer opened it, it all came tumbling out. She picked it up from the floor, most of it circulars, which went straight into the rubbish.

As she turned to walk up the stairs, she heard a knock on the street door behind her. Without turning round, she hurried up, not wanting to talk to anyone, but when the person outside began calling her name, she stopped.

Knut Reinertsen had rung several times, left phone messages too. She hadn't returned his calls. Now she let him in, held out a hand, stiff and reluctant. He shook it, dropped it immediately.

She had to offer him something or other, coffee, tea. Fortunately he declined both. Possibly because of the way she said it. She opened the balcony door; it seemed easier to deal with him out there.

– You've visited her? she said as he sat down.

– No.

She acted as though the answer didn't surprise her. – There are probably restrictions about who they allow into the embassy, she reasoned.

There was something different about his face. Maybe it was just the new glasses, small and round with black frames.

– I don't think the embassy is the problem.

Jennifer sat down too, leaned an elbow on the railing.

– Doesn't Lydia want you to visit?

– Hard to say what she wants. He thought a moment. – I called her on the phone yesterday.

Jennifer looked out into the grey air. A building site somewhere or other in the vicinity. The sound of pneumatic hammers pounding into the earth. She had started reading newspapers again. Saw a piece about how half a million people were expected to move into Oslo and the surrounding area over the next thirty years. And some would be moving out.

– What's happening to her? she asked.

He took off his glasses, rubbed his eyes.

– It's pretty much stalemate at the moment. There's no way she can leave there without being arrested. And she can't stay there for the rest of her life.

– Doesn't she understand that herself?

He glanced at her. – I've no idea what she understands. She keeps talking about a man her father once knew. It seems he fell into a rose bush and got his face scratched up. It's all about this man now, according to her. When I asked her about her own situation, it seemed hardly to worry her.

– Shouldn't that worry *you*?

– Of course. A flicker in his red-veined cheek, a tiny muscle quivering next to his eye. – There's something I promised to tell you, he said quickly. – I promised to tell you that she is sorry.

Jennifer filled her lungs with air; it filtered slowly out again.

– Is that why you wanted to talk to me?

– It was obviously very important for her. She repeated it several times. Insisted that she doesn't regret anything. That people who condemn her don't understand. You are the only one to whom she wishes to apologise. And I could hear that she meant it. She always liked you, Jenny. You are one of the few people she admires.

– Please.

– She said it earlier too. Before all this happened. Everything you managed to do, and always in the same conscientious way. And at the same time being the best mother to those boys that anyone could hope for.

Jennifer stood up abruptly. He raised a hand as though to detain her. – I do realise that an apology doesn't help in the least. But I decided to do as she asked me. Perhaps as much for my own sake as hers.

For a long time, she couldn't say anything. Knut Reinertsen was silent too, sat there staring into the air, still without his glasses on.

– I was interviewed again, two days ago, she finally said. – By the security service.

He nodded. – I'm sure the security forces are deeply involved in the case.

Is this now just a *case* to you? she felt like shouting.

– They asked me a number of questions about the research project, she said instead. – I was shocked. I've been thinking about it since.

She had been. It had become part of the stream of things that flowed through her head in the night. – Do you know anything about it?

– I've been asked about it too. Lydia has been in touch with researchers in other parts of the world.

– Nothing surprising about that.

– Places where there are no official codes of practice governing co-operation over research. One of the people she worked with in Bosnia is involved in a similar project in a country she refuses to name. The only other member of the group she was in that is still alive.

– That car crash . . . Jennifer started to say.

Knut Reinertsen put his glasses on again, looked at her. – That was arranged so that she could get away once the war was over down there. Someone got her a new identity.

Jennifer couldn't bring herself to ask how come he hadn't known anything about this.

– Is this whole thing credible at all? she said.

He sat a while, staring out, his jaw rotating slowly. It looked as though he was chewing something.

– No one can blame you, Jenny.

Of course she'd thought about that too. Somewhere in that stream of thoughts that never stopped boiling and bubbling as she sat in the chair, or lay in bed, or on the short walks to and from the neurological wing. She had contributed to a project without knowing what it was about. Left it to others to make use of the things she had discovered.

– Maybe not.

– All research can be used for something that was not its original purpose. And I'm not just thinking of the fact that the ethical boundaries are constantly changing.

It struck her that it was this didactic tone she had always found unbearable in him. Even now there was a whiff of it.

– Any research finding can become a weapon, he added. – It's one of the dilemmas we seem incapable of dealing with. It makes me fear the worst.

She opened the door to the living room, and finally he got to his feet as well.

– It was Zoran who found out about it.

She jumped at the sound of his name, supported herself against the frame of the door.

– He heard that phone message Ibro Hakanovic left.

– I know, she said.

– He got in touch with people he knew in Bosnia to find out if it was true.

She knew that too.

– He called me, Jenny. Asked what I thought.

Jennifer had to sit down again. She moistened her lips with the tip of her tongue. They were raw and cracked.

– Why didn't he go to the police immediately?

Knut Reinertsen shook his head. – He wanted to talk to her first. To make sure. You know Zoran, he didn't want to walk around feeling like a snitch.

For a moment she looked up into his dull eyes.

– I shouldn't have let him do it, he said.

Afterwards she sat at the table, went through her letters, regular bills in one pile, final reminders in another, along with a dentist's appointment for the previous week. In a third, letters from people she hadn't seen for a long time, some of whom she couldn't really remember any more.

She sat turning one over in her hands, a white envelope, no sender's address on the back. It had a Swedish stamp, and her name was spelled incorrectly, the letters slanting to the left. The address was wrong too, and attached to the envelope was a note from the post office asking her to get in touch if she was not the addressee.

Inside, a small photograph, an ultrasound image. Nothing else. On the back, in the same frail lettering as on the envelope:

Girl, 15 weeks.

Anamnesis

Emergency call-out to the Russian Embassy 11.08.14 at 21.12. Arrived with ambulance staff 21.21. Taken to a bathroom in one wing, found the body of a woman in the bath. The woman's name given as Lydia Reinertsen, 52 years old, residing at the embassy since June. Reportedly in a state of increasing psychic unbalance over recent weeks, has been seeing a psychiatrist.

Status praesens

Woman, slightly built, somewhat undernourished, found underwater in bathtub 21.21. Skin pale, no respiration or pulse. Stiff, dilated pupils, no reaction to light stimulation. No reaction to pain stimuli.

On the side of the bath and on the surrounding floor, two empty and one half-full bottles of diazepam, 60 tablets x 10mg. Tablet remains found floating in the bathwater.

Treatment

Cardiopulmonary resuscitation started, defibrillator × 3, treatment terminated after 32 mins.

Conclusion

52-year-old woman, reportedly mentally unbalanced, found in bathtub. Had probably lain under the water for over an hour before the arrival of the emergency team. Finds at the scene indicate ingestion of large quantities of anxiolytic.

Resuscitation attempted without success.

Journal entry, emergency medical service, 11 August 2014

Arash stood by the kiosk in the lobby. He had a fifteen-minute break, but didn't think that gave him time to eat in the canteen. In the newspaper stands, all the papers had the same story and almost identical headlines. She looked younger in the picture they used – it was probably taken some years earlier – but he would have recognised those eyes in any photograph.

The phone rang. He took the call immediately.

– Sorry, my friend, the voice said in English, – you're going to have to postpone your break.

Benjaminsen had started dropping these English phrases into his conversation over the summer. It had to signify something, but Arash had no need to know what that might be.

– Get right over to A and E, it's mayhem there. Insane.

– I'll sort it out.

– Arash, you're the man.

On his first day back at the hospital, he had spoken with his boss for over an hour. Benjaminsen obviously wanted to reassure himself that Arash was well enough to return to work as a porter. *I see you're wearing your ring, Arash*, he offered as his opening remark. *I guess that means people don't need to worry about their fingers.* Having said this, Benjaminsen sat there and looked at him, as though testing him. Suddenly he burst out laughing, and Arash had to laugh along with him. Afterwards, he didn't hear a word from a soul about what had taken place in the mortuary. That must have been Benjaminsen's doing.

As he hurried along the corridors, Arash ate the banana he had bought. He left the newspaper behind, but that front-page picture stayed with him. Early that morning, Knut Reinertsen had rung. He said he wanted to know how he was doing. Apologised that he couldn't offer any more conversations, *things being what they are*. Arash understood that, and didn't ask for any further explanation. But Knut Reinertsen explained anyway: he was going on sick leave for an indeterminate period, might even be travelling. And that was something Arash could well understand, too. He turned down the offer of a referral to one of Reinertsen's colleagues. He already had someone to talk to, someone with a similar background to his. His name was Shaygani, and he was a refugee from Iran. He'd come to Norway with nothing but his two empty hands, worked at the hospital, studied medicine, specialised in psychiatry. *That's the way I'm going to do it too*, Arash had said to him, and this doctor was in no doubt that he would make it.

The thing Arash had returned to in their conversations, over and over again, was that closed door.

– I should have climbed up and broken a window, he said to Shaygani. – Got inside somehow or other.

Shaygani let him say what he had to say before he spoke.

– You didn't know what had happened.

– I saw that woman come out of there. I should have realised it was urgent.

It had taken over an hour to get hold of a caretaker who could open the door to Zoran's flat.

– I read somewhere that after a stroke, one point nine million brain cells die every minute, he said to Shaygani. – Every second matters.

Shaygani didn't argue with him. Didn't take anything from him, didn't add anything.

The ongoing investigation is looking for answers to the question of whether results from the aforementioned research project may have been communicated to other parties whose intention is to use them for other purposes. Three independent experts in the fields of medical genetics and pregnancy have been approached for their opinions. An extract from Professor S. Mørland's response is given here:

'In other words, it would appear in principle possible to further develop the results of the research project in question. One of the discoveries that could turn out to be pioneering concerns a possible genetic basis for certain types of childlessness. This is related to the fact that in some rare cases the membrane of the egg cell does not become impenetrable after fertilisation. If it proves possible to influence the genes of the egg cell so that the membrane closes in the normal fashion, then the opposite will also be possible. In other words, the genes in a normally functioning egg cell could be changed such that subsequent to fertilisation the membrane of the cell is unable to prevent the entry of other sperm cells, resulting in the failure of the egg. The path from this to a "vaccine" that has these genes as its target, and which could therefore militate against pregnancy throughout an entire life, would seem to be very complex, but that such a thing could be developed, given sufficient resources, cannot be excluded. We are talking about, for example, changing the mRNA of the cell by means of vectors, preferably in the form of a virus. Should this turn out to be possible, the findings from the research project at Akershus University Hospital could be termed a step along the way.'

As is apparent from the attached documents, our anonymous source claims that several so-called independent laboratories in the two countries mentioned are working on a vaccine of this type. The purpose might be to control growth in certain sections of the population, even to bring about a reduction in the numbers in these sections. Over time, this will lead to certain ethnic

groups becoming more or less extinct. We put this
question to T. Eriksen, a senior researcher at the
Norwegian Defence Research Establishment (cf.
Appendix 4b). His conclusion includes these words:
'This is a type of ethnic cleansing that we have not so
far seen, and which could be implemented without war
or deportations or other physical measures against large
groups of a population. A vaccination-like substance
could be given to young females in the group in question, possibly mixed with other vaccinations with a
documented prophylactic effect and accepted as such
by the population at large. What such a preparation
would be worth if offered for sale to those cynical
enough to wish to use it must be a matter of speculation.
One must also bear in mind a situation in which the
population of the world as a whole is increasing, leading
to further pressure on available resources, not least if
changes in the environment make the production of
food and other necessities of life even more problematic
than it already is.'

So this is a project that was evaluated in the ordinary
way by the ethical committee of the regional research
body, and which was awarded funding by the Norwegian
Research Council.

As we know, all the data from Lydia Reinertsen's
computer was deleted on 19 June. Similarly the data
from Jennifer Woods Plåterud's computer. We have no
certain knowledge as to the current possible where-
abouts of this data, even though one of our sources indicates research institutions in two different countries.
This leads to speculation concerning Plåterud's role in
Lydia Reinertsen's research. It has been reported by
Romerike police that Plåterud obtained access to important information, and also that she withheld information

at a critical phase of the investigation that could have brought it to a more rapid conclusion. Her motives were apparently personal, but this is only one of several possible explanations. As of now, there is insufficient evidence to take the case to court, but we recommend that she be kept under observation.

From an Internal Police Security Service memorandum, 20 August 2014

Jennifer couldn't have gone there without him. She told herself that was why she had waited so long.

But there were other reasons, too.

– Are you comfortable?

She looked at him sitting there buckled up in the passenger seat. Perhaps he nodded. At least she couldn't see anything in his eyes to indicate discomfort. She had taken him out in the car once before; he'd been sick and thrown up. This time would be better, she had decided.

She turned off the motorway, drove on over the top of the hill. The cornfields were beginning to yellow, and the light above the copse was a darker, deeper grey.

– I have to tell you this, she said suddenly. – That day in the flat. You lay there unconscious. Every second mattered.

She slowed down.

– I could have called an ambulance. Lydia wouldn't have been able to stop me.

He sat there looking out the front window. No movement in his face at all.

– Afterwards she locked me in the bathroom. It was over an hour before someone came. That time could have been yours. You could've been helped.

He made a noise down in his throat. Perhaps he was trying to protest.

– You know why I let her go?

She turned into the car park.

– It was the only hope I had.

He turned his head towards her now. There was a light in his eyes she hadn't seen since it happened. He lifted a hand, moved it about as though writing something.

– Pen, she almost shouted, braking so sharply he was slung forward in his safety belt. – You want a pen.

She found one in her bag, put it into his hand. Found an envelope in the glove compartment, put it on the dashboard.

He leaned forward, his hand shaking, held the wrist with his other hand, forced it to be still. When he sank back again, the envelope fell to the floor. She picked it up.

You did right, she managed to read. *That's why I lo*

She turned to him. He had closed his eyes, as though the effort had drained all his strength.

She took out a handkerchief, dabbed a corner of his mouth, the one that drooped.

– Is that why? she said, and took his face in her hands. He opened his eyes again. He nodded, this time she was certain, and she heard a sound from his mouth, a word. *Jenny*, it might have been.

She wrapped a woollen blanket around him before getting out of the car.

As she passed the church door and carried on up the narrow gravel pathway, she pulled the thin jacket tightly around her and buttoned it up. It was the first day this year she'd felt the wind like that, the way it could blow through your clothes, all the way in through your skin.

Zoran was not the reason she hadn't been there since the burial. She hadn't been able to face it. Hadn't even been able to think about it. Not until that morning. She woke up and knew: I'm going there today. Didn't understand how she would manage. But she had slept. A few hours' continuous sleep. It had something to do with the light, that there was again a blind darkness there, in the depths of the night, a deep hole she could be drawn down into, without any thought of ever returning.

She walked among the graves in the lower part, with no memory of where they had walked the last time, that morning at the end of June. It didn't matter if she had to search for it. There was still a part of her that didn't believe there was a grave there at all.

At the top of the grassy slope there was an area that had recently been readied for use, and even before she saw the figure over by the fence, she knew where it was. But as she got closer, she felt an urge to turn back. To come here and meet Trym at the same time might be just too much. She stood there in the chilly wind until she felt the sweat freeze on her back.

He'd seen her by then. Raised a hand, and that movement was enough for her to get a grip on herself and walk on up.

He was standing there with a watering can in his hand. The ground in front of the gravestone had been turned over, the spade lying next to it. The flower bed dense with tiny flowers, all different colours. They formed an oval silver wreath, darker and darker towards the centre, and at its heart a deep yellow.

– Did you do that, Trym?

He looked down at her, seemingly embarrassed.

– It was all I could think of. And I owed him money, too.

She moved close to him, took his hand.

– My boy, she said.

He half turned away.

Acknowledgements

RESEARCHING FOR A novel is one of the most pleasurable aspects of the work involved. Wherever I have travelled, I have been made welcome, and people have shared their valuable time with me to illustrate things and answer my questions. Help like this has been a great encouragement.

Shahram Shaygani advised me with his insights on Iran and how Iranian refugees typically react to their first encounter with Norway. Mahmood Shaygani shared his knowledge of Rumi's life and poetry, and Joakim Palmkvist his expertise concerning the Malmö gangs. With Tobias Barkman, he is the author of *The Mafia wars: nine murder victims and the city they lived in*. Jeff Miller illuminated various aspects of mixed martial art and submission wrestling. Christoffer Tonning and Therese Ahlberg offered advice on Swedish matters.

Thanks to Ying Chen, Cecilie Arntsen and Bente Johansen at the pathology department of Akerhus University Hospital, Petter Arlo and Anders Damhaug of the hospital portering staff, and Robertino Ivanov of the security service. And thanks to Mona Hertzenberg and Tom Danielson of the Romerike district police force.

Thanks also to Rebecca and Joachim Damhaug.

And last but not least, to Helen Damhaug for all her help along the way.

THRILLINGLY GOOD BOOKS FROM CRIMINALLY GOOD WRITERS

CRIME FILES BRINGS YOU THE LATEST RELEASES FROM TOP CRIME AND THRILLER AUTHORS.

SIGN UP ONLINE FOR OUR MONTHLY NEWSLETTER AND BE THE FIRST TO KNOW ABOUT OUR COMPETITIONS, NEW BOOKS AND MORE.